Unknown Diners

by

Michael Walsh

Recent Fiction by Michael Walsh

Spilt Wine
Published 2017 – ISBN – 978-09940936-6-0

Posted As Missing
Published 2017 – ISBN – 978-09940936-2-2

Missing
Published 2017 - ISBN - 978-0-9940936-3-9

Back In Action
Published 2017 - ISBN - 978-09940936-5-3

Recent Non-Fiction by Michael Walsh

Sequitur – To Cape Horn in Comfort and Style
Published 2013 – ISBN – 978-09919556-0-2

Carefree on the European Canals
Published 2014 – ISBN – 978-09919556-4-0

Carefree Through 1001 French Locks
Published 2015 – ISBN – 978-09919556-7-1

Canal Cruising in France
Published 2015 – ISBN – 978-09919556-9-5

Unknown Diners

ISBN: 978-0-9940936-4-6

DARK INK PRESS

Published by Dark Ink Press, Canada

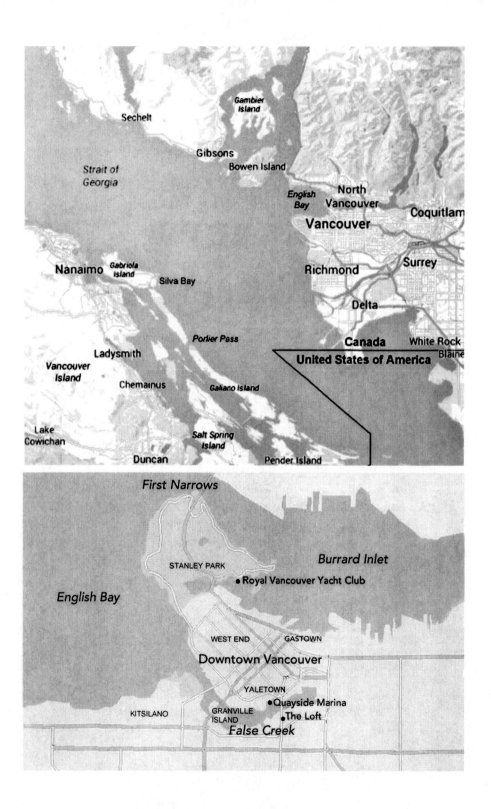

Author's Note

Although this is a piece of fiction, most of the geographic and historical background are real, as are some of the characters. The criminal activity and the criminal characters are all fictitious, and any resemblances to actual characters or incidents are coincidental.

Catherine nodded thanks to the man, stepped into the restaurant, and paused. *Do I still want to do this? Dammit, it's not want. I need to do it.* She blew out a deep breath as she approached the reception podium. "Catherine Isselstein," she said. *Wonder who Cynthia's seated me with.*

The hostess checked the list, then nodded to her right. "This way, please."

As Catherine was shown to her window table, a man rose from it and stepped forward, extending his hand.

Oh, thank God, it's Lorne. Catherine smiled and raised both arms as she neared. "I need a hug, Lorne. It's been too long." They merged and remained silent for a long while. *So strange. Being here. With him.*

They ended the hug, kissed cheeks, then stood back smiling, their eyes exploring each other. "People are looking."

"Good, so am I. That's a great dress." He ran his eyes over it again, then back up to her face, shivering as he did. "I find it difficult *not* to look at you."

"And your eyes are still as flattering. Come, let's sit." She turned her head and nodded. "We're holding up the wine round."

He held her chair, moved to his seat, and they watched as the bottle was presented. "We're starting with a Franciacorta from Ca' del Bosco, the 2011 Dosage Zéro," the sommelier said as she poured. Then wishing, "Tanti saluti," she continued to the next table.

Lorne held his glass toward Catherine. "To your re-emergence. We've missed you — I've missed you."

"It's strange being here again. Even stranger without Nathan. This was our favourite window."

"So Nathan? The police... Did they ever get any leads?"

"Nothing. They're calling it a cold case now. He went out to review a restaurant and didn't come back. No clues. Nothing."

"I saw so little about it. It seems there was a publication ban."

"It's been a recurring theme across the country. They're trying to keep the sensationalism out of the media."

"Sensationalism?"

She looked down at the table and shook her head. "He was found in garbage bags two weeks later, dumped in a lane in Gastown."

"In garbage bags?"

"Tortured... butchered." Her shoulders quaked as she lifted her napkin to her mouth and held it there.

"Are you okay? Please tell me what to do here. I've never had to handle... Are you sure you want to be here? Shouldn't you be with friends?"

"I *am* with friends." Catherine wiped her eyes. "I have so few. Two only. Isn't that sad? Two friends. You at these things and at the tastings, and Cynthia every few weeks for lunch. I hadn't realised how reclusive I'd become until..." She blew out a deep breath.

"Family? What about them?"

"On the Island. I went across with them after the services. My emotions were all over the place. I couldn't do anything. Couldn't read. Couldn't write. Couldn't be around people — not even my folks. I had to come back and crawl into a hole." She wiped her eyes again. "So sorry to be dumping this on you."

"Now that's an ironic twist, you being sorry for me." He reached across the table and touched her hand. "I wish I knew what to do here. I have no experience with comforting. I don't know what I should —"

"Just be here. Just be you. You've always made me happy." She tilted her head and gazed into his eyes. "Actually, I came this evening hoping you'd be here. Maybe talk... Sense your energy." She forced a smile. "I want to be happy again, Lorne."

She blew out another deep breath, shook her head, then lifted her wine glass. "This is great bubbly. Let's concentrate on being here. Enjoy this evening. It's been almost seven months now, time to carry on with life. Please help me move beyond this."

Chapter Two

Lorne smiled at Catherine and nodded. After nosing his wine again, he shook the glass and stared at the rising bubbles. *Good God! Where do I go from here? That was a big show stopper. What hells she must have gone through. Still going through them. Need a subject change. To what?* He ran his gaze around the room and back to his glass. "Five years now — where's the time gone? Can you believe it's been five years since Lumière closed?"

"Can't be five." Catherine took another sip of wine, then slowly nodded. "But I guess it is. That was while we were on the media junket through Chile and Argentina, wasn't it? God, how shocked we were when we returned."

For most of its sixteen years of existence, Lumière had been *the* hot spot. It was Zagat's top restaurant in Vancouver, consistent winner as Best French Restaurant in Western Canada, always at the top of the wine list awards... Then it failed.

Catherine and Lorne were sitting at a four-top set for two in the focal window during a promotional pre-opening of La Luce, a new Italian-themed restaurant taking over the space of the recently bankrupt Roberto. Five years previously this prime West Broadway location had housed Lumière.

She examined the details of the room. "Little change. Roberto had continued with Lumière's decor, and now so is La Luce. Odd, isn't it? They were doing so well, then bang! Closed. Both of them, so sudden, so unexpected. Both big surprises."

"But now we should be much less surprised. So many wonderful places have closed since Lumière. Too many, and it's increasing." He paused to pop a stuzzichino into his mouth, followed by a sip of wine. "I'm thinking there's something behind this. There are just too many of them."

"What do you mean, too many?" She looked up from her glass.

"Think of the past five years, the places that have closed. Good places. Great places. Places like Nu and C — Harry was at the top, he had helped create Northwest Cuisine back in the eighties with his Raincity Grill, and he was a leader in the Eat Local movement. His three restaurants were innovative, creative and always pushing the boundaries of fine dining. They were bustling, buzzing, then poof."

"That octopus bacon at C was inspired. I see what you mean. His places went from hot to not — physically not — so quick."

Lorne again studied the fine mousse in his glass. "Others, like gli Conti, Bistro du Midi, Cosecha. Appears now Nuance is about to close their doors. Great cuisine and ambience, well-run and thriving. But other places, hot places, like..."

"Like Roberto here. The food and service were both far beyond just good, and the place was buzzing. Why did it spiral down so fast? It seemed to be doing so well."

"There's something even stranger, though. When I started analysing this a few days ago, I realised the places which had..." Lorne paused mid-sentence and watched Catherine's face light up as they heard Cynthia's familiar voice.

"I'm so pleased you've both come. But you, Catherine, we've not seen you in months. God, when was the last?" Cynthia did a quick inhale. "Such a shock with Nathan. How are you doing?"

"Yes. Fine, I guess. Coming to grips with it. The shock, then the emptiness and..." She turned her head to gaze into Lorne's eyes. *Strength. Thank you.* Turning back to Cynthia, she continued, "Sorry, I've been ignoring you. Your invitations. I've been terribly unsocial." She winced a smile. "But I've been playing hermit too long now; I need to get on with living."

"I'll be back a little later, after I've finished my welcoming rounds." Cynthia turned and strode across the room, raising her arms in a greeting.

"She's always bubbling with energy and enthusiasm. A great marketer." Lorne shook his glass and nosed it, then took a sip to savour as he watched servers arrive with two dishes for each of them.

11

"Granseola alla veneziana on your right and farfalle con piselli, zaffera-no e capesante on your left. Buon appetito!"

Catherine waited for the servers to leave, then looked at Lorne. "You were saying before Cynthia, you realised..." She paused as the somme-lier arrived.

"We think the 2013 Gavi Le Marne from Chiarlo will complement both dishes." She showed them the label, then poured.

"You realised?" Catherine asked Lorne as the sommelier left.

"The places that replaced them. Most took over leases, bought the im-provements and the equipment out of receivership, likely for a pittance on the dollar. We've been to their opening promos, their media lunches and dinners."

"I see what you're saying. Nathan was talking of this before..." She paused and closed her eyes for a few moments, then shook her head and continued, "The face they present to us, and for the first few weeks to the public, is wonderful, but..."

"That's it, isn't it? The big *but*. A few weeks after the opening presenta-tions, the service, the food, most everything else is down a few notches. The only things up are the prices and the five-star reviews. There's too much of this, too much of a pattern here. Someone is diddling. Someone is manipulating reviews."

"A creative way to expand their business — begin by stifling the com-petition. Target a restaurant, write a series of damning online reviews." She shook her head. "No, not damning, but reviews with subtle under-tones of discontent to massage the gullible public. Then plant a few dark seeds among the concierges and watch as the restaurant flounders or fails."

Lorne looked around the room. "They'd have had minimal expenses here. The Art Nouveau decor is from Lumière. I'm sure the kitchen is also unchanged. No need to spend much."

Catherine scanned the room as she nodded. "Appears little more than re-freshing the chair upholstery and touching up the paint."

"People are wary of buying failed restaurants; the stigma scares them. The receivers have to sell them for ridiculous prices, often for little more than the salvage value of the equipment."

"Remember Lumière's renovation? Ignore the kitchen equipment, the decor alone, cost over a quarter million to install, and it was all thrown in for free when the new owner assumed the lease."

Lorne twisted his lips and nodded. "Yeah, and if someone is manipulating, they wouldn't be concerned by the stigma of a failed place. They'd know damned well why it failed. They need only reverse their tactics and generate a steady stream of glowing reviews, payoff the concierges and inbound tour operators and —"

"And manipulate us with presentations like this one. Get us writing praises. This crab dish is superb, the scallop one is sublime. I didn't realise Ortello could create like this."

"He can't." Lorne glanced at the plates, then back up to Catherine's eyes. "He's a good line cook; been around the big pubs and chains for years, but he's a technician, not an artist. When I read in the invitation that he's the executive chef, I almost told Cynthia I had a prior."

He shook his head and looked at the plates again. "But this isn't his cuisine; these dishes are artistry. There must be a plant, a ringer in the kitchen to do the promotional openings."

"So who's behind this place?" She took another bite of scallop.

"The owner wishes to remain in the background." He looked into her eyes and shrugged. "That was in the marketing blurb Cynthia sent with the invitation."

"There've been a few like that the past while. Another odd thing becoming common."

"Exactly. Part of the pattern I've been —"

"My God, this is superb. Have you tried the scallops?" She looked up from her plates and nodded toward the kitchen. "I'd love to know who's back there."

"Let's not spoil this wonderful food." He took another bite of the crab sampler. "Mmph! This is *so* good. Let's do the heavy thinking later. Let's just be here now. Enjoy the evening." He tilted his head and smiled at Catherine. *Enjoy sitting here with her. God, I've missed her. Wonder how she's holding up... Appears to be better now, looks more relaxed. Best I don't mention Nathan. My God, she's so gorgeous, she's so...*

"You seem in a trance, Lorne." Catherine smiled. "I've always loved the look in your eyes when you're off on another..."

He heard her pause mid-sentence as Cynthia's voice neared. "Great to see you out again. Hope you're enjoying the cuisine, the presentation, the... God, listen to me. Babbling my marketing. I haven't seen you in so long, and all I can do is dump."

"Delicious. The cooking, the presentation — everything is flawless. I'm beyond impressed. It appears you've another promising place in your portfolio." Catherine paused and glanced at Lorne, then returned her eyes to Cynthia. "So who's behind this one?"

"I'm not sure. It's a company back east — Montreal. I've worked with them before." She scanned the room. "The fellow over there at the end of the bar, Pierre — Pierre Nadeau. He's their marketing person out here. I'm hoping for follow-on this time, not simply another opening promotion."

Catherine swept her eyes around the room. "It's obvious you're starting well. The people you've attracted, the reviewers, the writers, the movers and shakers."

"I have great lists." Cynthia smiled at each of them. "Hey, they must be great — you're both on all of them." She laid a hand on Catherine's arm and lightly patted. "It's so good to see you out again. I'm up to my ears at the moment with these promos and with the public opening. We should lunch next week. I'll text you." She strode across the room toward another table.

They turned back to their sampler dishes and their wine, finishing them a short while before the busboy arrived. The waiter soon followed. "Did you enjoy the shellfish?"

Catherine looked up and nodded. "Splendid. The saffron sauce with the scallops was sublime."

"Next, we have cinghiale con porcini e cannellini, and here," reaching back to the tray held by his assistant, "filetto di manzo con tartufo bianco. My notes say you both like your tenderloin rare — correct?" He saw their nods, placed the plates in front of them and departed to be immediately replaced by the sommelier.

"The 2010 Poggio Antico. We thought a youngish Brunello di Montalcino would do wonders for both dishes," she said as she showed the label, then poured generously into the two fresh Riedel stems. She nodded, turned, and continued her rounds.

"Superbly orchestrated service," Lorne said as he picked up his glass and offered a toast, "To your re-emergence. I've missed you."

"It's strange coming back, getting into the reviewing again. Stranger still doing it without Nathan." She gazed into Lorne's eyes and tilted her head. "Really strange. I miss him, and I don't. Confusing messages, confusing feelings."

"You were a great team." He swirled the glass, which he still held high toward her, brought it to his nose and breathed in the bouquet. "But let's get into these plates. The aromas of white truffles are fighting a battle with the porcini and braised boar, and the Brunello is screaming *me too*."

Chapter Three

Lorne and Catherine turned to savouring the creations on the fresh plates and enjoying the Brunello, their conversation now focused on the flavours and flair and on the synergy with the wine. They discussed the artistic plating presentations and the service as their table was bussed and cleaned, and then set with dessert plates, cutlery and six wine glasses.

A waiter arrived with a large dessert sampler platter and placed it between them in the centre of the table. The sommelier followed with three bottles and showed them the labels before pouring the wines, lighter to heavier. "Moscato d'Asti, Vin Santo and Passito di Pantelleria. You two don't need explanations for these." She smiled, then continued around the room.

"And I was just getting back into my size fours," Catherine said, as she examined the platter and laughed. "God, it's good to get out again. I've been a hermit."

"I'm still a hermit, except when I come out for these things, and for the tastings, the junkets, the —"

"Yes, I suppose you are. I've never seen you with anyone." Catherine lifted her gaze from the platter. "A boyfriend?"

"Girlfriend. I've never done boys — except for the priest." He gave her a twisted smile, then took a bite from a crostata di fragole and followed it with a sip of Moscato.

"The priest?"

"An old Catholic tradition. We don't want to go there. This is delicious Moscato. I've had girlfriends, but never serious."

"Wonder why I pegged you as gay. Gentle, nonaggressive, kind and always helpful. Yeah, I guess. Trim, fit, well-groomed." She sat up in her chair, tilted her head and studied him. "You're a damned good looking man, Lorne. Devastating to be more accurate. Bright and witty — you've a great sense of humour. You've always made me happy. I've never heard you complain. You're obviously successful and prosperous. I would think there'd be hordes of women wanting to glom onto you and hang on. Why hasn't anyone?"

"It's never worked out with anyone I'm interested in. I guess that's it." He shrugged and took a spoonful of caffè pannacotta and another sip of the Moscato.

"So where have you searched? There are so many great dating sites on the web. I've been sifting through them, trying to figure out which one I should use."

"I haven't searched. Guess I've been too busy. Too focused on other things, the research, the writing. I've never looked."

"Focused. Yeah, you certainly are focused, but how the frick do you expect to find anyone if you don't search?" She eyed the dessert platter. "What's good here? I want a few nibbles only. I'm just getting used to my slim body again."

"The biscotti are light. They're a classic with the Vin Santo, and this one from Avignonesi is superb." He paused to look up and run his eyes over her. "You're gorgeous. But you've always been absolutely gorgeous to me. I could never figure out what you were seeing whenever you said you were too heavy."

"Ooh! I like that." She moved her scarf aside, then wiggled her shoulders as she flipped her thick red tresses around to her back. "Those are the eyes I need to have looking at me."

Lorne dipped a biscotto in his Vin Santo and let it soak a few seconds. "Here, bite the end off this." He reached it across the table toward her.

She took his hand to direct the piece to her mouth and continued holding while she savoured the bite, enjoying the complexity of flavours and the touch. "You're right, this *is* marvellous. Some things fit together *so* well." She squeezed his hand and felt a tingle and a shiver run up her thighs and down her belly.

He smiled. "So you've decided to start dating? I guess it's been a long time since Nathan... Sorry, we weren't going there."

She squeezed his hand again, kissed his fingers and took another nibble off the end of the biscotto. "Yeah, I'm tired of being alone. It's not natural. People are meant to be together."

He smiled at her and nodded. "I would love to find someone to share my life, someone's to share. More than a friend, though, a lover. I'm not getting any younger, thirty-four now, and it increasingly seems I'll continue the rest of the way as a bachelor."

"Why do that?" She wet her lips. "Look around, there's at least one woman in this room with an intense interest in you."

"Who do you... Oh, you mean Cynthia?" He scanned the room to spot her. "She asked me out a few times. It went nowhere. I found no magic. I guess she might still be interested."

"Okay, so there are at least two interested women in here, then."

"So who else? I can never tell." He swivelled his head to scan faces in the room. "I would love to find out."

Catherine squeezed his hand again, moved it to her lips and kissed it. "*Me*, Lorne... *Me*. We've known each other nearly forever, in the trade, in university, before that. I've always been interested in you, but you never saw me as anything beyond a friend as we tasted, wrote, wined, dined. You ignored everything about me beyond those things. Ignored everything but a warm friendship. A delightful friendship."

She shook her head and pouted. "There was never a hint of response to my flirting and advances. Nothing at all. I thought at first it was because I wasn't your type, then I thought you might be asexual, but you had too much fire for that. Finally, I assumed you must be gay, and I began dating Nathan and —"

"Not a gay cell in my body that I'm aware of." He stared into her eyes. "I'm a hundred percent hetero as far as I know." He ran his fingers through his hair, then shrugged as he began speaking, "This might sound weird to you..." He hesitated. "Creepy, even." He paused again and gave her a sheepish grin. "From the beginning, I've fantasised about holding you. Caressing you. Making love with you. So many wonderful fantasies — impossible fantasies. I never dreamed any of it was possible."

She nibbled on his forefinger, then put its tip in her mouth and ran her tongue over it before speaking again. "It's all possible, Lorne. All of it. I'd love you to begin playing through your fantasies with me." She flipped her hair off the back of her neck. "It's getting hot in here, isn't it? Which is closer? Your place or mine?"

Lorne took bites from each of the messier desserts on the platter while Catherine surreptitiously popped the more portable things into a zip-lock bag in her purse, both of them wanting to leave the sampler platter appearing well enjoyed. Their eyes were alive with passion as they raised their glasses of Passito to her toast, "Here's to many years of pent-up desire."

They drank to the toast, then rose from the table and caught Cynthia's eye. Lorne buttoned his double-breasted blazer as he stood, hiding an excitement he hadn't been able to dismiss. Feigning another engagement and begging off staying for coffees and grappas, they thanked Cynthia as she walked them to the front.

"Here, your kits," Pierre said as he handed them each a logoed canvas bag. "The menus, descriptions and profiles are all in here." He dropped a small ribboned box into each bag. "Also, an extra treat for each of you. You know how to reach us if you need anything further."

Cynthia took Catherine's hands, smiled into her eyes, then glanced at Lorne and back. "So good to see you again. Enjoy the rest of your evening."

Catherine smiled at her and winked. "We fully intend to."

Chapter Four

Lorne's iPhone pinged when the car he had paged pulled to the curb. Catherine took his hand as they started across the sidewalk. "We've not yet decided to whose place we're going." She tilted her head up to receive his kiss. "Where's yours?"

Pierre quickly stepped past to open the car door as Lorne began replying, "A block and a half from the Olympic Village Skytrain station." Then he continued loudly enough for the driver to hear, "the Exchange, Wylie and First."

They snuggled and kissed as they drove off, remaining quiet until Catherine said, "Funny, we're almost neighbours. I'm on Marinaside Crescent, a short walk from the Yaletown station."

"If you have a Creek view, you likely look out on my boat."

"You have a boat? You've never mentioned being a boater."

"No, I guess when I'm doing wine and food, I do wine and food. None in my boating world know I'm a wine writer."

"Yes, you're certainly single-minded in your focus." She gave him a wry smile. "So what type of boat?"

"She's a cutter-rigged sloop."

"Oh, thank God! If you'd said you're a powerboater, I would have given up on you." She giggled and tilted her head up to kiss him as she squeezed his hand, which hadn't let go of hers since they got into the cab. "My father has a sailboat. I love sailing. There are so few of them down there in the marina now. They're mostly huge powerboats. Dad calls them gin palaces."

He stroked her hand, prompting another kiss. "Would you rather go to the boat?"

"I'd love to. I haven't been aboard a sailboat for *so* long."

Lorne glanced up to see where they were. "Turn down Burrard, across the bridge to Pacific. We're going to Quayside Marina, foot of Davie, beyond Urban Fare." After he saw the driver nod, he caressed Catherine's hand as she snuggled into his chest. He moved his other hand to cup the back of her head.

"Is it big enough for what I have in mind doing with you?"

"It depends on what you have in mind. She's now the smallest sailboat in the marina since the eighteen-metre ketch left a few months ago."

"Smallest? Over eighteen metres? Most think Dad's is huge at fifteen metres." She sat up and smiled at him as she ran her hand across his chest, then ventured lower, exploring the hard rippled muscles of his abdomen through his shirt. Lorne jerked, and she abruptly stopped.

He turned away, his shoulders quaking. "Sorry, Catherine... I... I didn't mean to... it just... it won't go away... Sorry... So sorry."

She rubbed the back of his head, stroked his arm and tried to comfort him. "Tell me what's going on, Lorne. I'd love to help you with it."

"The priest... The effing pervert... Since then, I've had problems with..." He turned his head to look at her, a tortured expression on his wet face. "It's why I've shied away from women. We don't want to get into that, it's far too horrid."

She pulled his shoulder to gently turn his body toward her and eased his face down for a kiss. Then she sat staring at him, speechless for a long while, trying to sort things in her mind. *Oh, God! What have I triggered here? He seems so ashamed. Must be why there was no response all those years ago.*

Lorne finally broke the silence. "We can call it an evening and go back to simply being good friends. I really do enjoy you as a friend. You've been my favourite woman ever since I met you. I love you dearly, Catherine. I'll help you find a proper man."

"What the hell are you babbling about? I've found a proper man. A *very* proper man. The priest was a fucking pervert... Pardon my language, but the past doesn't matter. We can work through this."

The car pulled to a stop at the bottom of the circle across from the marina gate. Lorne touched the *Accept* on his phone to confirm the fee, added a tip, then got out and gave Catherine a hand.

They stood on the sidewalk, and she wrapped her arms around him, laying her cheek on his shoulder, looking up into his eyes. "Don't *ever* be ashamed of your body. The only things you should ever feel shame about are your actions. Never about you. *Never.*" She squeezed him tighter, aware of his fragility and trying to understand its source.

She felt him relaxing. "That's better." She squeezed him tighter. "Let's go aboard, I'm excited to get to know you in other ways."

He led the way to the gate, put his thumb on the pad and his eye up to the scanner. The lock clicked, he pushed the door open, ushered her through, and they headed arm-in-arm down the ramp. A few slips along, he stopped. "Here she is, *Tastevin*."

"I drool over this boat from my patio and balconies." She turned and pointed across the marina at the three-storey townhouse. "That's my place, the one with all the flowers on the balconies."

"Small world, amazingly small. Would you care to step aboard? Or would you rather head home?"

"Head home? Are you crazy? You're not going to back out of this anymore, Lorne. Whatever it is. I'm not giving up. Let's go aboard and work at moving beyond it."

"Simply checking." He shrugged. "I don't know how to read a woman's intentions." He led the way through the transom gate and into the cockpit, thumbing pads and getting green lights as he went. The companionway lock clicked, and he pulled the doors open, slid the cover forward and took Catherine's hand to lead her down the steps into the main saloon.

"Yup! A lot bigger than Dad's. This is huge. How big?"

"A centimetre less than twenty metres. It's easier on registration and other regulations being under twenty." He looked at her with a crooked smile. "I exaggerate the size, call her twenty."

"That's not unusual. Most men exaggerate size." She smiled at him and giggled.

He took her on a tour of the boat, starting aft and ending forward in the master cabin. "There's an ensuite head here where you can refresh. Let me get clean towels. The shower is over there, do you want to shower first?"

"No, I want to shower with you."

"I meant before we... Before."

"I know, silly. Only teasing." She removed his blazer and tie and laid them on the settee. "I've always loved you wearing suspenders, rather than a belt. So few wear them." She undid his shirt buttons, playing with his chest and abs along the way.

He continued to stand mesmerised as she slipped the suspenders off, undid the waist clasp, pulled the zipper down and allowed his trousers to fall to the cabin sole. "No underwear?"

"No, I stopped years ago. I kept getting tangled, so I carried on with the regimental tradition of my kilt." He glanced down as he shuffled his shoes off and stepped out of his trousers.

"I've never seen you in a kilt. Didn't know you were Scottish."

"Wilson is one of the three most common Scottish names." He shrugged. "Most miss it because it doesn't start with Mac."

Catherine slid his shirt off, picked up his trousers and laid them on the settee, then stood back looking at him and waiting.

Lorne stared at her for a while, then blew out a deep breath and asked, "Would you mind if I undressed you?"

"I've been expecting you to." She sighed. "I'd be delighted if you did, though, at this stage, Lorne, you needn't ask." She stepped out of her shoes and toed them aside, then stood eyeing him up and down as she waited.

"Where should I start? I'm not very good at this. Truth be told, I've never done it before."

"Never done what? Undress a woman?"

"That, never. Nor let a woman undress me. I've never gone beyond kissing, except in my imagination."

"I don't see that as a problem. I'd love to teach you. I had no idea you were so innocent. We can stop now if you wish."

"Do you want to stop?"

"Good God, no! What I want is you to relax and begin doing all the tender things you've dreamed of with me over the years." She saw the tears rolling down his cheeks and pulled his face down to hers to lick them away. "You're such a tender sweetheart, such a gentle soul. Come, I'll guide you."

He untied the silk scarf and removed it from her neck, then stood staring at her, speechless.

"The dress has hidden zippers up the sides, under these flaps. Undo them and peel it inside-out from the hem up over my head. It's simple."

He released the body-hugging black dress at the sides and peeled it up as she raised her arms.

"Let me show you how to undo my bra. It's easy, watch." She shook her released breasts, rubbed them to relieve the itch from their confinement, and smiled as she saw his eyes following them.

"May I? May I touch them also?"

"Of course, you may, that's one of the reasons they're there. They're meant to be touched, to be caressed, fondled, licked, sucked."

Catherine pulled her panties down and stepped out of them. Lorne's shoulders quaked. She wrapped her arms around him and gently rocked, cooing in a soft voice, "It's alright, everything's fine. Let it out."

His sobbing gradually eased. "I've dreamed of this since I first saw you all those years ago. Now I don't know what to do."

"You don't need to know, Lorne. Love is natural. Making love is instinct. Stop thinking about it and let it happen." She kissed his neck. "Nothing has to happen. Let's get into bed and cuddle. Hold each other. Be together and... We don't have to do anything except be together."

Chapter Five

Lorne and Catherine lay there quietly for a long while, cuddling and gently touching, relaxing, looking into each other's eyes and thinking. *This is so strange... I've always dreamed of this. Dreamed of lying with her, touching her, enjoying her body. God! She's even more gorgeous than I've imagined all these years...*

"What are you thinking, Lorne? You're far away, somewhere in your dreams. The look in your eyes. The throbbing." She shifted her hips and stroked his cheek.

"Sorry, I was just..."

"No need to be sorry. No need at all. It's perfectly natural."

"I was just thinking about how gorgeous you are. Absolutely gorgeous. Far more beautiful than I ever imagined."

"I love the way your eyes see me. I love the way your body signals its agreement." She shifted her hips again, lightly pressing, and he throbbed in response.

"Sorry... I don't mean..."

"Don't be ashamed of it. It's perfectly natural, normal, healthy. It's part of the design. A vital part of it." She felt him lightly push toward her. "That's better. Enjoy it."

"You've always been so easy to talk with, Catherine. So warm, so accepting and understanding. I've always been comfortable around you. I'm amazed at how comfortable I am now. A short while ago I was dreading this. Being nude with you. Now I'm..."

"Dreading? Why dreading? Am I that scary?"

"An interesting choice of word, *scary*." He shifted his eyes from his blank stare to gaze into hers. "I'm trying to think why I was so scared. There's nothing scary at all about this. It's my mind that's scary. Twisted from... I don't want to go there. Not now. Let's just cuddle. I'm wonderfully comfortable doing this."

"That's what we need. We need to feel comfortable, comforted, loved." She kissed his neck and nibbled on his earlobe. "We need to relax and begin getting to know each other on another level. We already share a marvellous friendship, a warm, trusting relationship mentally and spiritually. There's nothing scary there."

"No, and there shouldn't be anything scary — absolutely nothing scary about our physical relationship either. It's my mind saying there is. But I don't know what would be scary or why. I honestly don't. It's just there."

He gazed into her eyes. "May I look at you?"

"You already are. You needn't ask."

"No, I mean look at your body."

"You don't need to ask that either. I love your eyes on me." She flipped off the duvet and rolled onto her back.

He sat up and slowly ran his eyes from her face, down her neck, examining the little hollow at the bottom of her throat and the delicate bulges of her collarbones. He continued down and around each breast, pausing to watch as her nipples puckered tighter. Across her ribs and downward, the flat expanse of her torso captivated him, and he paused to marvel at her navel. *A tiny outie.* He examined how her pelvis bones framed the flat belly. The short red bush caused his eyes to linger, and he was about to move on when she bent her knees up and dropped them to the sides, exposing further. He looked up to her eyes to see a wide smile and a wink. His eyes went back down. "May I? May I touch you here?"

"Silly, of course, you may. I'd be disappointed if you didn't."

"This is surreal. From the beginning, I was enchanted with you. When was that? Third year UBC. The drop-dead gorgeous redhead in Creative Writing. You asked me to be your beta reader. I still remember your words: *You do mine, I'll do yours.* You were so adorably endearing. That's when you started calling me silly."

"I was completely smitten by you. I kept trying to tell you, but all you did was edit my steamier and steamier love letters which explicitly described what I wanted to do with you." Catherine did a Quebecois forehead slap.

"You were so thick. You kept finding mixed point-of-view and punctuation errors. I couldn't believe it."

"Why have we never talked of this? A dozen years of conversations. A dozen years of mutually reciprocal horniness."

"Lorne, Lorne, Lorne. Dear sweet Lorne. Don't you realise you're so channelled, so focused." She smiled up at him as he stared at her delicate folds. "So tell me, what gave you the fear of drop-dead gorgeous women?"

"Father Connolly. The Church protected him. It took five years to bring him to trial. The trial dragged on, and through it, I had to relive all the torture, the pain, the horror, the —"

"Whoa, whoa, whoa. Stop there. Forget the priest. He sounds completely twisted."

"He's dead now; died in the asylum last month. I found out only this week. It's all flooding back now. I had been dreading his release. Often seemed I was the one in prison. Maybe I still am."

She reached up and took his hand, pulling him down onto her and wrapping her arms around him. "I had no idea."

"I'm sorry, I..."

"Sorry? Lorne, why are *you* sorry?"

"Father Connolly insisted. I always had to be sorry for —"

"Whoa, Lorne. There's no need to be sorry any longer. He's dead."

"Yeah, you're right, he is." He blew out a deep breath "Let's just continue cuddling. I'm comfortable doing this."

They fell asleep entwined in each other. Lorne was awakened by her gentle attempt to untangle. "I didn't mean to wake you, but I need to pee. Any special instructions on the heads?"

"It's a simple electrical flush. The button is obvious."

He felt the urge himself, and after she had hopped back into bed, he trotted off. She was lying on her back with her knees splayed out when he returned. She smiled and softly said, "I've placed a bookmark, thinking you might want to continue from where we left off."

His gaze alternated between her eyes and the display between her legs. "I know all the theory here. God knows I've researched, studied and imagined it enough, but this is..." He paused as he lightly shuddered. "This is so far beyond my dreams." He gently placed two fingers in the patch of short red hair at the top of her cleft and moved them in a slow circle, watching the interaction of lips and hood, watching the ripples flow across her belly and listening to her quiet moans.

He tried things he had read about and had seen in videos, converting theory to practice and watching her response. All the while, he continued the slow circling of her mound, now gently, then with a bit more pressure, then gently again. Faster, then slower.

His alternating intensities continued until he saw her legs twitch and her toes curl. He fell in tune with her body, and a short while later, her belly started heaving and her hips thrusting. She scrunched the bed sheets in tight fists as she writhed in orgasmic ecstasy, then stared wide-eyed at him, mouth open wide with pulsating moans from deep in her throat.

He trembled with her, enraptured by her response. As she began regaining her composure, he asked, "So, does this mean I'm no longer a virgin?"

Chapter Six

"Oh!... My!... God!... Oh, my God, Oh my God... Oh my... My God," Catherine said through her panting as she continued staring wide-eyed at him.

Lorne lay down beside her and wrapped his arms around her as she continued a light quivering. "I've wanted to do this with you for so long. *So long.*" He started crying, his light sobs barely audible.

She held his face to kiss him, felt his wet cheeks and licked them. "Your tears taste so sweet."

"I don't know what they're for. Tears of release? Of relief? Of joy?" He caught her tongue with his, and they fenced a short while before merging into a deep, exploring kiss.

For a long while, they lay on the bed, cuddling, kissing caressing and murmuring endearments. He nibbled her earlobe and whispered into her ear, "I know it's a cliché, but was that good for you?"

"You have no idea how good." She turned her head to kiss him again. "You've always been my number one rub fantasy. And my number two and three." She sat up and stared at him. "I cannot believe how closely you played one of my favourite fantasies. Oh, my God!"

She turned her head and nodded. "You're still very proud down there. Can I do anything for you?"

An expression of anguish crossed his face, briefly, but she saw it. She lay back down and wrapped her arms around him and gently rocked.

Lorne pulled his face from her thick red hair and looked into her eyes. "It's past midnight. I should get some sleep. Will you stay here with me tonight?"

"I dare anyone to try to pry me away from here — from you." She squeezed him tighter. "I'm not going anywhere."

He awoke to the sound of the electric flush, with the sun slanting through the cabin portlights and hatch. The bulkhead clock showed eight thirty-five. *We've slept in. I've nothing scheduled. I wonder if she does.*

"Have you anything on your agenda?" Catherine asked as she hopped back onto the bed and kissed him good morning. "Mine's empty until Monday afternoon."

"I was just thinking the same thing. I've nothing before Authentic's portfolio tasting, is that yours?"

"Yes, the same. I was hoping I'd see you there. Until then I was going to vegetate and write. I've lots of research to do and —"

"I was going to go sailing. There's a marvellous satellite connection aboard. I regularly head out and anchor. Do most of my online research and writing in secluded anchorages. So peaceful. My thoughts had been to head out this morning. Would you care to come with me?"

"You're so silly. You're such an innocent child. You have no idea how endearing you are. God, I love you."

"So, does that mean you'll come with me?"

"Yes, silly; yes, yes, yes."

"We should get up, then. I'll make breakfast."

She nodded at the tenting of the duvet. "It appears you're up already. Is that all morning, or is some of it for me?" She chuckled as she leaned down and kissed his cheek.

"Both, I guess. You were so gorgeous crawling back onto the bed." He gave her a twisted smile. "I'll go take care of it."

"Do you need help?"

"We'll have to work up to that. I'm still..." He kissed her lightly on the lips, then plunged in and they writhed together on the bed as his passion grew. He stopped and shook his head. "I'll go take matters in hand... Still can't do..."

She watched as he rolled out of bed and walked toward the heads, then she lay there thinking, trying to sort out... *Trying to sort out... What? What am I trying to sort out? Why am I trying? Damn it, he's worth it, that's why. God, is he ever worth it. This is already heaven. If it never evolves beyond this, so? So don't push. Let it happen...* She continued running thoughts through her mind, trying to make sense of his reactions and the fears that seem so profound. *Whatever it is, he's such a gentle soul. My God, I love him...*

The sounds of the flushing and of the water pump running brought her back, and she turned her eyes to enjoy him swing as he walked toward the bed. "That appears to be much more relaxed."

He looked down, then blushed as he lifted his eyes to meet hers. "I'm sorry, I had to... I just... I don't know."

"No need to be sorry, none at all. Remember that. There's no need for you *ever* to be sorry about this. I'd love to take a shower. Would you like to join me? We could scrub each other's backs and —"

"Oh, God! That was in one of those stories I edited for you, wasn't it? How could I have missed it?"

As they stood in the shower, soaping and caressing each other, she looked down. "You're still as thick as my wrist, the length of my hand. Does it ever get any smaller than this?"

"A long swim in cold water will shrink it a bit, but mostly, this is its dangle. It's not rare. Statistically one or two per thousand is this size or bigger. There'd be millions like this on the planet."

"Yes, but how do you hide it? It must be obvious to others."

"You've known me for many years. We've spent a lot of time quite closely together at tastings, dinners, on junkets. Did you ever notice anything?"

"No, but now thinking — you've always worn baggy trousers, and I've always wondered why you didn't show-off your butt and goods. Gays like showing-off, and they enjoy looking at men's butts and crotches. So do I." She smiled sheepishly up at him. "I do enjoy it — but it seems I'm still working with the idea of you being gay."

They dried each other, taking their time to examine, explore and tease. As he slowly towelled her breasts again, she trembled then sighed. "I didn't realise they needed so much." She giggled. "In addition to the drying."

He kissed her lips lightly, licked them, then gazed into her eyes. "Do you mind if I tell you I love you?"

"Silly. I love you, I love everything about you. Do you mind if I tell you that?"

"No, why would I?"

"Well?"

"I guess you're right. Okay — I love you." He licked her lips again, slipped his tongue between them, and they merged in a long exploration. He paused the kiss to say, "I love you, Catherine. I always have. Ever since I first saw you."

Chapter Seven

Samir held Pierre by his throat and pushed him to his tiptoes up the wall. "You fucking let him slip away."

"We know where he lives... The Exchange... Olympic Village," Pierre wheezed through his constricted throat. "We're watching... Front and back... They have photos of him... We'll get him."

Samir lowered him, but still held his neck against the wall. "Why the fuck wasn't he nabbed when he got there?"

"The guys were there in plenty of time. The cab didn't arrive."

"You planted a tracker?"

"Yes, Sir... In the canvas bags. One in each."

"One in each?" He lifted Pierre again.

"Not everybody's... Just his... And his lady's."

"His lady?"

"They left together."

Samir lowered him. "So the fucking trackers? Where are they?"

"In the cab in a parking garage on Alberni. I've men watching. We'll make the driver tell us where he dropped them off."

"You don't like your fingers, do you?" He tightened his grip on Pierre's throat, then let it go. "Tomorrow. Get him to me by tomorrow, or..." He swung his hand like a cleaver. "Go on, get the fuck out of my sight."

◇◇◇

Part way through breakfast in the cockpit, Lorne pointed up the ramp of the marina. "Guess we were distracted last night when we arrived. We left the media kits on the floor of the cab."

"Nothing we can't replace. Probably another logo-embossed pen or corkscrew. Far too many of those. And the marketing fluff and bumf." She shrugged her shoulders. "I never review on openings or promos, anyway." She nodded across at her townhouse. "I need to get my computer and some changes of clothing. What's the forecast?"

"They show clear and warm through midday on Monday when it deteriorates with an approaching frontal system. I was thinking of being in the southern Gulf Islands on Sunday night to take advantage of the great broad reach across the Straits on Monday morning."

"Do you plan everything with such precision?"

"No, I see now I've not planned our relationship."

"Some things need no planning, Lorne. Our relationship simply needs to be allowed to blossom."

"People tell me that about many things. Guess it must be true."

As they walked around the crescent toward her townhouse, he ran over his plans so she would know what clothes to pack. "There's a new restaurant in Chemainus I've read great things about. I need to review it. I was also thinking of visiting two wineries in Maple Bay, one with a new restaurant."

"You review restaurants? I thought you did only wine."

"I've kept it secret. Much easier that way."

"Where do you write? I've never read you. You've a blog?"

"Doesn't everybody? But I also have some ink."

"Where?"

He pursed his lips as he looked at her and slowly inhaled, then he blew out a deep breath. "PacPress, The Coast. Many of the neighbourhood papers syndicate me. I love *your* columns. We're quite similar, actually. We're among the last of the dying breed of anonymous reviewers."

She grabbed his arm and spun him to a stop, shook her head and stared up into his eyes. "No! Are you? Oh!... My!... God! You're the Unknown Diner." She shook her head. "All these years I've told you you're my favourite reviewer, my model, my hero. You never let on." She took his hand, genuflected, kissed his fingers and lifted her eyes. "Oh, my God!

You *are* my god in *so* many ways." She wrapped her arms around his hips and snuggled her face into him, quiet in her thoughts.

She looked up. "Why haven't you ever told anyone?"

"I've had a lot of trouble with trusting others."

She rose from her knee, shaking her head. "So what else are you going to tell me?"

"I trust you."

"Whoa! That's *so* heavy. Who else do you trust?"

"Me — sometimes." He looked down into her eyes with a crooked smile. "That's it."

"Your parents?"

"Until the crash."

"Crash?"

"They died in a flight to the Okanagan in 1996."

"That must have been horrid for you."

"Much less horrid than what came." He winced. "I was placed in foster care."

"Relatives? You must have had relatives to take you in."

"Died in the crash too. It was a big family party celebrating my parent's twentieth anniversary. Grandfather was flying them to Penticton in his company jet for a round of tastings and a grand dinner with the top winemakers. They crashed near Princeton."

"You didn't go with them?"

"Obviously not." He shrugged his shoulders. "I was just starting high school. I stayed behind with the maid, my old nanny."

"How old were you? I should know that — you're thirty-four, so you were fourteen."

"And a quarter. Let's leave this for the moment. The whole thing's far too painful. Let's think of something lighter — much lighter. Think about sailing the next few days, maybe taking another look at you."

She squeezed his hand. "I'd like that. I'll make sure not to forget my birthday suit when I pack." She laughed. "Though with your full itinerary, will we have time to use it?"

"I'll make sure we have plenty of time for that. Your body's so mind-bogglingly beautiful. You need to teach me all about it. I'm quite ignorant about women, their bodies, their emotions, except in theory. We can forego the dining and tasting plans..."

"No need for that. I was only joking." She squeezed his hand again and smiled as they resumed walking. "I'm sure we'll welcome the brief tasting and dining breaks."

She unlocked the door and led him in. "A quick tour." She pointed to open plan layout arranged in an ell around the ten-metre ceiling up the front corner. "Down here's the kitchen, dining room, lounge and a small bathroom. Next floor, master bedroom and two guest rooms, all ensuite — the larger guest room was Nathan's office. The top floor is my office and yoga area with access to the upper patio."

"I'm always amazed by these places. Such creative architecture. Nobody'd guess what's unseen behind their façades."

She glanced down at his trousers and chuckled. "No, but now we're both aware of what's hidden from view."

He gave her a twisted smile. "You'll have to change clothes for sailing, won't you? Will you allow me to practice undressing you? I rather cocked-up with it last night, didn't I?"

"Of course, I'll allow you." She grinned. "We can both practice."

Later, as she was packing her duffel bag, still nude, she looked up and said, "I'm amazed by your tight body. Those abs are to die for. How do you keep so fit?"

"Sailing *Tastevin* solo takes a lot of work. I use it as my gym, and I still climb occasionally, but not as much now I've become so busy with the research and the —"

"I didn't know you climb."

"But you didn't know about the sailing, either — or the restaurant reviewing. I keep things separate."

"I understand that, but I've been part of the climbing community since I was a child. Dad introduced me — he had been very active, exploring up Island, through the Coast Ranges and far beyond."

"See, you hadn't told me about your climbing. You also keep things separate." He nodded to her butt. "There as you bend. I love the way your lips separate as you bend over that way." He shuddered. "May I touch you again?"

"Oh, please do." She looked over her shoulder at him and shook her butt as she smiled and nodded. "But you know we'll not get across the Straits today if we... Oh, God! Feels so good."

"The winds would be on our nose most of the way. I had thought to anchor at Keats this evening." He continued to stroke and gently play with her. "We'll cross the Straits tomorrow."

It was late afternoon when Lorne luffed the sails as he released the anchor in Plumper Cove on Keats Island and set a mark on the plot. He allowed the boat's remaining way to veer the chain to eighteen metres before he pushed the button to stop the windlass. *Tastevin's* inertia set the anchor and swung her around, perfectly centred in the bay.

"You've done this before," she said as she watched him furl the sails, deploy the snubbers, plot the swing circle and set the anchor alarm. "I'm in awe. You handle this huge sailboat solo far better than I see most handle their small ones with crew."

"The winds were favourable. I figured why furl sails and motor in." He chuckled. "After all, this isn't a gin palace."

He quickly finished the logbook, then wrapped her in a hug. "Would you care for some Champagne? We need to celebrate our first date."

Catherine arranged a small platter with the dessert titbits from the restaurant while Lorne added bowls of olives, cashews and almonds. They relaxed in the cockpit sipping Champagne, nibbling from the platter and on each other's lips, earlobes and witticisms. The angry raised voices coming across the bay from another boat's bungled anchoring attempt reminded them they weren't the only two souls on the planet.

Catherine shook her head at the sound, then watched bubbles rise from the bottom of her hollow stem. "La Grande Dame has always been one of my favourites, though I haven't had the 2006. It must have arrived while I was playing hermit."

"Clicquot launched it here about three or four months ago; after they had taken a few of us to Reims for P&P."

"Pee and pee?"

"It's for pampering and propaganda, my term for the splendid hospitality the producers offer us." He took another sip. "They leave the wine on its lees for eight to ten years before they disgorge... Have you been hosted at Clicquot's Hôtel du Marc?"

"Three visits. We had lunch there a couple of times and a splendid dinner, but we were never invited to stay. They showed us the rooms — I thought them more impressive than the ones in Moët's Château de Saran." She stared at the stream of rising bubbles for a long while and re-mained silent, then she shook her head and looked up from her memory trance. "Old days... Gone. I'm back here now. I love this wine — no, let me rephrase. I enjoy this wine — I love you."

He kissed her again and lingered, then ran a hand lightly across her breasts, teasing and retreating. "We've sailed these parallel courses for years, matching tack for tack, never drawing near. My klutziness kept us..."

"In the beginning, yes. But then I married Nathan and..."

"Was that good for you? Were you happy?"

"It was good, we were happy — mostly. But it lacked the friendship. It missed the easy friendship you and I have always shared. I was always so excited to see you at an event, at a wine dinner, at a tasting, on a junket."

"I guess I was safe company. If you thought I was gay, others must also have. So many in the trade are."

"No... Strange. I never heard that from the others, and I used to keep my ears close to the tell-a-woman net."

"Tellawomanette?"

"From an old joke of Dad's: What's the fastest means of communication? Not telegraph, not telephone, but tell-a-woman."

"Aah, from the pre-computer days, but still fast. Much faster now with texting, twitter, other apps. So the word wasn't that I was swish?"

"No, I guess it was only me — strange, I've not thought of this before — once I'd concluded you were, I stopped thinking about it. You became my safe, solid refuge... And my fantasy."

As they spoke, he played with her fingers, kissing and gently nipping them. "We should think of dinner, the sun will begin setting in less than an hour. We could cook something, or we could head across the inlet in the tender to a restaurant in Gibson's. Would you rather eat out?"

He grinned broadly, looked into her eyes and shook his head. "Eating out... Another of my fantasies with you. You're always the central char-acter. I'd love to do that to you sometime."

"Ooh... I'd love to have you do it to me. How about now?"

"Now?" He smiled. "You'll have to guide me. I know the theory. Thor-oughly. I've run it through my mind *so* many times."

Her face filled with a broad grin. "Two choices on the menu: Salty, sweaty and musky from a day's sailing and horniness, or squeaky clean from a shower."

"I'll go with the plate of the day. I've always wondered about the full flavour. Bland vegan doesn't excite me much at all."

"Oh, my God! I love you." She squeezed his thigh and kissed him. "I love your adventurousness. I love your quick way with creative imagery."

She led him down to the bed in the fore cabin and left him free to explore, having to teach him nothing. After her second orgasm, they cuddled and caressed gently as the light in the cabin dimmed toward the mid-June sunset.

"We could call a water taxi, go across to Gibson's — there's a new place I need to visit a third time to give it its fair shake. It's the new interpretation of Molly's Reach. I was surprised when the lawsuit failed and —"

"Is that another one of those? Like the ones you were talking about last night."

"No, this one's new, not taken over." He paused and thought. "Guess I hadn't looked at it this way before, but the difference between reality and the reviews is similar. Yes, it probably is. Let's go."

"Whoa, Lorne. Whoa, whoa, whoa. You need to learn to be less impulsive. We haven't finished here yet. You still need to come. I'd love to help you with it."

"Let me call the water taxi. It'll be twenty, twenty-five minutes... We need to shower and change."

The launch was approaching the transom as they stepped into the cockpit a little over twenty minutes later. As they headed across the narrow strait, Catherine kneaded his hands. "Your life is a focused schedule, isn't it?"

"Is it that bad? I guess it must be. I don't know how else to do it. Honestly, I don't. Ever since Connolly..." He contorted his face. "Damn, I don't want to go there."

"I love you, Lorne." She squeezed his hands and looked at his twisted face. "Forget that for now... Be here now... Us... Here... Now... I love you." She licked the tears from his cheeks, then held him in her arms, stroking the back of his head, murmuring. Soothing.

Chapter Eight

Lorne and Catherine stepped out of the launch at the float and walked up the ramp arm-in-arm. "Molly's Reach is slow this evening. Probably only locals, no tourists." She nodded toward the large false façade. "Looks like a new sign, though. Much bigger than I remember from the reruns."

"Yeah, my thought was they're trying to keep some business. All that built-in marketing from the TV series. My mother was hypnotised by it. She boasted she'd seen every episode, all eighteen years of them." He chuckled. "Then all the reruns."

"Dad said he used to watch the Beachcombers so he could poke fun at the errors in the boating scenes and to laugh at the hokey plots. But I guess that was CBC in the 1970s and 80s."

"Yes, but as hokey as the shows were, a booth or the counter at Molly's Reach was always central to the plot. A whole generation of TV watchers in Canada, the States and a dozen other countries know the restaurant. Those viewers are now the moneyed tourist."

Lorne pointed up the slope. "The new place is directly behind it, Molly's Beach. Clever play on words, picking up on the built-in marketing. I can't believe the name was allowed. I guess they brought in high-power lawyers to badger the small guy."

"Wow! It appears much busier, what time is it?"

He popped his iPhone from his pocket and thumbed it. "Twenty thirty-two. Yeah, it's really hopping. Hope we can get a table."

They were told it would be about a quarter hour, so they spent their time skimming the reviews, which were neatly arranged in frames on the wall of the waiting area.

He squeezed her hand "Were you ever in Molly's Reach?"

"We came over here once — I was still a kid. Mum wanted to see the old TV set after it had been turned into the story's diner. The only thing I remember of it was the strawberry milkshake."

"That building was the storage shed for the show. They dressed it up with a false façade as the diner for exterior shots. This new reception area, lounge and bar are decorated to look like the TV studio set, a gussied-up version of the diner from the series."

He pointed to a driftwood-framed doorway beyond the reception desk. "The restaurant runs across the waterfront through there."

"A lot of reviews here. Seems as though everyone has reviewed it but I haven't found yours yet"

"You won't find it. I've dined here only twice so far, but I've yet to find anything kind to say."

"Yeah, that's in the banner on the Unknown Diner blog — your blog." She squeezed his arm and lifted her face for a kiss. "You never write a bad review."

"I'd rather forgo the writing fees than say something damaging to a business." He bent to kiss her again. "The kindest thing I can do to some restaurants and wine producers is say nothing."

"Your silence speaks loudly, though. Most astute readers clearly interpret your lack of comment. You have a huge following."

"I let them make their own assumptions on my silence." He squeezed her waist, then nodded his head toward the restaurant entrance. "A large group coming out now. Looks like a tour bus load. Our table should be soon."

"You can see this as part of a great bus tour. Start in Vancouver, thread slowly through Stanley Park, across Lions Gate Bridge, along Marine Drive to Horseshoe Bay, then the ferry through the islands to Gibsons and Molly's for dinner, then the ferry back. The Beachcomber Tour. Do a lunch one too."

"There's another bus load," he nodded again. "Guess they're heading to the ferry. Let's ask if we can get a window."

A few minutes later they were led to a table overlooking the marina lit by the fading glow of sunset and a waxing gibbous moon. The room was decorated in driftwood, seashells, whalebones, seashell and driftwood sculptures and framed seashell pictures. Naïve wood carvings were caught in tatters of fishnet that framed the windows and hung from the ceilings.

Lorne smiled at the hostess and said, "I'll adjust the table to take better advantage of the space." He turned the pedestal two-top diagonally, and they took side-by-side chairs across the corner, looking out into the night. "That's better."

The hostess watched with a quizzical expression, shrugged her shoulders and pointed to the cocktail list. "Whatever... We have a special on cocktails and other mixed drinks this evening."

He handed the cocktail list back to her. "We'd prefer the wine list, please." She headed back to the front.

Lorne put his hand on Catherine's thigh. "This is better than sitting across from each other." He turned and ran his gaze around the room. "How would you describe this decor?"

"The long version or the short one?"

"Give me the long one, I love your eloquence." He leaned to kiss her cheek.

"Horrible kitsch."

"And the short version?"

"Either word, no preference, your choice." She squeezed his hand, which was lightly kneading her thigh. "What's yours?"

"Naïve tourist bait. Guess it would enthuse those not from the coast, and the die-hard Beachcombers and Gerussi fans who..." He interrupted himself when he saw the reflection of the waiter growing in the window. "Here's service."

"What can I get you to drink?"

"We had asked for the wine list. We still need one."

"We have a special on cocktails and highballs this —"

"And we'd still prefer the wine list." The waiter placed two cocktail lists in front of them and headed to tend other tables.

A few minutes later, another waiter came, but without the wine list. "Have you decided on drinks, yet?"

"Yes, we've asked for the wine list. Could you please bring us one?" Lorne said, handing him the cocktail lists.

After the waiter had left, Lorne ran a finger around Catherine's ear and played with her earlobe. "So far, the service compares to my previous visits... I love that you don't wear earrings. You've such lovely ears. Be a shame to spoil them."

"I've never been much for jewellery. Never understood the piercing craze. Have you ever been pierced?"

Lorne stiffened, took a deep breath and contorted his face trying to stop the tears and fighting his gag reflex. He grabbed his napkin and put his face down into it, his shoulders shuddering with his sobs.

Catherine moved her hand to the back of his bowed head and gently stroked, her other hand squeezing his thigh. "Let it out, Lorne. Don't try to hold it. I love you, Lorne. Let it out."

His sobs became more subdued and gradually subsided, but he continued to hold the napkin to his mouth, still fighting the urge to chuck. He mumbled through the napkin, then lifted his face to continue, "... all came back through my mind the other day when I heard he'd died. Guess it's still coming through... Sorry... I... It had been quiet for years... I'm so sorry to dump this on you."

"You're not the one to be sorry. Not in the least. Do you want to go back to the boat? We can fix a nice dinner there. Maybe grab some sushi, a pizza, some Chinese, some whatever in town to take back to —"

"I'm fine — these things are mercifully short. Give me another few moments... Have you looked at the menu?"

"You have no idea how silly that sounds, you silly man. I love you to bits. Have I looked at the menu? No, have you looked at the menu?"

Michael Walsh

"No... I guess not." He wiped his face again, then turned his crooked smile toward her. "Been a bit busy to look at it."

She smiled back at him, nodded and started into the menu. "My God! These prices. There can't be much local trade, all tourists. This is mostly pub food. Very expensive pub food."

"Those are the *Casual Favourites* pages. Flip over to the next page, *Fine Dining*. Tell me what you think."

"Some interesting items. Well maybe interesting with the less complimentary interpretation. Seems to be all old school. There are things I haven't seen except in historical menus: Shrimp Cocktail, Oysters Rockefeller, Halibut Belle Femme, Chicken Cordon Bleu, Veal Parmigiana, Beef Wellington for Two."

She looked up from the menu. "Great tour bus client fare. I would think the camper crowd too. Now they're retired, they can tie into some of that fancy grub like rich folk eat," she drawled out in a good imitation of a Midwest accent, then chuckled. "Plain to see what they're doing, isn't it? Look at the prices!"

"Don't order the halibut — I had it the last time. It looked and tasted like pangasius, basa, tra, swai... Whatever you want to call frozen farmed catfish from Vietnam. The Cordon Bleu I had the first time seemed to be frozen and deep-fryer ready."

"How could they eff-up a Beef Wellington, a tenderloin?"

"You want to find out?"

"I'd love a big piece of meat. Been craving one..." She squeezed his hand and let her mind wander, smiling, feeling a tingle in her... *Everywhere, I tingle all over at the thought of his big meat... Must remember not to mention piercing... Wonder what that's about... I'd love a big piece of meat...*

"You're off somewhere. I love the sublime expression on your face, but you're going to crush my hand."

"Sorry... I... I guess I was off exploring." She loosened her grip, picked up his hand and brought it to her lips. "The Beef Wellington will do — for now."

"We still need the wine list." He turned to see if he could find a server, and he spotted a clutch of them standing in a corner, talking. His waving finally caught an eye, and they all dispersed to head to their stations.

He asked again for the wine list. It arrived half a minute later, and he ordered two entrées followed by the Wellington rare. "Put in the order and come right back. I'll find a wine quickly."

He opened the wine list. "Still the cleverly crafted selection. Wines from poor producers in the famous appellations or poor showings from well-known producers. What's your preference?"

"I'd prefer a great wine from a great producer in a great area." She smiled at him and giggled. "Well, you asked."

"That page seems to be missing. How about an inexpensive Argentinian? Their economy is still bottom-feeding, offering great values. Here's Finca Los Primos Malbec, a nice wine, and even with the two hundred percent markup here, it's not far out of line."

He ordered the wine, and they resumed their light banter. They have never been short of words, always an easy flow, usually filled with clever turns of phrase, plays on words and fun. After five minutes, Lorne turned again to see where the wine was. They waited.

The two entrées arrived before it did, escargots bourguignon and paté maison. "Which do you want to start with?"

"The wine." She smiled. "Why do you continue doing this, Lorne? You know you won't review this place. Why punish yourself?"

"Fairness. Give every place the same three unbiased chances. Nobody knows me as a restaurant reviewer. They know me as a wine writer, a competition judge, a wine educator. I always dine anonymously and pay my own way —"

"But you get lots of freebies and —"

"Yes, but because of the wine and my reputation there. I never write reviews based on my freebies. Not even my editors know my identity — you're the only one I could trust."

She shook her head. "And I didn't know until..."

Michael Walsh

He leaned over and kissed her. "I'll divide these. Notice, no bread basket yet?" He began dividing the two appetiser plates. "The paté's commercial, probably from Oyama or Freybe. The escargots are canned. Tough to go wrong with them, add olive oil, garlic, parsley and... Finally, the wine's here," he said as he caught the movement of the waiter's reflection in the window.

"We're out of the Finca Los Primos but this is similar."

"I'm not familiar with the producer. What's the price?"

"It's also forty-two, Sir."

"I assume you're still out of all the other inexpensive wines on the list."

"Yes Sir, but we've recommended replacements for all of them."

"Okay, let's get on with this. We also need bread."

The waiter unscrewed the cap, poured a perfunctory taste and left, Lorne calling *bread* at his back as he went. The waiter nodded over his shoulder and was quickly back with a basket. Catherine checked it and sighed. "Freshly sliced this morning."

While Lorne finished dividing the two plates, Catherine poured the wine. They raised their glasses in a toast, had a sip and turned to their entrées. They had barely begun them when the main course arrived, wheeled in on an ornate trolley by a young man in a tall white toque. Seeing it was useless to buck the current, they resigned themselves to the inept timing as the carver bungled away with the tableside service. Lorne tapped Catherine's arm and nodded at the Wellington being carved, raised his eyebrows and whispered, "Rare?"

He caught the carver's eye. "This is much closer to grey than pink, and a long way from red."

"The kitchen's all out of rare, Sir. We just had two bus loads. This was the last medium."

"So this has been freshly microwaved?"

"Yessir, did it myself." He smiled proudly as he continued to fumble with the carving and plating.

They watched as the hacked mess was heaped onto plates and fingered around. The comedy continued as contents of pseudo-silver vessels were dumped with flourishes to further sully the plates, before they were ceremoniously presented by two waiters who had been standing by. The toque and the waiters bowed and marched the trolley away to the applause of several diners in the room.

"I cannot believe your patience, Lorne."

"I'm simply analysing what enthuses the gullible unwashed. The non-thinking people who automatically vote Conservative here, and Republican down south. They're such an easy market for the greedy, the corrupt, the sleazy. This place preys on them."

"This is definitely what you were talking about last evening at La Luce. Those reviews out there in the foyer, all glowing — probably all bought."

"Or self-written. Let's get the bill, pay it and leave. Would you prefer Chinese, some sushi or a pizza?"

Chapter Nine

"Nothing much. It seems we weren't in the mood this evening for abysmal service, a switch and boost wine list and exorbitant prices for packaged food," Lorne replied calmly to the question. The manager had been called by the hostess who had been called by the waiter as he had tried to get the bill so he could pay it. "It's nothing you've done. I'm sure it's far beyond you — in more than one way."

"But you've barely started. Is something wrong?"

He stared at the manager, doubting his listening and comprehension skills. "Your service, presentation and quality finished us before we had much of a chance to start."

They moved to the reception desk, the manager punched some buttons, tore the tape from the printer and read it. "But you're leaving a hundred and fifty-two dollars worth of food on the table. We can get you a doggy bag... A box."

"We're leaving fifty dollars worth on the table, less than that, including the wine. We'll take the wine. A rough red will do fine with our pizza."

"We can adjust the price if you're unhappy. I need to call and —"

"No need to expend any energy on it. That wouldn't match the work ethic we've seen." He glanced up to see Catherine was well into photographing all the framed reviews. He pulled out four fifties. "I need a receipt for expenses, for taxes."

The manager tried to generate a receipt from the interface, then buttonholed a waiter to do it for him. Catherine came over to join Lorne, nodding as she approached, then sidled up beside him, taking his arm.

"Tip?" The waiter looked up from the screen.

"Change please."

"But for the service?"

"Already far overpaid."

The manager elbowed the man, caught his eye and nodded. The waiter handed Lorne forty-eight dollars, then tore off the receipt and held it out as he droned his memorised prattle: "Thank you for dining with us. Come back soon. Tell your friends about Molly's Beach."

Lorne led Catherine toward the exit arm-in-arm and listened to the same spiel again as the door was opened for them.

He nodded to the doorman. "Thank you, that's a fine idea. We'll spread the word."

"Are you going to?" Catherine asked as they walked along the street looking for dinner.

"Somebody has to. I doubt there's been a chef in the kitchen since their opening smoke and mirrors dances. They've a gouging game with the wine list, but they were pushing cocktails. They must have a more profitable scam there."

He stopped, turned and put his arms around her. "On to other things." He leaned down to kiss her lips. "There's a great little sushi place around the corner and along. Want to do sushi? We still have the remains of the Veuve stoppered in the fridge — and a back-up — several backups."

They sat at the bar, and Lorne explained the Champagne, the boat and their hungers to the itamae and said *omakase*. Sipping green tea and chatting, they watched the creations evolve in front of them. The place was busy, but there appeared to be nobody at the bar or the tables unattended. "Good business."

"Have you reviewed this place?"

"Not yet. This is only my second visit. The first was great. Wait 'till you try this."

Michael Walsh

"There are so many things I want to try with you..." She trailed off dreamily. *So many things... So much pent-up... Anticipation... I'm wet... Oh God! Please God if you're there, please help Lorne through this — this whatever it is. So fricking horny for him. I can't believe his fingers... His tongue... Oh, my God... That schlong... Soon, please God, soon...*

The quiet beeps as he poked his phone brought her back. She listened to him ask for a water taxi in twelve minutes, across to the Keats anchorage. "Here you are scheduling again."

"And there you were dreaming. I love the look on your face when you do that. Where were you?"

"Just thinking about you. How fortunate I am to know you."

"I'm the lucky one. You're the only person I've felt safe around since... Stop!" He tensed. Stared at the wall, then shook his head and turned to peer into her eyes. Quietly.

She watched his face slowly relaxing, his crooked smile gradually unwrinkling. Still quiet. She rubbed his hand and felt his grip on the teacup relax, heard his quick, shallow breathing slow, watched his shoulders drop. *No tears this time... Seems lighter... I wish I knew what to do... God, I love him... Hunk! So hard, strong, confident outside, so tender, so fragile inside...*

"You're making that sublime face again. Our order's ready. Are you?"

Back aboard, she laid out the sushi on the porcelain plates he had taken from the cupboard. He poured soy into two small heart-shaped bowls and lifted hollow stems from the rack. "I love these wavy plates," she said. "Where did you find them?"

"In a little shop on Saltspring, they reminded me of a gently rippled sea. Still do. I'm pleased you like them. Much more pleased you like me."

"God! What's not to like? You're such a magnificent beast. So complex, yet so simple. So hard, firm, distant, yet so soft, warm and endearing. Loving... Caring..."

"You've that sublime face again. You really do love me, don't you?"

"God! What an understatement! You have no idea how much. How much I crave you." She wiped her hands on a tea towel and looked up.

"Hug?"

They merged. Her whole body shuddered. Tears rolled down her cheeks as she tilted her head up to him. He tasted them as he kissed her. "What are these about?"

"Joy... Ecstasy... You."

The kiss went deeper, the hug tighter, their bodies pressing, writhing, feeling the swelling. He paused the kiss but continued the hug. "Sushi? We've sushi to enjoy, and La Grande Dame... Actually, I've two great ladies to enjoy."

"Both of us widows."

"Hadn't thought of that. Shall we dine? I was thinking of over there with cushions." He nodded to the carved low teak table.

"I'd like to get into something more comfortable." She winked at him. "Care to help me with it?"

"I'd love to. I've some bathrobes. I'll go get —"

"No need for them unless we get chilly, but then I'd rather you keep me warm."

As they undressed each other teasingly, she giggled and said, "You're so much better at this than you were the first time."

"That seems so long ago — last night — so much since then. May I tell you again that I love you?"

"Silly, silly Lorne. So silly. You never need my permission for that. You don't need any permission to love. *Ever.*"

He nodded. Paused. Nodded again. "I love you. I always have. I feel I always will."

Michael Walsh

Chapter Ten

"This is superb sushi, so creative. The textures, the flavours... Mmph." Catherine put her hand up as she finished savouring the bite. "Sorry, I just had to have another. This is so delightfully appropriate, doing raw seafood in the raw. This is *so* good."

Lorne swallowed his bite. "It's still as good as I remember. Better. Appears the lower overhead is allowing him to pay up for quality. Way up. This is truly delicious."

"Lower overhead? Where was he before?"

"On Arbutus in Kits. He and his wife decided not to renew the lease. They rented out their Vancouver condo and bought this place. They now live upstairs."

"Wise move. The rents in Kitsilano have become ridiculous... That's why the name was familiar — this is eSushi, isn't it, but better?"

"It was always among my favourites in Vancouver. Known for freshness and quality." He laughed. "I remember sitting at the bar and hearing a know-it-all type ask if the uni was fresh. Hachirou picked an urchin out of his tray, put it on a board in front of the fellow and told him to watch as it slowly crawled toward him."

"That was fast thinking — probably an old trick. What was that, oma something you said to the itamae? That was such a brief order for this superb assortment."

"Omakase. It's Japanese for I'll leave it up to you. A talented itamae will assess the client and act accordingly. I mentioned yacht, Champagne and being very hungry, then nodded at you and smiled. He understood."

"I missed the nod." She smiled. "You didn't, did you?"

"Did too."

"Oh, my God. How to inspire a creative spread."

Lorne nodded down at her display. "But as wonderful as this spread is, that one is more intriguing to me." He shuddered. "I've not imagined what it would look like in a sukhasana."

She glanced down, then back up to his eyes, smiled, winked and took another sip of her Champagne. "I needed to cool it off. It's been so hot for you. And I see you've risen to the challenge, or is that its acknowledging salute?"

"You have such a marvellous way of phrasing such things. You should write women's fiction."

"I do."

"You do? You've never told me."

"And you've not told me about your restaurant reviews, your sailing, your climbing."

"True... You're published?"

"Thirty-two and counting. You edited my first one." She winked at him and popped a tako nigiri into her mouth. Then sipping her Champagne, she watched his expression change from puzzlement through amusement and into the contortions of his loud laughing.

"You published that?" He laughed again. "I got so hot reading your chapters. Rereading to edit, but more as jerk inspiration. My God! I still remember those steamy scenes." He shook his head. "Thirty-two of them? Under your name?"

"No, I was too embarrassed, so I did a pen name. They're much better now, but I kept the name. It had developed a following."

"So?"

"So?"

"Pen name? I need to know your alter ego so I can read her. God, she turned me on."

"Wouldn't you prefer hearing it straight from the source?"

"Oh my... Oh my my..."

As he stared at her, she began speaking in a soft, deep-throated voice through her actions. *"She winked back at him and licked her lips, shaking her shoulders just enough to swing her breasts across his vision and entice his eyes down from hers. He watched her buds pucker, invite, beg his hands, his lips. She swung her breasts gently again to confirm, to beg..."*

Lorne was quickly on his knees in front of her, one nipple in his mouth, the other being rolled between his fingers.

"So it seems you like my prose... Oh, God! That feels so good."

He looked up at her face as he continued licking, tongue flicking, sucking and tweaking. He paused his mouth to speak. "You're a hypnotist, an effing hot hypnotist. How did you do that?"

"Simply sensing what you want, knowing what I want."

"But that's easy — I want you."

"I know that, and I ache for you, I crave you... Desperately."

"I'd love to do something about it. You're the expert on these things. What would you suggest?"

"Whoa, Lorne. Whoa, whoa, whoa. I'm not an expert here at all... I write steamy novels. My postgrad is in psychology, not psychiatry. We can lie in bed and talk about it. Talking often loosens things. You know you can talk with me. You know I don't bite. You know I don't judge."

"I'd like that... I'd like it a lot." He watched his fingers tweaking her nipples and trembled lightly. "God, you're beautiful."

"And you're so good at doing that." She cupped the sides of his head and gently lifted his face to hers. "As much as I'd love you to continue doing that, let's finish this marvellous sushi, not leave a second dinner on the table. We haven't eaten much today, and we need the energy. I'm hoping we'll need lots of energy."

Chapter Eleven

"So where do we start?" Lorne asked as they finished the sushi and the remainder of the Champagne.

"We can lie in bed and cuddle and talk."

They lay silently, wrapped in each other under the duvet. After a few minutes, Catherine said softly, "Don't even need to talk. Just be together. Relax and allow our spirits to merge. Know we're here for each other. Safe, protected, loved."

They remained silent for a long while as Lorne thought. *Why am I so afraid of looking at this? Connolly's dead. He can't hurt me anymore. I no longer have to deal with the church lawyer or that psychiatrist, Doctor Frick... Doctor Sick, the sick-aitrist.* He laughed.

"What's funny?" she asked, kissing his shoulder.

"Doctor Sick, the sick-aitrist. His name was Frick, but sick was more appropriate."

"Frick... So that's where your curse word comes from, the one I've adopted. Frick the fricking sick sick-aitrist."

"That's good. I hadn't thought of that one. Fricking sick, he had to have been. He contorted reality in his testimony. Contrived twisted lies with the church lawyer, nearly convinced the court I was making up the whole thing. He damned near convinced the judge I was a self-abusing, mutilating pervert. He played Connolly as a gentle, saintly man. I again feared for my life, thinking they'd get Connolly off. He now knew where I was."

She rubbed the back of his head and snuggled her face into his chest. "He's dead now. You no longer have anything to fear."

He wiggled his body more tightly to hers. She wiggled tighter still, and they lay silent for another long while.

Lorne wandered back through his memories, slowly sorting and sifting. He started quietly speaking. "Mine was always big compared to other boys. Then with adolescence, it grew... A lot. In the school showers, I gained the names Allcock, and Hunguy. Father Connolly was often in locker room talking with us when we changed into and out of gym or sports strip. After Mum and Dad died, he applied to be my foster parent. The system didn't question the Church then. It certainly does now."

She squeezed him tighter, rubbed her face into his chest and kissed it, remaining silent as she waited. Waited a long time. Waited patiently.

"The fucking pervert shackled me to the floor." Lorne started convulsing in deep sobs, between them blurting, "Fucking pervert... God damned psycho... Christ's fucking representative? What fucking crap... Satan's servant suits better..."

Lorne's ranting convulsions continued as Catherine gently stroked the back of his head and murmured almost to herself, "Let it out, let it go... Free yourself... It's gone... It's behind you. You're safe, protected, loved... I love you... You're such a beautiful creature. I love you, Lorne... Let it all out."

She awoke a long while later from an urge to pee and looked across to the bulkhead clock. *0142.* She tried to untangle without waking him, but he reached up and rubbed her back as she rose to begin sidling toward the edge of the bed. She turned and kissed him, put a hand on his cheek, moved it to his ear and played. "We've slept. It's quarter to two — gotta pee. Don't go away, I'll be right back."

He shook the sleepiness away in time to enjoy her kiss and her gentle strokes. "Did I miss anything?" He laughed. "The last thing I remember was my blue language and... Was that stuff really coming from me?"

"That's the first time I've ever heard you use anything stronger than effing or frick. You're getting to be normal." She smiled at him, stroked his cheek and bent to kiss him, grazing her breasts across his chest as she did. "Gotta pee."

A minute later she was back and snuggled beside him again, resuming their entwined cuddle. "Champagne — any bubbly — does that to me. Do you want to sleep, orrrr?"

"Or what? You make it sound so exciting. That's the most exciting *or* I've ever heard."

"We could play doctor. You remember playing doctor as a kid?"

"The girl down the street — Kate. God! We were four, close to five. Innocent explorations. Delightful. Looked at my first pussy, got an examination in return. Can't remember, but I likely didn't even rise to the occasion, so innocent. I've forgotten those innocent days. Too much muck followed."

"We can go back. Pretend I'm little Kate and you're little Lorne."

"Could we?"

"It'll be fun. We'll make a game of it. I'm Kate, I'm almost pretty near going on five."

His eyes widened to match the smile on his face as he sat up to look at her. "How do we do it?"

"The same innocent way we did as children — curiosity."

"My curiosity was with the difference. Why Kate couldn't pee against the garage wall like me."

She rolled onto her back and spread her legs. "Well?"

He turned around and lay on his elbows between her legs and stared. For a long while, he did nothing but look, then he moved a tentative finger to touch her rounded lips, to poke at their softness. "This is so pretty. Like a small bum. You have two bums, one in back and one in front." He ran his finger lightly along her cleft, gently pulling one lip aside.

"It's my pee bum."

He looked up at her smiling face. "That's exactly what Kate called hers. I've never heard it since. Such a cute name. She had a pee bum and a poo bum."

"That's what Mum called them. I wonder if it's common, I've not thought about it. I'll have to ask the girls what they called theirs as kids."

Lorne resumed his exploring, two hands now, pulling aside the lips and minutely examining. "I love how your little lips are arranged. They're there to protect the delicate inside parts." He lightly tugged on one and watched it pull the hood of her clit. He moved the lip back and forth to study the action there. "These attach to your foreskin — I guess your hood's like a foreskin, a protective cover." He moved both inner lips now and watched the action. "These are here not only for protection, but also to move the hood over your clitoris — to excite it."

He drew a finger up her cleft, pushing lightly on the bottom of the nub, watching it poke out to greet his examination. He moved his finger side to side to study the now turgid clit's interactions with hood and lips. Satisfied he understood the layout and mechanics there, he moved his finger back along to the slight thickening of her pee hole. *Not an elegant name, but I prefer pee hole to urinary meatus. We have such strange language for our nether regions.*

He smiled up at the sublime expression on her face. "You've that wondrous face again. God, Catherine, I love you. I've been thinking; down here... That's another one... Just thinking of the strange language we use for such magnificent parts, down here, down there, nethers, unmentionables, puden-dum... What do you call your pee hole?" he asked as he touched it.

"Pee hole, I guess. I don't know what else it would be called."

"Urinary meatus is the Latin... Not elegant, but descriptive — a direct translation for pee hole, in fact. But the unmentionables, the pudendum? What's that about? Pudendum is from the Latin pudere, meaning to be ashamed. Why the shame? These are magnificent parts."

He continued his explorations, moving along to the glistening mois-ture, dipped a finger in it and brought it to his nose. "Such an intoxi-cating aroma." He shuddered. "You have such a marvellous bouquet." He leaned forward to more fully appreciate it. "Nature's perfume." He looked up and smiled.

Dipping his finger again in the moistness, he drew a slow circle around her opening, and again, and again, feeling the smooth slickness of the skin. He pushed his finger in and felt around, tingling with the warm sensation, feeling her tremble, hearing her moan.

Slowly he withdrew and sat up to take an overall view as he nosed his finger. "You have an absolutely gorgeous pee bum." He shuddered again and looked up to see her arms extend toward him.

He collapsed on top of her and they writhed in a tight embrace, kissing whatever came near their lips as they moved. "So much more interesting with a woman, than a little girl," he said after a long silence "You're *such* a beautiful woman. Thank you."

"You've grown up magnificently yourself. You're much better at it than you were the first time. I liked it then, we had fun, but I love this; it's far more exciting, and so much more comfortable than your garage on Cypress..."

"On Cypress?" He stiffened. Shook his head and rose onto an elbow. "You can't be... I... Oh, my frickin God..." He started laughing then flopped onto his back convulsing with laughter, tears streaming from his eyes. "I didn't..." He tried to speak but the belly-laughing prevented his words, so he stopped trying.

Catherine watched, puzzled at first, but then began suspecting he had forgotten. *I never thought he didn't know me when I asked him to be my beta reader. Oh, my God! It never entered my mind. He became such a sweet friend... I wanted more, but...* She watched as his laughing eased, then rolled on top of him. "I thought you knew. All these years, I thought you knew." She burst into laughter and they rolled, clasping tightly as their movements ground their bodies together.

"My little Kate is all grown up now. I never connected her to that drop-dead gorgeous woman who was so friendly to..."

"And I never thought you didn't remember me."

"So it was better this time?"

"Frickin God! You barely touched me, and I almost popped."

"So you're still the only girl I've touched down there... Damn there has to be a better term for that. When was it when you moved? Can't even remember where you went."

"I was ten, so 1992 when my folks bought the winery. Had to leave my best buddy when we moved."

Michael Walsh

"I don't know how I didn't connect you. We had such a sweet relationship back then."

"We still do, Lorne. Do you want to keep going? It's now my turn to play the doctor. I'd love to see how my best buddy, my little Lorne has grown up."

Catherine felt him tense, start shallow breathing, then slow and begin relaxing. She squeezed him gently and whispered, "We don't have to now. We can pause and get some sleep, then..."

"No, let's keep going. If I don't... If we don't work through this, it will always haunt me."

They kissed lips lightly as they had done as kids, playing mummy and daddy. Then untangling from their embrace, she rose as he rolled onto his back. "Close your eyes and relax, Lorne. Think of the garage on Cypress Street. No more comfortably, the old mattress in your attic." She giggled. "Without the dust."

She knelt beside his hips, her eyes admiring him. *My Greek god... No, my Canadian god.* She gently lifted his limpness from between his legs and laid it up his belly *A bit past his navel, well the puckered spout is, the head's a bit short of there... Like a bottle-nosed dolphin... I hope it fits... Of course it will, babies are bigger.* She shuddered and continued her slow examination along his length.

Not touching, only looking. Don't want to excite him yet... Check it out soft first, then I'll watch the hardening... I'm dripping... Calm down girl, this is supposed to be clinical. She ran her eyes down his raphe, remembering her anatomy classes. Her eyes stopped.

Looks like jagged scar tissue. She bent to more closely examine. *A big hole, a piercing. That's probably what that was about... No, not probably... That's what it was about. Dare I touch it? Will it trigger another? Yes, damn it. We have to get him beyond this.*

She extended a finger to lightly touch the edge of the scar tissue. *No response.* She ran her finger down the scrotal raphe and back up to the scar, touched it again, then put the tip of her finger through the piercing in the web.

Lorne tensed. Not much, and then he relaxed. "That's where he put the padlock through. To chain me to the floor — the first time. That was the easy one."

Chapter Twelve

Catherine stared at her finger through the hole, then closed her eyes as she fought her gag reflex. Lorne sat up and stroked her back. "It's alright, that's the easy one. I'd forgotten about it. Doesn't constantly remind me like the others." He felt her tense again then begin sobbing. He pulled her finger out of the hole and eased her down onto the bed, pulled the duvet over them, turned off the lights and they merged into another cuddle.

The sunlight through the portlight woke him, still wrapped in a wonderful tangle. He didn't want to turn his head to look at the clock. *It might wake her. She's so peaceful, so comfortable. Being alone is so... So alone, I guess... It must have been hard for her after Nathan... That was so sudden. I understand alone... God, do I understand it. But going from something as wonderful as this to alone, so quickly to...* He felt her stir.

She rubbed his chest, kissed his neck and laughed as she moved her hand to wipe his shoulder and her cheek. "I've been drooling on you." She giggled. "Guess it's not unusual for me to drool over you. God knows, I've had the practice."

He adjusted the cuddle to reach her lips and lick them teasingly. "My mouth's fuzzy and funky. Do other people kiss like this in the morning?"

"Lovers do. I don't know about ordinary folk." She caught his tongue with hers, prodded through his lips and continued on in, exploring, he reciprocating.

"Good morning, Gorgeous," he said after they finally paused. "Did you sleep well?"

"I guess I must have, I remember nothing except your trying to calm me. It seems you did that." She nibbled his lower lip and ran her hand down his back to his butt cheek, giving it a shake. "Let's move our butts, we've lots to do."

"What have you in mind?"

"First, we need to pee... At least I know I need to, you guys seem to have bigger tanks. Then a shower and breakfast. After that, I'd like to continue sorting things out. You now seem to be handling it easier than I am. You'll need to help me."

"I'll use one of the after heads, you use this one. I'll meet you in the shower."

A while later, as they luxuriated in each other's bodies under the spray from the triple shower nozzles, she said, "You seem to have unlimited hot water."

"Mostly from solar and wind, but there's an automatic back-up from an on-demand propane heater. I keep the watermaker on an automatic five-day purge cycle, so it's always ready to replenish on my longer trips."

She soaped his chest and abs again. "You've designed your life to be solo and independent, haven't you?"

"Life taught me that — forcefully." He made sure her breasts and vulva were well washed — once more just to be sure.

She soaped his penis again. "Yours is the only foreskin I've seen. Should I wash under it? I've read that needs to be done."

He looked at her with a twisted face. "I did it when I was in the head, after I peed. I always have to." He shrugged his shoulders, picked it up and examined it. "This may spoil your breakfast, but..." Then gazing into her eyes, he continued, "But we're here already. Tell me to stop whenever you want."

"Do you want to rinse and dry? Do this on the bed. Not a good idea to faint in the shower." She gave him a crooked smile.

"Are you okay with this? We could have breakfast first."

"No, let's just get on with it. We're already rolling, let's dry each other and get on with it."

They sat on the bed facing each other quietly for a while as Lorne gathered his thoughts. *Where do I start? Background information, the mutilation culture, perversion, child porn...* "You're aware of child porn, I'm sure?"

She nodded.

"And Catholic abuse — the perverted nuns and priests?"

She nodded again.

"How about the body modification culture?"

Another nod.

"Beyond the visible piercing?"

"Like clit rings, labial rings. One of my girlfriends has a ring through her hood and one in each of her lips joined by a chain."

"Have you heard of subincision?"

"The Australian Aborigine ritual?"

"Yes. How about penile splitting?"

"Nathan bumped into a gross site one night and said I had to see it. A collection of sick people who cut their penises and boast about it."

"That's a good description of Connolly."

"He had cut himself?"

"Then he started on me," he said as he rolled back his foreskin.

She slowly moved a hand to cradle his penis and sat there staring, remaining silent. *Okay... Pretend I'm in an anatomy lab examining a specimen. I can get through this. I haven't puked at one of these since first week Grade Eleven.* She moved her other hand and rolled the glans with a finger, separating the two halves a bit, then a bit more.

"You can go a lot wider. It doesn't hurt anymore."

She did and bent closer to examine. "This isn't as bad as I was expecting. Leading me to it gradually helped. The hole through your left half? What's this?"

"That was fresh, not fully healed when I escaped. It was to be the new leash anchor for when he started splitting my shaft."

She held the gag. "He was going to split your shaft? Just like that? Just slice it down the..."

"No, not all at once. A bit at a time. Let it heal, then cut another bit, like he did with my head." He paused and watched her. *She seems okay with this so far.*

"He took photos of the entire process. The entire seventeen months — thousands of photos. From every angle. His favourite poses were of me licking and sucking the split halves and..."

"You could lick yourself? I guess it's long enough for that." She lifted her head and smiled at him. "Can you still?"

"I've lost the flexibility of my youth, but I can still get most of the head in." He smiled crookedly and blushed.

"So he was going to split the entire thing?"

"I'm not sure. He kept talking about what he was going to do with the foreskin, wanting to keep it intact. I think he planned on seeing how far he could go and still be able to roll it back over and hide the split. He had made his first shaft cut and Crazy Glued the new surfaces a few hours before I escaped."

She spread the halves wide and ran a finger across the healed surfaces. "Doctors can repair this. I'm sure quite easily."

"Yeah, I know. But I had already endured too much pain by that point, mostly emotional. I retreated deep inside, I kept this hidden. The hospital treated my broken shoulder and wrist, concussion and amnesia, while I cared for my other wounds."

"So, you escaped?" She moved a hand down to the hole through his scrotal web, but decided not to put her finger through it this time. "How did you get free of the padlock?"

"It wasn't there anymore. He had made another hole when he started splitting my head, through here." He flipped his penis up across his thigh, exposing the bottom side, pulled the foreskin back farther and pointed to the jagged scars. "He pierced the shaft through the spongiosum under the urethra, just below the head."

Michael Walsh

Catherine was still in her imaginary anatomy lab, so she bent close to examine the scars, trying to make sense of them, tracing them with her finger. "So, how did you free yourself from the padlock?"

He pointed to the scar and said, "I chewed through here."

She gagged, held her mouth, but couldn't stop it and spewed through her fingers.

Lorne wrapped his arms around her and patted her back. "It's alright, I think we're through the tough part now. Do what you need to. Don't worry about the mess. I've a washer and dryer aboard, there's plenty of hot water in the shower."

Chapter Thirteen

"Good thing my stomach was nearly empty — sushi, not beef." Catherine looked up at Lorne sheepishly. "I haven't done that since Grade Eleven Anatomy."

He had pulled the sheet loose from the bottom of the bed and was wiping her with it. "I guess it was a bit gross dumping it as I did. I should have gone slower, but you seemed okay leading up to it. Are you okay now?"

"I'm fine... Now. I guess it was the suddenness of it." She shook her head at his wiping. "Don't worry about cleaning me, most of my spew ended up on you."

"Go jump in the shower, I'll throw this into the washer, then join you. Sure you're okay?"

"Yeah. Just shaken. How about you? Are you okay?"

"I think I've finally gotten rid of him — I hope I have."

Half an hour later, they sat in the sunny cockpit enjoying their espressos and eating thin slices of smoked sockeye on cream cheese sprinkled with capers and red onion on lightly toasted bagels.

"Is this the cold-smoked alder salmon from Quallicum? It must be. Still my favourite."

"They've expanded, kept the quality and lowered their prices. I don't know how the others will survive."

"How about buying reviews, raising prices to pay for them and pretending to be the best?"

Michael Walsh

"Seems to be the modern way, doesn't it?"

"Like the bagels. These must be Safeway Bakery. The reviews usually tout Solomon's and Beigel's. I've tried them so often to see if I could discover why."

He took another bite and put up a finger to mark his pause. "A large portion of the public is gullible. They don't trust their own taste. They'd rather distort their tastes to adapt to what they're told is good. Politicians play with this. Prey on them with it."

"And the other mass markets — women's clothing, cosmetics, yahoo vehicles, firearms, other ego boosters for the insecure. So much of modern marketing is preying on insecurity, on doubt, on fear."

They moved on to lighter banter as they enjoyed their leisurely breakfast. The morning had warmed quickly, as they often do in the late spring, and since the anchorage had emptied, Lorne took off his bathrobe. "I often sit here in the cockpit this way. Even with others in the anchorage. They'd see nothing... Likely wouldn't want to."

She shucked her robe and snuggled beside him, pulling his face to hers for a kiss. "So what do you have in mind?"

"I was thinking I could try using this thing for its other intended purpose."

She had no doubt what he meant by *this thing.* It was proudly standing front and centre. "Here?"

"We could. The cushions are soft, I'm hard and..."

"You're so impulsive." She smiled at him and gave a slow stroke up his length. "But as much as I'd love to have you turn me into quivering jelly right here, right now, let's approach this more slowly. Enjoy it more."

"We could use a berth in one of the aft cabins. They're queens."

"Do you have a fresh sheet for your bed?"

"There's another silk and a bamboo."

"Simple, then, let's do the king in the master cabin... Much more appropriate. Take our time with it, build up to it..." She shook her head and smiled. "God, this is so funny. I've been building up to this since I was four. Praying for it, begging for it for thirty years and now I slow... Probably right, though. Why rush it now?"

They stretched the fresh bottom sheet onto the bed, tossed the six pillows on, then stood gazing into each other's eyes. She changed to speaking in a deep-throated voice: *"The magnificent hunk stood in front of her, looking into her eyes, seeming to question. She raised a hand to her right breast and started slowly circling a finger around her nipple, trembling at the sensation as it puckered out. She looked at her lonely left breast, then to his eyes, inviting..."*

"Oh, my fuck..." His hand was on her breast and circling. "You're so fucking hot, I used to pull to your writing. I had trouble doing the editing without... Sometimes I had to wipe jizz off your pages. Oh, my God."

"She smiled at him, then pressed his hand into her breast, squeezing it lightly and rolling her eyes across to the bed, tilting her head for emphasis. He followed her, now more eager... How could she help seeing his eagerness?" They moved onto the bed.

"He knelt over her, between her spread legs as she lay back, head on the soft pillows, sensing the fresh silk sheet beneath her. He appeared to be wondering what to do next. She held a hand out toward him, he took it and she gently pulled him on top of her. They kissed..."

"See, this is easy," she said at the end of a long exploring kiss. "It's a matter of sensing what your lover wants and allowing them to sense what you want."

She led him through foreplay, popping once in the process, then they connected.

An hour and a half later they were still connected. She was kneeling astride as she gently rocked and rotated her hips, bending forward to swish her nipples across his chest. He watched her with wonder in his eyes as she climbed toward another shuddering release. "You're doing amazingly well... I told you... There's nothing to fear... This is wonderful... For me... Excuse me... Again..." she said with panting breath before she began convulsing with deep moans rising from her throat.

She collapsed onto him again, panting more deeply and twitching as a warmth spread through her soul. "Is it good? Am I pleasing you?" he asked, gently kneading her bum cheeks and kissing her neck. "Was I doing the breast massage thing correctly?"

"God, Lorne, this is so far beyond good." She kissed his face randomly, seeming to try not to miss any spot. "You are absolutely amazing. Nathan could rarely last long enough inside to please me, I could count the times. You've popped me nearly as often in the past while as he did in a decade."

Her face kissing continued as her breathing calmed, then she paused to say, "This exercise regime will keep me slim. My God, such a wonderful all-round exercise regime. Cardiovascular, flexibility, endurance, mental, spiritual, emotional."

She sat up and ran her hands lightly across his chest, teasing his nipples, then trailing her fingers over the firm ripples of his abdomen, through his navel to the curls of hair at their juncture. "We need to get you to come. So far it's been all me. It's your turn now."

"But what if I get you pregnant?"

"I told you before we started, this is a safe time." She giggled. "I know that's a long time ago now, but I'm still safe." Shrugging her shoulders and smiling, she gazed into his eyes. "Besides, I'd love to make babies with you."

Tears welled in his eyes then rolled down the sides of his head as he stared at her. "My ears are getting wet — sorry I'm so emotional." He raised a hand to wipe the tears, but she beat him to it as she bent to lick them away.

He continued to stare into her eyes. "I would love to do that. I would really love to. Do you want to start now?"

"We can practice until it happens. I'm not fertile for another while yet, but first, we need to get this seed machine of yours working. There'll be no crop unless you plant seeds."

"I can easily make it work, outside, solo. I've never done it inside — never been inside before. Guess I'll have to learn."

"So far you've been a quick learner. Show me what you do solo. From there, surely we can figure out how to work it together." She bent forward and licked his lips, then slowly lifted her hips and unplugged him, letting out a long sigh through the process. "You're so comfortable... No soreness... Amazingly, no soreness. I used to get so sore and raw from the friction with Nathan, even with his short sprints. We've just run a marathon, and I'm not sore." She fingered her vaginal entrance. "Not at all."

She turned to him, wrapped a hand around his penis and pulled the foreskin back to study the action as the spout opened to expose the tips of the head halves. With a firmer tug, she popped it over and behind the ridge. "This is a tight glove," she said, studying the action as she rolled it back up to cover the head and allowed it to purse out into a spout.

"I don't remember ever playing doctor with your foreskin. I guess we were completely innocent then. Yours is still the only one I've seen, and until now, I had no idea how they work — folding back on themselves. Guess I'd not thought about them. The rabbis cut these off the infant boys, so I thought they must be useless."

She rolled it off again and continued peeling the skin along his shaft, arriving at his pubes, paused to examine it again, then took a grip with her other hand farther up the shaft and continued pulling the skin back until it was taut. "That's a length and a half of skin I've pulled back. The rabbi's tiny snip is a huge amount of flesh." She stared at it and shook her head.

"This is how Nathan's was," she said, stretching the skin all the way off to make a smooth, shiny surface. "His was smaller... Much smaller, but similar. This is like a fricking knobbed broomstick, no wonder I got sore. Shoving that in and out, rubbing me raw. Him too. He became so raw trying to satisfy me. He finally gave up trying."

She released the skin and allowed it to move back up and gather in big wrinkles behind the rim. "The rabbis don't simply snip a piece off the end of this, as we've been told. They cut out a huge section from the middle, wrap-up the remains and hope the ends heal. That's why Nathan had those strange scars. What a horrid tradition."

She gazed into Lorne's eyes, which had been watching her with delighted wonder. "You have such a magnificent schlong. I love how it glides within its own sleeve." She fingered her entrance again. "No irritation. It'll be fun getting this to work for us both."

She rolled on top of him, and they wrapped together in a tangled embrace, lightly touching, caressing and murmuring pleasant thoughts. After twenty minutes Catherine said, "You still need to show me how you bring yourself off so we can figure out what'll work inside."

"You show me how you do yourself. That'll excite me." Lorne smiled at her. "I've dreamed of that so often."

She felt him throbbing again and she pressed toward it. "I feel it's already working. You've a marvellous response."

They untangled and he sat to watch as she began moving the skin around on her mound. "I do this first as a warm up. A general gentle rub... no, not a rub, just moving flesh around. Then I'll use my other hand to begin tweaking and pulling my nipples, rubbing. Depending on my mood, I may start lightly fingering my little lips, pulling them out gently and running them in circles. This moves the skin back-and-forth over my clit, which increases my wetness..."

She continued to demonstrate and explain, alternating her eyes back and forth between his face and his huge stiffness until her orgasm overtook her.

He was entranced watching her, captivated by her beauty, but more amazed with her awareness of her body, her confidence with it and her desire to share this. *To share this with me. This is so like my dreams.* His body shuddered with her as she climaxed.

As Catherine recovered, she saw him still staring at her with a strange expression on his face. "Lorne, you seem hypnotised. You're somewhere else."

"I've been mesmerised having one of my fondest dreams play out here in front of me. I kept pinching myself. Please tell me I'm not dreaming."

"It's real, Lorne. I'm real, you're real. You're really real, you're so genuinely you. You're so endearingly childlike in your innocence, in your curiosity, in your honesty."

"I love watching you. I could learn to do that for you. I'd love to... Would you like that?"

"You did a wonderful job of it yesterday... My God that was so wonderful. You've little to learn. Maybe more confidence, I don't know what else." She pointed at his pointing. "Show me what you do."

He wrapped both hands around it, one above the other, and began sliding the skin up and down. "I can go slow like this for hours — I often do. It keeps me on an excited edge, just short. The longer I do it, the more intensity when I come. When I want to finish, I simply pull back my foreskin to bare my heads and give them a few strokes. Pop. Relief. Mess." He looked into her eyes and smiled. "Do you want me to show you my geyser?"

"Why not reach down when you're in me, pull the skin off your to head? Convert yourself into a bare broomstick when you want to come. You'll get increased friction inside that way. God, Nathan's bare head rarely lasted more than a minute or two."

"That should work." He played with baring his heads by pulling the skin at the bottom of his shaft. "Three short pulls bares them." He smiled at her. "This'll work. Do you want to try it, or should I go ahead and pop out here?"

"Silly, silly you. You must be joking. Sometimes you're so silly, Lorne. You know damned well we both want you to come inside. Lay back. Let me straddle you again."

After they had adjusted postures and conjoined, she started gently churning, tilting and rotating her pelvis as she did short squats. "Let me know what you need. Direct me. Let me help you with it."

"You keep doing what you're doing, I'm already almost at the edge now from watching your lips in action. How close are you? Do you want us to come together? I think I can tell now when you're getting near the point."

"That would be sublime. Give me a few minutes."

He watched with fascination as she gradually built to the point he recognised, then he reached down and gave his skin three quick tugs. Less than a quarter minute later, they were writhing, twitching and convulsing together as a bellow built loudly from deep inside his throat, harmonising with her deep moans. Their faces were wet with tears as she collapsed onto him and they hugged tightly, both still gently rocking their hips.

Their panting turned to laughter, body-shaking laughter, which mimicked their earlier convulsions. "Yeah, that works. God, does that work."

Chapter Fourteen

"It's well past eleven," Lorne said, nodding to the bulkhead clock. "I could lie here forever playing with you, but we should add some less exciting activities for contrast." He kissed her neck and teased her earlobe with his tongue and teeth, then let out a loud laugh.

"What's up?"

"Just thinking... Last night in the restaurant, playing with your earlobe, leading to piercing. God, we've come a long way from there. Sorry to dump this stuff on you, but..."

"Silly, silly, silly... My silly Lorne. Don't be sorry for that, be grateful. It's gone, it's behind you now. You've no reason whatsoever to be sorry. I'm the one who should be sorry, I puked all over you." She shook her head.

He sat up and stared at her with a broad smile. "There you are, my dreams lying on the bed in front of me. You're so gorgeous. Gorgeous inside and out. Your spirit, your mind, your body. All so gorgeous." He put his hand on her flat abdomen, then shuddered. "I'd love to watch this as it swells and..."

"Oh, my God, Lorne. Oh! — My! — God! That is so beautiful. You're a magnificent beast, a tender sweetheart." She placed her hands on his, and she gently pulsed. "That would be awesome." She took his hand and guided him on top of her, and they writhed together, kissing, pressing into each other.

It was nearly an hour later when they separated and rolled onto their backs, still lightly panting from their exercises. "We were going to do something else." She laughed.

"How about a shower? We're rather sticky and sweaty. We can sort out the rest of our day there."

I still can't believe this is happening, he thought as he watched her kneeling in front of him, tenderly washing. *Treating it like it's normal, rolling the skin back, washing between the halves, washing the scars, accepting... My God, I love her... I need to tell her more often.*

"I can't see your... What did you call your pee hole? Urinary something?"

"Meatus. I rather buggered it when I escaped. It's this hole under here," he said as he turned it over and pointed at the mass of scars. "Let's do that later. Do easier stuff for now."

"Yeah, you're right, whenever you're ready. Just know I'm interested. I'm so pleased we got it working. So pleased for the both of us."

"It's a relief in so many ways for me — *so many.*" He looked down at her and shuddered. "*So many.*" He sighed as she continued washing it. "We should focus on something else. Maybe lower the tender and head over to Gibsons and poke around Molly's Beach, see if we can uncover anything."

"Like what?"

"Like check their garbage. Examine the packaging, confirm our suspicions — I don't know — we'll come up with other ideas when we're there. We could also go to eSushi, order takeout again to nibble as we sail. There's supposed to be a nice breeze this afternoon to take us across to the islands."

"That'll be your third visit. You could write a review."

"Good thought. Let's go."

"Whoa! Whoa, Lorne. My impulsive Lorne, remember? You were going to wash me." She rinsed it off, pulled the skin back into a spout and gave it a shake and a kiss. "Great schlong."

Twenty minutes later they were dried, dressed and setting off in the tender under a clear sky. "I wonder whether the same staff members are there for lunch." Lorne was musing aloud as he guided the tender across Shoal Channel. "Probably not, it would be too long a shift. They likely do a roster change late afternoon."

"If the reception staff is different, I could play reviewer..." She checked her pouch for a card. "See what their response is."

"That should be interesting. Great idea."

Lorne locked the tender to the dinghy dock, noting the thirty dollar fee beyond two hours. "We won't be more than an hour," he said as he extended his hand to steady her while she stepped out onto the float.

"Recognise anyone?" he asked as they stood in the restaurant's waiting area.

"No, do you?"

"Not yet. Let's wait a while longer and watch, pretend we're reading the reviews."

A few minutes later, after a small group had been ushered into the dining room and the reception area was clear, Catherine tugged his arm, tilted her head and lead him toward the desk. She presented her card to the hostess. "I write for the Courier and for two online review sites..."

"It's the chef's days off, it wouldn't be a fair time. We can make a reservation for another day." She glanced at her book, then back up. "He'll be here next Monday, Tuesday and Wednesday. What day would be good for you?"

"We're busy Monday..." She saw Lorne mouthing *Tuesday*. "Tuesday will work."

"I suggest dinner, the presentations are always better then."

"That would be our preference."

"What time would work best for you?"

"Twenty thirty is my favourite." She saw Lorne's nod.

The hostess read Catherine's card. "I'll email you a reminder. Can I get you anything now? Complementary drinks?"

"Thank you, no. I think we'll just wander up the street and find some sushi, or something."

"There's a great little sushi place around the corner. Doesn't do promos though. Doesn't need to. It's truly great. That's where I eat. It's rather new, the name's eSushi."

"Thanks, we'll try it. It's always good to get a personal recommendation. Have you a card? We could tell them it was you who recommended."

As they walked up the street holding hands, she turned her head to him. "Good game. Bring in their polished team to do the presentations. Likely in a private dining room. Wouldn't want us to be distracted by the crowds in the main dining rooms."

"With most of the reviewers these days using the system to get free lunches and dinners, they play right into their game."

"Or, more likely, they set up the system to use reviewers to help them manipulate diners who don't trust their own senses."

"Great scam."

She glanced at the card. "Barbara might be useful. She seems to understand what's going on. At the least, she's a great judge of sushi."

They sat at the sushi bar, and Lorne told the itamae they wanted takeout. They will be sailing across the Straits, hadn't yet had lunch and were hungry. They also wanted nibbling snacks for later in the day as they sailed and for evening in the cockpit with Champagne, all omakase.

The itamae smiled, extended his hand and rubbed its thumb across the balls of his fingers as he raised his eyebrows to Lorne.

Lorne smiled and pointed up, moving his finger slowly up and down for emphasis. The itamae pursed his lips and nodded, then bowed and began to work.

"Oh my, this is going to be good," Catherine said as she set her teacup on the bar. "I followed it so easily. What a wonderful way to order. He knows what he has, he knows what we want and his pride springs forth, creating."

Michael Walsh

They watched entranced as the itamae worked in front of them, selecting, slicing, shaping, rolling, arranging and making them salivate in anticipation. "This is wonderful dining foreplay," she said as she squeezed his thigh. "I love all kinds of foreplay."

Chapter Fifteen

"We'll get him." Pierre held his fists tightly clenched. "We're still staked out at his building on First. Front and back, around the clock. Still nothing."

"And the tracker pens?" Samir shook his head.

"The vehicle hasn't moved. Many of these drivers do it as a second job. We're watching the car around the clock."

"Give me a reason why I shouldn't take another knuckle."

Pierre thumbed his old pinkie stump. "A major agent's portfolio tasting Monday afternoon. I always see him at those."

"You be there. Give him the fucking pen this time. Understand?"

◇◇◇

A little past fourteen thirty Lorne sailed off the anchor, and once they had cleared Shoal Channel, he set-up *Tastevin* with the wind a few degrees abaft the starboard beam and adjusted the Hydrovane to steer the wind angle. The sixteen to eighteen knot northwesterly had them making hull speed.

"We're flying along. Dad's never goes this fast."

"It isn't able to. The maximum speed of a displacement hull is limited to its waterline length. The longer the waterline, the faster the boat can go. Planing stinkpots and gin palaces ignore this rule. For increased speed, they pull out their wallets and play with the exponential litres per hour thing."

"I guess I knew that — somewhat. He was always tweaking the sails and talking about moving closer to hull speed. What's the hull speed of this... Of *Tastevin*? Such an appropriate name for your boat, a wine tasting vessel."

"Ten point seven two knots, in theory, by the formula. We're blipping between ten five and ten six now. About as fast as she goes. She loves this wind angle, a..."

"Don't tell me. See if I can remember." Catherine looked up at the sails and the windvane, then out at the surface waves, pursed her lips and put her hand up to hold her pause as she thought. "We're on a beam reach, maybe a bit broad." She smiled at him as he nodded.

"Very good. She loves ten or twelve degrees either side of a beam reach. She has a wide sweet spot and is easy to please." He held a piece of hamachi sashimi with his chopsticks, just short of his mouth as he paused to speak. "Have you tried the yellowtail?"

"Amazing. Did you see how long he took finding the right piece? Cut, look, cull. Another piece, cut look, smell, cull. And another, cut look, smell, taste. All his culls seemed wonderful... Better than most other places serve."

"Easy review to write — well, maybe not. I'll have to tone my comments back. Otherwise, I'll sound like the other reviewers, the ones with greased palms and snouts in the trough." Lorne did another of his twisted smiles.

Catherine studied the chartplotter, then scanned ahead at the deep blue landmasses on the horizon. "Looks like we're headed for Porlier Pass."

"We're pointing at it, but the wind is slowly veering, and with the vane steering a wind angle, we'll gradually come starboard as we cross. The increasing flood tide will carry us up the Strait mid-afternoon and beyond. The currents aren't right to transit the passes until late evening, so I was thinking of the anchorage in Silva Bay." He smiled at her. "Have you ever been there?"

"I love the place. What's the crooked little entrance gut called? The one with all the rocks and reefs the yahoo power boaters always seem surprised to find."

"I call it Shipyard Rock Entrance. The passage is well-marked, the big rock in the middle is obvious. It's a fun little dogleg." He grinned and selected another piece of sashimi.

"Dad always did either the north or the south entrance." She raised her eyebrows. "He said *Swansea* was too big to take comfortably through the crooked one. Too many rocks and reefs."

"Guess it's a matter of levels of comfort."

"Comfort... Feeling safe... Confident." She smiled at him and paused while he finished the piece he had just popped into his mouth, then she kissed him. "You've always been so confident. Everybody notices it, comments on it. You exude confidence."

"Not always. For a big chunk of my teens, I was anything *but* confident."

"God that must have been horrid."

"Let's enjoy the sail. The sushi."

Lorne noted the time as seventeen twelve after he had sailed onto the anchor in Silva Bay, furled the sails, set the snubbers and the anchor alarm. He looked up after completing the logbook entry. "Told you it was easy."

"I couldn't believe it. Nobody sails through there."

"Sailors used to. I'm one who still does." He smiled at her. "Guess most now rely on their engines... *Tastevin* is a sailboat. I sail her. I have to use the engine to enter and leave the marina in False Creek because sailing's forbidden beyond the Burrard Bridge, but other than that, I try not to use the engine. I love the old expression, *iron spinnaker*."

"Dad often uses that one. His standard mid-afternoon summer quote: *Wind's died, time to haul out the old iron spinnaker.*"

"I love ghosting along in light airs, watching the surface ripples to spot the next zephyr and be ready to welcome it, rather than being surprised when it arrives. I love using the currents, rather than fighting them. We can learn a lot through quiet observation, absorbing what's happening around us. When it's time to act, we have the information — and the energy. We haven't squandered it uselessly. Take no action until the ultimate cusp."

Michael Walsh

"Dad taught me about that, tacking up through Sansum Narrows. I kept wanting to tack as we sailed toward the cliffs. He kept saying wait, pointing to the line of ripples indicating a wind shift. Or holding a beat at the edge of luff, trying to clear the next rocky point, watching the wind play on the surface ahead. Assessing it." She smiled at him. "I nearly had to wipe my poo bum a couple of times." She winked and smiled wider.

"Poo bum and pee bum. Delightful terms. What fond memories those are. So innocent, so gentle, so loving."

"We're there again, Lorne. Innocent, gentle, loving. We're still those curious exploring kids inside."

They were still in the loose hug they had adopted after he had completed the logbook entries. "We haven't done much since we arrived." He checked the clock on the gauge panel. "Nearly seventeen fifteen. What would you like to do?"

"Be with you."

"There's still the pack from eSushi in the fridge. I could open a bottle of Champagne..."

"I was thinking of being with you in the biblical sense." She kissed his neck and wiggled her body tighter to him, mashing her mound on his thigh.

Catherine led him down to the fore cabin and paused at the foot of the bed, then she smiled and shifted to talking in her husky voice. *"Lorne decided it was time for him to take the initiative. He knew what she wanted, what she longed for... And God, did he know what he wanted."*

"Fuck! You pump me up so fast. I can't believe it." He was all over her. Mouth, tongue, hands, his erection crushed into her belly, writhing.

"He paused in his passionate fervour, paused to reassess. Paused to see the wisdom of approaching this more gently, more lovingly. Softly pleasuring rather than playing a caveman or a Viking plunderer. Slowly... Gently... It leads to the same end, but much more enjoyably..."

Chapter Sixteen

Lorne and Catherine lay connected, cuddling and talking as they gently tilted and rotated their pelvises from time to time, enjoying the sensations and their closeness. The cabin had darkened, the mid-June sun gone, the light of the waxing gibbous moon through the skylight offering their only illumination.

"The caveman thing must be innate. I jumped straight into it."

"What I hear from the girls is many men never get over it. Many women have to endure being plundered. Raped, more accurately, when all they want is gentle loving. Sure, some get off on the rough stuff, but... You'll have to... Excuse me... Popping again... Oh fuuuuu..."

She melted into him, slowly regaining her breath as she sprinkled his face with kisses, licks and nips. After she had come down, she ground her mound into him and said, "Your turn, Lorne... I've been hogging the orgasms here. It's now well past your turn."

A few minutes later, as they writhed together recovering from their mutual explosions, she sighed and said, "Now that's the way to do a quickie — three hours of build-up." She grabbed his butt cheeks and pulled him closer. "I'm still hungry for more of you, but I have another hunger. We should eat."

"There's still the pack from eSushi in the fridge. I could open a bottle of Champagne..."

"Didn't you say that a while ago? Guess it's a few hours ago now." She pointed up at the deck hatch. "There's the moon almost straight above us — looks like four or five days to full."

"It's full on the twentieth, the same day as the solstice. It'll be near its perigee so we'll have a supermoon."

"You have a broad interest, a well-rounded education... Your captivity? Your schooling through that?"

"He was kind and gentle much of the time. Classically educated in Greek, Latin, philosophy, literature, history, the sciences. He loved teaching, sharing his knowledge. Being a teacher, he had easy access to textbooks and curriculum, and he also kept me supplied with wonderful books from the library. He was a great tutor and was always asking me what I wanted to study next. It was apparent he loved me, loved me in his sick and twisted way."

"But he kept you chained?"

"After the funeral and public stuff, he helped me organise the estate with Dad's lawyers, setting up the trust account and other details. Then he took me upstairs to the garret suite and padlocked a chain around my ankle and locked the other end to an eyepad on the floor. That would be my home for seventeen months... Well, changing the padlock arrangements."

Lorne paused and held her tightly for a while, then continued. "He'd spend a few hours a day teaching, always ending with sex education. He moved quickly into his twisted ideas as he fondled me, trying to arouse me. My response was revulsion."

"He sounds psychotic... Jekyll and Hyde. Did he get angry with your response? Violent? Hit you?"

"No, he was always calm and methodical. Gentle, actually. He had binders full of images from smut magazines and some he had printed from the internet. He showed them to me, trying to get a rise."

Lorne looked at her in the dim light. "We can stop here if you want... Come back to it later."

"Your choice, really. You stop when you want."

"He began by showing me truly gross stuff, mutilation and torture, but he soon realised those would garner nothing but revulsion from me. He tried gay porn and got nowhere, so he resorted to pretty porn, soft porn, beautiful women, natural, inviting, exciting. He received the rise he wanted from me for his photos."

Lorne paused, hugged her more tightly again, then said, "I think it's time for something much more pleasant. Some sushi and Champagne."

He turned on the lights, and they slowly untangled and unplugged. "I'm quite sloppy here," she said, holding herself and laughing. "I think we need to change the sheet again."

"You *should* be flooded. I thought I'd *never* stop coming. When are you fertile?"

"I normally ovulate with the full moon, bleed with the new moon... I've always been regular, my system is tied to the lunar cycle, so I don't mark the calendar. I simply watch the sky." She stared at him, her smile becoming increasingly sublime as she continued quietly calculating.

"Your little beasties will last four or five days in here." She rose into a shoulder stand. "Let's keep them all in, let the boat's gentle rocking help move them through my cervix to my tubes. Go get the sushi and the Champagne, you can feed me here."

He hugged her legs, she spread them a bit, then wrapped them around his neck. He stared at the sublime expression on her face, tears running down his cheeks, dripping off his chin whiskers and wetting her further.

Chapter Seventeen

"You won't be able to drink your Champagne like that, and swallowing the sushi uphill might be difficult." Catherine spread her legs to release Lorne's head, but he moved down, and between licks, said, "I've plenty more sperm. I'll keep topping you up. Five more days; I should manage twenty-five or thirty refills."

She gave him a crooked smile from her shoulder stand. "Nathan didn't want to have children early, and as the years passed, he became increasingly opposed to the idea. I guess I'm over-reacting at the opportunity." She giggled. "I'll come down if you promise to keep me topped up."

He picked her up and carried her toward the shower. "Time to clean up for dinner, silly girl. I'll do you. You do me." He laughed loudly, shaking them both as he did. "Your old pick up line, which I didn't pick up on. God, I was so dumb-ass dense then, wasn't I?"

"You had a lot going on in your head back then."

Later, up in the cockpit, he turned on the radiant heaters to take the chill off the evening as they enjoyed their moonlight dinner and continued talking. "I'll have to stop drinking soon. I'll miss the wonderful wines."

"Most doctors now say small amounts are not damaging. We can limit ourselves to glasses of magnificent wines. Give the kid an early taste of quality. Never too young to learn."

She stroked the back of his hand, which was resting on her thigh. "I love how comfortable you are with this. I used to fantasise about making babies with you, even before I understood the mechanics of it. When I first asked Mum, she told me that babies happen when mummies and daddies hold each other in a special way." She laughed and squeezed his hand. "Remember all the hugging and holding we used to do back then?" She leaned into him as he opened his arms. "Oh, my God, I love you, Lorne."

They hugged tightly for several minutes, sharing reminiscences of their childhood hugging, holding and touching, then they turned back to the last bits of their sushi.

"We're all grown-up now," Lorne said as he glanced at the level in her glass. "We know how it works. Do you want a top-up?"

"On the Champagne or the sperm?"

As they lay on the bed gently moving, holding each other in that once-elusive special way, she sighed, then said, "You're the one who has to come, Lorne, not me. The score is now three to zero. Want to make it four to one?"

He did want to, and they both did it noisily. They then lay more quiet, wrapped close together as they recovered. Once his speaking became easier, he said, "I'll leave the plug in. Leave no escape for those little wiggly guys."

She caught the worried expression on his face. "What's up? What's the face about?"

"Thinking about anatomy... The location of your cervix. The design is for the penis to ejaculate toward it. I'm shooting in the opposite direction. Maybe we can find a position where I'm turned around inside."

She stroked the back of his head. "There are lots of wonderful positions we can explore. I can think of a few right now, which will have you flipped over in here." She did a few small pelvis rotations. "I didn't think of this earlier. It must be awkward when you pee. Sort of backwards, isn't it?"

"I've adapted. I've tried twisting it, but that pinches the flow. Besides, it has a strange spray. No public urinals, always stalls. I normally squat, lay it across the seat and spray down. Alone in the wilds, I drop my trousers, squat and spray backwards."

Michael Walsh

She stroked his cheek and brushed her lips across his. "You should get it repaired. It's such a magnificent schlong. You seem much easier with it now. Surely they can reconstruct a urethra — why do we use Latin for body parts? A pee tube. Surely they can do that. They regularly build whole penises on the transsexuals now, including a proper pee hole in the proper place. I'm saddened seeing you still adapting and suffering with it."

"Maybe when your pregnancy gets to the stage when — and why isn't there an acceptable word for this? When sharing a comfortable fuck with you becomes awkward." He ran his tongue across her lips. "I wouldn't want to waste comfortable fucking time. God, not now, not when we're just beginning."

"Let's get pregnant first, then you can see a doctor about it. It's time to do something about it... It seriously is. It's been a long time, almost twenty years."

"Yeah, I've thought of it often, but, you know..." He paused and looked at her with his twisted smile, "I haven't seen a doctor since being examined and documented for the trial, thirteen, going on fourteen years ago now. Good thing I'm healthy."

"Frick, Lorne. That's not healthy. You need regular check-ups. I do one every six months. Blood work and basic cancer screening. Nathan's doctor had him on annual prostate examinations. You can't ignore your health."

"I've learned to care for myself. There's lots of information online, test kits in the pharmacies. Repair kits there too."

"There's that crooked smile again. I can read you so easily. You know that's not good enough." She shifted her pelvis gently. "We now have this working. You're so much easier with it. Seeing a doctor will only help." She continued her gentle movements, and he was soon matching her.

Chapter Eighteen

The alarm sounded at 0630, and Lorne untangled an arm to reach the snooze button, then turned back to kiss Catherine good morning. The fifteen-minute snooze alarm began harmonising with the deep throated tones of their orgasms, and they allowed it to continue sounding as they calmed.

"You can say good morning to me this way as often as you wish," she said as she stroked his cheek. "As many times a day as you want." She let out a deep moaning sigh. "Come! Up and at 'em, the tides won't wait."

They were soon up, showered, dressed and sailing slowly through the bay in the morning breezes toward South Entrance. "I never saw Dad do that. He always used the engine when weighing. You make it seem so simple."

"What, sailing off the anchor? That's how they did it for millennia if the air was moving at all, long before there were engines. It's a simple thing to do. I find it less complex than using the engine. I'll explain it for you the next time."

"Nobody seems to do it anymore. I've only ever seen it done twice. Yesterday and this morning." She smiled at him. "You do things your own way, don't you?"

"Yeah, guess I do. It's part of what happens doing things on one's own. Funny, I was thinking a couple of days ago that I had convinced myself I was happy living alone."

Michael Walsh

"Weren't you? You always seemed happy when I saw you at functions. Always upbeat."

"A lot of that was because you were there. You always lifted my happy level. Boosted it way up."

She moved behind him as he stood at the port helm wrapping her arms around his waist, pressing her breasts into his back. "I don't want you ever to be unhappy again." She pressed into him, and he moved his back against her to expand the contact.

"I wish the breeze would stiffen as quickly as I am. God, you rouse me." He reached around and squeezed her bum. "Once we clear the point, I can set-up the vane and relax from the helm. Too fickle yet for autopilot. Another ten or twelve minutes."

"Everyone else is motoring out."

"They're rushing to wait."

"Rushing to wait?"

"Most seem to head toward the passes early and sit outside waiting for predicted slack water. We'll continue sailing, take advantage of the last of the ebb and wash through Gabriola running with both the current and the breeze. Betcha we'll be well into Trincomali before they motor past us. The sailboats will then fumble in our bows to set their sails. Betcha."

"I'd be stupid to bet on that one. Dad always laughed at it." She gave him another squeeze. "Breakfast? When can I start on that?"

"We'll be tacking in a few minutes, so there's no sense starting before we've settled. You could start with coffee, though. I'd love a double espresso."

"I watched you the last couple of days. Give me a quickstart."

"The water feed is direct. Switch the machine on and let it heat. The hopper should have enough beans, the grinder button's obvious. The big portafilter, just rounded, second pressure setting on tamp, there's no need to change settings. You know where the cups are." He reached around again to squeeze her bum.

She disappeared and was back in the cockpit with two cups four minutes later. He took a sip. "You pull a great espresso."

90

"I had a great instructor." She winked at him. "I cheated. I have the same make at home, but a different model."

They had an easy passage through the narrows, two gybes in the following light breeze, while they enjoyed large ham, mushroom and red pepper three-egg omelettes and more espressos. He looked up from his plate. "You do a wonderful omelette." He winked at her. "Is the ham kosher?"

She laughed. "We stopped that when we were still on Cypress. Mum thought it was archaic. Following instructions which made sense millennia ago in completely different circumstances. She thought it would be stupid to continue them."

"Religious traditions certainly *are* stupid, aren't they? Like, try to rationalise things such as burkas, hajibs, halal, circumcision, kosher, subincision, female genital mutilation, turbans, kirpans, nun's habits, tonsures, celibacy, abusive priests..." He gave her his crooked smile. "Back to more sensible things, light things. Great omelette. You beat a dash of water into the eggs, didn't you? So fluffy and light."

The cockpit clock showed 0812 when Lorne rose to tack *Tastevin* between DeCourcy and Ruxton. Once through, he set a course down Stewart Channel to take advantage of the slowly building easterly sea breeze as Vancouver Island warmed to starboard.

"This is our third day out, and so far we've burnt a litre of diesel getting out of the marina," Lorne said as they sat cuddling on the starboard settee. "Everything else has been solar and wind. I don't even think the propane kicked in on the hot water with all our showering."

"Even your tender's motor is electric," she said as they shifted into sitting spoons on the settee. They continued watching ahead and monitoring the chartplotter with AIS and radar overlays. She felt him swelling against her back. "What's up? — That's silly, isn't it? I know what's up. Why's it up?"

"I'm thinking of this position, visualising. This will allow me to spray your cervix."

"Yes, this would be one of the easier positions." She mashed her back into him. "How much longer?"

"This is as long as it gets." He chuckled.

"Silly man. I meant time wise."

"Just joshing. A little under an hour with this wind."

She wiggled her back into him and moaned. "We need more wind."

Chapter Nineteen

Catherine shifted her hips again, ground more meat, still lightly panting. "You're getting better, Lorne. We're now doing two for one, but there's still too much me."

Immediately *Tastevin* had settled to her anchor in Chemainus, they had stripped and coupled. She was still sitting on his lap, leaning up his front in a modified spooned posture on the cockpit settee. He was still in her cockpit as he leaned back against the soft cushions.

"You seem to love your orgasms, and I'm enraptured feeling, watching and listening to you pop. But you keep begging me to come and end it. I'm confused."

She ran her hand over her flat abdomen, pausing a moment, then reached farther to feel where he disappeared inside, pressing there, then continued down to cradle his scrotum and gently heft it. "While there's any possibility of conception, I want you to keep flooding me. A thirty, forty million at a time. I want to give life a huge chance. After we've conceived, I'll gladly go back to three, four five to one... God ten to one, I'm easy." She let out a loud laugh.

"If only you could hear the moans and complaints of the girls — me too, I guess — God, those were also my stories." She paused and shook her head. "Oh, my God! Those were also my tales of woe, my complaints and my commiserations with the girls."

"So what's this story? What are the complaints?"

"Oh God, I love you, Lorne. Oh my fuck, my wonderful loving fuck. My hero, my sweetheart, you have no idea how desperate, how desolate

Michael Walsh

many women are. You're such an innocent man, a loving, caring person."

"I gather, then some women aren't happy with their men."

She reached up over her shoulder to stroke his cheek. "Lorne, you've always been the master of understatement, but that by a huge margin understated the largest of all understatements. From what I've experienced, read and heard, I think humanity needs a large portion of the men on the planet to be asking about this."

He ran his hands lightly up her front and cupped her breasts. "I'm still confused. I guess I've not spent any time thinking about these things... Relationship things. You really do need to explain."

"My dear innocent sweetie, my amazing lover, you have no idea how many men give little thought or effort to satisfying their women. The caveman approach: Bang, pop, grunt and retreat. They're fulfilled physically, but inside there's a void. The women don't even have the physical fulfilment to ease the emotional and spiritual void. I've done themes based on this in several of my novels."

Lorne gave another gentle pelvic thrust. "Thinking about what you were saying about Nathan... Being circumcised... His difficulty satisfying you. Muslims circumcise. The whole Islamic world is male-centred. They force their women to hide themselves, deny them rights. Because of their physical mutilation, many of the men are less able to sexually satisfy their women. No wonder there's so much anger there."

He teased her nipples between his spread fingers. "For more than a century now, the United States has had the highest non-religious circumcision rate in the world, over ninety percent of the men at one point. They're still by far the highest. That would lead to a lot of frustration."

"Wow! Oh, my. Where's most of the violence in the world? Israel, the Middle East, the USofA, the Islamic world and wherever they've spread. It seems to be where circumcision is most prevalent is also the most violent."

"The men have been disfigured, disabled by religious tradition or flaky Kellogg fervour. They have no idea of the cause of their frustration.

The USAians continue to arm themselves with more and more deadly weapons, shoot their neighbours, spray shopping malls and schools with bullets."

"The Jewish thing seems to be a contradiction here." Catherine shrugged. "Maybe the men work their frustrations out through their famed entrepreneurial fervour. That might satisfy their search for gratification."

"With the recent decline of circumcision in the States, I wouldn't be surprised to see the American Rifle Association resurrect some of Kellogg's flakier theories and practices to keep them supplied with frustrated and angry men."

"That's twice you've hinted at Kellogg's flakes. Is this the beginning of a serial?" She chuckled. "What's the connection?"

"It's a very sick story. Much sicker than your pun. Connolly introduced me to it." He cupped her breasts and gave them a gentle shake. "Let's finish anchoring first, I haven't yet set the snubbers or the alarm, and this is the first time I've not completed the logbook immediately."

She reached again to their juncture. "This might be messy on your seat cushions. We'll need to remember to keep towels handy."

"Swivel around and face me. I'll carry you below to the shower." He scooted to lay flat, she turned on his pintle as smoothly as a balanced rudder, and he sat again to cuddle, then he stood with her and carried her toward the shower.

"I always loved it when Dad carried me piggyback, but this piggyfront is much more exciting. No risk of sliding down." She giggled with delight. "Oh my God, I love you, Lorne."

They showered and dressed and while Lorne was finishing his anchoring routine, he explained as she watched. "You can do the snubbers the next time."

"You'd let me do that? Nathan didn't allow me to do anything that even hinted of being a man's job, as he called it." She rubbed his back. "Seems to be a simple system. Even a silly girl like me understands it." She giggled.

"No sense doing things awkwardly, keep them simple." As they walked back toward the cockpit, he asked, "It's ten past eleven, which do you prefer, tasting first or the restaurant?"

"Where are they? Their locations and the travel logistics might answer the question for us."

"The restaurant's a few doors along the waterfront from the head of the pier. The first winery's outside Cowichan Bay, Blue Grouse."

"Let's go to Blue Grouse first, then go see Mum and Dad, they're up at the end of the road from there. We could have lunch with them. I'll call and give a warning. We can do dinner in the restaurant."

Lorne's eyes widened as she talked. He stopped and stared at her. "You've always refused to tell me the name of their winery. You said you didn't want to influence my judgement. Mosscrop, I love their wines." He wrapped her in his arms. "Let's forget about Blue Grouse. Call your folks. I haven't been to visit Michael and Rachel this year yet. I love their wines... I love their daughter."

Chapter Twenty

"But Walsh isn't Jewish. I thought your father was Jewish."

"No, he's Irish. It's Mum who's Jewish. At first, she didn't want me playing with you, which made it more exciting... Isn't that the way. Prohibit something and it becomes more attractive."

Lorne laughed. "Yeah, think of marijuana. Since it's been legalised, its consumption has declined — I know mine has," he said as he set the anchor alarm.

"You toke? Yeah, I guess everyone does, or did before it became legal." Catherine laughed. "Strange, that... I rarely touch it now."

"I wonder where the drug pushers have gone, now even more with the new hard drug legislation."

"Could be into the corrupt restaurant business. That manager at Molly's seemed more like a Hell's Angel than anything."

Lorne paused from writing the log. "Did you see he was missing half of both his pinkies? Appeared to be either punishments or some depraved ritual."

He watched her do a finger gag imitation. "Lighter things. You should phone your folks."

She headed below to get her phone and was talking on it as she returned to the cockpit. "That would be great, Daddy, we can meet you at the head of the pier." She paused to listen. "Yes, Chemainus... Half an hour... Great."

She smiled at him. "Dad's coming to pick us up."

"This is so funny. You know all the glowing reviews I've written for your folks' wines. Always among my favourites. You never let on. I love your integrity." They merged in a tight hug.

"I have a great model of integrity right here." She squeezed him tighter and lifted her face for his kiss. "We should get ready."

She watched as he unplugged and unlashed the tender. "How long will a charge last?"

"The battery will last six or seven hours of slow motoring. Way more than needed, but the tops of the inflatable's tubes are photovoltaic. On a sunny day, the charge never drops. Nice system."

"Why are so many still using gasoline outboards? Noisy, stinky and polluting."

"Afraid of change, I guess."

She again watched the process as he lifted the tender from its deck chocks, flipped it over, swung it over the side and lowered it to the water. "Three button pushes and a hand manoeuvre, so simple and elegant. A child could do that." She snickered. "Even a woman."

"There are manual overrides on the whole system in case there's ever an electrical problem. I like simple. I'll let you do the recovery when we get back. We should be going."

He swung the accommodation ladder over the side and lowered it, undid the pelican hooks in the lifelines and led her down the gentle steps to the tender. "Do you want to drive?"

He set the boat alarms with his iPhone as she headed them toward the pier. She manoeuvred up to the dinghy dock on its far side, and he turned a mooring line to a cleat. He showed her the combination on the chain lock as he secured the tender to the float. "Easy to remember, it's the year we were both born."

He smiled up at her. *She has that sublime face again. I must tell her I love her. I wouldn't want her to think I don't.* "I love you, Catherine. Just thought I should remind you."

"Lorne, Lorne, sweet, sweet Lorne. You remind me every moment of your existence. You exude love. Your pores ooze it. Fuck, I love you.

Come here, hug me, lick my joyous tears."

"When you two finish down there..."

She broke from the kiss and laughed, turned her head to look up. "Hi, Daddy. You know Lorne."

"Appears you know him far better than I do." He chuckled. "Come on up, I haven't seen you in months. We were worrying about how you were holding up. Seems to be extremely well from this angle."

He walked along the pier beside them as they mounted the ramp, carrying on with their greetings. They paused at the top for a hug, a kiss and a handshake. "You've gone back to that pretty girl figure, so good to see you happy again. Come. Your mother is dying to see you."

They carried on a three-way banter during the quarter-hour drive. As they turned up the lane to the winery, Lorne asked, "Michael, I was wondering... Maybe I should say Sir or Mister Walsh, but would you mind if I married your daughter?"

Catherine screamed. She put her hands to her face and looked around at Lorne in the back seat, her mouth wide open, her wet eyes staring, her head nodding vigorously.

"I gather he just proposed to you."

"And I just accepted. Oh... My... God... Oh, my God, oh my God. Oh my my."

Michael Walsh

Chapter Twenty-One

They stood in the kitchen sharing the news with Rachel, and after hugs, kisses and congratulations, she asked, "So when did you two start seeing each other?"

Catherine gazed into Lorne's eyes, smiled and winked. "Thirty years ago on Cypress Street, playing doctor as four-year-olds in Lorne's garage. But recently, three days ago — maybe it's four. The time has been stuffed full."

"Kids and then a few days, that seems quick. I'm sure there's a story here. You always write wonderful twists in your novels."

"It's a long story, Mummy. In many ways with him, a long one." She winked at Lorne.

"So this is little Lorne down the street. He's certainly grown up superbly. I've always enjoyed seeing him at tastings and on his visits here. Good for my..." She giggled. "I'm reading too many of Kate's books. Why are we all standing around here? There are comfortable places waiting on the patio and lunch is nearly ready. You go on through, I'll be a few minutes here. So good to see you again. And so happy, both of you."

"I'll stay here and help Mum get the lunch ready and fill her in on the details, on the backstory. I'm sure she's dying to hear the girlie stuff."

Catherine gave a synopsis of the relationship, beginning with running into Lorne again in their third year of university and the steamy letters. Then she talked about her futile attempts to interest him beyond a wonderful friendship.

100

"And he never got the hint?" Rachel asked.

"No, and he didn't even connect me to little Kate on Cypress. The funny thing is that for a dozen years I thought he knew. To him, I was just a delightfully friendly woman."

"Oh my, that is funny."

"It's much more complex, though. He secretly adored me, fantasised about me, sexual fantasies. Much like mine about him. A dozen years of mutually unrequited horniness."

"Why didn't he do anything about it? He's always seemed so confident, so aware, so sharp."

"It's complex... Extremely complex. I don't want to spoil lunch. We'll talk later."

"This seems so soon after Nathan. Shouldn't you wait a..."

"Mummy, you know the frustrations I had with him. God! You and millions have read about them, his attitudes and his behaviour, his two-minute specials have been written into so many of my characters. He never caught on." Catherine turned to the counter. "Everything looks ready. Is there anything else?"

"No, this is it. Michael has the wine going out there already, I'm sure. Grab the other tray. Let's go join them."

Lorne and Michael were talking sailing when they arrived with the trays and set them on the cradles. The sailing conversation continued into the beginning of their lunch. "This goat cheese travelled the furthest to our plates," Rachel inserted in a lull in the sailing wind. "It's from Saltspring Island. If you stand, you can see their pasture." She raised an arm to point. "The walnuts are from the bottom of the hill here, the spelt for the crouton is from fields four kilometres away, and the greens are all from our garden. We love to eat local."

Michael looked at Rachel, then at his plate to see he had barely started his warm goat cheese salad, and the others had nearly finished. "Sorry, Dear... Not often I find a sailor I enjoy sharing with. I had no idea he sails. The salad is delicious." He took a bite and smiled sheepishly at her.

Michael Walsh

"You *should* enjoy it," she said. "You put them together before you drove down to the pier. All I did was heat the cheese. I'm simply reminding you to continue eating it. Go on back to your sailing talk. I always enjoy the look you get in your eyes when you're fully into something. I need to catch up with Kate, anyway."

The men returned to talking sailing while Catherine continued talking about her relationship with Lorne.

Partway into the quiche, Lorne paused and looked at Michael. "Catherine was telling me you've done some climbing."

"Not much anymore, at seventy-two, my joints are getting a bit stiff. I still get up Arrowsmith once or twice a year and..." He eyed Lorne's broad shoulders and muscular arms. "You climb?"

"Yes, but much less now. Too busy with my writing and my researching. A couple of days ago I decided I was done with my serious stuff. Sad, but it's time. I've done many wonderful climbs... Classic routes."

"What's your favourite?"

"Hands down, Mike's Folly on Colonel Foster. What a wonderful free-climb that is. It was the first route up the mountain after so many others had failed. Put up in 1968 — amazingly, solo. It's still the classic route. Have you done it?"

"Yeah, the first in 1968, then did the second ascent in '69, then..."

Lorne shouted, "NO! YOU CAN'T BE... Oh, my God! You're Mike! Oh, my God!"

Catherine put her hand on Lorne's arm. "What's up?"

"He's my climbing hero, my inspiration, the one who dragged me from the doldrums of despair after..." He paused and looked at her with questioning eyebrows, then he saw her understanding nod. "After my escape." She squeezed his hand and leaned to kiss it.

"Mike Walsh is such a common name — like John Doe. I never even thought... Wine and mountains are so far... Oh, my God!"

They all sat quietly until Catherine said, "There's a lot of story here. A lot of dark story. He's been through hell — several hells and survived. Let's continue lunch now. I'm excited to try the berry tarts."

Lorne and Michael's conversation switched from sailing to climbing. In the 1960s, 70s and early 80s, Michael had pioneered many of the routes that are now considered classic. His climbs are prominently written-up in the guidebooks, with such comments as Dick Culbert's: *Good to see a little insanity has survived in the march of climbing technology.*

"Repeating your routes gave me a focus, a challenge. I figured if they had been done solo once, they could be repeated the same way." Lorne paused and tilted his head. "One of the things that's always puzzled me. Why did you stop your serious climbing so suddenly? Your last was the first ascent of Noel in the Stikine."

Michael smiled and nodded toward Catherine. "Her. My sweet Katy. I didn't want to risk having her lose her father. I was into my late thirties, and the fates had been kind to me. I had seen too many climbers die..."

"You never told me that, Daddy." Catherine looked at her father with tears welling in her eyes. She rose and rushed around the table, knelt beside his chair and hugged him. "You're such a sweet, loving man. Such a wonderful father."

"I think Lorne said a few minutes ago he's doing the same thing... Stopping the high-risk climbing. Sounds as if you two are planning on finally giving us a grandchild."

She blushed, then peered into her father's eyes. "I'm fertile with the full moon, and he's been busy in the furrow planting seeds..." She gave him a sheepish grin. "We're hoping."

"You and your plot twists and your clever turns of phrase." Rachel was now kneeling at her side, joining the hug. "You said there'd be more good news."

Chapter Twenty-Two

They sat in the sun long after lunch, carrying on a rambling conversation, which Catherine diverted a few times from heavier things. Finally, she said, "Okay, enough dodging." She looked at Lorne, squeezed his hand and watched him nod.

"Lorne's parents, you remember the Wilsons down the street on Cypress? The whole family died in a crash on a flight to the Okanagan when he was fourteen. After the dust had settled, he went into the foster care of one of his school teachers, a priest. He was then held captive for a year and a half in a garret..."

"It was only seventeen months," Lorne corrected. He and Catherine then touched lightly on the behaviour of the priest, both the benevolently nurturing and the psychotically cruel.

"Once I was free from the chain, I inserted a stent and applied Crazy Glue to the wounds, like I'd watched him do so often..."

"What were the wounds?" Michael asked.

"From freeing myself..." He looked at Catherine, then back to Michael. "Some raw skin caused when I released myself from the shackling arrangement. Anyway, I climbed out through the garret window onto the roof. I must have slipped and fallen to the ground. It was dark when I regained consciousness. I had no idea where I was, who I was, what had happened. All I knew was I had an extremely sore head and what seemed to be a broken left shoulder and arm. I started walking in the dark, looking for help."

Lorne looked at Michael and Rachel. "Sorry to dump this stuff on you, but if we're going to be family..."

Catherine put her arm around his shoulder and kissed his cheek. "Keep it coming out. This is into new areas for me." She looked at her parents. "We're past the worst of it."

"I was found nude and huddled on a lawn by a man walking his dog. He called 9-1-1, and I was taken to the hospital with hypothermia, a severe concussion and a broken shoulder and wrist. My amnesia continued. There were no missing children reports to link me with, so I remained Little Johnny Doe." Lorne gave his crooked smile. "I guess the priest was afraid to step forward to..."

"When was that?" Michael asked. "I remember none of this in the news."

"March 1998. In June I was fostered by a family in Nanaimo and in September, I started school again. I had begun Grade Nine when I was locked-up, so that's where they started me. Within a few weeks, I was put in Grade Eleven and shortly after, into Twelve. Connolly was a great tutor if nothing else."

"Connolly. I remember that trial, a dozen or so years ago," Michael said. "Closed because of the minor involved, but the information that leaked out... Horrid." He winced at Lorne.

"Fortunately, little got out that I was aware of. The people who fostered me, the Martins, were wonderful. They were into outdoors activities, they were seriously into climbing and sailing. Do you know Peter and Elizabeth Martin?"

Michael thought for a while. "Not that I can recall." He chuckled. "But these days that means little."

"After graduation in 1999, my memory began coming back in nightmares... horrid nightmares that I gradually realised were reality. In mid-July, I ran away from my foster home, took my climbing gear and the small amount of money I had saved, and headed into the mountains, trying to run from the emerging reality." Lorne paused and looked around, bowed his head and put his hands to it. "That's enough for now."

They sat silently for a long while, pretending to be focusing on the wine in their glasses. After a couple of long minutes, Catherine said, "Tough act to follow, isn't it — but we have to — the Gewürztraminer, this the 2011 South Block, isn't it?"

"Yes, amazing late harvest that year. So much botrytis. I knew it was one of your favourites."

She swirled her glass again and nosed it, then took a bite of a field strawberry tart followed by a sip of wine. "What a heavenly match this is."

They slowly worked at regaining their earlier light banter while they continued enjoying the wine and tarts. As Michael was laughing again at Lorne's impromptu proposal to Catherine, he asked, "So when are you two getting married?"

Catherine snickered. "We could Google to find a marriage commissioner who's available this afternoon." She smiled at Lorne. "But there's no rush, we could wait until this evening."

They had a good laugh, further relieving the tensions, and they carried on into mid-afternoon. Catherine put her hand on Rachel's arm and leaned to whisper. "Should have gone again before I left the boat, but I need to pee."

"I'm sure we all do with these wines. Come, we'll use the bathrooms, the men can help the compost."

"The compost?" Catherine tilted her head.

"Michael, tell Kate about blessing the compost."

He broke off from a climbing story and smiled at Catherine. "Yeah, I suppose you wouldn't know about it. Different plumbing system, you girls. Very pretty, but different..."

"Michael! You're digressing." Rachel chuckled.

"Anyway, as I was leading up to... Urine is well-known as a compost activator — farmers call it liquid gold. Full of nitrogen, great for the plants." He smiled at her. "Which reminds me, I need to go. Come on, Lorne, I'll show you the compost heap. I'm sure you could also use it by now."

They rose from their seats. Lorne looked at Catherine and shrugged. She nodded and tilted her head toward the bottom of the garden. "Love you, Lorne... Go for it. You're my hero... *Your* hero will understand."

As they walked to the bottom of the garden, Lorne ran through his mind how to approach the situation. *She said he'd understand. What a beauti-*

ful relationship she has with her father, so relaxed and accepting. What the hell, I'll just let it evolve.

They stood side by side and Michael pulled his out to begin blessing the compost heap. Lorne pulled down his zipper, hauled out a bit of his length and chuckled. "I haven't done this with company since I was a teenager."

Lorne smiled sheepishly at Michael and shrugged his shoulders. *Makes no sense to continue hiding it.* He turned around, dropped his trousers to his knees and squatted. "Mind the spray, it goes all over the place."

"That's an awkward way to pee."

"I buggered myself a bit when I escaped. Catherine's convinced me I should get it repaired."

Michael finished and housed his hose, then he looked down at Lorne still in his squat. "How's it buggered?"

Lorne finished, then milked the underside to drain it, and after he had shaken the last drops off, he stood and lifted his penis to show Michael. "Connolly had a padlock through here, under the urethra, attaching me to the chain. It was my only way to escape." He spread the glans halves. "His next anchor was to be this hole when he started splitting my shaft. I decided to chew myself free."

"Jesus fucking Christ... The fucking pervert." Michael shook his head and closed his eyes. Then opening them, he bent to examine the penis more closely. "That can be repaired, Lorne. It should be easy with what surgeons do now. I can't believe you haven't had it done already. God, how long ago is it now? Must be getting on twenty years."

"I think he used hypnosis. From what I've been able to figure out, he had used it on other occasions with me. He was constantly reminding me I must always keep this hidden except from him. Whatever his hypnotic suggestion was, it was stronger than the amnesia. Much stronger — I've kept it hidden until this week. Catherine finally broke through."

"I'm sure she's pleased she did. Damn, that's certainly a hefty piece."

Lorne smiled, shook it again, covered the glans and raised his trousers, then they headed back up the slope toward the patio. Michael looked at him and nodded his head down. "The rest of your system? It works well?"

"She seems to think so, but I have no measure. She's the only girl I've ever played with." He shook his head. "I still cannot believe how I've never connected you to Mike."

Michael put his arm around Lorne's shoulder as they walked onto the patio to rejoin the women.

Chapter Twenty-Three

The women watched Lorne closely as the two men approached and sat. Catherine nodded to Rachel and smiled.

"So, Lorne... Kate was telling me nature smiled kindly on you, to use her first euphemism." She laughed. "The language she needs to use to keep her stories the shade of blue her editors want, often confuses me. I finally wheedled out of her that your schlong hangs halfway to your knees." She glanced toward his lap then up to his eyes with a smile.

Lorne smiled back and raised his eyebrows. "She exaggerates... A bit." Then he looked at Catherine and smiled wider.

"I have the report here from the compost heap," Michael said with a chuckle, as he pretended to read something in his hands. "It seems the ladies' room report is not far off."

Lorne looked eye to eye to eye. "This is so refreshing, so healthy and so very much non-Catholic. It's strange, isn't it? My parents' early prohibitions and shushings prompted my curiosity. I couldn't figure out why the taboo."

He looked at Catherine. "Strange, isn't it? If my curiosity causes me to examine your elbow joint to see how it works, or to see how your hair grows the wondrous shapes of your eyebrows, is that wrong? Is it evil to study the junction between your skin and toenail? The intricate folds and curves of your ear? Why can I look at your nose in innocence? Marvel at the change of skin between chin and lip? Why are these permitted, but we're denied even acknowledging the existence of the parts we use to create life? Religion sucks — all religions. Catholics don't have the monopoly on hypocrisy and perversion."

Catherine squeezed his thigh, then rubbed it. "We need to get back to the simple, healthy attitude we had as kids. Innocent, accepting. A body part is a body part. Unfortunately, you had a lot of Catholic shit dumped on you."

Catherine looked into her father's eyes, raised an eyebrow and saw the light nod. "So Daddy? You saw?"

"A simple fix. I'm far from being a surgeon, but I don't think it would be difficult to put that thing right." He chuckled. "With its size, they won't need microsurgery."

Earlier, in her phone call from the boat, Catherine had briefed her father about Lorne's fragility and hinted of its source as she talked with him below decks. She had spoken of encouragement, support, acceptance, humour, lightness, deep-seated fear, mutilation, abuse, horror, loving, protecting, enfolding. She had run out of words as she approached the steps leading into the cockpit. "You'll know how to do it, Daddy," she had said.

She smiled at her father and nodded, then relaxed further. The men resumed talking about climbing, and Catherine continued discussing with her mother about pregnancy and what to look forward to.

The late afternoon sun started moving behind the trees in the hedgerow, shading them and prompting Michael to glance at his watch. "Seventeen forty. What are your plans for the evening? We could do dinner here."

Catherine turned to Lorne, saw his light shrug, and said, "We had been thinking of having dinner at the new place by the pier in Chemainus — what's it called, Lorne?"

"The Driftwood."

Michael curled his lip and shook his head. "Fancy menu, but you'd do better at a White Spot. God, even at a Denny's."

"I suspected it was another of those." Lorne sneered as he nodded at Catherine. "The reviews seem to follow the pattern."

Michael listened with a puzzled expression. "Another of those? The pattern?"

Lorne explained what they suspected was happening with restaurants, with reviews and the apparent manipulation, while Michael and Rachel nodded. "We've seen an increasing amount of that. Couldn't believe most of the reviews horrid places were receiving," Rachel said. "Remember that one in Victoria a few weeks ago after the first night of the Wine Festival? That took the meaning of awful to another level."

"We've decided to always seek personal recommendations from people whose palates we trust." Michael stroked his beard and continued, "So you suspect there might be something widespread behind this?"

"Lorne mentioned it last week at a restaurant opening. Another place trying in the old Lumière location."

"What happened to Roberto? That was a thriving place. They sold a lot of our wine." Michael stroked his chin whiskers more vigorously. "How long have you suspected something? That somebody might be manipulating?"

"A week and a bit, maybe two..."

"It's strange, I haven't thought of this much, but Nathan was hinting at something odd before he headed out that night." Catherine stared at Lorne, opened her mouth wide and sat speechless.

Lorne put his hand on hers and pulsed it gently as he tilted his head. He could almost hear her mind grinding.

She shook her head. "I was hyper busy. I had a lot of research to do. Probably wasn't listening — missed the details. He wanted me to come with him. I begged off. Too busy with a big rewrite and my editor pressing. He went on his own... God, I wish I could remember where it was. I tried to for so long to remember for the police."

She put her hands to her face, slumped her shoulders and remained silent for a long while, then began in a monotone, "His dismembered body was found two weeks later by a vagrant in a Gastown alley. Apparent cause of death, blood loss. Pieces missing. Those are all the clues they have. I wish I could remember where he had been going that night."

She lay her head on Lorne's shoulder, and he held her.

"His computer... No hints in it?"

"He had it with him. He often wrote on the go. Disappeared, and his iPhone also."

"Backups? Sticks?"

"Nothing. We've been through everything many times. There was not a hint of where he had been going. His office is still as he left it. Sifted through by the investigators, but it's all still there."

She reached up and stroked his cheek. "This hasn't gotten us far with our plans for dinner — except not to go to The Driftwood."

"Well this is easy then," Rachel said. "Stay here, dine with us."

"Spend the night. Kate still has her bedroom here." Michael laughed loudly. "Maybe you two can play doctor again."

"Or mummy and daddy." Catherine giggled, then told them about how she and Lorne as kids had tried so many different ways, searching for the special way to hold. The one Mummy had said made babies. She broke out laughing as she finished, "We were so innocent then." She turned her head to receive Lorne's kiss. "We still want to make babies. Innocent ones."

Chapter Twenty-Four

"So, will that work with your schedule?" Michael asked.

"We're going to Authentic Wine's portfolio tasting tomorrow afternoon in Vancouver." Lorne took out his iPhone and looked at the tidal currents. "Slack is shortly after nine in Porlier, turning to flood." He switched to his wind app. "We should weigh by seven. Winds are rather light until mid-morning. Great blow across the Straits starting late morning. We'll be early into False Creek. We can walk to the tasting."

Catherine stroked his cheek. "My mister programmed life. I'll have to do something about that. We don't have to be anywhere or do anything except enjoy, Lorne. You move well with the tides, the currents, the winds. It should be easy for you to move with the ebb and flow of life, of people."

Michael looked at Lorne and winked. "I'm usually up early. No problem for me to drive you to the pier any time you want. What about your tender — is it safe moored there?"

"It would be the thief's last choice with no outboard hanging off its transom. Even if it were chosen, without the proper thumb scans, the drive is disabled. It would have to be paddled. I've left it in some really sleazy places, but I've now sworn off going to the States again until they get their act together."

"It's settled then," Rachel said. "You're spending the night. Kate, you take Lorne over to the asparagus plots. Get about three dozen. Eight or ten big oyster mushrooms off the logs while you're there. We'll do scallops. We've always plenty of Fanny Bay iqf in the freezer... What else?"

Lorne and Catherine looked at each other and grinned. "Guess we're staying for dinner. You can see that Mummy's never been the indecisive type — it runs in the family. I'll grab a basket and knife."

Halfway across the slope, Catherine pointed to the bench. "Let's pause here a while and talk. There's been a lot of stuff, heavy stuff, quite quickly. Not a lot of quiet time to absorb it."

He sat, and she lay along the bench beside him with her head in his lap. "I used to lie here and stare up into the trees looking at all the branches. I'd follow them with my eyes counting all the forks, all the decisions. Carry on along this one or take that branch? Where does it lead? Life's like that, isn't it? Each moment presents a decision."

"I used to think of that in the mountains. Still do everywhere." He looked down at her face and moved a lock of wayward hair across her forehead. "I like to take the time to appreciate the surroundings, to observe and absorb everything, to be fully present and sense the evolution, the broadening picture, the tangential possibilities." He smiled and stroked her cheek. "Not dwelling on any of them, simply allowing the information to flow through. This way, when it's time for a decision, I know it, and I'm ready."

"You gob-smacked me with that proposal. Dad was his normal calm self — accepting. I was near shock."

"I thought the timing made sense. We both knew we wanted to, and there was a lull in the conversation." With his little finger, he caught a tear that had started rolling down her cheek. "I hope this is for joy."

"One of many to follow. I want us to never cry tears of sadness again — we've had far too many. Tears are for joy from now on... Both of us... Promise?"

"I promise."

"So that was okay? You and Dad at the compost?"

"I can't believe how easy it was. Like no big deal. He's such a wonderful man. And your mother, a loving sweetheart with such an easy frankness. It's no wonder you've turned out so magnificently."

"I think they've a good idea of some of the horrors you've been through, and I see no need to go into it any further with them. But I'd like to help you through the rest of the story — your running away, the mountains, and whatever followed, right up to when I started writing you those steamy love letters."

"There's a lot of sick stuff in there I'd love you to help me get rid of." He stroked her cheek and laid his finger on her lips for a kiss. "We should go get mushrooms and asparagus."

She sat up, turned, and they merged in a long probing kiss, their hands exploring. When they finally paused, she still had her hand down the front of his trousers. She laughed as she stroked him again. "How are we going to sneak this into the house?"

"I can walk behind you or carry the basket high." He chuckled and looked down. "This is why I always wear one of my double-breasted blazers when I know you'll be at an event. Sometimes you surprised me and showed up unexpectedly..." He chuckled. "And this showed up at seeing you. God, you turn me on."

"No... You're joshing me." She gazed up to his eyes, paused and tilted her head. "You're not kidding, are you?"

"It wasn't all the time. Only when my fantasies clicked in."

"How often was that?"

"Most of the time."

"Christ, my major rub fantasy, there next to me all those years with an invisible attraction that had been erected especially for me."

"I always had to walk it home alone, then shake hands with it. Confused and lonely."

She brushed her lips across his and gave him another squeeze. "I'd write this as a proposal for a novel plot, but my editors would reject it as unbelievable."

"I rarely read fantasy, but I've lived it a lot." He looked at her with a twisted smile on his lips.

"We're both finished with the fantasy of this now. We need to adjust to the reality of it. Let's go get the asparagus and mushrooms." She eased her grip on him and brushed her lips again across his.

He caught her tongue with his, and they were back into another jaw lock. A few minutes later, when they unclenched, he said, "Asparagus."

"Yeah, a giant white Alto Adige asparagus." Her hand was still gripping him firmly. "Have you ever seen the asparagus from the Südtirol? So huge — so phallic."

"Climbed there several times, but in the summer. Wrong season for asparagus. The Dolomite peaks of the Rosengarten group there, Catinaccio, the Vajolet Towers are rather phallic. They're damned good climbing. Love to do them with you some day."

Chapter Twenty-Five

After a delicious dinner, they moved in to sit in front of the fire and continue the conversation there. When the grandmother clock on the wall struck ten, Catherine put her hand on Lorne's shoulder. "We should let these old folks get some sleep. We have things to do, and we need to be up early in the morning."

They confirmed the six thirty departure and had a round of hugs, then Catherine led Lorne up the stairs. "You'll have to make up for lost time." She pulled him along the hallway to her room. "You're behind schedule with your top-ups."

She opened her room door, and he followed her in. "Wow, this is nice. Huge. This is what you moved into from Cypress?"

"No, my first bedroom was much simpler, very much simpler. All the energy was spent upgrading the winery, and we moved into the old trailer the previous owner had lived in. I was halfway through high school before Dad finished the house."

"It appears as if you still sleep here. So neat and tidy."

"Mum came up to clean, make the bed, put fresh towels in the ensuite... Arrange it while you and I were preparing dinner."

They headed across the room, both leaving a trail of clothing on the rug as they went. He helped her out of her panties at the foot of the bed, and they merged in a tangled hug, hands and lips exploring. At his urging, she sat on the edge of the bed and lay back to welcome his tongue and hands.

"This isn't about making me pop," she sighed. "It's about getting me pregnant." Nonetheless, she relented, and he continued.

Lorne freed his mouth for a moment. "This has been on my mind all afternoon. Fantasising." He resumed where he had left off, his hands now finding her breasts. Close in front of his eyes, the flat expanse of her belly began undulating while the sounds of her breathing quickened and deepened.

"Oh my God... I don't think... I've ever come... So quickly... Your fantasising... Oh, my fuck..."

He moved up, moved in and felt her waning pulses as they rolled on the bed together. "It's been a long time," he said between kisses.

"Even in my steamiest novels, you don't exist. I'd never dare write you, you'd never get past the editors. Oh, my God."

When she had calmed, he rolled onto his back with her, still attached, and pivoted her halfway around into a cross. She caught on and swung a leg around, then continued the turn and rose onto her knees to straddle him, her back to him. He held her waist and guided her as she began churning while slowly moving up and down.

"Wonderful view of the action from here. I love the movement of your folds." He ran a hand forward past their junction, pausing to play with her lips before ending on her clit.

She hung her head down to watch his length move in and out. "Your turn, Lorne... You need to... Come now... Oh fuuuu..."

She collapsed forward, hugged his calves and kissed his feet as she convulsed. He sat up to stroke her back as she continued her heavy breathing. "Hair trigger," she panted. "Hah, it's the men who... Who're supposed to have..." She continued panting, though lighter now.

"Hair trigger? Okay, this time, I'll peel it before we start. I'll show you a real hair trigger." He chuckled as he sat, extended his hand to her neck and lightly pulsed it.

She bent her head over to squeeze his hand. "Fuck do I ever want your baby." She moved up into a squat and did deep knee bends above him as he lay back on the stacked pillows, cupping her breasts and teasing her nipples. "Forget me, Lorne. Peel it... Now."

Within half a minute he erupted inside her, muffling his howl not to disturb Michael and Rachel. He collapsed back onto the bed, and she laid back on him, still gently rocking her hips. He reached around, found her mound and slowly moved it in circles while his other hand cupped a breast.

"I cannot believe you haven't done this your entire life. You do it with such compassion, with so much concern for me, sensing what I want, what I need. You've led me through position changes I've never explored, led my body, my soul into areas I've never imagined possible."

"I've a vivid imagination, and I've done a lot of research online, preparing in case I ever had the opportunity to do some of these things with you."

"If you keep doing that, I'll pop again." She gave a deep sigh and wiggled her hips.

"Okay, hang on." He chuckled as he grazed his forefinger across her clit.

After she had recovered, they remained connected, lying on their backs with her butt on his hips and their heads on pillows as they stroked and talked. They were giving every opportunity to make it easier for the sperm to find their way downhill to her cervix.

"What do they say online about this? About maximising the chances of conception?"

"I was never willing to look. I didn't want to get my hopes up and then dashed. Nathan was so opposed to the idea from the beginning. There must be a lot of information on the web."

"Is there a wifi connection here? Surely there must be."

She smiled as she pointed to the box of tissues which had been placed at the edge of the bedside table. "Can you reach the box of Mum's thoughtfulness?"

They disconnected, Lorne wrapped himself in a turban of tissue while Catherine poked a wad of it between her lips. He dug-out both their computers, and they sat on the bed, leaning back against the stacked pillows and surfing.

Michael Walsh

"This is interesting. Listen at this. This site says having sex too frequently can reduce the chance of becoming pregnant. Once a week may not be often enough, while every day is too frequent, as daily sex can reduce the quality of sperm. Instead, aim to make love every two or three days."

"Where's that?" She looked across to his screen.

"At babycentre.co.uk. Seems the Brits still remember Queen Victoria." He chuckled. "I'll send you the link."

"Here's another one: *Make a point to have sex every other day starting around day ten. A positive result on your ovulation predictor kit occurs the day before ovulation. Have sex that day and on the next two days. These are the prime days to conceive.*"

"What's an ovulation predictor kit?"

"Also new to me. Sounds like it would be useful."

"Listen to this one: *Reduce the frequency of sex - because it takes time for sperm to both mature and accumulate.* This is on webmd.com - *Having sex every day even during ovulation will not necessarily increase your chances of getting pregnant. In general, every other night around the time of ovulation helps increase your chance of getting pregnant.* It says here that sperm can live up to 72 hours after intercourse."

"Three days? I thought it was four or five days."

"Here's an interesting one: *The amount of sperm in men's semen increases if you wait a few days between ejaculations.* Here's where it gets interesting, though.*" Lorne looked up from his computer, smiled then returned to the screen and continued, "*But they also found that a high sperm count alone doesn't necessarily improve the likelihood of conception. The longer you wait between ejaculations, the greater the decrease in motility, the ability of the sperm to swim and meet the egg. Sperm motility is one of the most important aspects for conception.*"

"That makes a lot of sense to me. And also to this writer: *It is also possible that a man who doesn't ejaculate enough can have problems with infertility as well. For lack of a better term, sperm that are "fresher" seem to be stronger and faster swimmers. Sperm that have been produced but remained in the body for a while can be less viable.*"

"Hey, I'd rather have a small army of healthy, aggressive wigglers than a huge army of tired old farts. I say send in the special forces." He stroked her cheek and smiled.

"I was just reading that one. It continues here, answering a reader's comment: *So, what does this mean for you? You and your wife had sex shortly after you ejaculated on your own. If the way your body works is similar to the men in the research study, when you had sex with your wife, your sperm count may have been slightly lower... but the sperm that you did ejaculate when you had sex with her were likely better swimmers.*" Catherine nodded. "Makes sense."

"This one puts it well: *...studies reveal that delaying ejaculation may increase the total concentration of sperm and perhaps the volume of semen. However, the percentage of normal sperm and the percentage of motile sperm both decrease with infrequent ejaculation.*"

"Listen to this one, it's the results from a study related to abstaining from sex and the ability to conceive: *...looked at sperm samples from around six thousand men who had abstained from sex from one day to over two weeks. The researchers found that if men had low sperm counts their sperm steadily became less mobile after an average of one day's abstinence. Their sperm were going stale...*"

"So where are we? These sites are all over the place."

"Normal internet. Everyone has an opinion. A huge filter is needed." Catherine shrugged as she curled her lips. "Like some of the intentionally mucked up stuff on Wikipedia, done to drive someone's personal agenda."

"The religious prudes are likely pushing the infrequent sex stuff. The motility thing makes more sense to me. Think of evolution... The fellows who came most often left the biggest trail of children. It would seem the more attractive males, however you want to define attractiveness, would be the freshest and more likely to impregnate... Both from frequency and freshness."

"Giving sperm no opportunity to deteriorate makes a lot of sense to me. I've been trying to find how quickly they're replaced. Seems to be little on it except nebulous statements."

Michael Walsh

"Here, I've found a medical blog entry titled How Sperm Are Made: *The testes contain over two hundred metres of tubing for the production of sperm. Approximately a hundred and twenty million are started every day. This is equivalent to making about twelve hundred sperm per heartbeat.*"

"Wow! Twelve hundred per heart beat. Continuously. So much for the waiting between pops." She reached down, hefted his scrotum and counted ten seconds. "There's another twelve thousand."

"That feels nice, your hand there to welcome the new ones. They may not all make it, the article continues: *They take approximately two months to mature, with quality control throughout the production process to ensure genetic and biological integrity of finished product before ejaculation. The final two weeks of maturation are spent in the coiled ducts near the bottom of the scrotum, joining the queue of a billion or more readying to be ejaculated.*"

"My God, how can we not get pregnant?" She ran her fingers lightly across the bottom of a testicle. "So this is where they're waiting, this lumpy stuff under here. It makes sense to me that if the ones that are ready just sit there, they'll deteriorate under the old idea of waiting to build volume."

"Daily seems better... Even twice a day for added freshness." He rolled to cup her breast and kiss her. "I can live with that."

Chapter Twenty-Six

Lorne's iPhone alarm woke them at six, and after a quickie, they showered and headed downstairs. They were greeting Rachel good morning in the kitchen as Michael came in the back door. "Compost habit — unless it's pouring rain. Good morning. Have you changed your mind on breakfast?"

"We're running on a schedule, Daddy," Catherine said as she kissed him. She snickered and added, "Time and tide wait for no man, not even for Lorne."

They hugged Rachel goodbye. "Don't be strangers. Your bedroom is always here. You can back come and cook like that for us as often as you wish."

The tender was where they had secured it, and after a hug from her father, Catherine stepped aboard and opened the chain lock. "So how do I start this thing?"

"I'll code the thumb pads for you later." Lorne did a sequence of touches and received a green light, then he undid the mooring lines and pushed away from the float. She pulled the lever back and slowly backed into open water as they waved at Michael.

"So down-to-earth, both of them. What delightful parents you have. And what a magnificent daughter they have." He put his arm around her waist as she headed the tender toward *Tastevin*.

Alongside, he talked her through attaching the hoisting slings and disabling the tender's drive. As they walked up the steps of the accommodation ladder, he asked her, "Do you remember the lowering sequence?"

"It seemed simple when you did it."

"That's because it is simple. The toggle switches are labelled, and everything is logical." They arrived at the panel. "Take your time and think it through while I raise and stow the accommodation ladder. I'll show you that next time."

She smiled at him as he returned half a minute later. "Seems logical I start here. *Hoist Up Down*." She pushed *Up*, and they watched the tender rise from the water.

"There's a cut-out switch at the top, so you can't raise it too far. Run it until it switches off." He bent and kissed her cheek.

"Next is *Travel In Out*, again logical." She tilted the toggle to *In*, and they watched the tender move across the deck and stop directly above the chocks. "I figured there'd be another cut-out switch here."

He kissed her lips lightly and patted her bum. "You finish here, I'll go release the snubbers."

"What about the lashing strops?"

"You should be able to figure those out."

She was finishing the last of the lashing when he returned from the bow. "Elegantly simple system. A child could sort it out and operate it."

"No need to make it complex. That complex stuff is for those who want to play macho."

He began shortening the scope on the rode as he rolled out the staysail, explaining as he worked. "The sail will move us forward toward the anchor, easing the load on the windlass. With this breeze, there should be sufficient momentum to pop the anchor free as we sail over it." He continued shortening the chain, gradually swinging the bow toward the anchor. "Next we pull out a piece of the main to catch more of the breeze. We should now be nearly up-and-down on the anchor."

The bow dipped a bit then rebounded, and he pushed the *Auto* button for the windlass to recover the weighed anchor. "There's a great auto-house system in the bow, again with a cut-out. I can let it carry-on while I tend to other things."

"This seems so simple. No noisy and smelly engine, no scurrying around, Dad would love this."

"I'd love to have them out sailing."

"That would be nice... Coffee time?"

"Hug time first."

"You amaze me, Lorne. You really amaze me." She wrapped her arms around him. "Nathan wouldn't let me do anything he considered men's stuff. Here with *Tastevin* he would have done everything himself, quietly, not sharing, not showing how, not caring. He would have told me to go make coffee, tidy-up below. I would have had to ask him for a hug."

"It pained me over the years to see your frustrations increase as I read between the lines of our conversations and watched you with him. But you always appeared happy."

"Happy to see you. That was my happiness. I wasn't dying inside like some of the girls, but..." Catherine tilted her head up to receive his kiss.

Lorne did a visual and instrument sweep, then pushed the autopilot button before taking the kiss further.

He raised his head to do another horizon sweep and check the chartplotter. She asked again, "Coffee?"

"Great idea."

Two hours later they were through Porlier Pass and set-up on a beam reach making hull speed and pointed at Point Atkinson. They lounged back in a cuddle in the corner of the cockpit settee and chatted.

"I've spent so much time dreaming about this, about sharing this. Strange thinking of it now, but for the last while I had been increasingly thinking this would be impossible for me."

"What was holding you from it? Keeping you from doing something about your penis?"

"I hadn't thought about why until I was at the compost with your father. He questioned why I had done nothing for nearly two decades. I started realising Connolly had used hypnosis. He was always telling me I must keep this hidden except from him. He must have used it on me for other things."

"That makes sense. It was such a strong force. I was startled — shocked, actually by your reaction in the taxi."

"Whatever his hypnotic suggestion was, it was stronger than the amnesia. I kept my wounds hidden in the hospital, from my foster parents, from everybody."

She reached down and put her hand on the bulge along his thigh. "I'm so pleased it's finally free."

"A few days ago, after my episode at Molly's — the piercing reaction — a thought ran through my head: *He's dead now, he wouldn't know.* The same thought came more strongly when we were sitting at eSushi a while later."

He enjoyed the light pulse of her hand and swelled to it. "Thinking now, Connolly must have used hypnosis. That's how he was able to shoot that video."

"What video?"

Lorne checked the instruments and did a visual horizon, then sat back into the cuddle. "Connolly tried for months in the beginning to make me enjoy playing with his butchered penis. He was still splitting his own shaft at the time and made me watch the process, then play with it. He was gentle and accepted my revulsion, but told me I would eventually enjoy it. Told me it's a learning process, a necessary part of our sacred covenant."

"The video?"

"I guess that's where the hypnosis comes in. He showed me a long video of me happily licking and sucking him through all stages of his self-mutilation. He was a sick man."

"Psychotic."

"He insisted I call him Father. In the beginning, it made sense, he was a priest and also my foster parent."

"That doesn't seem nurturing for a father."

"But he was, though. He was caring and always concerned about my education. Strange thinking about it now. I'm sure he loved me. It's when he took me to the garret and locked a chain around my ankle that the situation became strange. But his love and his caring seemed to continue."

"How did he explain the chain, the isolation?"

"He said it was part of the covenant process. I had to endure deprivation and hardship to be accepted. It was a necessary part through which all had to pass."

"You didn't question him?"

"I was young, fourteen, and likely still in shock from the deaths of my parents, grandparents, aunts, uncles. He was a priest. I went along with it. The place was comfortable; an old illegal rental suite, a bed-sitting room and a small bathroom. There was a bar fridge with a microwave and toaster oven stacked on top."

"What about food?"

"He kept the fridge and freezer stocked with quick-prep items for the ovens, and there was always a selection of fresh fruit and vegetables. The chain gave me access to them and to the desk, the bookshelves and the lounge chairs. Plus the bathroom and bed, but the dormer window was out of range."

"Sounds basic, but I guess many live less comfortably than that." She stood and did a sweep of the horizon. "The Cross Island ferry in our port bow?"

He glanced over at the instruments. "Both the radar and the AIS still show it will cross well clear astern."

She bent to kiss him, then sat on his lap and snuggled into his chest. "Let's talk about something easier for a while. Do this stuff in small doses."

Chapter Twenty-Seven

They enjoyed the remainder of the sail across the Straits with much lighter conversation and a fine wind that allowed them to make English Bay with only minor sail adjustments. They fell off to a wallowing run up the bay in the building following wind and seas, then shortly past noon Lorne rolled in the sails at the entrance to False Creek and motored toward the marina.

As they found lee from the wind, Catherine looked up at him at the port helm. "Seems to be a good blow coming."

"A few hours earlier than previous forecasts. That's why I was playing your mister programmed life." He smiled at her and chuckled. "In a couple of hours, it'll be quite nasty out there."

A while later, he noted the 1226 showing on the cockpit clock as they arrived alongside his slip. He stepped off with the breast line and secured it to the float cleat.

"Do you always make it that easy for your line handlers?" Catherine called from the bow after she had dropped a bight of the line over the cleat on the float.

"I don't know... You're the first line handler I've ever had. Guess I'll have to become accustomed to having one." He walked along the float toward the bow and took the back spring off its hook, then paused and looked up at her. "I'd like to do that."

"Have to be careful, then. Have you ever noted, the more line handlers at the rails, the sloppier the skipper's approach?"

"Seems it sometimes, doesn't it? And the louder." He reached up and brushed her ankle with the back of his hand, smiled and pointed to the cleated line. "Take the bow line turns off the cleat and ease it out to the red mark, then turn it down. That allows the stern to sit just off the cross float."

"I guess you need many tricks when you solo a boat this size. The tricks and systems have become your crew."

"I'll gladly replace all of them for one of you." He continued with the mooring, securing the springs and the stern lines, showing her the marks on the lines and explaining his process as he did.

He checked the time on the cockpit clock as he completed the log. "We've nearly an hour and a half before the tasting begins and five hours before it ends. I've fresh clothes here aboard."

"I still have the outfit I'd packed for The Driftwood. It's hanging in the locker. I'm okay for clothes here."

"Do you need to go home for anything?"

"I've everything I need here, packed for tastings and dining. The only thing I can think of needing at home..." She paused and put her hand on his butt. "Need to see how you fit in my bed."

"Fuck! You know where my switch is and how to flip it — so fast." He sent a hand down to adjust himself. "You've damn near made me rip my trousers." Their hands and lips were all over each other as they merged.

They grabbed their garment bags from the lockers, and he picked up her small duffel. He locked up the boat, set the silent alarms, and they stepped out through transom gate to the float. As they walked around the crescent hand-in-hand, he asked her, "So the inspiration for your novels, you have such a marvellous turn of phrase, creative imagery — Here I am reviewing your novels, and I've not read any of them, only listened to you do impromptu excerpts — So hot. Where's the inspiration?"

"I wrote from frustration. The central heartthrob in every one of my novels is based on you, and on my fantasies with you."

He spun her gently into a hug in the middle of the sidewalk, and they explored mouths. For a long time. A very long time.

Michael Walsh

"People are staring at us," she said as they unlocked and moved to random face kissing.

"Good. Let them see love, see bliss, see communion. Let them see reality, not fantasy."

They continued more briskly around the crescent to her townhouse, where she unlocked and opened the door to lead him in. She flopped her garment bag to the floor, kicked off her shoes and looked at the stairs. He set down her duffel, laid his garment bag on top of it and submitted to the tug of her hand, kicking off his shoes as he followed her.

The stairs were left littered with discarded garments as she led the way up to her bedroom. She flipped the duvet off the bed and now nude, stepped onto it, moved to the middle and stopped, then turned slowly, speaking in her low voice. *"She turned to face him, taking a wide, defiant stance, hands on her hips and lifting her chin at him. So you think you can take me, do you?"*

He peeled off his last sock as he watched her, mesmerised, fully stiffened and wondering what was coming.

She stared at him. "Fuck, I can't do this kind of fantasy with you, Lorne. You're too gentle and tender, too loving." She extended her hand. "Come, make love *with* me, not *to* me. Softly, lovingly."

As she lay on top of him recovering from her third orgasm, she said in a quiet voice, "Crazy of me, I didn't even think... That kind of thing always worked for Nathan when he was hot. But it's the difference between plundering and sharing... My God, I love you, Lorne."

"We should think of showering and dressing. Do you want to come again?"

"Silly question. Silly, silly, silly. What about you? Are you sure you're okay holding off until this evening?"

"I'm happy if it gives the next thirty of forty million in line an extra bit of time to mature." He smiled at her as he began slowly thrusting his hips and tweaking her nipples.

Half an hour later they were showered and dressed and heading out the front door. He pointed to the darkening sky. "Appears we've time to make it on foot before the arrival of the deluge from the front. Or do you want to take the SkyTrain?"

"I've missed my walks the last few days." She tugged his arm, and they started up through Yaletown. "Do you realise we're still on our first date?" She smiled as she looked up at him. "Lots of exercise, but not much walking."

They arrived at the hotel in building blustery winds which were announcing the imminent start of rain. In the lobby, he pointed to the sign, and they followed its arrow toward the ballroom. As they approached the registration table, they saw many familiar faces. "This will be interesting." She squeezed the arm she was holding. "I hadn't even thought."

"Act normally." He patted her hand on his arm. "Most everyone knows we've known each other for years. We're usually a close pair at these events, anyway."

"I guess you're right. Besides, we've nothing at all to hide." She smiled up at him. "It'll be fun seeing how long it takes for someone to notice. If Cynthia's here, I bet she's the first. She must have sensed something was cooking the other night. God, that seems so long ago now."

They picked up their badges, nodding to and greeting others and engaging some in light pleasantries as they moved toward the door. They were among the first wave of tasters, the full-time trade. The full-time writers, the store owners and managers and a few others who'd managed to beg off work mid-afternoon from day jobs. Soon, in the lull between lunch and dinner, the restaurant managers and sommeliers would arrive.

"Start with Champagne?"

"Always," she smiled back at him.

Chapter Twenty-Eight

At the Roederer stand, Richard poured Lorne and Catherine flutes, then pointing under the table, he mouthed *Crystal*. They smiled back and nodded, then after raising their glasses in a toast to him, they headed to the centre of the ballroom. "Seems the 2006 Crystal has arrived," he said as they paused to taste and survey the layout.

"You always do this, don't you?"

"What, stand in the middle of the room?"

"That, and a bubbly."

"Helps me plan my tasting strategy." He took a sip from his flute and looked at her. "My God, you're gorgeous."

"You're a damned gorgeous hunk, yourself. What's your strategy today? Do you need to taste anything?"

"Besides you?"

"Fuck!"

"That too."

"Too public here for that." She looked up at his face and offered an impish grin. "You're making me cream."

"Good thing I've worn my double-breast."

"You're not?"

"Am so."

She looked at his blazer front and giggled. "You hide it so well."

"Always had to around you."

"Fuck!"

"Okay." He smiled at her and pursed his lips.

"Hot in here, isn't it?" She took another sip of her Champagne.

"You two seem friendly," Cynthia said as she neared.

They turned to greet her. "So how was the public opening?" Lorne asked as they *fait la bise.*

"Busy. Very busy. We had huge Twitter traffic, glowing reviews on all the online sites. The place is fully booked — a few tables available at unfashionable hours a week and more away..." She paused to look at them, then grinned. "But you guys. When you left Thursday evening, the fire in your eyes."

Catherine chuckled and winked at Cynthia. "We've been busy doing research for my writing."

"The steamy scenes?" She looked at Lorne and shivered. "How exciting. Very exciting..." She trailed off and shook herself. "Great to see you've finally nabbed him."

Cynthia laughed and hugged each of them in turn, pausing for a long while with Lorne. "I've always thought you two were made for each other." She nuzzled into him. "Do you have any clones?"

They stood chatting for several minutes, Cynthia setting up a lunch date with Catherine on Friday, before she headed off to taste.

"Cynthia's been a dear friend almost forever — my only close girlfriend. We've always shared everything... Well nearly." Catherine took another sip of Champagne. "She knows of my frustrating relationship with Nathan, but I'm surprised she never told me about her hots for you."

"Because it never went anywhere except in her mind."

"But you dated, didn't you?"

"She asked me out many times, but I accepted only twice. She rang none of my bells." He chuckled, "But God, did she try."

Catherine snuggled up to him for a hug. "My my, that's obvious this way, isn't it?" She laughed and wiggled into him. "I'm sure she didn't miss it."

"We should go taste the Crystal. Richard will be disappointed if we don't." He led her back to the Roederer stand.

Richard watched them approach. "So good to see you two together." He reached down to the ice tub beneath the table and motioned them to the curtain at the back. "Shipment's delayed clearing through. Another week. We had this couriered."

He unzipped the foil, undid the cage, eased the cork out and poured generously into fresh flutes, including one for himself. "To you two... Wow, we always said you two belong together."

"It's obvious?"

"The blind might miss it... No, they'd pick up the vibrations." He laughed and raised his glass to them.

She blushed as she looked at her glass to assess the mousse before taking a sip. "How's Marion?"

"Great, she's loving her retirement. She'll be here a bit later to help when the crowd thickens. She'll be excited... Wow!"

While the other two chatted, Lorne quietly spoke his tasting comments into the note app on his iPhone. He clicked off and pocketed it, then took another sip. "Great year. Have to go back a long way to find one as good. The price remaining the same?"

"We're still managing to hold it under three hundred. Not much margin left for us. Mostly prestige now."

Richard stoppered the Champagne as he walked them around to the front of the stand. Lorne took another sip of Crystal. "What else should we look at? I need to find a few more low-end wines for a summer sippers piece I'm writing."

"We've samples of the new vintage of the Primitivo and the Sangiovese over there." Richard pointed across the room. "The shipment should be clearing in two or three weeks. They'll tell you where to go next. Great seeing you... So happy."

Over the next two hours, Lorne and Catherine spent more time talking with friends and colleagues than they did tasting. Few missed the new relationship. "I've never spent so much time to get so few tasting notes."

She squeezed his arm and laughed. "But you were always so focused on tasting before, Lorne. Get all your tasting in quickly before you began to socialise."

"Yeah, I guess. Like a one-program automaton."

"I learned to wait until I thought you were finished before I approached."

"Your approach always finished my tasting and started other things. I looked forward to it. How did you know when I had finished?"

"Middle of the room, looking around."

"Yeah, I guess. That's what I did when I was trying to decide what to do next."

"It seemed always to be with me. We'd stand there and share notes, discuss the wines, then head over to tables to re-taste, re-assess. I was constantly in awe of your passion for wine, the fire in your eyes as you spoke of it and of the people who made it. The rambling wine discussions we had, refining my knowledge and creaming my panties."

"You didn't?"

"Did too."

"Fuck!"

"Yeah, let's."

Michael Walsh

Chapter Twenty-Nine

Lorne and Catherine did a quick circuit of the tables and bade farewell to those whose eyes they caught, then left. It was pouring rain when they reached the lobby and looked outside. Lorne pulled out his phone, glanced at the time, *1652,* and opened the weather radar. "The rear end of the front is over Bowen, it'll be half an hour before the system has passed over."

"We could do the passage to the SkyTrain."

"Then there's a block and a half walk, nearly two, in the downpour from Roundhouse to the boat." He looked at his blazer.

"Same to my place." She looked at her suit.

"We could take a cab, or we could stay on the train to Marine Drive, get off and head back. That'll consume a good half hour. I love people watching."

"You too? I love it. Draw my characters from people watching."

"Another option: We could head up to the restaurant here. We barely managed a nibble at the buffet."

"I've often wondered why people stand there eating, rather than moving back to make room for others."

"Yeah, selfish — maybe only unthinking... Restaurant?"

"I read a great review of the place several months ago." She smiled at him as she led him to the escalator. "The Unknown Diner had glowing comments on it. Crazy, I never guessed."

The dining room was nearly empty as they were shown to a window table overlooking the harbour and were told it would be a few minutes before dinner service began. "Appears we're ahead of the early-dining tourists."

"It'll soon start filling, it's just coming up to seventeen hundred. Many of these hotel restaurants get two full sittings of tourists before Vancouver comes out to dine," he said as they examined the room.

They watched the rain pelt against the windows, driven by the blusters. She pointed out over his shoulder. "There's the line of bright now starting to show through the rain."

He turned to look. "The clear behind the front. It'll be a good evening for sailing. I've a far finer sport in mind, though."

Catherine squeezed his hand, and he turned back to look at her, listening to her dusky voice. *"He turned to look at her, watching her mouth move as she looked longingly at him. She crossed her legs and squeezed... No relief. She lowered a hand and pressed... Then more firmly, wishing it was his hand."*

Lorne shifted in his chair and rearranged himself. "You'll rip the front out of my trousers if you keep doing that." He shuffled his chair around from opposite her to facing out the window and leaned across to lay a light kiss on her lips and a hand on her thigh under the drape of the tablecloth. "Is this better?"

"Getting there." Catherine placed her hand on his and slowly moved it up and across her thigh as she slouched farther in her chair, spread her legs and tilted her pelvis. "Just a little pressure, Lorne... Connection... Ease the buzz... Oh, God!"

He leaned forward farther in his chair and pretended to be pointing at something on the waterfront as he pressed his other hand on her mound. "Better now?"

"I always get so horny when my fertile time approaches." She pulled her mouth back into a dimpled smile. "So fucking hot for you right now."

"We can forget about eating here. Head back now. Grab a cab."

"No, it's fine. Your hand... The connection with you. The rush has eased now. Need to keep my mind off... Let's talk about sailing plans for tomorrow, to Gibsons, dinner at Molly's."

"They — what was her name — Barbara was going to email you a reminder."

Catherine reached for her phone from her waist pouch. "I've left it switched off the past few days. I'm sure there's a million emails and texts." She pressed Lorne's hand into her mound, then eased it and guided it down her thigh. "I'm fine now."

They both straightened up, then leaned in to brush lips. Her phone finally cycled on, and she scrolled through her inbox. "Nothing, that's strange, she seemed competent... Stupid me. Been away from this too long. The email on my reviewer card is a web-based one for greater anonymity."

She browsed to the site, logged in and quickly found the email. "After all the fluff, it confirms 2030 Tuesday 20 June, table for two." She did a quick thanking reply, pushing *Send* as the waiter arrived with menus and a wine list.

Lorne clicked off his phone as he arrived, and in response to the question about drinks, he pointed to the wine list. "We'll be quick, give us a minute, two at the most."

They opened the menus and scanned the daily sheet. "How about sharing a selection of entrées and a half carafe of wine?"

They quickly chose five seafood starters and a half litre of the WaveCrest Pinot Gris, then closed the menus and wine list. The waiter saw the signal, returned to the table, and Lorne gave him the order, telling him they wanted them simultaneously to share.

Partway through writing the order, the waiter shook his pen. "I'll have to get another. This one's dead."

"Here use this." Lorne pulled a pen from his blazer's pocket.

"La Luce. That's the new place on Broadway. You from there?"

"No, it's one of their promotional giveaways. You keep it, I've far too many pens, and I'm constantly being given more."

As soon as the waiter had gone, Lorne said, "I was checking the forecasts. The winds behind the front will decrease overnight becoming near still by noon. We could leave early to take advantage of what breezes remain."

"What's early?"

"Eight should be early enough. It's only twenty miles the shortest route. Mid-morning the dying circulation winds will be replaced by the increasing anabatic winds as the day warms."

"Anabatic, what's that?"

"The winds caused by the rising air over the land as it warms. The cooler air over the water moves inland to replace the risen air, giving us what are commonly called sea breezes."

"Yeah, I know the sea breezes and also the land breezes in the evening. I'm sure you have a technical name for those." She giggled. "You really don't like motoring, do you?"

"Yeah, katabatic." He grinned. "We could motor there in two and a half hours but where's the challenge? The enjoyment?"

"How long will it take us sailing the whole way?"

"With an eight o'clock start, we'd have twelve hours. We'd use four or five of them if we took the short way, across the south of Bowen."

"And the long way?"

"If we ghost up Howe Sound with the sea breezes until early afternoon and then reach across and run back down the west side of Gambier as the squamish begins, it'll take six to eight hours. It's beautiful. Have you been through there?"

"No, my first time is tomorrow." She smiled at him, tilted her head and sighed. "You're a dream. Do you know that?"

"I thought you were the dream. My dozen year dream."

"Yes, okay, I've one starry-eyed dreamer. You have millions of my readers who idolise thirty-two versions of you as their strong, gentle, loving dream hunk."

"Thirty-two? You've cloned me? Maybe Cynthia would want..."

Michael Walsh

The waiter arrived with the carafe and poured. "The plates should be only another minute or so."

"Cynthia has all thirty-two clones of you. She's the only one who knows you're my model."

"You told her?"

"Didn't have to. She guessed it soon after she learned I wrote women's fiction, and I had signed one of my early books for her. God, that has to be eight or nine years ago."

Chapter Thirty

The rain had stopped, and the sky had begun clearing as Lorne and Catherine stepped out onto the sidewalk in front of the hotel and walked toward the SkyTrain station. "I need to review that place. Everything about it was superlative. Great setting, smooth, efficient service, the appetiser plates were all delicious."

Lorne squeezed her hand and nodded. "That's my favourite way of sampling restaurants. Get to taste a broad variety without being stuffed."

The sidewalks were quiet, the after-work crowd having gone, and the evening crowd not yet arrived. Catherine squeezed his hand. "Let's walk, I love the fresh air after a storm."

They strolled in silence for a while toward Gastown heading to Beattie to skirt the hill. "Along here somewhere? Nathan?"

"Yeah, I haven't been through here since."

"We can head up Richards."

"No, I'm fine." She gripped his hand more tightly and stroked his arm. "Really, I am."

They continued quietly for another block and a bit. "Does your cycle always affect you like that?"

"Only when I'm sitting across from my dream lover and I start fantasising." She laughed. "Maybe we should take a taxi."

"There's one waiting just ahead..."

"Kidding, Lorne, only kidding. But we could walk faster."

Michael Walsh

It was shortly past 1915 when she led him into her townhouse, and they paused for a long, gentle hug in the foyer. "How about a long hot shower first to wash away the walk and relax us?"

"You're the boss, you know what works. Remember, I'm the neophyte with this stuff."

"The world needs more neophytes like you." She slipped out of her shoes as they continued the hug. He followed her example, then with his toes, he peeled off his socks to add to the ante.

She dropped a hand to his butt and shook his firm cheek. "Come on, shower time." She led him up the stairs and along to her bedroom where she began undressing him, carefully laying his blazer, trousers and shirt over the back of the wing chair.

He again followed her example, and after he had finished, they stood examining each other and smiling. He stepped back to get a better view and sighed. "My dream. My fantasy, so recently impossible. Standing here in front of me. Wanting me. Wanting my baby."

Her three quick, long strides had them in a tangle of limbs and searching hands and lips. "Forget the shower for now," she panted as she began unwrapping. "We can do that after."

She pulled him to the bed, peeled back his foreskin and lowered herself onto him to churn and do shallow knee bends. He lasted less than a minute. When the throbbing had eased, she lay back, her butt on his hips, her back on the bed beside him as he still twitched. She stroked her belly. "That's better. I think I've been laying an egg."

"You think?"

"Yeah, sure seemed it. Feelings were too intense."

"Well, I've surely sent in a huge welcoming party. I thought I'd never stop coming." He reached down, pressed a hand on her mound and began slowly moving it as his other hand tweaked a nipple. "So what do men usually do after a quickie?"

"Nothing."

"Nothing?"

"Well, very little. Nathan would lie there for a while relaxing, then depending on the time of day, either get up or roll over and go to sleep."

"Always?"

"In the beginning, he was better. He tried to last longer — tried to satisfy me — tried other things. He became increasingly frustrated and gradually stopped trying. His one or two-minute specials became the routine. No frills, no add-ons."

"*He* became frustrated? My God, what about you? What did he do about you? Surely not just leave you there?"

"You have no idea how common that is, Lorne." She pressed her hands onto his. "No idea. Many of us are left to paddle the canoe alone."

"Wow." He continued his slow hand motion, sending an occasional finger along to titillate. "Why did you stay?"

"You know... I guess I didn't realise how frustrated I was until I was with you a few days ago. Fuck, I love you." She reached down and cupped his scrotum. "Did we get all the fresh ones?"

"Must have. I think I turned my balls inside-out." He shifted his hips. "That feels so wonderful, your hand there." He slid a finger lightly across her clit again. She moved to it.

Twenty minutes later they still lay there, lightly pleasuring each other. "That should have given all the strong swimmers a chance." She ran a hand over her belly and laughed. "We don't want the slow swimmers, anyway. Shower?"

"That'll be nice," He looked around. "Tissue? Towel?"

"Forgot. Bit of a rush." She giggled.

"Sit up, spin around. I'll carry you. No sense risking messing the bed sheet."

They stood in the shower for a long time, washing, exploring and enjoying bodies, then they teasingly dried each other, and she finished by hanging a towel on the prominent peg he had erected.

He glanced down at it, pulled the towel off and led her to the bed. "I think we can both find more active uses for this."

They did. An hour and a quarter later, as she lay sprawled on top of him, recovering from another orgasm, she said, "Surely this is how it's meant to be, not a quick duo followed by a long, sad solo."

It was dark when he awoke, and it took him a while to realise he wasn't dreaming. He shifted gently in their cuddle to ease a kink, careful not to slip out, not to wake her. *Wonder how long we've slept. Sky's dark... Moon's risen above the windows... Close to midnight? Past?* He felt her stir, shift her hips and press, then sigh a low moan. He swelled inside her, and she moved more vigorously.

"You can wake me this way anytime you wish." She turned her head to kiss him. "I love this dream." She squeezed him more tightly. "Roll over. Let me ride my stallion again."

He rolled to his back. "We've slept a long while, any idea what time it is?"

"You've slept a long while, but you kept waking me."

"I snore? I didn't know.... Sorry."

"Not snoring." She sighed. "Your erections. God, you rise frequently... So wonderfully... Inside... Popping... Oh God..." Deep moans filled the room as she trembled.

As she collapsed on him, he wrapped his arms around her. "My, that was a quickie."

She panted, "Three hours... Intermittent... Building... Oh, my God..." Her entire body trembled again, then she slowly melted into him.

"Sorry to disturb your sleep with my..."

"God, Lorne! You have no idea how silly that sounds to me."

Chapter Thirty-One

After Catherine's breathing had settled, Lorne said, "Makes sense for me to pull out. Let you sleep."

"No way! It's such a heavenly sensation having you stretch me awake like that. Then the throbbing — my God! You sure do your nightly exercises with vigour."

"Guess I'm never awake for them." He laughed. "They come in deep sleep, REM sleep, I read. Three, four, five times a night, sometimes more."

"I'll gladly keep count for you. You've done three already. Stay in my cockpit." She laughed loudly. "I can catch-up on my sleep tomorrow in *Tastevin's* cockpit as we sail." She did a few Kegels.

"Oh, my God! God you're strong." He rocked his hips. "That's quite the grip."

"Been doing Doctor Kegel's exercises for a long while... Five years, maybe six." She squeezed him again. "My yoga teacher told me it makes orgasms easier and more intense. By that time, Nathan had lost interest. Do you like it?" She did another and held it.

"Oh, my God! Yes! That's so exciting. You grabbing me like that."

"Nathan said it made him lose concentration."

"Christ! It jacks mine way up." Lorne kissed her neck and shoulder as he reached his hands down and grabbed her butt cheeks. "We're all made so differently. So amazingly differently. I love your differences — all of them."

He woke with the alarm. She was already awake enjoying his morning stiffness, so he moved to increase her enjoyment.

"Morning," Catherine said as she moved into synch with his gentle thrusts. "This is nine."

"Nine?" He tried to shake off his sleep. "What's nine?"

"Your count." She snickered. "And this in the old British measurements." She ground more vigorously.

"You get any sleep?"

"A bit. Between arisings. You're so much more interesting to exercise with than are my resistance balls and bulb."

"Balls and bulb?"

"Inserted devices for exercising and measuring my progress."

"Fuck! You trained yourself, and he ignored you. Squeeze me."

He rolled onto his back, taking her with him. "Sit up, spin around, I've another twelve-hour load hanging down there in case none of last night's team made the swim."

They were a bit late to the boat, slipping at 0820. She brought espressos up as they passed Spruce Harbour, and they sipped them as they passed Granville Island. It was clear and nearly calm as Lorne pulled out the sails to ghost along in light airs past Kits Point. The sails were beginning to draw more steadily as *Tastevin* moved clear of the land and farther into English Bay.

Lorne pointed the bows across to West Bay to find early North Shore breezes while Catherine prepared a board of fresh fruit, nuts, cheeses, cold cuts and breads for their breakfast.

They sat in the cockpit nibbling and talking. "I love these Dutch breakfasts. I guess it's German and French and the rest. Healthier than North American." She laughed. "Dry cereal... Funny, you never see corn flakes, rice crisps or frosted craps in Europe. Well, except in the tourist hotels which cater to Americans."

"Another crazy thing leftover from Doctor Kellogg."

"Is that the flaky reference you made? God, when was that? Our time measurement has melted into a meaningless lump. You mentioned Kellogg, but a doctor?"

"A sick doctor. A very sick one. Unfortunately, he was also very widely accepted."

"Where? When?"

He looked at her with a crooked smile and shook his head. "It's horridly sick. Twisted. Unbelievable, except it's true."

"Do you need to move it through? Part of your catharsis?"

"Guess so. Yeah." He nodded to her, paused and then shrugged. "Let's finish breakfast first. Let it settle."

It was 1045 when they passed close under the Point Atkinson lighthouse, using the wind drawing around the point and waving to the walkers, joggers and tourists in Lighthouse Park.

Once clearly past, he relaxed from the helm and adjusted the Hydrovane to steer. She looked at him as he rejoined her on the starboard settee, a questioning expression on her face.

"Seems you're ready for a flaky Kellogg story."

"Are you?"

"Yeah. Get your computer, it'll be easier there."

She was back a minute later, her MackBook flashed and ready.

"See my wifi?"

"*Tastevin*, yes."

"Password's Nuits, as in Nuits-Saint-Georges. Uppercase N."

A few seconds later, "I'm in."

"Google doctor kellogg plain facts."

"Got it. Plain Facts for Old and Young. Excerpt: pp. 106-7."

"Read it. Better, read it aloud to refresh my memory. See how it is with me now. Now I'm rid of Connolly."

She started reading:

Masturbation — In younger children, with whom moral considerations will have no particular weight, other devices may be used. Bandaging the parts has been practised with success. Tying the hands is also successful in some

Michael Walsh

cases; but this will not always succeed, for they will often contrive to continue the habit in other ways, as by working the limbs, or lying upon the abdomen. Covering the organs with a cage has been practised with entire success. A remedy which is almost always successful in small boys is circumcision, especially when there is any degree of phimosis. The operation should be performed without administering an anaesthetic, as the brief pain attending the operation will have a salutary effect upon the mind, especially if it be connected with the idea of punishment, as it may well be in some cases. The soreness which continues for several weeks interrupts the practice, and if it had not previously become too firmly fixed, it may be forgotten and not resumed. ...

"Who is this sick person?"

"Doctor Kellogg. The man who brought us Kellogg's Corn Flakes. There's an urban legend they were invented by him to put in the boys' beds to make noise when they moved while masturbating. In reality, they were part of a diet to kill sex drive. Whichever you believe, USAians breakfast on anti-wank flakes." He looked at her and raised his eyebrows. "It gets worse... Do you want to stop?"

She looked up from the screen and offered a wrinkled face. "No, let's press on." She scrolled down the page:

Infibulation — Through the courtesy of Dr Archibald, Superintendent of the Iowa Asylum for Feeble-Minded Children, we have become acquainted with a method of treatment of this disorder which is applicable in refractory cases, and we have employed it with entire satisfaction. It consists in the application of one or more silver sutures in such a away as to prevent erection. The prepuce, or foreskin, is drawn forward over the glans, and the needle to which the wire is attached is passed through from one side to the other. After drawing the wire through, the ends are twisted together, and cut off close. It is now impossible for an erection to occur, and the slight irritation thus produced acts as a most powerful means of overcoming the disposition to resort to the practice.

"This is real? When was this?"

"Published in 1877 in the US Mid-West. You want to stop?"

"This is unbelievable. Horridly cruel punishment for something so natural, so necessary to health."

"Do you want to keep going? The next part is women."

"It can't get worse, can it?"

"Yes." He put a hand on her shoulder.

She looked up and grimaced. "Fuck! Okay."

Treatment of females — In females, the author has found the application of pure carbolic acid to the clitoris an excellent means of allaying...

"Fuck, fuck, fuck. What a sick man. This can't be real."

"Unfortunately, it is."

She continued, her hand to her mouth.

... pure carbolic acid to the clitoris an excellent means of allaying the abnormal excitement, and preventing the recurrence of the practice in those whose will power has become so weakened that the patient is unable to exercise entire self-control.

The worst cases among young women are those in which the disease has advanced so far that erotic thoughts are attended by the same voluptuous sensations which accompany the practice. The author has met many cases of this sort in young women, who acknowledged that the sexual orgasm was thus produced, often several times daily. The application of carbolic acid in the manner described is also useful in these cases in allaying the abnormal excitement, which is a frequent provocation of the practice of this form of mental masturbation.

"Why didn't anyone do anything?"

"They did. They adopted Kellogg's ideas as the way to proceed. Other *medical authorities* soon jumped aboard this insanity. The US quickly became the largest non-religious circumciser on the planet. By the 1950s, over ninety percent of the boys had their penises cut, mutilated, ruined. This disease spread to other countries. Fortunately, many there began questioning."

"The girls? The carbolic acid? My God."

"I've found no more about it. I've always hoped it was squashed early."

"Fucking sick."

"Yeah."

Chapter Thirty-Two

Samir shouted into the phone. "Who the fuck is this?"

"Who? Who you talking about?"

"The fellow strapped to the table, that's who."

"That's Lorne. They said they nabbed him as he came off the escalator a little before midnight. Took him to the room, recovered the tracker."

"This isn't him, you fucking incompetent Quebecois asshole. Can't you idiots do anything right? Decide on which finger."

"Please. Give me a bit. We got the cab driver. Pretends he can't remember them. I'll get Cheng to come and coax him. He'll talk."

◇◇◇

Catherine and Lorne sailed silently for a while as she absorbed the Doctor Kellogg information. After they had tacked to point up Queen Charlotte Channel, she asked, "Is there other stuff on this? There must be... How did you run across it?"

"Connolly made me read through it as part of my sex education. That was early on, I guess to prepare me for what was to come. The medical literature is filled with stuff like this. There's a good summary... It's been years now, but it should still be there." He brushed the back of his hand across her cheek and leaned to kiss her. "You want to carry on? We can stop now."

She looked at him and twisted her lips. "No, let's keep going."

"Okay..." He paused to think. "Google circumcision history USA. That should do it."

Catherine clicked in the search and entered it. "Over two million hits. Seems popular."

He read the screen, then pointed. "That one, the one after the wiki — whale.to."

She clicked the link, and they watched the text load. "That's the one. It's a good summary of the spread of the aberration." They read the page together:

1860: 0.1% of the U.S. male population circumcised — In cases of masturbation we must, I believe, break the habit by inducing such a condition of the parts as will cause too much local suffering to allow of the practice being continued. For this purpose, if the prepuce is long, we may circumcise the male patient with present and probably with future advantage; the operation, too, should not be performed under chloroform, so that the pain experienced may be associated with the habit we wish to eradicate." Athol A. W. Johnson, On An Injurious Habit Occasionally Met with in Infancy and Early Childhood, The Lancet, vol. 1 (7 April 1860): pp. 344-345.

"Fuck! Published in The Lancet, the authority," she said after reading the first entry.

1871: 1% of the U.S. male population circumcised — I refer to masturbation as one of the effects of a long prepuce; not that this vice is entirely absent in those who have undergone circumcision, though I never saw an instance in a Jewish child of very tender years, except as the result of association with children whose covered glans have naturally impelled them to the habit." M. J. Moses, The Value of Circumcision as a Hygienic and Therapeutic Measure, NY Medical Journal, vol. 14 (1871): pp. 368-374.

"You can't make this stuff up can you? Except it appears they did, and people started believing it." She looked at him and furrowed her brow.

He stroked her back. "I've always wondered what their motive was with this. They were legitimizing mutilation and torture."

1887: 10% of the U.S. male population circumcised — Hip trouble is from falling down, an accident that children with tight foreskins are especially liable to owing to the weakening of the muscles produced by the condition of the genitals." Lewis L. Sayer, Circumcision For the Cure of Enuresis, Journal of the American Medical Association, vol. 7 (1887): pp. 631-633.

"This is hilarious. Hip trouble caused by weakened muscles from having a tight foreskin. Who did this one get to write his humour?" She squeezed his thigh. "I'd laugh if it weren't so sad. The AMA Journal. So very sad."

There can be no doubt of [masturbation's] injurious effect, and of the proneness to practice it on the part of children with defective brains. Circumcision should always be practiced. It may be necessary to make the genitals so sore by blistering fluids that pain results from attempts to rub the parts." Angel Money, Treatment of Disease in Children. Philadelphia: P. Blakiston. 1887, p. 421.

"So sore by blistering? These are very sick people." She did a mock finger gag.

"Unfortunately, they were also the medical experts of the time."

1888: 15% of the U.S. male population circumcised — A remedy [for masturbation] which is almost always successful in small boys is circumcision. The operation should be performed by a surgeon without administering an anesthetic, as the pain attending the operation will have a salutary effect upon the mind, especially if it be connected with the idea of punishment." John Harvey Kellogg [the breakfast cereal tycoon], Treatment for Self-Abuse and Its Effects, Plain Facts for Old and Young, Burlington, Iowa: P. Segner & Co. 1888, p. 295.

"So there's Doctor Kellogg."

"Yeah, and it continues."

... It is well authenticated that the foreskin ... is a fruitful cause of the habit of masturbation in children ... I conclude that the foreskin is detrimental to health, and that circumcision is a wise measure of hygiene." Jefferson C. Crossland, The Hygiene of Circumcision, NY Medical Journal, vol. 53 (1891): pp. 484-485.

"Why not chop off the hand? It's an equal party to the party."

"I'm sure some thought of it. Tough to get published, though."

Measures more radical than circumcision would, if public opinion permitted their adoption, be a true kindness to many patients of both sexes." Jonathan Hutchinson, On Circumcision as Preventive of Masturbation, Archives of Surgery, vol. 2 (1891): pp. 267-268.

"More radical? Is this hinting at chopping off the boys' hands? Maybe only their penises. I'd laugh if it weren't so... so..."

"Sick?"

"Yeah. Really sick. But they're the medical authorities, the professionals who know what's best." Lorne checked the horizon.

In all cases in which male children are suffering nerve tension, confirmed derangement of the digestive organs, restlessness, irritability, and other disturbances of the nervous system, even to chorea, convulsions, and paralysis, or where through nerve waste the nutritive facilities of the general system are below par and structural diseases are occurring, circumcision should be considered as among the lines of treatment to be pursued." Charles E. Fisher, Circumcision, in A Hand-Book On the Diseases of Children and Their Homeopathic Treatment. Chicago: Medical Century Co., 1895. p. 875.

"Where the fuck did these idiots get their ideas. They all seem deranged." She shook her head and screwed her face.

In all cases of masturbation circumcision is undoubtedly the physicians' closest friend and ally ... To obtain the best results one must cut away enough skin and mucous membrane to rather put it on the stretch when erections come later. There must be no play in the skin after the wound has thoroughly healed, but it must fit tightly over the penis, for should there be any play the patient will be found to readily resume his practice, not begrudging the time and extra energy required to produce the orgasm. It is true, however, that the longer it takes to have an orgasm, the less frequently it will be attempted, consequently the greater the benefit gained ... The younger the patient operated upon the more pronounced the benefit, though occasionally we find patients who were circumcised before puberty that require a resection of the skin, as it has grown loose

Michael Walsh

and pliant after that epoch." E. J. Spratling, Masturbation in the Adult, Medical Record, vol. 24 (1895): pp. 442-443.

"Great, cut more away. Make the offending thing into a fucking irritating broomstick." Catherine shook her head.

Local indications for circumcision: Hygienic, phimosis, paraphimosis, redundancy (where the prepuce more than covers the glans), adhesions, papillomata, eczema (acute and chronic), oedema, chancre, chancroid, cicatrices, inflammatory thickening, elephantiasis, naevus, epithelioma, gangrene, tuberculosis, preputial calculi, hip-joint disease, hernia. Systemic indications: Onanism [masturbation], seminal emissions, enuresis, dysuria, retention, general nervousness, impotence, convulsions, hystero-epilepsy." Editor, Medical Record, Circumscisus, Medical Record, vol. 49 (1896): p. 430.

"They missed acne and warts. The things which actually concern adolescents." She laughed.

"Also missed the healthy necessity of masturbation, let alone the pleasure it brings. Physical and emotional."

The prepuce is an important factor in the production of phthisis [tuberculosis]. This can be proven by the immunity of the Jewish race from tubercular affections." S. G. A. Brown, A Plea for Circumcision, Medical World, vol. 15 (1897): pp. 124-125.

"Now they bring in tuberculosis. Guess it was a growing concern back then."

Clarence B. was addicted to the secret vise practiced among boys. I performed an orificial operation, consisting of circumcision ... He needed the rightful punishment of cutting pains after his illicit pleasures." N. Bergman, Report of a Few Cases of Circumcision, Journal of Orificial Surgery, vol. 7 (1898): pp. 249-251.

"What a bunch of torturing perverts. What the fuck is Orificial Surgery?"

"Go to a new tab and Google it."

"Wow, look at all the results."

"That one, the first one: *historyofcircumcision.net.*"

Catherine clicked and they read:

The Orificial Surgery Society - A symptom of the late Victorian vogue for surgical solutions to health problems was the Chicago-based Orificial Surgery Society, which was active from the late 1880s until the early 1920s and published a number of textbooks by prominent members (all with MDs), and the Journal of Orificial Surgery from 1892 to 1901. Its particular obsession was the influence of the lower orifices on the nervous system, meaning that it targeted the foreskin (in both males and females) and the rectum as the focal points for disease generation and control. Any tightness or other disorder in these sphincters caused nervous irritation, and the cure was forcible dilation or amputation.

"And these quacks were allowed their perverted practice? Truly unbelievable." She lifted her head and shook it, then did a monitoring sweep of the horizon and instruments, before going back to the computer screen.

The society was particularly insistent on the need for circumcision, in both males and females, and was concerned that, while its health advantages for boys was well understood by the medical profession, there was less appreciation of its value for girls. As one textbook advised:

The condition of the foreskin of boys has received more or less attention, at least since the days of Moses. But the girls have been neglected. ... I do feel an irresistible impulse to cry out against the shameful neglect of the clitoris and its hood, because of the vast amount of sickness and suffering which could be saved the gentler sex, if this important subject received proper attention and appreciation at the hands of the profession. Circumcision for the girl or woman of any age is as necessary as for the boy or man.

"Wonderful. Play God with the women as well. And the people went along with this?"

"Seems there were a lot of gullible assholes and foreskins in the States." Lorne put a hand on her shoulder. "Fortunately, this school of quackery died-out in the early twenties. Click back over to the history page."

Not infrequently marital unhappiness would be better relieved by circumcising the husband than by suing for divorce." A. W. Taylor, Circumcision - Its Moral and Physical Necessities and Advantages, Medical Record, vol. 56 (1899): p. 174.

Michael Walsh

"Now the marriage counsellors jump into the fray."

1900: 25% of the U.S. male population circumcised — Finally, circumcision probably tends to increase the power of sexual control. The only physiological advantages which the prepuce can be supposed to confer is that of maintaining the penis in a condition susceptible to more acute sensation than would otherwise exist. It may increase the pleasure of coition and the impulse to it: but these are advantages which in the present state of society can well be spared. If in their loss, increase in sexual control should result, one should be thankful." Editor, Medical News. (A Plea for Circumcision) Medical News, vol. 77 (1900): pp. 707-708.

"Sure, society needs to be spared from the pleasures of sex." Lorne kissed her cheek and stood to scan the horizon.

Another advantage of circumcision ... is the lessened liability to masturbation. A long foreskin is irritating per se, as it necessitates more manipulation of the parts in bathing ... This leads the child to handle the parts, and as a rule, pleasurable sensations are elicited from the extremely sensitive mucous membrane, with resultant manipulation and masturbation. The exposure of the glans penis following circumcision ... lessens the sensitiveness of the organ ... It therefore lies with the physician, the family adviser in affairs hygienic and medical, to urge its acceptance." Ernest G. Mark, Circumcision, American Practitioner and News, vol. 31 (1901): pp. 121-126.

"Great! Now we get the blind leading the blind. This is horridly sick, isn't it?" She gazed into his eyes with a blank face. "Did it kept growing?"

"Yeah. Lot of repeated themes through here as it built. Scroll down a decade and a half."

Circumcision not only reduces the irritability of the child's penis, but also the so-called passion of which so many married men are so extremely proud, to the detriment of their wives and their married life. Many youthful rapes could be prevented, many separations, and divorces also, and many an unhappy marriage improved if this unnatural passion was cut down by a timely circumcision." L. W. Wuesthoff, Benefits of Circumcision, Medical World, vol. 33 (1915): p. 434.

"What the fuck? Prevent the kids from rampant raping. Prevent the men from pleasing their wives."

"Watch the progress... Scroll down a few pages."

1935: 55% of the U.S. male population circumcised — I suggest that all male children should be circumcised. This is 'against nature', but that is exactly the reason why it should be done. Nature intends that the adolescent male shall copulate as often and as promiscuously as possible, and to that end covers the sensitive glans so that it shall be ever ready to receive stimuli. Civilization, on the contrary, requires chastity, and the glans of the circumcised rapidly assumes a leathery texture less sensitive than skin. Thus the adolescent has his attention drawn to his penis much less often. I am convinced that masturbation is much less common in the circumcised. With these considerations in view it does not seem apt to argue that 'God knows best how to make little boys.'" R. W. Cockshut, Circumcision, British Medical Journal, vol. 2 (1935): 764.

"Good God. Thinking he knows how to make little boys, and God doesn't." She squeezed his thigh then ran her hand down to his bulge. "I love how yours works."

"So do I." He began swelling along her hand. "Scroll down the screen farther. Down to the 1970s."

1971: 90% of the U.S. male population circumcised — There are no valid medical indications for circumcision in the neonatal period." Committee On Fetus and Newborn. Standards and Recommendations for Hospital Care of Newborn Infants, 5th edition. Evanston, IL: American Academy of Pediatrics. 1971. p. 110.

"Fuck, ninety percent mutilated. But the thrust of the argument has turned completely around. When did that happen?"

"During the mid-sixties, when baby boomers began questioning its purpose. They're still trying to stop the barbaric practice. Neonatal snipping in the States is now around sixty percent and the overall percentage of those with genital mutilations is down to slightly below eighty."

She smiled. "At least the trend is going in the right direction."

"Going to be tough to go further... There's now a huge lobby promoting circumcision. The medical industry uses the snipped infant foreskins for stem cell work and research, but worse, the cosmetics industry use these baby penis trimmings as an important ingredient in their anti-aging skin care products."

"Fuck! This can't be." She looked at him and grimaced.

He wrinkled his face and nodded. "Unfortunately, it's true. The hospitals make billions of dollars a year from circumcisions. Remember, medicine's an industry in the States, not a health care. Both the research and the cosmetics industries need a steady supply of raw materials. There's a huge multi-interest lobby."

"I would think the lube manufacturers are also lobbying." She put a hand to her crotch and stared at him as she nodded. "It's just occurred to me; we've used no lube at all, you and I. My God, Nathan and I used so much lube... We both had bad skin reactions to K-Y Jelly. That stuff's so full of harsh chemicals. We had to find something more natural."

Lorne nodded. "Strange, I haven't thought of this, but I don't slide in and out of you, I glide back-and-forth in my own skin. No lube needed." He looked at her as he continued nodding. "I guess mutilated men also need lube for masturbation. What a stupid practice, circumcision."

"Idiotic. I had no idea." She tilted her head. "What about the research showing that circumcision prevents AIDS?"

"Those results have now been shown as false. In fact, most new research shows it's the other way around. Specialised cells in the foreskin produce antibacterial and antiviral proteins. With the foreskin amputated, these are no longer present. But also, the chance of infection increases from cracks and lesions in the dried, unprotected glans, which is meant to be an internal organ."

Chapter Thirty-Three

Catherine shook her head. "So, that's why the corn flakes references the other day?"

"Yeah, Doctor Kellogg was a big part of the beginning of the entire horrid mess."

"God that's heavy shit. Time for lighter stuff for a while."

"Sorry to dump this on you, but it's a part of..."

"Don't be sorry, Lorne. You need to move through it — to get rid of it." She closed her MacBook, set it down and turned to lay her head on his chest and kiss his neck. "You need to do this."

"Yeah, a bit at a time, it's not so bad this way. I wasn't going to go into the whole circumcision thing. Only the stitching-up with silver wire."

"That was in the Kellogg excerpt, wasn't it?"

"Yeah. The first thing Connolly did to me."

"You want to continue?"

"No... Let's stop and enjoy each other, enjoy the sail."

"Horseshoe Bay's the other side of that point, isn't it?"

"And we'll be in the ferry lanes shortly. The inbound from Nanaimo is in our port quarter." Lorne pointed to it, then glanced at the deck clock. "The outbound should be leaving in the next few minutes." He checked the plotter. "We're privileged to both because of the sails, but we'll fall off to starboard to keep clear anyway."

"Dad does that too. Give the big guys an easier time." Catherine pointed to the small sailboats ahead. "Want to bet they're going to force the ferries to alter?"

"Unfair bet. You need to give me ten to one on that one; better twenty to one." He laughed. "I'm always amused it's the smallest boats that most often do it."

"Dad says they're trying to show how macho they are." She laughed. "Small pricks pretending to be big pricks. He says that also about the yahoo drivers with their jacked-up pickup trucks." She reached down his thigh and giggled. "Guess you don't have to pretend."

Lorne moved into her hand, both voluntarily and involuntarily, kissed the top of her head and held her closer to his chest. "Have I told you recently I love you?"

"You haven't stopped showing me since we started this date. Do you realise we're still on our first date?"

"Never want it to end."

"Funny, thinking about it now — Cynthia. She sat us together at the La Luce dinner." She lifted her head to look at him.

"Hunh..." He stared at her with widening eyes and a growing smile. "Yeah, you're right. You think she was playing matchmaker? She's known for a long I had no interest in her."

"It'll come out at lunch on Friday, I'm sure."

"Yeah." He glanced at the chartplotter. "We need to fall off for the ferries. Let me show you how to adjust the wind vane."

Catherine gave him a little squeeze then rose to her feet. He led her to the transom. "We need to fall-off only fifteen degrees or so to parallel the ferry lane. On small changes like this, I prefer to use the vane rather than the helm."

"I've seen vane steering before, but never up close. Dad uses an electric autopilot."

"*Tastevin* has one of those also, but I prefer the vane. It's more organic, in tune with nature." He put his hand on the loop of line. "This is the adjusting line. Watch the vane when I pull it."

He gave the line a pull. "Each length between blocks is about three degrees."

She watched the vane swivel a few degrees. He pulled four more lengths. "The right side of the loop turns us to starboard. Now we ease the sails and fine-tune. Simple."

As the boat slowly swung to starboard, she nodded. "That's so simple. Even I could do that." She giggled, then watched him bark the main sheet around its winch drum and do the same with the genoa sheet.

He looked up at the sails, checked the ship's head and nodded. "Good, we'll let her settle in on this for a couple of minutes, then adjust if needed. Seems pretty good now as she is."

Two minutes later, after taking a turn on the genoa sheet and easing the main outhaul a bit, they returned to the settee. "A minor trim or two should take us to Loins Bay before we need to tack. Six miles — an hour and a half. It's five to noon, we'll catch the beginning of the squamish by the time we get there."

"Squamish? I know the town and the Chief — Dad talked a lot about climbing on the Squamish Chief. How does that help us with sailing?"

"The town is named after the Squamish people who've lived there for millennia. Their legends say they come from the Mother of the Wind. Nearly every afternoon, strong winds fall down the canyon from the mountains. Cold air descends from the glaciers and snowfields of the Tantalus Range, the Garibaldi peaks and the areas around Whistler, and blow out Howe Sound to the Straits. In the winter, the winds can be violent; in the summer, they make for wonderful sailing."

"How strong are they this time of the year?"

"With these conditions..." He looked up at the sky and around the rim of mountains. "We'll see around twenty knots, maybe twenty-five. Farther up the sound, they'll see thirty and more. The wind surfers and kite surfers love that area."

"I should fix lunch for us so we can finish it while we're still on this gentle course. What would you like to eat?"

"You."

Michael Walsh

"I know that. Besides me?"

"There's lots of fresh fruit. How about a big fruit salad and yoghurt? I'm sure Molly's going to try to stuff us tonight."

"Sounds great. To drink?"

"You like rooibos?"

"Love it."

"Tin box in the cupboard above the... Wait, you take the watch. I'll go put lunch together."

Catherine smiled, then started crying, still smiling. She collapsed onto him, kissing anything of him her lips could reach. "God! You are... You're a god... My god. Nathan would never let me do anything unless it had to do with cleaning, cooking or lying there as his fuck hole."

"But you appeared happy together."

"On the outside, yes. I'm a great actress. But inside... Besides you, Nathan's the only one I've been intimate with, and I accepted him and his behaviour as reality." She shuddered and wiped her tears. "I've lived vicariously through my novels, created a fantasy perfection and tried to live it with no idea reality could be this sublime."

"We're beyond the fantasy now. Both of us." He leaned and kissed her. "Take the watch; I'll go below and fix lunch."

Chapter Thirty-Four

"You trust me with a two million dollar boat. Nathan wouldn't trust me with his old beat-up motor scooter."

"That's so sad. All that time I thought you were happy. You were always my happy untouchable dream girl. It made me happy simply to see you. To fantasise about you."

"If only I'd known... I..."

Lorne held Catherine tighter. "That's gone. We're here. We're happy."

"Ecstatic."

He did a scan of the horizon, checked the chartplotter and then merged his mouth with hers as they writhed together on the settee.

A few minutes later as they paused their kiss, Catherine asked, "Could we?"

"Here?"

"Yeah. Now."

"I can keep watch while you sit on me."

She was undressing as he finished speaking, and he was soon following her example. "Too many clothes for the heat, anyway. I often sail in the nude on nice days. Good all-over tan."

Lorne sat on the settee. Catherine stepped up onto it, straddling his thighs to lower herself onto him. She paused as his tongue found her folds. "You don't miss a trick, do you? You'll not keep a proper lookout with your face buried in me like that."

Michael Walsh

He withdrew his mouth to speak. "An amuse-bouche. Always a nice entry to things that follow; gets the appetite going."

She continued settling to impale herself on him, and they sat there like that for a long while enjoying, melding.

He made another sweep of the horizon, checked the sails and the plotter, then he leaned back against the cushions. "I'll play sailboat here, you play whatever suits your fancy." He chuckled as he looked down. "You have such a fancy fancy. I love the short red hairdo."

"You like the hair?"

"I love the way you trim. It frames your lips so beautifully."

"Nathan always wanted me to shave. Everything. It looked like the bald pee bum you played with on Cypress. I haven't shaved or waxed my lips since he was killed." She let out a deep sigh. "You know, that's the first time I've managed to get the whole sentence out — his being killed."

"That's good. We both have things to put behind us." He turned his face up to receive her kiss, then looked back down and ran his fingers through her patch. "This is how I always visualised you. Redhead through and through."

"Fuck! You didn't?" She squeezed him in a Kegel and held it.

"Did too. Oh, my! That's so hot."

She began shifting her hips, gently churning. He swept the horizon again and checked the plotter screen. Once he was satisfied with their safety, he paid attention to her breasts, lightly tracing their shapes with his fingers as his thumbs grazed occasionally across her nipples.

"Oh, my God. That is so, so heavenly like that. They're always tender this time of the month." She sighed again. "Nathan used to damned near rip them off. Fuck!" She gave him three slow, tight Kegels.

"Fuck! Oh God!" He thrust a bit deeper, then slowly withdrew his advance to savour the last long squeeze. "Oh, my fuck!"

He refocused on her breasts, tweaking the nipples lightly as she began her orgasmic convulsions. He held her tightly as she slumped onto him, moaning a soprano foghorn.

Lorne checked the port quarter to see the inbound ferry where he expected it, parallel about a cable and a half off. "Ferry'll be overtaking us in a couple of minutes."

Catherine glanced out across the quarter. "Close." She panted, then laid her head back on his shoulder, still breathing deeply. "Wave for me... I'm busy... Melting."

He monitored the ferry visually and on the plotter screen, and as it passed well clear of their beam, he waved back at the passengers lining the rails. "Nice day, lots of people out on deck enjoying the scenery."

She sat up, still lightly panting, and joined in the waving, knowing that at over two hundred metres, nobody would see detail. "I've never dreamed of sailing this way."

"I have. Often. With you."

She stared at him with her eyes stretched open to their limits. "Fuck!" She shook her head and collapsed back on him. "You didn't?"

"Did too."

"Fuck!"

"We are." He gave a small thrust for emphasis.

Catherine did a fluttering Kegel. "Yeah. Guess I forgot. It's been well over my accustomed minute or two." She sighed.

"Sad. Such a magnificent creature deprived for so long." He watched as the ferry passed clear ahead, then scanned the horizon and checked the plotter. "The AIS symbol for the outbound ferry shows it's left its berth. We should see it around the point in a few minutes."

They continued sailing in this relaxed manner past Horseshoe Bay and up between Bowyer Island and the mainland coast. From time to time she decided she wanted another orgasm, but mostly they remained passively connected, cuddling, pleasuring and talking. As they passed Bowyer, the wind changed, and they needed vane and sail adjustments. He chuckled as he pointed up to the beginning luff on the main. "Haven't done much with lunch either, have we?"

"Been busy catching up on a lost decade. My God, I love you." She gave him a big fluttering Kegel. "I'll do lunch, you do the sails."

Michael Walsh

Lorne had settled *Tastevin* on a starboard reach across the sound in the beginnings of the squamish when Catherine brought up two spoons and a huge bowl of fruit salad with yoghurt in the centre. "The tea's ready — in the thermos. I'll bring it up when we've finished this."

"Looks great. Great big too." He smiled. "You must be hungry."

"Been getting lots of exercise." She sighed. "Such wonderful exercise. We'll have to go shopping, we're now out of fruit."

After enjoying several spoonfuls, Lorne got up to tweak the vane and adjust the sheets to trim the sails as they moved farther into the Sound and the wind built. "Moving up toward nine knots. Less than an hour — fifty minutes we'll be on a broad reach across the top of Gambier." He sat and took another spoonful. "Delicious fruit salad."

"Great ingredients to work with."

"But it's how you put them together."

"Yeah. I guess."

"Look at us. We've been together in a friendship for over a dozen years. More than that if you think of our six years as kids. A dozen and a half years. Great individual ingredients. We simply hadn't been placed together properly until a few days ago."

She giggled. "Mum's elusive special way."

Chapter Thirty-Five

Catherine's iPhone chimed as they sipped their tea. She pulled it out from her computer sheath, thumbed it on and saw the flashing icon. "New email on WebMail. That must be Barbara." She opened the browser, tapped to the site and logged in.

Sorry, didn't think... If you're doing the walk-on ferry, we can pick you up at the terminal. Save a taxi.

She replied: *Sailing over, anchoring in Plumper Cove on Keats.*

Ten minutes later, another chime. *We have guest moorage here in the marina. How big are you?*

She replied: *20 metres.*

Three minutes later: *Big... Give me a few minutes.*

Twenty minutes later: *We'll send our tender over for you in the anchorage at 2010. I'm sure you're hard to miss, what's the boat's name?*

Catherine saw Lorne's nod and sent a confirming email. *Burgundy hull, the name Tastevin is on the bows and stern.*

Lorne regained his seat from his tweaks after falling off and adjusting the sails and the vane to start running down the west side of Gambier. "They seem to be professional and efficient."

"Fancy outer garments. We've seen their dirty underwear."

The wind served them well, and mid-afternoon they sailed onto the anchor in the marine park. After they had settled in and Lorne had completed the logbook, they sat cuddling, pleasuring and talking. She reached down and hefted his sack. "The next team ready yet?"

"That feels so good when you hold me like that." He nodded at the clock on the panel. "Sixteen ten. Been a little over eight hours. Maybe wait another three or so to keep closer to the twelve hours. Add another ten or fifteen million to the team."

"My eternal scheduler. You have no idea how endearing you are. How much I love you." She gave his balls a gentle massage. "Keep working, guys." She looked up into his eyes and giggled. "The boss says you're not finished yet."

They continued their light conversation as they lay on the settee tenderly touching and caressing each other. After half an hour or so, Catherine asked, "So he stitched you up? With wire?"

"Yeah."

"I've been trying to sort out the mechanics of it. I can visualise sewing up a woman's vulval lips — some Muslims still do that. Fuck! They even cut away the clitoris. What a horrible ritual. So sick. But a penis? How?"

"Connolly pushed it back inside, squeezing the foreskin and..."

"Back inside?"

He sat up and shifted. "Like this." He worked his penis into his pubes, and she stared at the gathered empty skin. "He stitched through here, at the base of the skin, trapped me inside."

"Fuck! Hurt? I'm sure it must have."

"Not as much as when most of the stitches ripped out with the first of my nightly erections."

"Fuck!"

"Do you want to stop here?"

"Do you?"

"I can keep going a bit if you can." He brought her hand down. "Here, hold this." She took the gathered empty skin from him. "Feel the pressure?"

She nodded. "A lot of it. It certainly wants to escape."

"Imagine it with the force of an unstoppable nocturnal erection behind it."

"Fuck!"

"Let your hand loose. Watch."

"Fast. I can't imagine that with an erection's force behind it."

"You can still see the scars from the ripped stitches."

She bent down to examine and then kiss them. "So, that's the stitching thing Doctor Kellogg was writing about?"

"Yeah. Connolly had talked about how circumcision hadn't worked on him. He had done himself, but he still masturbated."

"Done himself?"

"Yeah. His early sex education lessons included showing me pictures of him cutting his away."

"Fuck!"

"Stop for now?"

"Yeah."

They lay back in the cushions and cuddled. Silently.

They were awakened by loud shouting coming from a boat anchoring in the small bay. Catherine sighed as she turned to kiss his neck. "So common, isn't it? It's almost always the man... I shouldn't laugh. It's actually sad."

"Yeah, it is. I've always wondered what the woman was feeling. I still do."

She squeezed him tighter. "Embarrassed, diminished, belittled, emptied. That's some of it."

"Fuck."

"Yeah, at least for me, when Nathan... God, I love you."

He pointed to the clock. Eighteen forty five. "Let's send in the next team a bit early."

Michael Walsh

She grabbed his hand. "Yeah, down in the cabin. Less disruption." They rose from the settee and headed below.

As she was kneeling and washing him in the shower an hour and a bit later, she said, "I'm amazed by how well this works, after all it's been through."

"I'm delighted you enjoy it. It's funny now, thinking of how revolted I was at the thought of your seeing it. Had to have been hypnosis."

"Sure makes sense to me." She rinsed it off, licked it and took the heads into her mouth, then backed off. "Quite a mouthful, even soft." She licked it again. "Once we can spare seeds to spill on fallow ground..." She giggled. "Torah training. Once we're past my fertile period, I'll be all over this." She took it into her mouth again and looked up into his eyes as she slowly nodded.

"Oh, my fuck. Oh God!" He cradled the sides of her head as he trembled. Then he backed her slowly off. "We need to finish here, dry and dress. Molly's tender is due shortly."

Chapter Thirty-Six

The tender was approaching their stern as Lorne and Catherine stepped into the cockpit. After locking up, he led her down to the transom step as the tender came up to it. He handed her aboard to the crewman and followed her in, setting the alarms with his iPhone as they motored away.

"Good to see you again. I didn't get your names the other night."

Both Lorne and Catherine were surprised. They hadn't looked closely at the man who had helped them aboard, but they now recognised him as the restaurant manager.

"Kate and Lorne," he said. "She's the Kate part."

"Obviously. And a beautiful example of one. I'm George." He laughed. "Pity it was Chef's night off when you were here before. Two bus loads ahead of you, late hour and a tired staff."

As George continued, Lorne smiled, nodded and thought. *Smooth, quick-thinking, obvious marketing training.* He refocused to hear the end of the spiel.

"... give you a better idea of what we offer here."

"We're looking forward to it," Catherine said.

They rode silently for several minutes, then Catherine asked, "Your bus tours, do you also do lunch?"

"We've been doing two since we opened, but we're moving to three per day, both at lunch and at dinner, the beginning of July. We've prepared a package for you. All the information is in it. Contacts for the tour operators, special deals for the motor campers."

"Sounds like a big operation."

"Based back east... But enough about us. That's quite the boat. Yours or his?"

"Ours," Lorne said. "We love sailing and exploring."

"Never done any sailing. Too many other things." They continued a light conversation as the tender operator drove them into the harbour and up to the restaurant's courtesy float.

As they alit, George said, "We have free dinghy moorage while dining. We're now starting our promotion to the yacht clubs and marinas." He led the way up the ramp and along toward Molly's Beach. Molly's Reach was nearly abandoned as they passed.

Inside, he guided them through the waiting crowd and into the packed restaurant. "We seat two eighty down here in three rooms," he said as he led them through to a cordoned staircase which wound up in a corner of the second dining room. "Another seventy to eighty in four private dining rooms upstairs, all with harbour views. There's an access elevator over there."

"All the same size?" Catherine asked as they climbed the carved driftwood stairs.

"No, there's an eight, a sixteen and two twenty-fours. The two big ones can be combined to seat about sixty. We're licensed for four hundred seats, including the bar in the reception lounge." He quietly opened a door and allowed them a peek. "Dinner meeting in progress — for fifty." Lorne and Catherine acknowledged nods from several familiar tourist industry faces.

George led them along the hallway. "We'll put you in here; it's near full downstairs," he said as he opened the door.

There was one large four-top set diagonally at the glass wall, overlooking the marina. Two chairs were set across the table corner, facing the window. Lorne examined the setup and mused. *Not only smooth. Observant also. How did they connect us?*

George continued, "We can set up a long table for eight in here."

Catherine looked through the glass wall. "Great view."

"With a day's notice, we can move boats around down there, fit you in." George pointed to the marina. "Next time."

He motioned to the table and held the chair for Catherine, and after they had been seated, he said, "We'll start you with some Champagne. I'll send in the sommelier. Enjoy your evening."

After George had left, Lorne looked at Catherine, raised his eyebrows and asked, "How did they know?"

"Thinking the same thing myself." She took his offered hand and put it to her lips. "George is a gentle soul for such an intimidating appearance. The missing pinkies, the disc in his ear, the tattoos up his neck."

"He's certainly smoother than his appearance. Well, except for his shaved and polished head. I keep trying to place him. Trying to think of where I've seen him."

The sommelier came in with a bottle of Taittinger, opened it and poured a taste into Catherine's flute. She picked it up, examined the mousse, nosed the glass and took a sip, then nodded. "This is another of my favourites."

A waitress came in with two plates and set them on the table in front of them. "Here's a sampling of Chef's amuse-bouches."

After the sommelier and waitress had left the room, Catherine lifted her glass in a toast. "Full marks so far for service and presentation. Here's to us."

Lorne looked into Catherine's eyes, then down at her belly. "To all three of us."

"Fuck! Oh, my God. You do that to me so often. Flip my whole insides. Fuck, I love you." He reached over and wiped one of the tears which had rolled onto her lip.

She raised her glass again. "All three." They touched glasses, locked eyes, touched lips, then sipped.

Catherine set her glass on the table and dabbed her eyes and cheeks with her napkin. "I'm so glad I don't wear makeup; I'd be a streaky mess."

"I've always wondered what that is all about — makeup."

Michael Walsh

"Money."

"Yes, but beyond that?"

"Marketing to women's emotions, fears, insecurities, dreams."

Lorne squeezed her hand. "You're absolutely gorgeous. I'm delighted you don't mess yourself up with that stuff."

"Dad's attitude. He would frequently remind me I'm far too pretty ever to spoil with makeup."

He squeezed her hand again and nodded at the plates in front of them. "Amuse-bouches. Won't be as exciting as my earlier one today, but..."

"Fuck! You've done it again. Jolt straight to the clit. Tongue at twenty lengths. Fuck."

Lorne pressed his hand on her thigh. "Want to keep you happy. I'm working on more than a decade and a half of fantasies, of theories, of study, of..."

"Oh, my fuck!" She shook her head. "I'm going to slide off this chair. I'm sure the back of my skirt has a big wet patch."

He picked up one of her amuse-bouches and moved it toward her mouth. "Choo-choo train coming, open up."

Tears streamed down her cheeks as she opened her mouth. She savoured the morsel as she wiped her face again, then swallowed. "Dad used to do that."

"Mine too." Lorne sat staring blankly. Silent.

Catherine squeezed his hand, then took his head as he laid it on her shoulder. She gently stroked the back of it.

"We should eat," he said after a long silent spell.

"Yeah. Looks good."

Shortly after they had finished the last of their amuse-bouches, the busser came in to clear their plates, followed closely by the waitress. She handed them the menus and from notes, recited a litany of special entrées and main courses Chef would love to prepare: *Dungeness crab ravioli with truffle beurre blanc, seared Texada scallops with lemongrass, torchon of Lasquiti foie gras with Sechelt huckleberry purée, line-caught Howe Sound red snapper, grilled Pemberton free-range venison chop...* These were the ones that stuck in Lorne's mind.

She finished her recitation and said, "I'll give you a few minutes," then turned to leave, stopping at the door to look back. "Can I send the sommelier in with more Champagne?"

"Thank you, no. We need to go lightly," Lorne said. "We're pregnant."

Catherine put her napkin to her mouth and froze while the waitress left. "We are?" She turned to look at him as she wiped her eyes. "Are we?"

He stood, she followed, and they merged in a deep kiss and an enveloping hug. As they unlocked the kiss, she asked, "You think so?"

"Too many feelings not to be. Both you and me."

"Yeah."

"I've never before had feelings like these. Maybe it's only the love. But I've loved you forever, Catherine. This is... I don't know..." He laughed. "I've never been pregnant before."

Chapter Thirty-Seven

Lorne and Catherine finished their hug, he held her chair for her, and they sat again at the table to read the menus. He paused partway through scanning the same menu he had read on three previous occasions. "The specials — they all sound wonderful." He leaned to kiss her ear and whisper, "Don't look around. The timing of service. We're on camera." He nibbled her earlobe. "Maybe sound. Also, likely a camera at the reception desk the other day."

She nodded and stroked his cheek. "Yeah, I agree. We should decide what to order."

"Want to give them another chance with the Wellington?"

"You?"

"There's a much better chance to get it rare tonight, though the venison chop sounds good."

"Let's be fair. We should give them the opportunity to do the Wellington again."

"What about the entrées? Same ones?"

"Canned escargots are no real challenge. Let's see what Chef can do searing and presenting jumbo scallops. They're a wonderful ingredient, but easy to mess up."

"What about the crab? Isn't that the plate which was so popular with all the judges when Feenie beat Morimoto?"

"Yeah, old history. I've watched that episode so many times. A real classic. When was that? Our final undergrad year, so early 2005.

That's what hooked me into reviewing dining."

"Crazy, isn't it? Feenie's the first of only two Canadian Iron Chefs. One of the few from anywhere ever to beat Morimoto, and then a few years later his Lumière fails. He was at the top with everything. Celebrity dinners, cookbooks, TV cooking series. Then the partnership coup and Lumière, poof."

"Let's have the chef show us the crab. I've had many others attempt their versions of it. So few get it right."

"Okay... Scallops and crab to share, then the Wellington."

They closed their menus and within half a minute, they heard the click of the door opening.

Catherine leaned to kiss Lorne's cheek and nibble his earlobe. "Yeah, way too obvious," she whispered.

"Ready to order?" the waitress asked as she approached.

Lorne ordered for them, mentioning they wished to share the entrées.

"That's automatically shared. The Wellington is prepared for two."

"I'm not talking about the main. We want to share the entrées, the entries to the meal, the appetisers."

"Sorry, Sir." The waitress shook her head and laughed. "We have so many American tourists here. Guess I got waylaid." With an impish grin, she continued, "Ignorant, aren't they?" She quietly mouthed as she wrote, "Share entrées."

She left and was soon replaced by the sommelier who stood at the table checking his notes. "A big Viognier would show both seafood plates to advantage. The 2012 Liquidity is one of the best matches for the crab. It's magical with the scallops."

Catherine nodded. "That sounds wonderful. I love their wines. Their Viognier has moved steadily toward the northern Rhône style."

"It always reminds me of Condrieu now," the sommelier agreed, then left to get the wine.

A waiter brought in a basket with a selection of bread rolls and an iced dish with curls of butter and placed them on the table. After he had left, Lorne leaned to kiss Catherine and whispered, "Notice? The foil-wrapped butter pats didn't make it up the stairs."

She snickered as she selected a dark multi-grain roll and broke it. "Very fresh. Seems house baked."

The sommelier came in with the wine, opened it and poured.

"So pleased to see everybody finally getting rid of corks," Catherine said, as she nosed her glass and nodded.

"Not everyone." Lorne chuckled. "Many French still insist on spoiling their wines, particularly the high-priced ones."

As the sommelier began pouring her glass, she put up a hand. "Only a bit for me." She smiled, looked down and patted her belly. "Early pregnancy."

He smiled back and stopped, then began pouring Lorne's glass. "Same amount for me." He smiled up at the sommelier. "Early fatherhood."

As the sommelier left, the waitress returned. "Chef said there was a run on the beef Wellington this evening, he's out of beef tenderloin. He suggests he replace it with venison tenderloin. He's started on it already."

"I like his initiative. Quick thinking, adaptable." Catherine smiled up at her. "Sounds wonderful. We were deliberating between the beef Wellington and the venison chop anyway. Great compromise."

After the waitress had left, they sat staring at each other and lightly touching as they talked about the pregnancy. "My breasts always get tender when I ovulate. Yesterday, today." She put a hand to her right breast and lightly pressed, then a bit harder. "Still a bit, but not so much now." She lowered her hand to her belly and rubbed. "The egg is here." She nodded and smiled at him. "Yeah, it's here."

They kissed again. He put his hand on hers, and together they stroked her belly. "Early, though, you said you're in tune with the moon. It's not full for a little while yet." He pointed out the window at the glow from the sunset. "It should rise over there, above the islands in a few minutes."

She followed his point with her eyes. "They say deep emotional upheaval can change the timing. Sounds like me the last few days. Such intense emotions. Fuck! So intense." She took his extended hand and put it to her breast and pressed it. "God, I love you."

The click of the door behind them interrupted their kiss. The waitress and an assistant came in with four plates. "Sorry to disturb your rapture." They set two plates in front of each of them. "Chef says bon appétit. Anything I can bring you?"

Catherine looked up at her. "Not that I can think of, thank you. This looks superb. Beautiful presentations."

She took out her iPhone and shot photos of the plates from a variety of angles, with and without flash. "Always good to have food porn images on the blogs."

They each began with the crab ravioli. "He got the mayonnaise right — Japanese tang — delicious."

"Great texture on the pasta. Delicate."

"The beurre blanc with the black truffle. Superb balance."

"He's nailed this one. How's the scallop dish?"

"Just heading there. Superb plating. Love the little plaited basket with the sauce. Looks to be woven lemongrass."

She cut a scallop in two and examined it. "Seems perfectly done, fast seared ends, slightly warmed centres. Exactly as you did them at Mum and Dad's."

Spearing a half, she dipped it in the sauce and popped it into her mouth. "Great sauce, Wow! It balances the sweetness of the scallop superbly." She took a sip of her Viognier. "Sublime combination."

As they enjoyed their entrées, they spotted the full moon peek its rim over the hills of Bowen Island. They put their cutlery down in unison and moved their hands to her belly. "We must be... So many messages. So ethereal."

They gazed into each other's eyes with tears streaming down their cheeks as they rose, faces wide with smiles. After another long hug and kiss, they sat, wiped their faces and continued with the plates as they watched the moon emerge above the horizon. "We must be."

Chapter Thirty-Eight

Shortly after Lorne and Catherine finished their entrées, a busboy came in and cleared their places. He was followed by the waitress who asked for their comments to pass on to the kitchen. "Sommelier told me you were going light on the wines. Can I bring you some water, San Pellegrino, Evian, Clearbrook?"

"Clearbrook would be great," Catherine said. "They won it again this year. Best-Tasting Water in the World."

"Amazing isn't it? The biggest water tasting competition on the planet, and our little BC town keeps on winning."

She returned in a minute with the water. "Chef says the Wellington should be another ten or twelve minutes. Can I bring you anything?"

"The moon's enough to keep us happy."

Less than a quarter hour later, as the trolley with the Wellington was rolled up to the table, Lorne's phone vibrated. He automatically took it out and read the message. *Pressure stern step.* He thought a moment. *Probably another sea lion on the...*

His thought was interrupted by the carver asking, "Is this the degree of rare you prefer?" as he pointed the knife tip to the cut.

"That looks perfect," Catherine replied.

As the carver continued, the sommelier arrived and presented a bottle to Catherine. "We thought the '11 Howling Bluff Pinot Noir would show the venison to best advantage. Chef agreed and has cooked toward it."

As Catherine was tasting the sample, Lorne's phone vibrated again. *Could be the sea lion leaving, or possibly the mate arriving.* He ignored it and watched her in awe. *My dream... She's even more beautiful in the moonlight.* His thoughts were interrupted by the sommelier's voice, "Short pour again, Sir?"

He nodded. "Please."

"You had that face again, Lorne." She reached over and brushed his cheek.

"I was thinking how beautiful you are with the full moon."

"Designed that way. Nature timing attraction with fertility."

"Sure works."

"Yeah."

They watched as the carver plated and garnished and then as two waiters laid their plates in front of them. The carver said, "Bon appétit," and wheeled the trolley out, led by the waiters.

"This looks splendid. Classic plating. Hard to fault." She shot a series of photos, then stood and shot another series. "Some of those should work. I'm salivating."

She laid a hand on his shoulder as she moved back to her chair. He caught it, pushed his chair back and swung her onto his lap to kiss her. "We'll not get to taste the venison while it's still hot if we continue like this." She sighed. "Tough choice."

"I'm sure you and I will stay hot much longer than the venison. Maybe we should do that first." He chuckled and kissed her again.

Lorne and Catherine each began slowly dissecting a slice. "This mushroom, shallot, garlic purée is divine, it's spot on with the touch of thyme." She sliced a small piece of venison to savour with it. "Moist, succulent, nice char from the hot searing. The meat is perfection."

"Must have gone into nitrogen for a while after searing. This was prepared and ready too quickly for normal cooling. The pâte feuilletée is perfect, not the soggy pastry we often see from wrapping warm meat. Nice technique. Delicious."

Michael Walsh

Once they'd analysed the plate, they began eating as diners, rather than as scientists. They nodded, uttering unintelligible sounds of enjoyment as they did, pausing from time to time to speak a few coherent complimentary words.

"Superb, full marks," Catherine said as she dabbed her mouth with her napkin after her last bite.

"Delicious. Beautifully prepared and presented." He laid his utensils on his empty plate. "So how do you rate this place?"

"Even if dessert totally flops, I'd still have to give it five stars. We all know things can go strange sometimes."

They were leaning the sides of their heads together and watching the moon as the two busboys came in to clear and clean the table. The waitress entered as the busboys were leaving. "From those emptied plates, it appears you enjoyed the venison."

"Truly superb! The presentation, the flavours, the flair. All of it." Catherine looked at the waitress. "Tell the chef it's one of the best we've ever had."

"I will." She laid dessert menus in front of them. "Chef would like to do a dessert sampler platter for you, so you won't have to decide." She smiled.

Catherine saw Lorne's nod, then looked up at the waitress. "That would be wonderful."

"I'll send in the sommelier," the waitress said as she left.

They leaned their heads together again to look at the moon. "An hour or so short of an eclipse."

"Yeah, guess it is. Dad's really into that stuff. He explained a lot of it to me. We used to lie on a blanket on the back lawn, and he'd explain the sky. The tides will be relatively large now with the full moon and the solstice so close together, won't they?"

"I studied the sky a lot in the mountains when I..." Lorne felt his phone vibrate again.

"When you..?"

"Phone's doing a lot of vibrating." He took it out, thumbed it on and thumbed in, then held it above his lap, tilting it toward Catherine so she could follow the slowly evolving sequence:

Pressure stern step
Pressure area 7
Pressure area 5
Pressure area 3
Pressure area 1
Cable locker hatch open
Radio transmit detect
Pressure area 2
Cable locker hatch shut
Pressure area 1
Pressure area 3
Pressure area 5
Pressure area 7
Pressure stern step

He whispered, "Seems good now."

"What is it?" she whispered back.

He turned to look at her. "I love that you don't wear earrings. Such beautiful earlobes to nibble." She leaned her ear to him, and he whispered between nips and licks, "Been boarded. A transmitter, likely a GPS tracker's been planted. Boarder's gone." He ran his tongue around the outside of her ear, then inside to explore. "I love exploring all your intricate folds. Everywhere. Upstairs and down."

"Oh, God! So hot," she sighed. "We okay?"

"Yeah."

Chapter Thirty-Nine

The sommelier arrived with two bottles and four glasses. "We thought you'd find it interesting to play the desserts against a totally botrytis affected Gewürztraminer and a Riesling Ice Wine." He showed them the labels and poured.

"The chef has challenged himself with this. Tough to match the intensity of these wines." Lorne looked at the sommelier. "We haven't seen the packages, the literature yet. Who's the chef?"

"He prefers to remain in the background..." The sommelier paused and glanced around. "This is private, but they rotate and prefer to kept their identities quiet."

"You know me, Geoff. You can trust it won't go beyond here."

"My job. I'd love to, but..."

"Okay. No problem. I've been following your career progress, pleased you've continued so well. Congratulations on the SWE."

"Thanks. Your courses and mentoring made it so simple for me to..." He looked down and clicked the buzzing light button on his belt pack. "Being called." Geoff left, and Lorne and Catherine sat gazing at the moon and nosing their wines.

Lorne held the glass of Gewürztraminer to his nose again. "Seems strange to me. So much more complexity, greater depth of aroma and flavour, so much more excitement in the botrytis late harvest wines than in the Ice Wines. Huge complexity versus simple balanced sweet."

"Marketing. There's so much more Ice Wine than TBA. Ice Wine has to be pushed, so the consumers have to pay the marketing costs. Simple market economics. There's nowhere near enough TBA produced for marketing expenses to make sense, so the prices for their magnificence languish in comparison. Stupid, isn't it?"

"Yeah."

They nosed again between the two. "Complexity, multi-layered subtleness or monotone expensiveness. I guess the generic Ice Wines attract the insecure who relate price with quality."

"The generic, yes. But there are a few great ones which deserve their strong prices. The rest of them seem to ride on their coat tails. Even the counterfeit Chinese chem lab ones are as good as the following herd, sometimes better."

"I wonder..." She was interrupted by the click of the door opening behind them.

"You wonder?"

"Wonder at many things marketing related, most marketing — bafflegab overriding reality. Manipulating emotions and doubt and insecurity. Replacing them with perceived gratification. Justifying the gratifications and polishing the egos of the deceived. It's a great money mill. Keep turning the crank and grinding out the gold, leaving the chaff thinking they're happy."

The waitress stood listening, and when Catherine had finished speaking, she said, "I agree fully, it's so obvious..." She stopped herself. "Sorry, not my place... Your dessert sampler." She placed the platter on the table between them.

"What a splendid assortment." Catherine turned and smiled up at the waitress. "Any special instructions?"

"You both know what it's about. I love your energy, the both of you. Chef hopes you enjoy these samplings."

Lorne and Catherine explored the assortment, enjoying the wide range of sensations, from harmonious to complementary tension of flavours with each wine. All the while, they looked out over the marina at the moon, now much higher and around toward the south.

"Look at the moonlight playing with the wake down there... Not moonlight, but a trail of phosphorescence behind the boat."

"I've always loved watching that at night, bioluminescence Dad called it." As the boat entered the small harbour and moored at the float, Catherine asked, "Isn't that Molly's tender?"

"Yeah." He took out his iPhone, held it in his lap, thumbed on and in and selected his alarm app. "All green now."

Catherine glanced down at his phone and shook her head as she nudged him and nodded out the window. He followed her prompt and looked out at the moon with her as she caressed his cheek and purred, "I'm as full as the moon. This has been a splendid evening. Memorable."

They leaned to kiss, then sat with hands on each other's thighs, caressing. The door clicked behind them, and they heard the waitress. "It appears the platter finished you. It was huge, wasn't it? Can I get you Porto, Cognac, liqueurs, coffee?"

Catherine smiled at Lorne and silently mouthed *coffee?* He nodded, and she looked up at the waitress. "Two espressos."

She returned in three minutes with the coffees, followed closely by George. "Sorry, I had no time to pop in earlier. It's been a busy evening." He placed a folder on the table next to Catherine. "I'm told you've been enjoying Chef's cooking."

"Absolutely splendid evening. The ambience, the service, the presentation, the food... All superb."

"We've prepared a dossier here for you." He opened the folder. "You'll find an overview and the philosophy of Molly's Beach and there are interior and exterior photos you can use. Here's the menu, and tucked inside are pages of detailed descriptions of many of the items, including tasting notes. There are also studio photos of many of the more popular menu selections. Feel free to use any or all of these."

"Everything about this evening has been professional, smooth, polished and superbly delicious." She nodded out the window. "Even the full moon." She laughed. "You've done a splendid job here."

"Thank you. We look forward to seeing your reviews. Anything else we can offer you this evening?"

"I'd love to meet the chef. Congratulate him on his cuisine."

"Unfortunately, he left a short while ago. Long day for him."

"Another time then."

"Relax here for a bit, I've a busy evening. I'll send someone up shortly to take you to the tender. Thank you for coming."

Lorne and Catherine stood to shake George's hand and thank him again.

Thirty-five minutes later, as they approached *Tastevin's* stern, Lorne opened his alarm app and checked the display. *All green.* He entered the code and smiled as the lights all changed to blue. The operator steadied the tender as Lorne stepped out and gave Catherine a hand across to *Tastevin's* stern platform. They paused there to bid the operator good night.

Lorne thumbed the pads, relieved to see the lights turn green as he led Catherine through the cockpit to the companionway. "That's quite the sophisticated alarm system. What were the messages you showed me?"

"I've weight sensors around the deck that are set for twenty kilos so they don't announce the birds. Number one at the bow, number six the port quarter and seven the starboard. The stern step, cockpit and all the hatches are also in the system."

"So what happened? What did it report?"

"George boarded at the stern, walked along the starboard side deck, switched on a radio transmitter, I'll bet a GPS tracker, put it in the cable locker and headed back the way he had come."

"Why do you think it was George?"

"His hand was still cold when we shook. It fits the timing."

"Yeah, it was cold, wasn't it? That's why the tender... But why would he want to track us?"

"I don't know. Want to view the video of him doing it?"

"Complex system. Why so much?"

"I looked over my shoulder a lot after... Let's playback the loop. What was that, about an hour ago?"

"Close."

"We could do it on the phone, but the MacBook has a much bigger image." He led her below, opened his computer, logged in and selected the program. They watched the alarm scroll, then he went back to the first one. "As I thought, a sea lion."

"A sea lion?"

"Phone vibrated when the carver was doing the venison. I dismissed it. Get a lot of sea lions on the stern platform. Sometimes quite messy." He scrolled to the next alarm, and they watched.

"That's not a sea lion unless it has a good George disguise." She giggled.

The image switched between cameras, as it showed George walk forward, open the hatch, switch on the device then kneel and stick his head inside the locker. "Is that a roll of duct tape?"

"Yeah, taping it under the lip of the deck. That's easy. Let's go remove it."

"No, I've set my alarm system to ignore its transmissions. Let's leave it there while we dream up a way to have a bit of fun with him and see if we can figure out what he's up to. I'm still trying to place him, where I've seen him."

"Not in the trade. Not around this region, anyway. I know pretty well all the faces, and I've not seen him before."

He closed the computer. "Lighter things now. Time for us."

She pressed up against him and kissed his neck. "Let's do something different tonight."

"What have you in mind?"

"Let's go to bed and just fuck, just passionate, wild unfocused fucking. We've not done much of that yet; we've been far too focused."

"You going to talk to me?"

"Yeah."

"Fuck!"

"Yeah."

Chapter Forty

Lorne and Catherine slept in until shortly past nine, having been active well into the wee hours before they fell asleep. They woke to loud foul language out in the anchorage. "Sounds like mister macho is blaming his stupid, incompetent mate for his own foul-ups." He turned his head to kiss her. "Good morning, Gorgeous."

They lay in a tight cuddle, touching, teasing and kissing. "We must be. I had no desperate craving for you to come last night."

"Yeah, I was thinking the same thing. I've stopped monitoring my balls."

"Ooh! Listen to that. Now, she's an idiot."

"Why do some men choose stupid, incompetent idiots to sail with?" He chuckled.

"They're the men who end up single-handing after they've run out of willing crew. Dad used to point them out. Derelict men in derelict boats in backwater bays."

"But I single-hand."

"Different. Very different. This isn't a derelict, and you certainly aren't. I can't think of a woman who wouldn't give her soul to sail with you." She rolled on top of him. "Pee first?"

"Yeah. What's second?"

"I can do some more talking."

"Fuck!"

"Yeah, but pee first."

After a casual brunch, Catherine sailed off the anchor and pointed *Tastevin* out of Plumper Cove toward Shoal Channel. "That's amazingly easy. Why doesn't everyone do it that way?"

"Sometimes it's a bit more difficult. The wind isn't always favourable."

She laughed. "The wind must have been very unfavourable in here earlier this morning when the other boat weighed."

Five minutes later, once they had cleared the point, they set-up the vane and pointed to the deepest part of the shoal. "The tide's risen enough now to make it easily across. If you tweak the sails, I'll bring up our computers."

She looked up at the main, then headed to its sheet winch. "Yeah, I'm dying to start my blog entry."

"I've mine half written in my head."

They sat on the settee and wrote, Lorne monitoring the plotter and instruments every few minutes while Catherine made the horizon sweeps.

Half an hour later they fell off around Paisley Island to a new course to clear Cape Roger Curtis. Lorne looked up from the winch. "I've thought of what to do with the GPS transmitter. Let's head into Coal Harbour, to the Royal Van. Pause there long enough to leave it taped under the edge of a guest float."

"That'll be fun. I wonder why he wants to track us. How's your blog coming?"

"Finished the draft, and I've just started the editing."

"I'll read it with you. We'll edit together as we go."

The Unknown Diner

This article is a departure for me. This will be more editorial than review. I'll describe a trend I find disturbing in the dining scene. I won't mention any names or locations here... Yet.

"Why not in the first sentence: This article is a departure for me *semicolon* it's more an editorial than a review."

"Yeah, that's better." He corrected the text.

Marketing is a huge industry with many businesses relying on it to remain profitable. For restaurants, marketing may be promotional coupons, two-for-one deals, lower prices at unfashionable hours and other price-related themes. Another thrust is advertising be it online, on radio and television, in magazines and papers, or with mail flyers. These all have their costs and their levels of success.

"You need a comma after the advertising."

"Thanks, added."

By far the best marketing for restaurants is positive reviews. These can be online, on air or in print, it doesn't matter. The dining public sees them, then repeatedly sees the better ones on the restaurants' websites and in all their subsequent marketing.

"Hmm... Is it *is* positive reviews or *are* positive reviews?"

"Yeah, I played back and forth with that. The word *is* agrees with *best marketing*, so it's correct, but it's too close to *positive reviews,* so it looks and sounds wrong."

"Tumble it."

"Yeah. *Positive reviews are by far the best marketing.* Done."

Fine, I review restaurants and have for many years. Those who have followed me will know I dine unannounced and anonymously, I always pay my own way, I never write a review on a restaurant unless I've dined there at least three times in the weeks leading to the review. Also, my loyal readers know I never write a negative review. If I have little or nothing positive to say about a place, I say and write nothing.

"Good. Direct."

Most of the other reviews online and in print are now written by people who announce themselves in advance. Okay, this has been an increasing trend for many years. The secret diner is nearly extinct. With integrity, the restaurant will show its normal quality and service. With equal integrity, the reviewer will not accept free dining or other gratuity. The result is a fair review. But fair reviews and integrity also seem to be on the endangered list.

Michael Walsh

This brings me to my dilemma. I have a large file of my unpublished negative comments about restaurants. It's been growing much faster the last several months, so I started analysing the contents three weeks ago, and what I saw disturbed me. I saw similar patterns, I looked deeper, and I grew increasingly concerned.

I recently dined at a place four times, the first three occasions in my usual unannounced fashion. On my fourth visit, I accompanied an acquaintance who also reviews restaurants.

"So I've dropped to being an acquaintance now you've knocked me up." She laughed and kissed his cheek.

Lorne laughed with her, then continued. *On each of the first three visits, I received poor service and low-quality food. Some of it was misrepresented on the menu and all of it decidedly over-priced. I have nothing against pub food and pre-prepared foods that are microwave or deep-fryer ready. But this place was not a pub. It was and is a place that has positioned itself in the fine-dining arena, both with its marketing and its pricing. Unfortunately, neither the quality of the food nor the service followed it there.*

"You might want to put a *was* before the decidedly. I like that last sentence." She stood and did a horizon sweep.

"Good... I've inserted *was*."

The higher-priced selections on their wine list are largely either from poor producers in the famous regions or poor showings from well-known producers. All of them very much over-priced. They were out of stock on each of the lower priced wines I ordered, but for each, they had their own special-labelled substitution.

On each of those first three visits, I left much of the food barely touched, paid the ransom and left to find some dinner. In the days following each of those visits, I had read the online and printed reviews trying to make sense of my experience. I questioned whether critic had turned hypo-critic. Was I out in left field somewhere, alone after the dining scene had gone right?

"Shouldn't that be hypocritical?"

"It could be. But hypocritic is also correct, though a much less common word. Same meaning, but it fits better with critic."

On the fourth visit, my acquaintance was announced and reserved as a reviewer. We were escorted past the waiting crowd, through the packed restaurant rooms and upstairs to a private dining room with a superb view. Only the two of us.

Over the next three hours, we dined in two and three Michelin star style, had superb wines and exemplary service. The food e were served was obviously all made from scratch with top quality ingredients. None of it was on the restaurant menu.

"Dropped a letter, second sentence. The food *we* were served."

"Got it... Fixed."

At the end of the evening, my colleague was given a thick dossier of papers, which included an overview and the philosophy of the restaurant. There was a packet of interior and exterior photos, all with links to online jpeg and pdf print-ready images. Inside the menu were pages of detailed descriptions of the items, including tasting notes and a packet of studio photos of the more popular menu selections, again with links. There were suggested phrases, sentences and short paragraphs to include in the reviews.

Our dinner cost them much less than the price of buying a small ad in a magazine, or a few spots on the radio. The expected review would reach many more people, last longer and would receive greater positive response.

So, back to the dilemma. Is doing what they're doing wrong? Is this any different from bait and switch, which is illegal under the Competition Act? Or is it simply the evolution of modern marketing?

The restaurant offers two dining options. One is for the restaurant reviewers, the hotel concierges and the inbound tourism operators. The other is for the public these newly recruited marketers suck-in.

Why don't we all become hypocritic diners? Who said there's no such thing as a free lunch? Let's all join the free lunch brigade, and the free dinner brigade while we're at it. Let's swamp them, then maybe we can move restaurant reviews back toward reality.

Michael Walsh

HOW TO BECOME A HYPOCRITIC DINER

- *Start a blog;*
- *Post a few dining reviews, McDonald's, Wendy's, whatever;*
- *Use a template to create a restaurant reviewer business card;*
- *Buy a pack of business card blanks and print your cards;*
- *Reserve some free lunches and dinners;*
- *For the best selection, go to highly rated places I haven't reviewed;*
- *Dine often before the trough dries up;*
- *Enjoy.*

"Wow! You're going to publish that?"

"Needs to be said."

"Yeah."

Chapter Forty-One

Lorne read the article again, then saved it, closed his computer and put it in the settee pocket. "How's your blog post coming?"

"It ground to a halt after I saw yours. Haven't been able to get it going again."

"Where were you heading with it?"

"The same duplicity thing as yours, but without the context or the depth. Without the hypocritic recruiting. I love that part. Mine seems totally flat now."

"Why don't you review a mystery place? Do a glowing review of last evening's dinner, but without the naming the restaurant. Start a guessing contest or whatever. There are other places you can review later to add to the theme."

"Hmm... Might be a way to salvage what I've already written... Hmm..." Catherine nodded to him and smiled.

"What have you so far?"

"Last night's dinner drafted. Needs the details and polishing. I was struggling writing about that terrible... Yeah, I like that."

He leaned over and kissed her cheek. "Read me your draft — dinner last night."

By the time they were off Dundarave she had finished crafting, editing and polishing it. "Should be fun." She smiled as she closed her computer.

"It sounds marvellous. Love the way you've built the mystery through the piece. Get them increasingly salivating and wondering at the same time. Should be a lot of fun."

They did another horizon scan, checked the sails and the instruments, then sat cuddling on the lee settee as they sailed toward Lion's Gate. "We'll have to motor through the Narrows."

"Regulations?"

"Yeah. Designed to keep incompetent sailors from impeding the commercial ship traffic." He smiled at her. "We're allowed one sail sheeted home for stability through First Narrows. It's the same for Second Narrows."

"The current? I remember the currents under the bridge. We okay?"

"A small part of dawdling in bed." He leaned to kiss her neck and shoulder. "A tiny part was to wait for the tides to help us across English Bay to False Creek. We'll be in First Narrows toward the end of the flood." He clicked the tide symbol on the chartplotter, and they examined the current graph.

"Looks like a bit over three knots."

He pointed across the graph. "See it decreasing? It'll be below two by the time we arrive, and for the Narrows, that's almost as good as it gets, giving us a nice boost to help us through."

"Coming back out... What about then?" She ran her finger across the screen. "Turns at 1720. Spend a couple of hours in the harbour and head out with the beginning of the ebb." She smiled. "I love your way of moving with rhythms and cycles."

"Far better than fighting them." They kissed, scanned the horizon and returned to their cuddle.

Off Prospect Point, they luffed up into the wind. Lorne started the engine, furled the jib and staysail and sheeted the main home while Catherine handled the helm. As they were motoring under the bridge, steering by electrical autopilot, Catherine asked, "So when are you going to publish it?"

"I'm sure it's cooked enough now, two hours and a bit to..."

"You do that too? Leave it sit for an hour or two, then go back to it? I've been doing that for years."

"Saves publishing impulsive writing, the old sober second thought thing. It always looks different once the rush to write has passed."

"Yeah, same. I sometimes question whether I wrote some of the stuff." She chuckled. "Both the good and the ugly."

He took out his computer, logged in and read the piece. "This is good."

"Read it to me."

He read it aloud, seeing her nods in his peripheral vision, and when he had finished, they were silent for several seconds. "Publish?"

"Definitely publish, Lorne. It's needed."

He made a visual sweep, checked the plotter and turned back to his computer, clicked the *Publish* button and watched the confirmation. He clicked *View Blog*, and they examined it. "Looks good."

"Looks great. What's your normal response? How many hits?"

He made another visual sweep, checked the plotter again. "Depends on how many tweets and re-tweets it gets, how many Facebook posts, shares and likes, but usually, it's eighty to a hundred thousand in the first few days."

"Fuck! I barely get ten thousand."

"Great! Way more than most. Lots of room for growth." He chuckled, and they merged in a hug, then he looked up. "We can roll out the sails again, we're through the Narrows."

"So that was the tricky part?"

"Yeah, a fearsome white-knuckle passage for many."

He rolled out the jib, eased the main and shut down the engine. "That's better. Much more peaceful."

They sailed around Brockton Point and into Coal Harbour, flashing the engine and furling the sails as the waters became more restricted, and the winds became increasingly fickle. He radioed the yacht club and announced their pending arrival, giving his membership number and asking for a temporary mooring for a couple of hours.

"Screen says you need twenty metres. Correct, Sir? Over."

"Yes, still the same boat. We're dropping off something and then stretching our legs while we wait for the current in First Narrows. Over."

"I can put you on H-3. Over."

"Great! Easy approach. Over."

"I'll send line handlers. Over."

"No need, we're fine. Over."

"Very good, Sir. Over."

"Thank you. *Tastevin* Out."

"So you're a member of the Royal Van?"

"My parents gave me a junior membership for my fourteenth..." He stopped and stared. "Take the helm... I need a few moments, can't see... Some tissue."

He dabbed his eyes after she had taken the wheel from him. "Point the right edge of the Bayshore tower." He moved behind her and circled her waist with his hands before bending to kiss her neck. "Sorry... I..."

"No need to be sorry. You've a lot of heavy stuff back there."

"Yeah. A lot... See the Rowing Club?" He raised his arm and pointed off the starboard bow.

"Yeah."

"Come starboard a bit now to steer on its right edge. Pull the engine lever back to the click."

"You want to take over again?"

"Why?"

"I've never done an approach."

"Great! No preconceptions, then."

"Fuck!"

"A bit later, you bring us alongside first."

"Fuck! All the way?"

"We've gone all the way before. Here's another version."

"Fuck. You're going to talk me through it, aren't you?"

"If you wish. You watched me do it the other day at Quayside. I'm sure you watched your father many times. Remember, everything dead slow. No need for anything quick. Feel the boat, become part of her."

"Dad loves to say: *Never approach land faster than you wish to hit it.* It's always made sense to me."

"Good one. My thoughts too. She has a left-hand screw — her stern kicks to starboard, astern."

"Yeah, Dad's too."

A few minutes later, Lorne stepped off onto the float with the breast line and turned it to a bollard, then smiled up at her.

Michael Walsh

Chapter Forty-Two

Lorne rejoined Catherine in the cockpit, and they hugged. "Well done, Ma'am. You didn't yell at me at all." He laughed.

"Your confidence is infectious. I'd never think of doing that."

"Great, don't think about doing things. Do them. Doing does things, thinking doesn't. Often prevents."

"Engine shut down?"

"Yeah, button here, then the key." Catherine quickly shut down, then in the silence, they resumed their hug.

A while later, he lifted his head from her hair, nodded toward the float and said, "We should finish mooring."

"Interesting. Only the breast line. We're stable."

"Her side is held tightly to the float. There's no way for the bow or the stern to swing out."

"Why do the others use two, three or more lines when they come in? Dad always has us bow and stern with lines."

"Possibly because that's what the books and the courses teach. Maybe it's so everyone can look busy. I honestly don't know."

He gave her a hand down to the float and showed her his line arrangements, all easily reached from ashore. He led the bow line forward to loop a bollard and then back to secure it to a staghorn at chest level on *Tastevin's* deck a few metres aft of the bow. "We don't need springs... Two hours, near calm in here." They walked aft and secured the stern

200

line in a similar way, then he undid the breast, coiled it and hung it on its hooks.

"Why do you undo the breast line? I saw you do that the other day too."

"It's a temporary mooring. It holds the boat in place while we properly moor. Another thing is that it's secured to the float, so we'd have to step ashore to undo it when we leave."

"The GPS thing?"

"Let's look at the video again, confirm that's all that was done." They sat in the cockpit and watched as Lorne keyed to the first alarm. "Sea lions. Still have to find a way to keep them off without doing them harm." He keyed forward to the next alarm, and they studied the sequence. "No pauses from boarding to foredeck. Knew where he was going." Lorne paused the video.

"But he said he had no sailing experience. Maybe power boats."

"Could be he had advice. Doesn't seem bright enough to be into this on his own." Lorne resumed the video, and they viewed the action on split screen, the pulpit camera and one of the lower spreader cameras. "It appears George planted only one item."

They followed the video sequence back to the stern and into the tender. "I see one only. You?"

"Yeah, no other stops. It seems as if he knew exactly where to put it. Little hesitation." Lorne closed the computer. "It's probably common to have the rode stowage without a lock. What's your father's like?"

"No lock. No need, only the anchor chain in it."

"Yeah, most are likely that way. Whatever, I'll go remove the thing. You search for a better place for it on the float. I'll get zip ties and duct tape and meet you there."

After they'd zip-tied the tracker to a diagonal reinforcing cable under the float, Lorne locked *Tastevin* and they walked along to the office to book in. Then out through the gate and up the ramp, they headed into Stanley Park for a stroll.

"There's an enchanting old growth grove through here." He pointed off to the left and led her. "I used to wander through it, looking up in awe at the red cedars and Douglas firs, some four metres and more thick. There's a beautiful little nook I would lie in. Deep duff and moss forest floor. I'd lie on my back and sink in. Dream of you as I reached to the sky like the trees."

"Oh fuck!"

"Yeah, that's what I was thinking. It's along here a short distance, well hidden."

An hour and a bit later, as he was handing her onto the transom step, she said, "I love the way you commune with nature."

"Much better doing it with company. So much better."

"You spent a lot of time alone, didn't you?"

"Far too much."

"You always seemed so happy."

"So did you."

"Yeah, I guess. Sad, isn't it?"

"Yeah, quiet sadness inside. Happy crust around it. Protecting it. That's strange, isn't it? Protecting it? From what? Not letting the sadness out, or not letting others in?"

"But you always let me in, Lorne."

"Partway, yeah. Same with you, I saw you were frustrated, but never suspected you were unhappy. You and Nathan."

"I told you I was a good actress."

"No more acting, promise?"

Catherine stroked Lorne's cheek. "Not even with my steamy talking?"

"Oh fuck..! Okay, one exception." He wrapped his arms around her, and they swayed. "We should get going. Time and tide and the rest of the quote. You take her out."

"Sure?"

"Yeah. You brought her in here, that's the hard part. You know how to start the engine and the chartplotter, you've seen me do them."

"Yeah."

"Good, the rest is easy, intuitive."

She switched on the instruments, flashed the engine and looked at him. "Mooring lines... You do the bow."

"I'll show you a little trick." He walked forward, took the bow line's turns from the staghorns and said loudly enough that she could hear, "Watch." He pulled steadily on the line, swinging the bow in to compress the fenders, then released and flipped the line off the bollard and onto the deck. The bow rebounded and slowly swung out as he coiled the line, hung it then walked aft. He smiled as he saw her flip the stern line off the bollard and aboard.

"Neat trick." Catherine slipped the lever to slow ahead and watched the starboard quarter as she increasingly added port helm to swing *Tastevin* into the fairway between the lines of floats.

Lorne stood behind her, framing her waist in his hands and lightly pressing himself into her back as she steered through the narrow passage and out into the more open waters of Coal Harbour. "Yeah, I guess it is easy. All those years I watched Dad, and I never had the courage to say yes when he offered."

"Courage. Confidence. Missing ingredients often."

"Where do I go here?"

"Stay a bit to the right of centre, blend with the traffic. Most boaters here know what they're doing. Stay clear of the seaplane zone." He pointed to the lines on the plotter. "They're clearly marked. We're in sufficiently open water now to steer with the autopilot."

"This button, the *Set*?"

"That's the one. Steer with those two lines of buttons. One, five and ten degrees per push." He squeezed her waist and nibbled her earlobe. "You're smart enough to figure this out."

"And you're brave enough to let me try." She pushed the button, let go of the wheel and monitored for a while, before she turned to receive his kiss.

As they motored out of Coal Harbour and into more open waters, Lorne was checking the wind. "Looks like we'll have to motor the whole way through the Narrows, wind's too light and fickle. An extra twenty minutes on the engine won't hurt."

Through the Narrows and out into English Bay, they shut down the engine as they picked up a westerly wind and hauled out the sails to beat up into it. Catherine smiled at him from the jib sheet winch. "God, you're good at giving me confidence."

"Not giving, simply allowing you to see it. It's been there all along. You need to let it out."

"Yeah, true. Doubt, self-doubt is so common and seems so easy to accept. We undersell ourselves... No, I undersell myself."

"You should publish your blog piece. It's great."

"You think so?"

"Confidence?"

"Yes, it's great piece, isn't it?" She giggled and reached for her computer. "I'll read it through again."

A few minutes later, after two minor corrections, Catherine pushed *Publish* and smiled at the confirmation. "Done. No comments yet, though." She laughed. "I remember checking the hit counter every few minutes after my first posts. Got nothing else done. Stupid, eh?"

They finally made enough westings to fall off on a reach across the bay past the cardinal buoy marking the edge of foul water. At 1950 they arrived at the entrance to False Creek, furled the sails and began motoring in toward the marina.

Catherine's iPhone pinged as they were passing Spruce Harbour. She read the text: *"Gr8 blog post. Whosit? See u at lunch, Cynth.* Well that's good, at least one person's read it." She laughed. "Cynthia's curious. I'm looking forward to lunch."

Her WebMail app icon showed *14*, so she selected it and scrolled through the emails. "Don't like this one." She turned her screen toward Lorne and he read:

Don't fuck with our restaurants. We're bigger and meaner than you. Bottom Line

Chapter Forty-Three

Catherine clicked off her phone, and they continued the remaining five minutes to the marina entrance, talking of possible libel, but they could think of nothing she'd written that even hinted at it. "We were always so careful. Nathan and I discussed this so many times. Write nothing that even the sickest interpretation of the law might contort as libel."

"They're using bully tactics. You've pointed to no one, named no one. They're pointing at themselves." Lorne motioned to the helm. "You want to take her alongside?"

"A little disturbed at the moment. I'll watch you, though." She gave him a crooked smile.

"Who's the email from?"

She opened her laptop, browsed to the site and scrolled down. "Here it is. Give me a sec... No, nothing, it's not showing a sender." She dug further, then looked up and shrugged.

"We can search through the routeing and... Later, we're here now." A minute later he gave the engine a final kick astern, then shifted to neutral, stepped off with the breast and turned it to the float cleat.

They secured the bow and stern lines and the springs in silence then stood on the float at *Tastevin's* stern and hugged, still silent.

Finally, he spoke, "I can dig out the source — I spent several years teaching myself hacking. Became quite the expert."

"Hacking? Why?"

"Tracking down Connolly, then searching for evidence." Lorne gazed into Catherine's eyes. "Heavy stuff. Really sick stuff." He looked away.

She hugged him tighter, her face tilted up, chin on his chest. "Let's ignore the email. A crank, a troll. Get lots of those."

"It's not only the email. We need to find who's behind this stuff, manipulating the reviews. We're too far into this now to stop, to be scared off by bullies."

She squeezed him tighter still. "Go below and dig it out? Or head over to my... Over to *our* townhouse to do it?"

"Below. It's closer."

He sat at her computer and started analysing the routeing on the email. "It's likely a proxy IP through one of the anonymous SMTP servers." He clicked further and scrolled down the strings of text and code. "Here... *AnonyMail*."

"How'd you get all that stuff on the screen?"

"Practice. Did it a lot, starting fifteen years ago. Hard to forget things like this." He continued scrolling and reading. "Here it is, the sender's address: *zxcvbnm@iam-ru.ru*. Fuck!" He sat back quickly on the couch as his arms flopped to the side, and his head banged into the bulkhead. "Fuck, fuck, fuuuu..."

"What is it?" She reached over to him. "You hurt your head?"

"Head's the least of it." He lay back, rolling his head side to side, eyes strained wide. "Not good. Not at all good. Fuck!"

"What did you see?" She rubbed his chest. "What's going on?"

"George — his server was *iam-ru.ru*. That's where his pages were." He looked at her and curled his lips. "This isn't his email, though. Too clever for him. I don't recognise Bottom Line."

"Who's Bottom Line?"

"Don't know — zxcvbnm, the bottom line on qwerty keyboards. Clever. Too clever for George. I can do more digging."

"So George? You recognise him now?"

"Yeah. The neck tattoo. He had only one chopped pinkie and a much smaller ear disc then. And a huge afro mop that... Fuck!"

"When's then?"

"A decade and more ago now. When I started digging, I tracked online images of me to his pages. Connolly's photos of me."

"Fuck! Sounds deranged."

"He was into child porn, torture and mutilation, both self and to others. Through his pages, I found my first leads to Connolly."

"Fuck! He recognised you last night. That's the reason for planting the GPS, isn't it?"

"Yeah. He must have recognised me from the trial. I had to testify against him. Child porn charges involving me. I was twenty-three by the time it went to trial, the Youth Criminal Justice Act no longer pertained, so I had to appear in court to testify against Nutcracker and..."

"Nutcracker?"

"Yeah, George's screen name. He's famous for his video of hammering a fellow's testicles to mush."

Catherine clapped her hands to her mouth, trying to control her gag. She rose and rushed toward the galley, much of her spew making it to the sink. Lorne rose behind her and rubbed her back. "Sorry, I do need to go slower with this crud."

She slowly recovered and turned her bowed head to look at him as he offered her a tea towel. "You've been through so many hells."

He rubbed her back and shoulders. "I don't want to drag you into any of them."

"I'm already in, Lorne. I'm part of you. We'll work through this together." She started cleaning the counter top.

"Don't worry about that. Let's clean you up. I'll do that." He turned her and kissed her forehead. "You go start a shower, I'll finish here."

"But it's my mess, I'll..."

"I caused the mess, you were only the messenger." He chuckled as he reached down and gave her bum a couple of taps. "Go. I'll meet you in there."

Michael Walsh

When he joined her in the shower, she was laughing. "Look at that stuff." She pointed down at the drain strainer. "I brought half the forest floor with me. Such a wonderful nook."

"Yeah. Kind of sweaty and sticky when we finished, weren't we?" They watched the accumulation build at the strainer.

He started soaping her back. "It's about a quarter to nine, we need dinner. Thoughts?"

"Let's pack up here and head home. Think of eating options as we go."

"Sounds good. Turn around, let me do your front. God, you're gorgeous."

They finished, dried and dressed, then packed the laundry and their computers and headed ashore. "We could pick up some things at Urban Fare to cook for dinner." She nodded up the street. "I don't feel like dining out right now."

"Bit late for cooking. Not into another restaurant either. We could order in something." They continued their walk around the crescent.

"Or get a selection from Urban's hot bar."

"Yeah, let's do that. I do it often after a long sail."

She unlocked the door, led him in, and they stood in the foyer hugging. A long minute later he said, "Strange, I felt unsafe back there — aboard. I've not felt that before, I've always felt safe in *Tastevin*. Until now."

"Spooked by the boarding, the GPS thing, by your memories of George."

"Yeah, guess so." He squeezed her. "Dinner, what should I get?"

"Food." She giggled.

"Yeah, how stupid of me." He kissed the top of her head. "I love you to bits, you silly girl. I hope you know that."

"What, that I'm silly?"

"That too."

He was back in twenty minutes with an assortment. "Way too much, but I didn't know what I felt like. Sort of all over the place tonight."

She took the large bag from him and glanced in. "Now you've a hint of what women go through with our cycles." She laughed. "Wait until this starts developing." She put a hand on her belly, and they both looked at it, then mashed together in a hug.

"Here I am, left holding the bag." She laughed, loosened her arm from around him, squatted to set the bag on the floor, then rose back to the hug.

He lowered a hand to her butt cheek. "We should eat."

"Yeah. Lots of options, the kitchen counter, the dining room, the coffee table with cushions, up on the patio."

"Your choice, you know them better than I do."

"Upper patio. It's a nice clear night, and we've radiant heaters up there."

"Great, the moon's up in less than an hour — still full."

She assembled a tray with plates, cutlery, glasses, napkins, a carafe of water and some candles and led him up to the top floor and out onto the patio. "I'll set this up; you bring up the computers. I'm curious to see the hit counts. Guess that's never left, wanting the confirmation, the acknowledgement and the acceptance."

The table was laid, the food ranged, the candles lit, and the heaters warming when he returned. He stood staring at the welcoming setting, then turned to her. "My God, I love you."

"We think so similarly," she said as they merged in another hug. "We should eat while it's still warm. This seems to be a global sampling. Samosas, pad Thai, tiddy oggies, souvlaki, pizza slices... What's the theme?"

"Confusion. Couldn't decide."

"Yeah, been there."

They sat and began eating, picking from their buffet. "Good timing for this. A bit stale and dry in the afternoon, after the lunch crowd. Late evening also, but always fresh with the crowds midday and mid-evening." She looked at him with a crooked smile. "This was my diet after Nathan was murdered. I had lots of practice getting to know the good timing." She laughed. "Also added quite a few kilos."

"That must have been a tough time for you."

"So many mixed emotions, sad, released, desolate, free, alone, unshackled, depressed, elated. Up down, up down, up down. So strange."

"And you played hermit?"

"Yeah. Stupid, eh? After the first few weeks, didn't want to see anyone, not even my folks. I couldn't trust myself to not inappropriately burst out into happy."

"Behind you now."

"Yeah. God, you're good for me." She leaned to kiss him.

A while later, she put her cutlery down and stared at him. "I can't believe how patient you are."

"How so?"

"Hit counts. Aren't you curious?"

"A bit, I suppose. We should check."

She reached for their computers and handed him his. Half a minute later, she shook his arm. "Look at this, the hits. Over seven thousand already. Two hours. How's yours?"

"Seems to be going viral. All over Twitter, Facebook, I haven't checked the others yet. Seems popular."

"Hits? How many blog hits?"

He clicked to Blogger stats. "Over a quarter million. The last hour. Fuck!"

"You're kidding. Let me see." He turned the screen to her.

"Fuck!" She put her hand to her mouth and spoke through it. "Told you it was needed."

"Yeah, guess it was. How are your comments?"

"Let me check." She saw her WebMail icon blinking, clicked it, logged in and scrolled through the messages, opening each to scan, then mark as unread for later. Partway down the page she opened one and stiffened, then put her napkin to her mouth to hold her gag.

Lorne watched her as she struggled, put his hand on her back and pulsed it. "Another strange one?"

She nodded and turned her screen toward him..

Tell your fucking stud to delete his blog post. If he keeps messing with us, we'll have to delete his crotch post. We'd love that double-headed monster in our trophy case.

Bottom Line

Chapter Forty-Four

Lorne and Catherine sat staring at the screen in silence for a long while. Finally, he spoke, "Your email? Any link to you? To here?"

"We set them up a couple of years ago when Nathan was being harassed by a restaurant owner. Had a security consultant do them." She took her eyes off the screen to look at him. "He said we were untraceable."

"Your business card, the one you gave Molly's. What's on it?"

"Name, well my logo *K ate*." She glanced around. "Here in my computer sheath." She pulled a card out and gave it to him.

"I've always loved that, your logo. Simple, to the point. So no name on it. The email address, your blog url and the Courier and VanEats logos."

"Same security consultant."

"Your blog profile. Anything there?"

She clicked to her blog, and they read through her *About Me* paragraph: *I'm Vancouver born, and I grew up on West Coast cuisine and Eat Local thinking. I love the ethnic mix which has added magic to our tables, and I want to celebrate the finest of these with you. K*

"Squeaky clean. No clues." He smiled at her. "This place is safer than the boat. Guess our loft is too."

"Loft?"

"Across the bridge, the Exchange, the old telephone building."

"You're in there? We had... Nathan had a friend with a place across the street. Yours is a listed Heritage Site, isn't it?"

"Yes, it's the oldest in the area, built in 1914 as the telephone exchange. I'm on the top floor with the original massive ceiling beams and the old brick walls. Funny, thinking about it now, that's where we were headed from La Luce before we diverted to the boat. Seems so long ago." He took a bite from a pizza wedge.

"You realise, don't you, we're still on our first date?"

He sat silent for several seconds, staring at her. "I've just counted. Not even a week yet. Six days. Six very full days."

"Yeah, and getting fuller." She pointed to her computer. "What do we do about Bottom Line?"

"Stay off *Tastevin*. I switched off her AIS transmitter when we arrived at Royal Van. It's still off." He ran his fingers through his hair. "They think she's there."

"So she's safe here, then."

"Until they want to do something. Stake-out the boat to watch for me... For us. They'll see we've foiled their tracking plan. That'll piss them further. They'll search."

"But there are so many marinas to search, so many boats."

"How many burgundy-hulled twenty-metre sailboats like her are around? She's easy to spot." He laughed. "The name on her hull also helps."

"Yeah, a day or two. So what do we do?"

"Stay away from *Tastevin*. Also away from here. Once they find her, they'll stake the area. We should think of moving to the loft tomorrow."

"Then what?" She stared at the samosa in her hand.

"Call the Mounties."

"I like that. Will they listen?"

"Took me several months to convince them to. Now I've a number and a code that take me straight to Ottawa."

"You've been doing this a long while, haven't you? Dodging the Georges and the Bottom Lines."

"Too long. You know the British game, Whack-a-Mole?"

"Yeah, I had the Mexican version of it, Guacamole. I loved playing with it, but impossible to beat."

"I've been doing the real one."

"Fuck! How long?"

"Since the end of my amnesia — 1999, when I started digging."

"So that led to the trial?"

"The trials." He picked up the pizza wedge again.

"How many?"

"I've stopped counting. I don't have to appear anymore, simply present my research to the Mounties."

"Surely you've whacked most of them now."

"You know Hydra?" He looked at the pizza and put it down.

"Yeah, the..." She sat up, wide-eyed. "Fuck, no!"

"Yeah, unfortunately. Big sympathetic brotherhood among these people. Big support. Take one down, a few more appear seeking revenge."

"Fuck!" She reached for his hand. "Come, cuddle time."

They held each other in a tight hug, gently rocking, then they lay back against the cushions in a cuddle as he started talking again. "The Mounties had me bait them, reposting Connolly's photos of me and leading them in. Child porn is the easiest conviction. It's tough to prove torture and causing bodily harm unless there are videos or photo sequences of them doing it with their face clearly showing, like Geor..."

There was a loud, sharp crack followed by a muffled explosion. They sat up, startled, then they stood to see what it was, but saw nothing except others on the balconies and on the walkway also looking around.

"Too loud for a car backfire. I don't know if cars even do that anymore." He looked at her and shrugged. They sat again on the patio couch, and Catherine opened her computer to check the hits on her blog.

"Wow, look at this. It's now..."

She was interrupted by Lorne jumping to his feet and rushing to the rail as he muttered, "Fuck! The bastards."

She looked up and saw the billow of black smoke rising from the marina. "No! Oh, fuck!" She rushed to join him at the rail as black smoke poured out through *Tastevin's* ventilation cowls, followed soon by flames.

She grabbed his arm. "We should go down to..."

"Last thing we should do. They want us to." He hugged her, and they watched. He pulled out his phone and punched 9-1-1. "Swamped already with this, I'm sure."

Catherine's iPhone pinged. She looked across at it, then back at Lorne when he said, "Check it. Could be them."

She opened her computer, logged in, opened the new email and sat staring at it with a hand to her mouth.

"Them?" He disconnected the 9-1-1 and sat beside her.

She nodded as she turned the screen to him.

In case you weren't aboard for the big bang... That was our Boat-no-Boat demonstration. Next it's Penis-no-Penis. Delete your post or we delete yours.

Bottom Line

Chapter Forty-Five

Lorne and Catherine returned to the patio rail and watched in silence as two men ran along the float, cut *Tastevin's* mooring lines and pushed her away from the float. Someone in a tender put a line to a bow cleat and towed her out into open water. "I like that sort of initiative," he said as he hugged her into his side.

"Fire trucks aren't there yet. Who are they?"

"Thinking boat owners. Preventing the fire's spread. The marina does a safety and fire-fighting seminar every six months." He turned her into his chest, and they hugged.

"By the time the firemen arrive, the fire would have spread to other boats, then accelerated."

"They work quickly."

"Saving their own boats."

"No, I mean Bottom Line."

"Yeah. We're into the professionals now."

"The professionals?"

"The Mafia, the biker gangs, whoever was cut-out of the business when drugs moved toward regulated distribution."

"Yeah. Had to go somewhere, didn't they? Not just shrug and walk away."

"Whoever Bottom Line is, he's well connected and fast acting."

"So what do we do now?"

He turned them in their hug and said, "Stand here and watch the fire — and the moon, it's beginning to rise."

She lifted her head from his chest and turned it. "But what about them? Bottom Line, George, the others?"

"Nothing."

"Nothing?"

"Not now. They expect us to react. They're waiting for us to react, in fact. In the crowds down there, watch for people watching people, not the fire."

"Scary. See two right away. Fuck!"

He kissed her forehead. "We're safe here. Look along the lines of balconies, up the condo towers. Everybody's out watching. Up here we're lost in the background. They expect to see us running around in a flap down there."

"Yeah."

"They're also hoping we were aboard."

"Oh, fuck!" She squeezed tighter. "Probably."

"Investigators are going to find two charred corpses aboard."

"What? Who? What are you saying?"

"Cool the trail. I'm calling the Mounties. We'll play dead."

"Then what?"

"Search and hack until I find Bottom Line. Get enough on him for the Mounties to deal with — attempted murder. I've never presented them with one of those."

They stood watching as *Tastevin* burned. "Could have been done from a dinghy or a kayak, a limpet would be easy to place from a small boat, maybe a diver approached. Whatever, from the rapid spread of the fire, it was likely an incendiary limpet. Pierce and ignite. Hull's likely holed below the waterline, so..."

"So she's sinking?"

"Yeah, but the moon's rising."

"God, I can't believe how stoic you are with this."

"Many years of practice."

"Yeah, I guess... So the Mounties?"

"Yeah, should get onto that. It's past midnight in Ottawa, but I can get the night desk, get the thing rolling."

Lorne switched on his phone, thumbed in and selected *Contacts*, scrolled down, selected and pressed *Call*. He gave his code to the receptionist and waited for the line transfer. He gave his code again to the Staff Sergeant and did the two-step authentication. "Thank you, Sir. I'll connect you to the Duty Superintendent."

"You've another NCECC case for us? Seems pressing, middle of the night."

"Yes, but this time with attempted murder."

"You have my attention. You?"

"Yes. And my wife." Lorne grimaced.

"When?"

"A few minutes ago. Vancouver. False Creek boat explosion and fire."

"Give me a sec." Lorne heard him talking on the intercom to the Staff Sergeant. "Boat fire, Vancouver False Creek. Happening now. Need information."

He heard the confirmation and continued. "I was thinking it would be helpful to the investigation if two charred bodies were found aboard. Delayed identification. Let them believe they've succeeded."

"You have an idea on who they are?"

"Know one of them. Nutcracker, George Hundsmann. Appears he received an early parole. The other one is new, calls himself Bottom Line. He seems very heavy. Swift. Decisive."

"Let me check..."

"Vancouver should know before things start. The boat should be sinking in a quarter hour or sooner. Vancouver Police will have divers heading there now. Fire Department also."

"Here's my Staff Sergeant. I'll get him onto Vancouver. Are you safe, do you need protective custody again?"

"I think we're good. Much better if they think we're dead."

"You're going invisible again?"

"Yeah, we need to. Bottom Line seems to be the top line or very near to it. God, he's fast."

"This number still safe?"

Lorne paused, then nodded. "I still have your scrambler on it."

"So what's your next step?"

"Watch my boat sink with our charred bodies aboard."

"Yeah, I... Fuck, they're persistent."

"We'll win."

"E Division will call you."

"Thanks."

"Thank you."

Lorne clicked off, then turned off his phone and looked at Catherine. She stared back, silent, slowly shaking her head. "You hide so much. You've carried a heavy load alone for so long." She picked up his hand and brought it to her lips. "You continue to floor me with these glimpses of what you've been through."

"It's complex."

"Fuck! Now that's an understatement." They moved back to the rail, their arms around each other's waists and watched *Tastevin* burn.

"I should do steel with the next one. Fibreglass feeds on itself and accelerates the fire."

"Next one?"

He nodded out at the fire. "That one will never sail again."

"I can see that. But you want to continue sailing?"

"I love the freedom, the independence, the oneness with nature. It gives me a feeling of place, of peace, of belonging."

"I'd love to give you all those — to share all of them with you." She squeezed his arm. "There she goes." They watched the clouds of steam rising from the bubbling water, watched her hull disappear, and her mast follow it down, then stop. The mast hesitated before it slowly tilted to the right with the ebbing tide. It stopped at a steep angle, the top spreaders just clear of the surface.

They looked up at the full moon in silence, then hugged.

Chapter Forty-Six

Lorne and Catherine watched as the assembly of waiting boats and launches began to approach the scene. A pollution containment boom, which had been ranged out, was towed into a circle and moored around the wreck. Divers went down as cameras flashed from the shorelines, from the Cambie Bridge and from the gartering boats. The traffic helicopter continued to circle the scene. Flashing blue lights became more common.

"This should be all over the media by now, mainstream and social. There's a feeding frenzy of photographers down there. Lots of selfies with dark, blurry backgrounds on Facebook and Twitter tonight." He kissed her cheek. "We should get back under the heaters. The evening's become chilly."

"You finished eating?"

"Must have. Not hungry anymore. Lost my appetite. You?"

"Yeah, me too." They stood by the table, looking at the food.

Two minutes later, they were still staring at it. He turned his eyes to hers. "Heavy stuff, eh?"

"Yeah, real heavy." They merged in another silent hug.

A few minutes later, he lowered a hand to her butt and tapped. "I'll pack up the leftovers, you do the tray with the other stuff. We've things to do."

"Things? Like what?"

"Like forget this crud for a while. Sink myself into you."

"I'd like that." She kissed his neck, nipped it and ran her tongue across it. "Yeah, really like that."

They lay in bed under the duvet, connected and slowly shifting their hips as they wandered their hands and mouths over each other. "I always wondered what the frenzy was all about. I tried to get Nathan to slow down. To be gentle."

"I love it like this. Relaxing, sharing, enjoying."

"So different from the videos."

"Videos?"

"Nathan used to find them online to show me his frenzied fucking was normal. You ever watch any of those?"

"Watched a bit. Seemed like torture, the expressions on their faces, so I went back to the educational ones. More sharing."

"Fuck! I love you. You have no idea how much I love you." She gave three quick Kegels then held a tight one.

"Oh my God." He tugged at it and she held. "Fuck! And those distracted him? God, we're put together so differently. Those to me are exciting, challenging, heavenly."

"You know Morse code?"

"Yeah, why?"

"Sending."

"Fuck!" He read her message and sent back: *Luv u 2*.

She moaned a deep sigh. "I want to come again... Join me this time?"

"Yeah, we need some sleep."

His phone woke him at eight forty. He answered it and listened to the message, spoke his code into the phone and pressed the octothorpe, then he waited for the prompt and entered his authentication.

"Good morning, hope I didn't wake you."

"Yeah... Okay. I'm still a bit fuzzy." Lorne worked his tongue and lips to freshen his mouth.

"Okay otherwise?"

"Yeah. Short a boat, but we're good."

"You've hooked a serious one this time, haven't you?"

"Deadly serious." He turned and faced Catherine, giving her an air kiss. "I have this on speaker so my wife can follow along. We're private."

"Good with me."

"Thanks, she's part of this. She has a quick, sharp mind."

"You'll see that the press conference and the media release both reported two charred bodies. Oh, and the Commissioner sends his thanks. Again. Very clever thinking on that."

"I thought it would give us extra time." Lorne nodded and blew out a deep breath.

"Ottawa said you felt safe. Still true?"

"I don't know. We're about two hundred metres from the scene, overlooking it. We saw lots of suspicious activity in the crowd of lookie-loos and gawkers last night. I'm thinking someone connected is in the condo towers or townhouses along here. The response was too fast, otherwise."

"Let us know if you need moving. We can quickly do that."

"Yeah, let me get up and get my bearings. Get a feel. I'll call you back within a couple of hours if it feels funny."

"Don't worry about the boat. We'll be recovering and impounding it for forensic investigation and... Your insurance. Who's your insurer?"

"Dolphin."

"We'll inform them. Be safe."

"We intend to." Lorne clicked his phone off and rolled to kiss Catherine.

"You're in this deeply, aren't you?"

"Been getting progressively deeper. More than fifteen years now. I sense we're almost there, almost to the bottom line."

She ran a finger down his nose, over his lips and chin and continued down. "So, you've called me your wife twice now." She circled his left nipple with her finger, then continued down.

Michael Walsh

"Yeah, guess I have. Seems easy. How else do I describe you?" He rolled onto his back to allow her finger fuller range.

"Right swipe, bed warmer, current hook-up, girlfriend, mistress, partner, soul mate, lots of options." She giggled as she pushed his penis aside to wiggle her finger in his navel.

"And your preference?"

"I like wife. Call me that the third time and it's for keeps." She laughed and ran her finger up his length and played with the spout, then paused and looked into his eyes. "I really need to pee. You?"

"Yeah, I've been holding it, not wanting you to stop that exquisite touching. So intense like that, amazing mix of sensations."

They rolled out of bed, peed and were soon back doing their slow sensual exercises.

It was nearly nine thirty when he said, "We need to take a look out there, down in the marina and around the crescent, see how it is, feel how it is. The Mounties can quickly move us to a safer place if we want."

"You need to come first, release some of your tension. Want to do a quick pop?"

"Yeah. Let's do that, start the day fresh."

Chapter Forty-Seven

Lorne and Catherine stood on the balcony a while later surveying the scene below. Two tugs were moving a barge with a crane into position beside the wreck. Down on the waterfront walkway, activity seemed normal except for the people stopped at vantage points to watch.

"See anything unusual? Anybody checking out people?"

"Not yet. You?"

"No."

They watched for a few minutes longer, then he looked at her. "Anything strange?"

"Nothing except you in my kimono." She sniggered.

He glanced down and laughed. "Yeah, I *am* a bit large for it."

A while later as they were showering, he asked, "Can we trust Cynthia?"

"How do you mean?"

"I don't know... thinking. She represents some of the restaurants that... Whatever you call it. That are like Molly's."

"Like that dinner at La Luce."

"Yeah. That and Greystone, Zack's, Gavroche, others. They're all similar. I was at her opening promotions, then back later, but I haven't been able to write reviews on them."

"I've missed those. My hermit phase. Last of her soft openings I did before La Luce was Dalliance down in Gastown."

"That's another of those. Kept going back, never could..."

"Fuck! Oh, my fuck..." Catherine froze.

Lorne held her. "What? What is it?"

"Oh, my God. That's probably where Nathan was going the night that..."

They stood holding each other under the shower nozzles, still and silent.

"You think?" She looked up at him a long while later.

"Think what? Dalliance? Cynthia?"

"Yeah, both."

"We need to find out. Come, let's finish here." He kissed her, then grabbed the soap and started washing her. "You look at your relationship with Cynthia, I'll run the strange restaurants through my head."

Later as they sat sipping their espressos at the kitchen island, after she had rambled through her friendship with Cynthia, he said, "Unless she's a great actress, she seems straight. No change? You've noticed no change in her behaviour, her attitude toward you?"

"Nothing that pops out. Same easy sharing."

"She share much about her business?"

"Not much, we didn't talk work. That's one of the neat things. She's always been a good break from work. We celebrate our victories and blow off our frustrations, but no details."

"Like what? Frustrations, what were hers?"

"Finding a man. Cynthia was constantly on that." Catherine ran her finger around the rim of her cup. "Always bemoaned her lack of anything long-term. All short flings, no follow-on. Like her restaurant opening promos." She nodded and tilted her head. "Yeah, I can see that."

"Interesting."

"The only business stuff she mentioned was her concern for the future. She was getting fewer long-term marketing contracts, her business was becoming mostly opening promos."

"She knows you're K ate?"

"Yeah."

"Who else?"

"My parents, my editors, you. That's it."

"What about, Mark It, Promot Ink, the others?"

"No, I decided to do only Cynthia's promotions. I never write based on them, anyway. It was more a friend thing."

He glanced at the clock on the oven front. "What time's your lunch with her?"

"Twelve thirty at Saguaro."

"The Tex-Mex on Granville?"

"Yeah. It's still one of her long-terms."

"You trust her?"

"With everything, until now."

"And now?"

"Don't know." She looked down at her finger doing rim circles. "I'm going to wear-out this cup." She gave a tight laugh. "Fuck!"

"Yeah. Trust could mean death." They sat staring at each other.

She nodded her head slowly, tipped her cup toward her and looked in. "Another coffee? There are croissants in the freezer. We could zap some, shave some slices of Appenzeller, there's still a bit of Tuscan ham and... Fuck!"

"Strange isn't it?"

"Yeah. You've been doing this a long time, haven't you?"

"Sometimes seems too long."

"Sure builds strength and stoicism."

"Either that or give up and die."

"Fuck! And you've always seemed so happy, so upbeat."

"Ever watch a swan glide swiftly across the water?"

"Yeah, so smooth, graceful. Why?"

"Paddling like hell underneath."

"Good analogy. Surface appearance gives little clue what lies beneath." She nodded down at his crotch and smiled. "Can't tell what's hidden beneath the surface."

"Nor what's hidden in the mind, in the heart, in the soul." He stood, moved behind her and wrapped her in his arms, kissing her neck and shoulder.

"Cynthia will text me at twelve forty. We give each other ten minutes grace."

"Unless she knows you're dead."

"Fuck, that seems so strange to think about."

"Yeah, I've been dead before. Never quite got used to the idea of it, though."

"What if they've kept her out of the loop on this? If she's even part of this thing." She turned her head to stare at him. "Mixed messages, aren't there. So much doubt. Unknown."

He leaned in to kiss her. "We were going to do brunch."

A quarter hour later as they sat eating their croissant sandwiches, she said, "Good idea, that, slicing them frozen."

"The croissants, yeah. It's tricky to get the defrosting time right. Often awkward to slice after. So, Cynthia? More thoughts?"

"My feeling is she's not involved, but I'm far too close to see. I hope it's only a business thing. Innocent business."

"Also my thoughts. Why would they trust her with information beyond the surface? They most likely share only enough to do the openings and initial promotions."

She stared at her coffee cup as she twirled a lock of her hair around her finger and unwound it. "Yeah, unaware what's behind them."

"Doesn't fit the profile." He laughed. "Nutcracker and Bottom Line are into mutilation."

"Fuck!" Catherine put her napkin to her mouth to hold the gag.

Lorne's hand was quickly on her back. "Sorry, have to stop mentioning —"

"Not that... Cynthia... Fuck!"

"Cynthia?"

"Girls' spa day. A few years ago. Fuck!" She looked at him and shook her head. "She's the one I told you about. Pierced lips, chain. Fuck. She proudly showed them to us in the sauna. Has a clit ring, nipple rings, scar drawings. Fuck! A big snarling tiger tattoo crawling around her hip, down her belly and onto her lips. She calls it her pussy cat."

"She know where you live?"

"Yeah, ladies' lunch here two or three years ago."

Lorne had his phone out, on and starting a redial as she finished talking. He went through the authentication process and was connected. "You need to pick us up now. We're located... Here, Catherine, you give him the address."

She took the phone and gave the address, "Car access along Aquarius Mews, number's on the garage door. Call on arrival, we'll open it." She handed the phone back to him.

"Have them text this number as they arrive... Great, we'll be ready... Thank you."

Chapter Forty-Eight

"Computer, phone, wallet. Passport; we may need it. Basics; a few changes of clothes. We can buy stuff. We can send them back for things." Lorne paused and looked at Catherine. "We could be over-reacting, but the consequences are too severe to not do this."

"Yeah, my feeling too. We need to shuffle some items around in the garage for the car. You do that, I'll pack. The last door in the hallway."

Less than twenty minutes later, they were seated at the kitchen island when Lorne's phone pinged. He read the text message. "They're outside."

They went to the garage, she pushed the button, and the door lifted. After a van drove in, she closed the door behind it.

Two uniformed Mounties stepped out and introduced themselves as Staff Sergeant O'Brien and Constable Yuen. They shook hands and O'Brien said, "We've a place in Surrey we can take you to unless you have other ideas."

"We have a secure place across the Cambie Bridge." He felt his pocket again to confirm he had the fob and keys. "We can unload in the underground parking, next to the elevator."

"Sure it's safe?"

"Yeah, I've been hiding there for many years now. I moved there after my last trial appearance. Yeah, it's safe."

They loaded the three bags, Catherine picked up the remote clicker from the shelf, and they all climbed into the van. She clicked to open the garage door. "I love these tinted windows."

Lorne gave O'Brien the address.

"Know it well. My husband and I are on the third floor — in the new side. You in the old or the new?"

"Top floor, in the old side. Small world."

"Your groceries — what do you do when you hide? I could shop for you."

"That'll save wear and tear on my niqab, hijab and chador."

"You don't?" She laughed.

"Can you think of a better disguise?"

"A burka." They all laughed.

Constable Yuen remained in the van in the parkade while O'Brien escorted them up the elevator to the loft, helping them with their bags. Lorne stopped in front of his door and extended his hand to shake. "Thank you, Staff Sergeant O'Brien. Very kind of you to assist."

"Denise, call me Denise. I mean it with the shopping. From the little I was told about your situation on the way over, it's not safe for you outside."

"This is my wife, Catherine. I'm Lorne." They shook hands and smiled.

"I was going to do groceries this evening, anyway. Put together a list. Be pleased to do it for you." Denise wrote his phone number as he gave it to her. "I'll call around seventeen thirty." She headed along the hall toward the elevator.

Lorne unlocked and opened the door, set the bags inside and motioned for Catherine to enter. She stood still, staring at him, head tilted to the side. "Aren't you forgetting something?"

He smiled at her, then shrugged. "A kiss? A hug?"

"Those are good for a start."

He bent to kiss her, wrapped her in a hug, released her and motioned his arm into the loft. She stood and shifted her eyes from his face to his extended arm, to the threshold and back to his face, and tilted her head again in question.

He stared at her. "What?"

"Some vague clues for you: *Wife. Threshold. Carry.*"

He swept her into his arms and stepped across the threshold. "That was the third, wasn't it?" He continued into the loft, laid her on his bed and began undressing her.

"The door, you should lock the door."

"Be right back."

Catherine was nude when he returned and began speaking in her low voice. "*She was nude when he returned, sprawled seductively on the bed and eyeing him as he stood staring at her. Running her eyes slowly down from his face, her nods urged him on as he began undoing his shirt, button by button, exposing more of his chest, then the tip of his manhood as it quickly grew above his waistband...* Fuck! You turn me on. Just strip. Let's get on with it."

His rush to finish undressing showed his agreement. The pace slowed as they merged and began gently churning, losing themselves in each other.

Forty minutes later, they heard her phone ping. "Text from Cynthia. I can quote it for you: *where r u.*"

"You think she's part of it?"

"Still don't know. I've never sensed anything mean about her. She's kind, caring, concerned, always willing to listen. To look at her, the little ball in her nostril, the rings in her eyebrows, the multiple earrings. Not unusual. But below... Fuck!"

"Would you recognise the tattoo, the pussy cat?"

"Yeah, most likely. Hard to forget. Why?"

"I need to start searching for Bottom Line, I'll set you up searching for Cynthia. See if you can catch her tiger by the tail."

"I wonder if her kinks are why she's not found a steady man."

"Sounds like she needs an unsteady one." He laughed.

"So how do I search?"

"Let's finish here, then I'll show you. Care to pop with me?"

"Silly question."

They ignored another text ping and the sounds of her phone vibrating on the floor as she knelt above him, gyrating toward much more interesting vibrations.

After a quick shower, they dressed, and he gave her a tour of the loft. Then at the counter with their computers, they logged in to his wifi, and he directed her to *bmexx.com*. "This is a good place to start. *Body Modification Extreme*. These people love showing off, sharing their self-mutilation."

"God! Look at the strange headings: *Piercing Tattoos Scarification Culture Ritual Surgical Hard*. The subtopics for piercing: *Ear Eyebrow Female Lip Male Microdermals Navel Nipple Nose Pocketing Stapling Tongue*."

"Look at the counts, over two million photos, over ten thousand videos. Click on *Tattoos*."

"Wow, must be a lot of categories, the first eight of them take the alphabet only to the beginning of the Cs."

"Scroll across."

"No cats under C. Look at this, third page, *Genital Tattooing*."

"Click it, look at the subheads."

"Oh, my God! *Anal Female Male*."

"Back and continue scrolling."

She scrolled through seven pages to the last category: *Wildlife and Nature*. "This has to be it. Over twenty thousand photos." She clicked on it to view the subheadings. "Fuck, there aren't any subs. So, this means I'll have to go through more than twenty thousand pictures?"

"No, most people do multiple photos. Some do dozens. Statistically, you have to comb through only half the photos." He smiled at her. "Problem is statistics don't tell us which half we need, or if it's at the beginning or end."

"Like searching for a needle in a haystack."

Michael Walsh

"Yeah, it's a bit like that. But first, we have to find the hayfield, then the haystacks, then determine the correct haystack before we can start searching for the needle."

"Fuck! You did this?" She put her hand on his shoulder and squeezed.

"Still do." He pulled her hand to his lips and kissed it. "Likely easier for you to start your search with *Genital Tattooing Female*."

"So if I find her tattoo, what do I do?"

"We'll then have her screen name, so we can find other photos, videos, stories she's posted, search through the comments on her posts. See who the comments are from, follow them and so on. Maybe find pages she's created. Dig and follow the trail."

"Fuck! You've been doing this for fifteen years?"

"Yeah, close to sixteen now. I've seen a lot of sick stuff. Even started understanding motivations, drives, compulsions."

"You see reason in this?"

"Yeah, when they do it to themselves or have it done willingly."

She looked at him. "But what motivates them to do it?"

"A lot of them searching for their gender identification, some running from bullying, others fighting insecurity. There are those trying to add to their image or trying to change it."

"I can see a lot of that. Unhappy, confused, wanting change." She rubbed his shoulder and laid her head on it. "That's the ones who want it. What about the unwilling?"

"That's where it gets sick."

Chapter Forty-Nine

Lorne and Catherine sat side-by-side with arms around each other's shoulders, heads leaning together. "So where are you starting?" She turned her head and nibbled his ear. "I like these adjustable stools — I can reach you now without craning my neck. So where?"

"I'm thinking of Shufflr."

"Shufflr? Why there? Table settings, cute puppy shots, tropical sunsets?"

"Depends on what you're searching for. I'll start with Bottom Line's fixation: *penectomy, nullification, neutering.* It's all there."

She sat up, turned and stared at him. "No! You're joking." She tilted her head and furrowed her brow. "You're not, are you?"

He shook his head slowly. "No. Great source. Damned near every image on the net has been copied and posted there, tagged, then shuffled, tumbled and re-shuffled. It's a great mine site with histories and links, just takes a lot of digging."

"You're indefatigable, aren't you?"

"Among other things."

"Fuck! I'll show you photos of cute kitties, you show me some of penis amputations. Fuck. Where's society going?"

"Same diversity of direction it's always followed, but now able to communicate it more easily, more broadly. Simple as that."

"Yeah, I suppose it's remained hidden through the ages. Now people can share it anonymously."

Michael Walsh

"That's what they believe. That's why so much of this stuff is posted, shared, liked, commented on, copied, pasted, reposted, shuffled. Most think they're doing this in anonymity."

"And you can track it?" She was back to rubbing his shoulder.

"For most of this stuff I don't even need to hack into the servers. It's all lying there for those who know what to search for and how to search."

"So what if I type in *pussytattoo.shufflr.com*?"

"Try it."

She typed and hit enter. "It's come back with a *Nope Not Here* message."

"Try *tattoopussy* or *pussytat* or Tweety's *puddytat*, be creative."

"Those stupid sixties cartoons... Wow, *tattoopussy*, look at this. Look at these. This one, her lips look like the snarling cat's tongue." She sat slowly shaking her head. "They really *do* want to show off, don't they? Look at all of these."

"Over there, on the right side, *People I Follow*, all those icons. There must be two hundred of them. Roll over each to see their names. Right click a new tab on any interesting ones. Watch what comes up."

"I never realised there was such a broad variety of pussy. Thin lips, thick lips, long ones, short ones. A lot of sad looking lips, though, pierced, ringed, chained... And the tattoos, from crude to creative, some quite pretty."

"Look at this one, Castro on her belly... His beard her hair. That's creative. Click on it, it'll blow up on a new page. There, all the comments, the reposts. It tracks them all. If you dig, you can find where the original came from. It might take you many clicks, but it's there. Everything's there."

"What amazes me is so many of them show their faces also, not hiding, not ashamed. They seem to be boasting."

"Yeah, I used to think that strange also. Now I accept it as part of the... The whatever you call it, disorder, derangement, illness, I don't know. Some of this stuff seems a cry for help." He looked at her, ran his fingers through his hair and shrugged. "Ready to start digging?"

"Hug first. I need some courage."

They stood and hugged, gently swaying. "You need to glaze your eyes to what you see. Focus on the road, the goal at the end of it, not on the dung and litter along the way." He gave her a light squeeze. "You're searching for Cynthia, for pussy cat."

"Yeah, and you're searching for Bottom Line. I'd rather look at pussies than where you're going. Fuck! So sick."

They sat at the counter digging quietly for over an hour, then she squeezed his arm. "Look at this." She turned her screen toward him. "*Pussyman*, an archive of men with pussies."

"Photoshopped, most of them. That's one aspect I've seen with the *nullo* and the *penectomy* stuff. Playing with their dreams or fantasies of getting rid of their junk. Lot of it in the States with the poor social health care. Many trans women looking desperately for ways to remove their unwanted parts."

"Fuck!" She stared to his eyes. "Most of them? What about the others?"

He leaned to kiss her cheek. "Some stop fantasising and actually do it."

"Just lop the thing off?"

"Lots of different ways. A common one is to tie it off tight, stop the blood flow. Let necrosis set in, let it die, then go to Emergency for acute care to cut off the dead meat and stop the spread of decaying flesh. Lots of stories about this on the *penectomy* sites."

"Penectomy sites? You say that as if they were common."

"They are." He grimaced.

"Fuck. So how are you going to find Bottom Line with so many places to search?"

"Persistence. Keep looking. Keep searching. I have nothing to go on except he's mentioned lopping me twice, and he knows about my split and my size."

"How so?"

"His second email, *double-headed monster*. That's one of the tags Connolly used on my photos... I should follow that, dig through the comments, shuffles, tumbles."

Michael Walsh

"I wonder if that's..." She paused, tilted her head and nodded. "Yeah, that's likely where they went."

"What went?"

"Nathan's missing parts. In the garbage bags in the alley. Only parts they didn't find..." She paused again and put a hand to her mouth to fight the gag reflex. "They found everything except his right hand and his penis, scrotum and testicles. Fuck! What a sick man we're after."

He put his arms around her and held her tightly. "They'd be for the trophy case he mentioned."

"Yeah, the police had told me there had been a growing number of cases across the country... Missing parts. They didn't go into details, but it's obvious now."

"You want to stop for a break?"

"No, let's keep going a while longer. We'll not get there unless we keep going."

They continued searching, quiet but for their clicks and keystrokes. A quarter hour later, she laughed and stroked his forearm. "You have to see this tattoo. A huge schlong down her thigh. In the side view, it looks real." She turned her computer toward him.

"Does, doesn't it? Could be a male inside wanting to get out. We're all made so differently. Most of the time the outside matches the inside, sometimes it's a near miss, other times it's way off the mark. Woman inside, man out, or vice versa."

"Must be confusing. I can't imagine what that would be like."

"I watched Connolly's torment and listened to it. He talked about when he had circumcised himself to stop his focus on his penis, to forget he had one, to stop him from masturbating."

"So, that's the Kellogg thing?"

"Yeah. He said his circumcision didn't work, it didn't stop the reminding or stop the urge. He started cutting himself further. That's where I came in."

"When he confined you?"

"Yeah. He made me watch and take photos as he did a subincision on himself. He had already split his scrotum, and he continued the split up, cut by cut over the months, cutting and sculpting."

"Oh, my fuck! And you had to watch?"

"He kept asking me if he looked like a woman yet. He kept watching for my erection. Sad. Woman inside wanting out."

Catherine nodded. "Really sad. Tormented. But he was also twisted and sick."

"You want to stop for a while and cuddle?"

"Yeah."

Chapter Fifty

Lorne lounged back in the corner of the couch, and Catherine settled in against him, legs entwined, her head on his chest. They remained silent for a long time, gently stroking each other, then she said, "We haven't even thought to check our blog hits."

"Been a bit distracted the last while."

"Yeah. You curious?"

"A bit. You?"

"Not as much as before." She snuggled closer and pulsed her hand on his left pec. "Such a solid chest. Such a solid man. God, I love you."

He pulled her closer. "Wonderful feeling, isn't it? I thought this would never happen. To hold you like this. To know you like this. To love you like this."

"Yeah, same." She sighed. "Remember lying and cuddling on Cypress Street? So innocent, trying to find the special way to hold. I'd watch Mum and Dad hug and touch and kiss, trying to see the way, then I'd try them with you."

"Delightful innocent days."

"Mmmm."

A quarter hour later they were still lightly stroking when the phone rang. He checked the clock. "Seventeen ten." She rolled off, and he rose from the couch to answer it. "Hello."

"Lorne, Denise here. I'm running late. Be closer to eighteen hundred by the time I get there."

"No problem, whenever. We're not going anywhere."

She laughed. "Gotta go. See you in a bit." She clicked off the call, and Lorne stood looking at his phone as he thought.

"Denise?"

"Yeah, running a bit late." He smiled and put the phone down. "Gives us a chance to do the shopping list. I'd forgotten."

He checked the fridge and freezer then sat down at the counter to begin the list as she watched over his shoulder. "Anything else?"

She read down the list again, opened the fridge door. "Nothing. I can't think of anything else missing. Toilet paper?"

"Bought a big bale last week. Soap's good too." He looked around. "Dishwasher, laundry, it appears we've got it all." He clicked *Print*, and they listened to the printer head running through its warm up cycles.

"Much easier these days than sending a messenger into the streets searching for a scribe." She laughed.

"Yeah, everything's easier and quicker. Like ferreting out the perverts and sorting them from the wandering souls."

"Wandering souls, how do you mean?"

"Think of all the pretty pictures you've seen this afternoon. Nice tasteful images. Art, much of them."

"Yeah, lots of butterflies, flower petals blending with lips, things like that Castro face, the thigh piece and... Creative."

"Then there's the sick stuff."

"Fuck, there was one with a trompe de l'oeil of a knife half done cutting out her vulva. Well done tattoo, but the thought process to motivate her. Fuck, I can't imagine what would..."

"And that's only the tattoos. Think of the actual genital cutting categories. Then there's the *Surgical* and the *Hard* categories."

"I'll stick with the tattoos for now, thanks."

"Any luck finding tigers?"

"I've seen some fanged faces on mounds and quite a few lower down with vulvas as mouths looking ready to chomp off any intruder. Seems to be a common theme. I've been wondering if they actually mean it."

He looked up from printed shopping list. "If they mean what?"

"Scare off those who approach. Like, would you want to stick your penis into a snarling tiger's mouth?"

"Interesting thought. Guarding the access. Cynthia's tattoo? Same theme? Intimidating?"

"I thought it was. Crawling around her hip and down her belly. Big snarling face tattooed over her outer lips and inner thighs. She splayed her legs out and in to show us the opening and closing mouth. Yeah, I'd say it was intimidating."

"And her lip piercings? Small?"

"Huge. That's a better word for them. I couldn't believe what I was seeing." She did a finger gag motion. "They must be four or five centimetres across."

"No, I meant her small or large lips. The inner or outer lips?"

"Inner. You seem very interested." She smiled at him.

"They're different categories. The outer are usually bondage or chastity stuff, the inner are often for stretching. You said she had a chain?"

"A thick one with a big ring in the middle. It appeared it would be very heavy."

"Stretching. Great, we'll find her quicker there. They show off a lot more, showing their progress."

"Progress?"

"How much weight they can bear or how..."

"Fuck! No?"

"Yeah."

"I cut you off. You said *or how* before I interrupted."

"Or how far they can stretch them."

"Surely this is rare."

"It's common enough that the small percentage who take the time to post online provide tens of thousands of images."

"You want me to start digging through that?"

"No, you stay with the tattoos, I'll do the labial stretching. I know my way around that stuff now. I tracked down a paedophile couple through that two years ago."

"Fuck!" She looked at him and shook her head. "My graceful swan, calm, placid, gliding along. You've been churning through shit all these years, keeping it hidden." She bent her head to his shoulder, still slowly shaking it.

He stood from the stool, picked her up and headed to the couch. "Time for another cuddle break."

Chapter Fifty-One

They were only a few minutes into the cuddle when the phone rang. Lorne reached for it and clicked it on. "Hello."

"Denise here. I don't have access to the fourth. My fob works only for the third."

"Where are you?"

"In the lobby now. Figured it would be easier for you to bring the list here. I'll wait at the elevator."

"Yeah. Great building security, but awkward sometimes. Be down in a minute." He clicked off, kissed Catherine, grabbed his fob, the shopping list and two cloth tote bags, and headed toward the door. "I'll be right back."

"I'll miss you." Catherine smiled and giggled.

He briefly outlined the building security system to her when he returned. "Electronic fob access to the outside doors and the parking and owner's floor in the elevator. One-way stairwell doors giving access only to ground level except to the owner's floor by key."

"So you'll have to go down again when she comes back. You keep leaving me." She pouted and laughed.

"No, she'll push our code on the entry phone, and I'll buzz her in, giving her access to the fourth floor. It's a good system, filters out the unwanted as long as owners are careful with it."

They resumed their cuddle on the couch.

"So the lip stretching thing? What's that about?"

"Some of it is the desire to have something dangling down there." He looked at her and shrugged. "But then there's the craze by those who think their lips are too large. They have them surgically reduced. Many do it to themselves."

"Fuck? Really?" She lifted her head and stared into his eyes. "I'm so glad I'm in the middle. I love my body."

"That's why it's so beautiful, why you're so beautiful. Your beauty radiates from within you, it oozes out through every pore." He gave her a little squeeze. "Your beauty blesses everything around you. I've always been amazed by your grace, your poise, your ease."

"Wow! I love the way you see things. You're so good for my ego." She squeezed him back and kissed his neck.

"You're genuine, not pretence. You don't wear make-up, your breasts are real, not plastic, you don't pay three or four times too much for bags, purses or clothing simply because they have labels stitched on the outside instead of in."

"Crazy, those things, aren't they?"

"Yeah. What I've been seeing is that the fuzzier the dividing line is between being male or being female, the crazier the stuff."

"Yeah, there are many shades between blue and pink."

"Many shades of purple in the middle."

"You ready to dig through at more purple?"

He ran a hand inside the front of her yoga pants and found moist warmth. "I'd rather do pure pink at the moment."

"Oh, God! How far's the supermarket?"

"Far enough. Early evening crowd usually thick."

"Here?"

"Bed." He picked her up and carried her into the bedroom. She was undoing his shirt as they went.

Twenty-five minutes later, the phone rang as they were relaxing in the afterglow of a mutual. He withdrew, quickly wrapped himself in a turban of Kleenex and picked up the bedside phone. "Hello."

Michael Walsh

"Hi, it's Denise. I'm downstairs."

"I'll buzz you in." He entered the code and clicked off, then turned to Catherine. "We've thirty seconds, maybe forty. My spare bathrobe's in the bottom left drawer. It's the red thing, hard to miss."

She finished stuffing a lip wad. "I'm sure it'll cover me better than my kimono did you." She chuckled as she rose and opened the drawer. "I won't dangle out the bottom."

He returned from the bathroom tying his robe sash. "There's a brush in there if you want to do your hair... It looks wonderful to me as it is."

Taking his wallet from his trouser pocket, he walked toward the door, arriving as Denise knocked.

He unlocked and opened it and she walked in pulling a caddy. "Surprisingly light crowd this evening." She smiled at him, eyeing his gown. "Glad to see you're able to relax."

"We're trying to. It's so good of you to do this. Makes it much easier for us."

She lifted the flap to pull out his two bags. "These are yours. There was a special on the snapper, looked really good, so I got you two kilos instead of one."

He lifted the bags, took the register tape from one and checked the amount. "Hang onto the change, and here's another fifty. I'd love you to do this again in two or three days. I'll run a total."

She stared at him quietly for a while, then shrugged. "I realised this afternoon, back in the office. Remembered you from the courtroom. One of my early duties was escorting you to and from safe custody." She stood trembling, tears running down her cheeks. "Sorry... I..." She shook herself. "Sorry."

He stepped forward and hugged her, a hand on the back of her head. "It's okay. We all need to work through it."

Catherine came up to them with a box of Kleenex. "You want to sit for a while?"

Denise lifted her head from Lorne's shoulder, and took three pulls from the box of tissues. "Silly of me. An emotional time. I've never been able to forget some of that evidence." She began dabbing her eyes and wiping her cheeks.

"Come in, sit for a while." Lorne motioned an arm up the hall.

"Thank you, I'm fine now. I need to put my groceries away." She looked down, put her hand on her belly. "Second month. Emotions all over the place."

Catherine laughed, ran a hand across her own belly and smiled at Denise. "Second day. Waiting for mine to start going crazy."

"Maybe I will sit for a bit. Jim's away, groceries can wait."

They sat at the counter of the kitchen island, sipping rooibos and chatting. "Our first, yes," Denise answered. "We were so focused on careers that we didn't have time to... Didn't want to take the time is more like it." She nodded at Catherine's belly. "But you? You think you are?"

"We have to be. Just felt so... So like it." She smiled at Lorne, put a hand on his arm and the other on her belly. "We are. Silly isn't it, but we know we are."

"Not silly. I felt the same. Couldn't describe it. Just knew. We both knew."

"Yeah." Lorne nodded. "A very clear message." He turned to Denise. "I remember you now from the trial. Sorry you had to sit through all that stuff."

She shook her head. "That's so funny, you being sorry for me. I only had to listen. You had to relive it. I couldn't believe how horrid that lawyer was to you, how... How distorted. That psychiatrist. What an evil man."

"Interesting thinking of it now — actually, it's crazy." He ran his fingers through his hair. "Connolly seemed the least evil of the lot. A confused, befuddled man."

"I guess he's still in forensic custody in Coquitlam."

"He died there last month."

"What about the psychiatrist and the lawyer?"

Michael Walsh

"I don't know, I've not kept track of them. Probably my relief at Connolly being found criminally insane. I wanted to forget, so I didn't follow the results of their charges."

"I know they were both convicted. I followed their trials hoping... Shouldn't say that; prejudiced. But I *was* hoping their evil would be properly punished."

Catherine had followed the exchange quietly to this point, but her curiosity got her. "What were they charged with?"

Denise scowled. "Initially, perjury, falsifying evidence and contempt of court..."

"Initially?" Lorne tilted his head. "I'm aware of those, but there were further charges?"

"Paedophilia, both of them. Investigators found a lot of child porn stuff in their seized computers."

"Interesting. Guess I've never thought to follow them, and I've never run across them in my investigations."

"Your investigations?"

"I've been doing some paedophile digging for Ottawa."

"Sick stuff, isn't it? I was handed the paedophile portfolio at headquarters last year, immediately after my promotion. Had to beg out of the section after a few weeks. My system couldn't take it. Too disturbing."

"Frick and Robotham... Their additional charges? Were they related to Connolly's online images?"

"Yes, they were both distributing them."

Catherine and Lorne smiled at each other as they nodded.

Chapter Fifty-Two

"It's public record, but much easier for you to get access than me," Lorne said as he looked at Denise. "Robotham and Frick, their sentence details, time served, release dates."

"Even though it's public information, I can't." Denise pursed her lips. "I'd love to, but we're not allowed."

"Yeah, it's better I go to the Commissioner. Do this through the proper channels." He glanced at the oven clock. "Nineteen ten, twenty-two ten in Ottawa. He's long gone for the day. The evening watch can get it started."

Denise watched him with her head tilted as he rose to get his iPhone. "Commissioner?"

"Yeah, Harold." Lorne thumbed his phone on, thumbed in, then scrolled to *Recent* and pushed *Ottawa Duty Desk*. He gave his code, waited for the line to be answered, then proceeded through the authentication.

"You're safe?"

"Yes, settled in at the loft again."

"I see that. I've your dossier on my screen. How can I help you?"

"Connolly's 2003 trial. The aftermath, the charges against Frick and Robotham. I need details of the charges, sentences and releases. A contact in E Division to work with on this, and also permission to work directly with their paedophile people again."

"We'll have them contact you. Onto something?"

"Yeah, a real heavy one this time."

"Keep us in the loop."

"Thanks, I will." He ended the call, clicked off his phone and put it in the pocket of his bathrobe.

Denise was still watching him, her eyes now stretched wider. "Connected, aren't you?" she said, still shaking her head.

"We've been helping each other over the years." He smiled at her and shrugged.

"So Frick and Robotham are into things again?"

"Don't know about Frick, but Robotham's flashing bright red at the moment. Can I get you more tea?"

She looked into her cup, then at both of them. "I really do need to get going." She glanced at her watch. "Jim's calling in a short while. Groceries need putting away."

Catherine put a hand on Denise's arm and gave it a little shake. "If you've some free time the next while, I'd love you to come over and talk. I think I've just lost my best girlfriend, and I need to find another."

They stood and hugged. "Yeah, I'd like that. The contact's kind of sterile with the job. I'll call you tomorrow."

After Denise had left, Lorne and Catherine stood in the hall by the door and hugged. "Makes sense, doesn't it? Robotham, Bottom Line. Clever, lawyer, corrupt, paedophile, wants revenge. Appears he won't stop at..." Lorne's phone interrupted him. He pulled it out, thumbed on and in and slid the answer.

"Staff Sergeant Watson, Duty Officer, E Division. Ottawa told us to call you."

Lorne gave Watson the details and an email address for him to send the information. He clicked off and pocketed his phone, then resumed the hug. "You have no idea how much easier it is for me to handle this stuff having you for comfort."

"I can't imagine how lonely, how awful that must have been. All these years." She released her hug, undid her sash and his, letting their robes fall open and wiggled into a closer hug. "That's better."

"Oh my God! Such an amazing way to comfort. You're such an amazing woman. I love everything about you."

They stood pressing their flesh into each other, gently swaying and caressing. Enjoying the warmth and comfort. Several minutes later, she kissed his neck and wiggled her face into it. "We should do something."

"We are."

"Yeah. Wonderful something." She trailed her lips across his chest and bent to nibble a nipple.

He shifted his hips to allow nature a little more turning room. "We could continue the hug on the bed." He pressed himself into her belly.

She wiggled into it, then stepped back and looked down. "Is this gift wrapping or a white flag of surrender?" She giggled as she began unwrapping the winds of Kleenex from his penis. "It's a bit stuck."

"We could continue in the shower." He shrugged his robe off his shoulders, then slid hers off, picked her up and headed to the bathroom.

Nearly an hour later, as they began cooking dinner, she lifted her head from quartering the criminis. "Didn't think in there, but the hot water seemed to be limitless. You must have a huge tank."

"No tank. And it is near limitless. This building was one of the first hooked-up to NEU."

"Any you? What's that?"

"N-E-U. It's the acronym for Neighbourhood Energy Utility, the system which recovers heat from grey water. You must have heard about it."

"Yeah. Seems I forgot about it. So your heat and hot water are all from recycled waste heat. That's this whole area now, isn't it?"

"Yeah. Supplies more than we can use. The building developers jumped on it — cheaper to buy into NEU than to install heating systems in their buildings."

"And you're left enjoying near limitless inexpensive heat and hot water, knowing it's bright green and recycled."

"That was among the things which attracted me to this place." He glanced over at the chopping board in front of her. "How are the mushrooms coming along?"

She looked down. "Got a bit distracted. Another half minute." She turned her attention to the quartering. "You're fully into this, aren't you? Natural energy, recycling, things green." She chuckled. "I'm still chopping."

"Simply makes sense. Use the wind, the sun, the tides, recycle and use again. Crazy not to use what's given."

"There's still a lot of crazy in the world." She passed him the board of mushrooms, he slid them off into the sizzling butter and gave the pan a few tosses.

They heard his phone do a bing-bong. He turned from the stove to look toward it. "That's likely the information on two of the crazier crazies."

"You want to get that? I'll do the sauté."

"Dinner first. I'm not crazy."

Chapter Fifty-Three

"Do you miss having wine with your meals?" Catherine ran a finger around the rim of her water glass and gazed into Lorne's eyes as they sat after dinner.

"Not as much as I thought I would." Lorne hooked his finger under hers and led it to his lips to kiss. "A week ago right now we drove past here, heading to the boat. So much stuffed into such a short time. Hard to believe it's only a week." He kissed her finger again, then played with it.

"Remember me playing with your fingers up in the attic?"

He laughed. "You were so serious, rubbing and squeezing and kissing them. Kissing my lips. So sweet looking back at it."

"I watched Mum and Dad sitting on the patio, playing with each other's fingers as they talked and kissed. I thought that was the special way to hold... It had to be, they seemed so happy. I could hardly wait to try it with you. I really wanted us to have a baby." Tears streamed down her cheeks. "Oh God, do I ever want that."

He put his arm around her shoulder and pulled her into his chest. "Yeah, don't we?" He stood, lifting her as he did and carried her across to the couch to lie and cuddle. "Yeah, really, really, really, like we used to say."

They lay there reminiscing about their play all those years ago, laughing at the things they did together. "Strange, all the stuff we did and how little of that was playing doctor."

"It seems once our curiosities were satisfied, my pee pee and your pee bum were only parts. Interesting — I wonder what would have happened if we had been caught into each other's pants."

Michael Walsh

"I think Mum knew from what I told her and from the questions I asked. She had to. I need to ask her about it."

"Very healthy attitude, that. I didn't dare mention any of it to Mom or Dad. Already had stern warnings to cover myself, to always keep it private. Later the priests and nuns added shame and sin to it. How different — accepting or denying."

"That must have been..." She stopped at the bing-bong of his phone. "That's another email, isn't it? You should look at them." She gave him a squeeze and rolled off.

"Yeah, should do that." He rose from the couch, picked up his phone and thumbed it on to check. "Yeah, two from rcmp-grc. Easier to do them on the computer."

"Giarcy?"

"G-R-C... It's a federal site, so it has to use a bilingual url. The translation for Gendarmerie royale du Canada. It's necessary they communicate in both official languages."

They sat side by side at the island counter as they read through the first email. It acknowledged their conversation and confirmed a search would be done through the central database, with the records being forwarded when retrieved.

He opened the second email. "Here it is... On Frick." He opened the attachment, and they read:

FRICK, Gustav Johannes
Charged: 2003 09 03: 131 Perjury;
137 Fabricating evidence;
139 Obstructing justice;
366 Making false document (3);
Contempt of court.
Charged: 2003 09 07: 163.1 (2) Making child pornography (364);
163.1 (3) Distribution, or sale of child pornography (3817);
163.1 (4) Possession of child pornography (3817).

Convicted: 2003 10 29:   All charges.

Sentenced: 2003: 11 12: 12 years confinement.

Parole Denied:	*2012 11 21*
Parole Granted:	*2013 11 19*
Released:	*2013 11 20*

"Not a pretty record, is it?" She pointed to his computer screen. "What are these numbers in brackets?"

"The number of counts for each charge, the number of times he was charged for each one." He ran the cursor down the list. "This one, making three false documents. He presented forged assessments from three psychiatrists supporting his own findings on my self-inflicted injuries and my captivity delusions. They almost succeeded with their fraudulent defence. Even my lawyer started believing them."

"Fuck. I can't imagine what you had to go through. You must have had someone to talk with, to share your torment."

"Not until the week after Connolly was convicted, starting third year UBC when you approached me to be your beta reader. You were the first ray of light I had seen in a very long time."

"Oh, my God!" She stared at him with eyes strained wide. "And you never let on. Not a hint of any of this."

"I needed something to take my mind off the horrors I had been living through, so I buried myself in fantasies about you. I see now that's why I missed the reality of you. It's also why I didn't follow these trials, Frick's and Robotham's. I needed to forget."

"Let me get this straight in my mind. Frick, the fricking sick psychiatrist, was Connolly's defence witness. His only one?"

"No, there was a series of character witnesses, the teachers he taught with, fellow priests, even the bishop. Connolly was painted as a saintly man, gentle, kind, helpful. Wouldn't hurt a fly. They all seemed genuine, I'm sure they had no idea of his other side. They knew only his Jekyll, not his Hyde."

"How could they have missed it?"

Michael Walsh

"Easy. Most of the time he was a sweet, gentle person with me." Lorne clicked to open the email which had arrived while they were talking:

ROBOTHAM, William Charles

Charged: 2003 09 03: 131 Perjury;

> *137 Fabricating evidence;*
>
> *139 Obstructing justice;*
>
> *298 Defamatory libel;*
>
> *Contempt of court.*

Charged: 2003 09 07: 163.1 (3) Distribution, or sale of child pornography (158);

> *163.1 (4) Possession of child pornography (158).*

Convicted: 2003 10 23: All charges.

Sentenced: 2003: 11 03: 10 years confinement.

Parole Granted: 2010 11 09

Released: 2010 11 10

"So he's been out four and a half years."

"Yeah, lots of time for him to get established." Lorne nodded at Catherine and sighed. "He would have made many connections during his seven years in Kingston."

She tilted her head. "So where do we start?"

He closed his computer, stood and picked her up. "With us. Bed, cuddle, relax, sleep. Be fresh for tomorrow."

Chapter Fifty-Four

After their morning exercises and a long shower, Lorne and Catherine were busy at their computers as the sun peeked in at them through the balcony windows. "Seems he's still disbarred. Nowhere among the lists of lawyers. Maybe didn't reapply."

"Or his application wasn't approved."

Lorne laughed. "Have to be much more corrupt than him not to be welcomed back into... But that's into lawyer joke territory."

"He might have stayed back east." Catherine lifted her eyes from her screen and turned to look at Lorne. "Have you searched the Quebec and Ontario lists? The Maritimes? The Prairies?"

"Yeah, searched those too... Nothing. I've Googled him, but all I can find is the 2003 stuff. His trail dies after that."

"Could have changed his name."

"Good thought." He checked the time on his computer screen. "Too early to phone E Division. I'll do that when I call for access to his hard drive archive."

"Hard drive archive?"

"The child porn evidence. From the charges on his record, it seems his computers were seized. Justice should still have the data that was used as evidence of the child porn."

"Complicated twists and turns you follow." She tipped her cup to peer in, then smiled at him. "More coffee? Breakfast?"

"Both. And a hug." They got up and merged.

"How about I do a big frittata?"

"Great. What can I do?"

"Stand around so I can ogle at you." She wiggled closer. "You're real eye candy for me. You could pull more espressos while you're at it."

As she diced the red pepper, she paused and looked up at him. "Your blog. The hits. Responses. You should check what's happening with it."

He activated his computer, opened his Blogger and clicked *Stats*. "Look at this, it's gone crazy." He swivelled the computer around toward her. "Over seven hundred thousand already today."

"That can't be today." She leaned closer. "My fuck! It is! Over two million on the week. What is it? Not two days yet. Fuck!"

He walked around the island to stand beside her and clicked to Twitter. "God, *#Hypocritic* is at the top of Trends."

"There, number two, *#DiningFraud.*"

"Let me change the location — it's set on *Current*." He clicked *Change* and selected *Canada*. "Wow! No difference I'm the top two. It appears we've been missing the action."

"It seems also as if people were suspecting something. Most of them are too insecure about their own tastes to say anything." She looked at him and shook her head. "You've certainly opened the floodgates."

"How's your response?" He reached across the island, picked up her computer and put it in front of her.

She opened her Blogger and clicked *Stats, Overview*, and they looked at the graph. "Not millions, but I've never before topped a hundred thousand."

He clicked back to his Twitter and changed the location back to *Current*. "Look here, *#MysteryDinner* number seven in Trends."

"That's in Vancouver. How's it in Canada?"

"Not in the top ten. Yet."

"What do you mean, yet?"

"I've two spare Twitter accounts I can use to point people from my blog to yours and vice versa. It shouldn't take long." He smiled at her. "It's called marketing."

"I wonder how Bottom Line is liking the attention. I'm sure he wishes he hadn't killed us. Now he has no way to stop this."

"Except to crash the servers. Robotham says he's bigger than us." He looked at her and chuckled. "But Google's Blogger is much bigger than he'll ever be."

"You're pretty sure it's Robotham, aren't you?" She turned back to her dicing.

"Too many things pointing at him. Corruption, child porn, his knowing me. Be interesting to see what his other kinks are."

"Other kinks?"

"Yeah. The criminal record. Possession and distribution, but not making or accessing child porn. There has to be something else, another reason he had kiddie porn."

"What about George, Nutcracker? Fuck, I still go queasy when I think of that."

"I'm sure he disappeared from Molly's soon after they realised we'd found the GPS thing."

"Yeah, you're right; he wouldn't stay around."

"I can go back through my files to find his trial, but I thought the paedophilia unit would locate him easier. We'll likely find him through Bottom Line as we dig." He glanced at the clock. "I'll do that after breakfast. What can I do?"

"You can crack and beat the eggs while I sauté this. Five should do it. Seven or eight grinds of pepper and throw in a smidge of dried tarragon. No need for salt; the ham will add enough."

"A bit of water to steam and add fluffiness, that okay?"

"Exactly what I do. We're so much alike."

He stepped across to her and ran a hand up her thigh, paused on her mound and then continued up to her left breast. "Yes, but we've marvellous differences."

She trembled and turned to hug him, and they stood swaying and mashing bodies. After a minute or so, she sighed. "Well, there's another fresh pair creamed." They kissed, then continued their beating and tossing.

After breakfast they returned to their computers, Catherine continuing through lip stretching images while Lorne phoned E Division headquarters. He was on his second call when she whooped and waved her arms.

He glanced over at the screen she had turned toward him, smiled and grabbed her hand. "I have to go. Something's come up here. Anything else?... I'll watch for it, thanks." He clicked off.

"My God, she could set-up a scrapyard with all that. What's she do at airports?" He laughed. "She probably enjoys the personal searches."

Catherine clicked back to the previous image. "Here's her tiger, her pussy cat. I'd say it's intimidating."

"*CynCat*. Good screen name. Plays on Cynthia, sin and her pussy cat. God, what a mess she's made of herself." He took Catherine's hand, pulled her up, and they hugged. "Not so hard to track down these people, is it? They want to show off."

"The hard part is choking back the sick."

"Yeah, let's hope we're nearing the end of it." He lifted her up by the waist and kissed her, putting an arm under her butt to hold her as she clung to his neck and wrapped her legs around him. They locked in a deep kiss.

Chapter Fifty-Five

Lorne and Catherine held their hugging kiss until his phone bing-bonged. He pulled his mouth away long enough to say *email*. He took two short steps, set her butt on the island, and they played kissy face.

"We'll have to try this one without our clothes in the way." Catherine wrapped her legs tighter. "Damned near came only thinking about it." She laid her head on his shoulder and kissed his neck. "So what's the email?"

"It's likely the name change. Too soon to be the court archive contents."

"You want to check?"

"Guess we should get back at it. Before I start mine, I can set you up combing CynCat's posts for comments, likes, follows. Find out who she follows, comments to, and so on. See if she uses the same name on Shufflr and do the same there. It's a great tangled web. They spread more than their legs all over it."

He showed her the basics and left her to it, then turned to his own computer. "Yup, this is what I thought it would be. The name change was approved on 1 December 2010 from *ROBOTHAM, William Charles to CHARLES, William.*"

"That was soon after he was released, wasn't it?"

He tabbed to the criminal record. "Yeah, released tenth of November. Name change to William Charles three weeks later."

"Yeah, the time it took to submit the application and have it approved."

"Interesting. He failed to report the name change. They're investigating."

Michael Walsh

"Failed to report?"

"The Sex Offender Registry. They have to report annually and within a week of any change of address, employment, volunteering. I'm sure name change is also a requirement."

"Is he still reporting as Robotham?"

"Don't know, but I'm going to find out." He opened the email, hit *Reply* and started typing.

Catherine returned to her searching, reading through the comments on each of the posted images. When she saw that Lorne had sent the email, she said, "This is quite funny, these comments. The women talking technique back and forth with each other, like discussing quilt stitches or how to grow better basil."

"I've seen a lot of that, making it seem doing this stuff is normal. It's always struck me as strange. We don't post pictures of trimming our toenails and discuss the different techniques."

She tapped Lorne's arm. "Look at this. She's showing how she clips her weights on, and in the comments, she's discussing the benefits of going regimental. Allows her to do weight stretching as she works. Fuck! The image of her with dangling weights swinging as she hosts. Fuck, guess that's why she wears long skirts most of the time."

"I can see why she has trouble keeping..." His phone bing-bonged, and he turned to the computer to open the new email. "Slippery fellow. Shows here he reported twice as Robotham, 2010 a week after he was released and his annual in 2011, then he stopped." He continued reading, shaking his head slowly. "So much for the Sex Offender Registry. They lost track of him shortly after his release."

"At least we have his new name, William Charles, to work with." She looked up from her computer and caught his frustration.

"Very stale. He would have used it only long enough to get a whole new identity. Prison's a great networking place, connections to the whole organised crime world. Likely had everything set-up before he left."

"The basic structure for the restaurant thing, anticipating the move from the drug distribution monopoly that the idiocy of the war on drugs had created for them." She shrugged. "Yanks!"

"Stupid, isn't it? The USAians still defending that, protecting the rights of organised crime to distribute. Gun lobby, I guess."

"Yeah, incredibly stupid. Defending their God-given right to shoot their neighbours. God, I wish they'd come up with a name for themselves. Yanks is limiting, USAian sounds... Sounds hokey. They keep insisting, but the rest of the Americas no longer tolerate their usurping American and America, sullying, debasing and despoiling our reputation." She shrugged. "USofAins from USofAia? I don't know."

They resumed digging in their computers, quietly focusing on their quests. Near noon, his phone bing-bonged again. He waited for the email to arrive in his computer, then opened it and scanned it quickly. "The data from Roboth... From Bottom Line's computer. Three hundred and eighty-seven Gigs. They've received a copy."

"God, three eighty-seven. Take a long time to send that."

"They've asked me if I have room."

"Do you?"

"Yeah, but it'll nearly stuff my drive."

"The Cloud?"

"Too much breach."

"Yeah."

"I'll ask them to send over a physical drive." He turned back to his computer, typed a reply and sent it, then looked up at her. "Anything interesting with our sinister cat?"

"Other than way too much focus on her cunt?"

"Strange stuff, isn't it?"

"I had no idea."

"Break?"

"Fuck, yes."

"Both those?"

"Yes."

Chapter Fifty-Six

At thirteen forty, while Lorne and Catherine were enjoying a big fruit salad with yoghurt, the phone rang. Lorne looked at the time as he stood. "Must be the hard drive copy, they said it would take over an hour to complete." He picked up the phone. "Hello."

"Hi, Lorne, it's Denise... Wondering if I could come up."

He turned to Catherine. "It's Denise." He nodded as he passed the phone to her.

"Sure, come on up, we're just finishing lunch. Fifteen minutes we'll be clear." She listened. "No, not at all, we'd love to see you." She listened again. "Yeah, Lorne understands that stuff." She clicked off and looked up. "Said she'll buzz us from the entry phone."

"Yeah, that's the easiest." They returned their attention to the fruit salad, and he was putting the dishes and cutlery in the washer when the phone rang again. "Quick fifteen minutes." He glanced at the clock as he answered. "Hello."

"Wilor."

"What's the date?"

"Twenty-three June."

"Three five nine."

"Package for you."

"I'll buzz you in." He turned to Catherine. "Robotham's hard drive."

He was heading toward the door to wait for the package when the phone rang again. "If that's Denise, press *nine*."

Half a minute later there was a knock on the door, and Lorne looked through the peephole to see Denise and a man amiably chatting.

He opened the door and smiled at them. "Is this a raid?" He laughed and motioned them in.

"This is Corporal Abadzu," Denise introduced. "Worked with him before my promotion... Small world."

Lorne shook hands, signed for the package, thanked the Corporal and locked the door behind him after he had left.

"Always so busy?" Denise laughed.

"Only when I'm onto... When we're onto something." He smiled at her and motioned along the hall. "Come in."

She nodded at the package. "You need to handle that?"

"Yeah, heavy stuff. Computer contents from Robotham, the defence lawyer. He's out now, but he skipped NSOR four years ago. No trace of him until he tried to kill us Wednesday night."

"God, I should leave and let you go at it."

He put a hand on her shoulder and guided her along the hall. "I need breaks, I have to allow myself big pieces of reality to punctuate stuff like this. It helps me keep my sanity." He led her to the couch and motioned her to sit.

"Tea? Would you like a cup of rooibos?" Catherine asked from the sink as she began filling the kettle with water.

"Lovely, thank you." Denise stared blankly for a short while. "So lonely without Jim..." She looked down at her hand on her belly. "Three weeks into this, he was off to Haiti as part of the United Nations stabilisation force."

"Jim's in the military?"

"No, RCMP like me. People warned us marriage and service life don't mix well. Fifth anniversary's next week. He'll be away for that and for most of this." She rubbed her belly.

Michael Walsh

Catherine brought Denise the box of Kleenex. "Tea'll be ready shortly." She sat on the couch beside her.

Lorne waved the package. "Work calls. You two relax." He cut the security tape, undid the wrapping, pulled out the USB drive and connected it to a port to begin sifting through it. A search for *jpg* led to a huge archive of images in Robotham's Documents folder, named *Other*. He clicked to the list of subfolders: *Big, Huge, HugeBoy, Incuse, Me, Micros, Nullos, Penectomy, SelfSuck, Stubs, Trophies.* He nodded his head as he scanned their names, then he opened one and scrolled through the images.

Catherine heard his mutter and saw his grimace. "Have you found something?"

He looked across at her and slowly nodded. "Yeah, it looks like he fits the profile."

"How so? What profile?"

"Too heavy for the moment. I'd love more tea." He rose from his seat, picked up the teapot and offered some to Denise and Catherine, poured a fresh cup for himself and sat on the couch, leaning back and sighing.

Catherine stroked his chest. "It's much lighter over here. Leave that for a while."

"Yeah." He sat up and shook his head. "There are some horridly twisted people out there."

"Are you getting a better picture of him?"

"Yeah. He's gay, the bottom half, so he would have been popular in prison. He has a size fixation, both extremes from incuse to huge. He's into penectomies and he collects penises..." Lorne stopped when he heard the gasps.

Catherine and Denise both managed to control their gags, and they sat staring at him.

"Sorry, I've been doing this on my own too long." Lorne's eyes revealed his distress as they flicked from face to face. "Sorry, I didn't stop to think."

Catherine put her hand on his knee and offered him a crooked smile. "Take a long break from it. Denise is telling me about early pregnancy symptoms. That's weird enough for now."

They sat lightly chatting and sharing for much of another hour, then Denise glanced at her watch. "I should be going. Things to do. All of us."

After they had seen her out and locked the door, they stood and hugged. "She's a nice woman. So soft and genuine. It must be hard on her handling the shit her duty brings."

Catherine stared into his eyes. "She was telling me how hard she has to work to remain detached from it. And you. You wallow in much worse crap voluntarily." She squeezed him and rose to her toes. "Kiss me, you crazy man."

They went back to their computers and focused. Nearly two hours later, Lorne thrust a fist into the air. "Yes! Got him!"

She looked over at him. "Watcha got?"

"His avatar. He named the image file *BotMan.jpg* so we now know *Bot-Man* was his screen name then. Maybe it still is. He's a bottom, an asshole with a fixation on big stuff to cram into it."

"Botman, Robotham, Bottom Line. So stupidly transparent."

"It seems to be part of the excitement for some. Showing off and riding the edge of discovery."

"So where do we go now?"

"See if we can find posts, likes, comments from *BotMan*. One word, uppercase *B* and *M*. What theme do you want to start with, the penectomies or the huge?"

She reached a hand across to his crotch and pressed. "Huge. Let's start with this one. We need a break."

Chapter Fifty-Seven

An hour and a quarter later, they resumed their searching in the computers. Catherine continued with the huge penis theme, searching through Shufflr archives for mentions of BotMan. Lorne browsed to bmexx, typed BotMan into the login and received the *Enter Correct User Name* result. He tried changing cases, still nothing. "Any luck with BotMan on Shufflr?"

"The account exists, but the page is blank, except for a link to Archive. There are no posts there. I've struck out. I'm now scanning through HiredBum." Catherine gave him an eew expression. "God, there are a lot of exhibitionist assholes out there."

"Yeah, no BotMan on bmexx." He ran his fingers through his hair, then went again to Robotham's data and scrolled down the list of folders. He opened HugeBoy. "Yeah, what I thought. This is what got him the child porn charges." He turned his screen toward Catherine. "Pictures of me at fourteen and fifteen."

"So, he would have gotten those from Connolly."

"Or copied them off other sites on the net. Most of the images on sites like Shufflr, Tumblr, Pinterest and the ilk are copied from elsewhere. These are in HugeBoy. You search for that, see if that account exists, I'll start on SelfSuck."

"Self suck?"

"One of his other folders here." He looked at her with a twisted smile. "Me sucking me."

"You still have to demonstrate that for me." She smiled at him, then turned back to her computer and typed: *hugeboy.shufflr.com* and received a *Nope Not Here* comment. "I find nothing here."

"Yeah, the court would have ordered it removed after the convictions. Likely scrubbed from most places." He turned back to his computer to see a page of images had loaded. "Appears SelfSuck is here." He clicked *Archive* and hit *Command* and the *Down* arrow. "Let's find out how far back they go." He continued to command scroll toward the end as the page loaded.

She watched as he scrolled down through the years. "There are a lot fewer images per month than I've been seeing. It's certainly not as common." She laughed. "Everyone has a butt hole, but not many can suck themselves."

"Damn. Didn't think. Shufflr's too new, a decade or so old." He Googled *shufflr wiki* and clicked the Wikipedia entry. "Yeah, founded 2007. Have to do this through bmexx, it goes back to 2000."

He tabbed to the USB data drive and clicked on *BigBoy*. "These are what we're searching for." He scrolled slowly through the dozens of images.

"He was a sick man, forcing you to do that, then spreading it to the world."

"Most of the time he was very kind and..."

"Fuck! How can you say that after what he did to you?"

"He was." Lorne continued to sequence through the images. "We need to find some of these — even one of them on bmexx."

He tabbed back over to Chrome and logged into the site, clicked to *Surgical*, then to *Subincisions & Genital Splitting*.

"God! I cannot believe all these categories exist, let alone all the stuff that's posted under them. Thousands of images of splitting dicks." She shook her head. "So sick."

Lorne clicked to the last page. "We'll start at the beginning and work forward. The first posts here are in 2000." He expanded the browser window four clicks for a larger view of the thumbnails, then clicked to the previous page.

"There!" She pointed. "That's you."

He clicked the image to expand it in a new tab.

"Fuck! Your face. Your eyes rolled up to look into the camera."

"He always wanted me to look at the camera."

"Fuck! The pervert."

"Here, look at all the comments." He started scrolling down. "Long scroll, lots of likes and comments. I'll head to the end and see if I can find its origin." He continued to click *Load More* as the scroll bottomed-out.

"So many comments."

"Yeah, more than fifteen years to gather them."

"Fuck! This has been spreading exponentially all that time."

"Haven't looked at this since I gave the files and links to the Mounties to get them moving on Connolly." He continued clicking *Load More* each time the scroll ended and finally reached the bottom. "Here, comment from BotMan to PussMakr 10/5 2000." *Love the image. Still one of your best. Have you more?*

"So who's PussMakr?"

"We'll find out. This is a USAian site, so the date's backwards. The fifth of October 2000. That's two months before I contacted the Mounties, six months before he was charged."

"He? Who?"

"Connolly."

"Connolly... PussMakr... His slicing?" She put her hand to her mouth to quell a gag. "Trying to make his stuff into a pussy?"

He put his arm around her shoulder and pulled her to his chest. "Yeah, that makes sense... Lie down for a while?"

"Yeah. A long while."

It was eighteen fifty when they returned to the computers after a comforting cuddle and a refreshing nap. "You still seem a bit shell-shocked from this." He stood behind her and massaged her neck and shoulders. "Why don't you read through your blog comments, get a feel for what's happening."

"Yeah. I should browse the news too. We've been out of the loop for a few days. I'll see if the world still exists." She pressed a hand on his. "Feels so nice. You should also check your blog."

"Yeah, but first I'm going to follow your idea on Bottom Line's email server, see where that leads."

He woke his computer, logged in and entered *www.iam-ru.ru*. "Look at this, a gay porn site. Clever name, like it's saying: *I am. Are you?*"

"It's in English? That's a Russian url."

"Doesn't mean it's in Russia, though."

"Yeah. No real borders to the internet, are there?"

He looked at the buttons on the welcome page: *Log In, Free Tour, Join* and clicked *Free Tour*. Inside was a list of category buttons with images and he read down the column: *Bears, B-Jays, Bottoms, HunGuys, Selfies, TinyTims, Twinks*. At the bottom was a red button with *Our Hard Site* on it.

He clicked on *Twinks*, watched a page of thumbnails load and scanned through them. He magnified his browser four clicks to expand the images, then back down one to stop the pixelation. "Found me again." He clicked on the thumbnail.

"Let's see." She leaned over and looked at the image. "At least your face is out of focus in this one. What's this mean, the title: *Twink EE YY?* Sounds like one of those horrid things the Yanks called pastry when we were young."

"Gay code. Twink is officially young-looking, but means young. They hide a lot of child porn there."

"And the EE and YY?"

"More code. E is endowed, and Y is young."

"So very endowed and very young."

"Yeah, basically."

"Sick people."

"Yeah, basically."

She pointed to the url in the browser window. "So is this Bottom Line's site?"

"Could be. Could also be offering emails as part of the site membership."

"Did you join to get here?"

"No, I'm on a free tour."

"Find out how far it takes you."

"Great idea." He clicked *Back* and selected *Our Hard Site*.

Another tab opened, and they watched as the images slowly populated the page. "Graphics intensive, not good for slow connections." She pointed to the Chrome window. "Look at the url: *imBMEX.ru*. Appears they want to emulate bmexx.com."

"Similar selection of categories. Very similar." He clicked *Join*, and they looked at the page. "This is clever marketing. Wow! Look at that: *Free Week Membership for Transfer from other bmex site.*"

"And this one: *Only one approved posted image per week to maintain your free membership.* It seems they're harvesting members and images."

He smiled at the screen, closed his computer, then hugged her. "Tomorrow. The rest of today is us." In a low, purring voice he continued, *"He leaned to kiss her, his hand moving to cup a breast and tease the nipple between his fingers..."*

Catherine's giggle was muffled by his lips.

Chapter Fifty-Eight

Lorne and Catherine lay in bed long after they woke in the morning, enjoying each other and finding new ways to pleasure. "What's so complicated about this?" He nibbled her earlobe and gave another gentle pelvic thrust. "I guess we're blessed knowing who we are, accepting who we are and feeling confident."

"I wonder whether all the marketing, the planting of doubt, the feeding of insecurity leads to some of the crap we're seeing. My tits are too small, my ears are too plain, my face needs a slathering of goo, I need labels on the outside of my clothes, my hair's the wrong colour. Fuck!" She gave him a long, tight Kegel.

He responded with a light tug. "You're not going to bite it off like Cyn-Cat threatens, are you?" He laughed.

"We need to see if we can link her to the asshole." She rotated her hips.

"Yeah. Possibly through the new bmexx site."

"Find George there too. What about Frick?" She rocked her hips.

"Don't know. Guess we should search for him too." He gave a series of long slow thrusts. "You want to finish and get up?"

She looked at the bedside clock. "Yeah, we should, it's almost ten thirty."

Forty minutes later, they sat enjoying espressos with their ham and cheese croissants on the balcony. "I love the gentle warmth of late June and early July before the summer fully kicks in."

"Do you sunbathe out here often?"

Michael Walsh

"Whenever the weather allows. It's a marvellously private place. I guess a telescope up there might see something, a block away, but if that's their thing, it would be much easier for them on the net."

"I'm amazed at how much stuff is posted there. The variety of it, and the willingness of people to spread themselves all over the web." She looked at him with pursed lips and a frown. "You're spread rather broadly out there. Involuntarily, unwillingly."

"Yeah, even with the court-ordered scrubbing, the images are still common, still slowly spreading." He put his cup to his lips and paused. "It's tough, though, to recognise me from those early teen shots. I'm thankful for that."

"Yeah, the long stubble on your face changes the impression immediately. People wouldn't relate back. Your face is craggier now too, devastatingly handsome instead of pretty boy." She glanced down at his crotch, nodded and laughed. "That hasn't changed much, though."

He looked down, then up to her eyes. "I show my face in public now, but that is between you and me." He smiled.

"There must be a lot of malicious posting of other's images. Think of the paparazzi and their photos of the famous, they've a viral spread quite often."

"Impossible to stop once it starts."

She laughed. "Have you seen any of those videos of the girls' night out at the male strip club? Ones like Dancing Bears?"

"Not sure what you mean."

"Women, grown women out and partying. An office party or a girls' stag. They're all over the net. Even mainline sites."

He shook his head. "Not familiar."

"They usually start with music, booze and dancing with each other, then male strippers start circulating among the women and enticing them. Let me get my computer; you have to watch one. It's too hard to explain."

She came back with her computer, logged in, entered a search, selected one of the results and clicked the arrow. "Here's one, *Office Party*. I've

274

seen it before, researching for one of my books. This one gets right into it. Watch how that blonde loses herself with him, does it in front of all the women from her office."

He watched quietly for a while, then shook his head. "How does she face her co-workers after that?"

"Or face her friends, her family after it spreads. This one was up over five million views two years ago when I modelled one of my characters on her, on that blonde. I'm sure it's much higher now." She clicked the *Back* arrow and checked. "Yeah, up over eighteen million now."

"Blow a stripper, blow your reputation. Wow! In front of her whole office. Now in front of the whole world."

"Several of the others soon joined in, so at least she had some support back at the office." She shook her head and shrugged. "There are a lot of videos like this out there."

"That's amazing. It'll be there forever, always reminding her. She'll always wonder who's watched her stroke, lick and suck a stranger in public. She's ruined all chances for any public office. Actually, for anything in public."

"The stupidity of it is she knew the video was being shot. She waved at the camera with a mouthful of him in one sequence. Comical if it weren't so serious." She closed her computer and gave him a twisted face. "Ready for more of the heavier stuff?"

"No, but I have to keep at it." He stood, picked up their plates and cups and followed her inside.

Back at the counter in front of their computers, he browsed again to imBMEX.ru. "I'll set-up a new account for each of us. Who do you want to be, *6and7eighths or 175soft*?"

"What are those?"

"Sorry. New accounts I'm setting up on imBMEX.ru." He smiled at her. "One for the Yanks and one for the rest of the world."

She stared at him with a puzzled face, then laughed. "Good names, inches and millimetres. Guess the name needs to entice, doesn't it?"

Michael Walsh

"Yeah, some use gobbledygook, but to get better response, it's best to put out a piece of bait. People scanning screen names will quickly click on an intriguing one. Common sense."

"It's like marketing." She shrugged. "Make mine metric."

He Photoshopped four images of himself from the USB drive, set-up a new account as *175soft*, uploaded two faceless photos, then waited for the confirming email. He clicked the link to activate it. "One done. See if you can log in."

She clicked to the site in her computer and entered *175soft*. "Password?"

"Sorry... Push the Shift key, type *6h6*, then release the Shift and type *245*."

She entered and clicked. "I'm in. Look at this: *You have 13.9 days of pleasure remaining. Top-up anytime.*"

"Great way to harvest images."

"So where should I start?"

"CynCat is a good place... Check if she's there, I'll set-up and search for PussMakr to see if I can find Robotham and him commenting. They must have known each other before the trial. How else would he be conspiring with and defending him?"

"Isn't this site too new for that? Connolly died in captivity. No access to this site."

"Yeah, stupid of me, didn't think. His *BigSplitBoy* account on bmexx would have been taken down with the child porn conviction. But I bet his PussMakr is still there."

He logged in to bmexx and searched. "Yup."

Chapter Fifty-Nine

Lorne browsed through the PussMakr images on bmexx. "Christ, Connolly was still updating this stuff after he was charged. The newest one is 20 August 2003, during his trial, a week before he was convicted."

"Dedicated." Catherine shook her head.

"He was likely screaming for help in the only way he knew. He was so calm in the courtroom. Anything interesting with the comments on Cynthia's posts?"

"Mundane. *Nice, cool, rad*, and comments like that. A few questions, technique and pain related, mainly. I'll keep scrolling."

Lorne expanded an image, took a screenshot and saved it. He repeated this a few more times with other images Connolly had posted of himself, then he set-up a new PussMakr account on imBMEX.ru. "Time for the new PussMakr to go bottom fishing."

"Let's see."

He clicked on the first image and turned his screen toward her. She sat staring at the picture with her hand to her mouth. He put his arm around her shoulders and hugged. "Not pretty at all, is it?"

"And he made you watch as he did this to himself? Fuck!"

"Guess I slowly became numbed to it. He treated the sessions as anatomy lectures, explaining the layers as he cut..." He felt her tense and stopped. "Time for another break." He picked her up and carried her to the bed. "Cuddle and nap time."

A little past fourteen thirty he sat again at his computer as she put the kettle on for tea. "Here we go. One comment already. Listen to this: *Pleased to see you're out. Welcome to the site. I'll PM you. rubme.*"

"Rub me? Is that inviting a tug job?" She laughed. "Hey! One picks up on the jargon going through this stuff."

"A clever name, *rubme*, asking are you bme and implying the Russian site."

"Do you think it's Robotham?" She walked around the island to stand beside him and look at his screen.

"We'll find out." He pointed to the small flashing flag on his screen. "Connolly has a private message." He clicked the flag, and a half-screen window opened.

Hi Francis: How do you like my new site? When were you released? Tried to track you, but couldn't get any information. Where are you? Bill.

"Bill?" She looked at him. "William Charles. That was it, wasn't it? His name."

"Yeah. A lot of things pointing."

"How are you going to reply? Surely you'll reply."

"Oh, for sure. I need to research first, though. We need a strong line. There's too much risk of losing the fish without it."

"How? What do you need?"

"A storyline, conversation history from a decade and a half ago. I can't risk jumping into the conversation without it. I'll have to dig back through cunt maker's postings and responses. See if I can find comments from Robotham, whatever he called himself. We're back to searching for the needle, but at least we have the haystacks now." He turned his head up and gave her crooked smile.

She bent and kissed the smile. "What about his email files?" She pointed to the USB drive.

"Stupid me. Of course." He stood and hugged her.

"See, there's another reason to keep me around."

He clicked to the drive and started searching. She brought him a tea and sat beside him to watch as he worked his way through trees of contents. Several minutes later, he turned to her with a frown. "As I'd feared, I need to fire-up my old Microsoft clunker to get into this, it's in Outlook."

"At least you've found it."

"Let's hope he did all his email on Outlook, not on a web-based place. A lawyer, early 2000s, most likely." He opened a cupboard, pulled out an old Toshiba and plugged it in. "I haven't been into this in two years or more. It'll take a good ten or fifteen minutes before the battery comes up enough to start the system. You ever use Microsoft?"

"Only when forced to... Libraries and such. I find it awkward."

"Yeah, I bought this piece of crap five or six years ago when I needed to access some emails." He returned to browsing in imBMEX.ru, bringing up rubme's posts. "Take a look at this. It appears he's either stumped himself or he's been lopped."

"Do I want to look?"

"Maybe not." He looked at her. "I'm dragging you into a lot of crap, aren't I?"

She looked at his screen. "This is rather benign compared to some of the crud I've been looking at. At least this isn't still raw and bleeding like Connolly's."

"Yeah, it appears to be fully healed. His files, the USB drive, the image folders. Stubs." He clicked the drive open and scrolled to the document folder and found the image tree. *Big, Huge, HugeBoy, Incuse, Me, Micros, Nullos, Penectomy, SelfSuck, Stubs, Trophies.* He clicked *Me* and then on the first thumbnail. "He looks the same now as he did back then."

"Why would he have done that to himself?"

"It could have been done to him."

"Yeah, that's possible. An accident. An angry lover. Fuck!"

"A way to find out here. One of the other folders, *Penectomy.*" He clicked *Back*, then opened the folder and looked at the first image. After scrolling through a few, he stopped and returned to the first one. "This is what it was like before he started on himself. You don't want to see the rest of them."

She looked up from her own screen and across to his. "He was rather huge — once. I wonder why he would have done it."

"Why do people pierce their ears? Get breast implants? Dye their hair, wear makeup?"

"Yeah. Unhappy with themselves. He must have been very, very unhappy." Catherine turned back to her computer to continue searching while Lorne opened the Toshiba and clicked it on, then waited for it to load.

"I wonder whether they've ever fixed this long load time." He watched the spinning. "Three or four minutes to start and nearly the same to shut down."

"No, still the same. I can open my MacBook, do my emails, Blogger, Facebook and Twitter, and close it before Cynthia can even get into her machine. She still swears by Microsoft, though at times it seems she's closer to swearing at it."

The Toshiba finally cycled on, and Lorne logged in to close a long series of update pop-ups as they bred on the screen. When he finally convinced the ghost of Gates that he didn't want to update, and he had stopped the other harassments, he connected the USB drive. He searched for *PST* and quickly found his way back to the email files, then clicked around and finally got Outlook to open.

He clicked contacts and scrolled down. "Got him. Here's Francis Connolly." He typed *fr* and hit *Enter*. "And here's Gustav Frick. This is going to be interesting."

Chapter Sixty

Lorne started reading through the email exchanges between Robotham and Connolly, gaining an understanding of their professional and personal relationships. He read a few of them to Catherine and after an hour and three-quarters, he drafted a reply to the PM and read it aloud.

Hi, Bill... Thought that was you. Very nice site, better than the other. A few weeks now, still trying to settle-in. Tough. God bless, Francis.

"What do you think? Does that carry the tone?" He watched her nodding.

"Yeah, that sounds like him. I'd say send it."

He read it again silently, then pressed *Send*. "Gone." He glanced at the time on his computer screen. "Sixteen forty, how long do you think?" He leaned to kiss her.

"I would guess within the hour. What about Doctor Sick? Have you read any of those emails?"

"A lot of the later ones were among the three of them as they scrambled. I'll continue back to see how far it goes. See if I can find where their relationship started."

"Did you find the beginning of Robotham's with Connolly?"

"Yeah." He put his arm around her shoulder again and gave a little squeeze. "I don't think you'd enjoy it."

"My guess is they were talking about relieving Connolly of an unwanted part."

"Yeah. Robotham was going to do him when the Mounties brought charges."

"So Robotham switched from cutting to defending. Where does Frick come in?"

"I'm going to find out." He pointed to his screen. "I'm sure it's all here." He stood, moved behind her and reached his hands around to cup her breasts. "I need a break."

She turned her face to meet his lips as he bent. "A naked cuddle would be nice. I'm frazzed."

It was nineteen ten when she woke, still entangled and connected. "Amazing how tiring that stuff is. Emotionally and physically draining. You been awake long?"

"Not long. A few minutes. I was lying here thinking how much you mean to me. How much I love you."

"How much?" She giggled and squeezed a Kegel.

"They haven't invented the word for it yet, but a lot more than that." He chuckled. "Squeeze me up, Katy."

"Oh God, what was that? Space Wars or Sky Trek or something? Beam me up, Scotty." She did a slow series and felt him expand.

He began a gentle in and out to speed the process. Forty minutes later, they were back at the island counter reading the new message from *rubme*.

Hi, Francis... You back in Vancouver? Where? I can give you a room for a while. Do you still need my help with the excess bit? Bill.

"So it seems Robotham's in Vancouver."

"Appears to be, unless he simply has a connection here who has a room he can offer."

"Yeah, but the help thing. Sounds as if he's offering his cutting services to... Fuck! I'm getting numbed to this. Seems almost like discussing a carpentry project." She did a mock finger gag.

"I guess to them it *is* nothing but a project."

She stroked his forearm and nodded to the computer. "So what are you going to answer?"

"I'm going to read through the email exchange with Frick first to get a larger picture."

"Good thought. They must go back to before the trial for their manipulative conspiracy. I'll start dinner." She stood, kissed him, and walked to the fridge to explore. "There are still two pieces of snapper. How's that?"

"Huh! You say something?" He looked up from the screen.

"I said we're having snapper for dinner."

"Great." He refocused on the computer, then abruptly turned his head toward her. "I love you. You know that, don't you?"

"Silly question. How could I ever not know that?"

Twenty odd minutes later, he looked up from his screen. "Mine wasn't the first case they've played their scam with, just the first one they were caught with."

"What have you found?"

"So far, I've found that he and Frick played this defence and expert witness game twice before, both of them priests. Got them both off. They must have been working for the Church, but I haven't found anything connecting them. Yet."

"How far back into it are you?"

"Three years, back to 2000. That's as far as I've gone. So sickening going through their conniving and scheming, twisting innocent boys into being the guilty ones." He put the Toshiba to sleep. "What can I do to help?"

"Wash your hands and sit. It's ready in two minutes."

After dinner, they leaned back on the couch relaxing as the dishwasher hummed in the background. She watched her hand as she stroked his chest. "You know enough about Frick now to mention him in your reply?"

"Yeah, there were long, three-way email conversations leading to and through the trial. I've a good sense now of the relationships among them. Clearly more than only the trial."

Michael Walsh

"How so?"

"There were small things through the text, but the major thing was their exchange of bmexx user names. BotMan, PussMakr and BorNullo."

"Bornullo? That sounds like a Tuscan wine?" She laughed. "You needn't give up wine with meals just because I have, Lorne."

"I want to keep you company. Besides, I don't miss it as much as I thought I would. A dozen years as part of my diet, but it seems unimportant now. How about you?"

"Same, I rarely missed having it, but now..." She looked down as their hands arrived on her belly at the same time. "Snap!" She grinned. "We're being silly. What's the Brunello thing?"

"BorNullo. I made a note to search, but got bogged down in the emails."

"Curious?"

"Cuddle?"

"Yeah."

A dozen silent minutes later, he reached down and squeezed her butt cheek. "Gotta write a reply to rubme and see what the frick Frick's about."

"What are you going to say?"

"I don't know. I didn't want to spoil our cuddle by thinking of anything but you."

"Oh, my God! You are so... So... God, I love you." She squeezed him tighter.

A few minutes later they were back at the computers. "You go search for BorNullo in imBMEX.ru, I'll comb through bmexx.com." He spelled it for her. "Upper case B and N, no spaces."

Half a minute later she said, "Nothing there."

He glanced over at her screen and laughed. "Yeah, same thing I found. He has an innie. Good name for himself; born nullo."

"What's nullo mean? I've seen that before in your headings. In the headings on Robotham's drive."

"From nullified. Eunuchs. Most often it refers to everything being removed, but sometimes only castrated or just the penis lopped off. His, though, is simply incuse. Born that way. Here, he's pierced the head and added a ring. Likely so he can pull it out a bit to pee without dribbling all over himself. God that would be messy."

"Yeah, look at this one, he's pulling it out with the ring, and this one, a big weight attached. I didn't realise penises came that short."

"Scarce, bordering on rare. Statistically quite similar to my end of the range." He nodded toward his crotch. "There are many of them posted across the net. A lot of sites, Shufflr pages and so on are dedicated to micros and minis. They also hide a lot of little boy images there. Child porn. But among the adults, there's a significant number whose penises don't quite reach the surface or barely peek out. I prefer my end of the range."

"Oh, God! So do I." She shivered lightly and smiled, then pointed to her screen. "It appears he wants his to be bigger, the other two don't seem to even want theirs. Three unhappy men."

Lorne sat and composed a reply in his notepad app and read it through a few times. Then he read it aloud to Catherine.

Hi, Bill... I'm with an old friend now in Kits, but feel I'm imposing. Where are you? You in touch with Gustav? God bless, Francis.

"I like that, but you've not mentioned the trimming."

"I thought I'd leave Robotham wondering. Keep his interest."

"Yeah, I can see that. Clever. I'd say send it."

He pasted the text into the IM reply box, read it through again, then clicked *Send*.

Chapter Sixty-One

The next morning, Lorne and Catherine lay in bed a long time, luxu-riating in each other before they showered and dressed, and it was ten past nine when Lorne turned on the espresso machine, then opened the freezer. "Only three croissants left, we need another shopping trip."

"Almost out of everything fresh too. Do you actually use a niqab and chador to go shopping?"

"Yeah, it's one of the best disguises. Most turn their eyes away. Few dare question them anymore, there've been too many religious discrim-ination charges. It's gone overboard."

"Strange, how overboard it's gone. The Quran tells them to dress with modesty by covering their breasts and genitals. They must be huge down there to need all that cover." She giggled.

"I can go out after breakfast, unless Denise calls. I don't want to impose on her to do more shopping." He looked in the fridge. "We could do ham and cheese croissants again, there's a nice piece of goat's cheese here for variety. How's that sound?"

She looked up from grinding the coffee. "Good for me. Maybe I could do..." She was interrupted by the phone's ring.

He clicked to speaker. "Hello."

"Hi Lorne, it's Denise. I'm really... I'd love to come up and talk with Catherine again."

"Have you had breakfast?" Catherine called as she moved toward the phone.

"Coffee only so far. Sort of feeling..."

"Come on up, we're trying to sort out what we're going to have ourselves."

Catherine sat on the couch with Denise, calming and comforting her as Lorne prepared the open-faced croissant sandwiches. Then they all moved to the balcony to share from the platter and sip their espressos.

"Tough to do alone." Denise looked at each in turn. "I really appreciate your allowing me to barge in like this."

"Funny, a while ago we were talking of phoning you, but didn't want to impose." She laughed. "Lorne was thinking of converting to Islam to go shopping."

"Damn! I was feeling so sorry for myself being alone with this, that I forgot you're like prisoners here. You must be out of everything. I'm not on 'til noon. I can do my own shopping while I'm there."

"Relax. We won't starve. I've stocked this place for long sieges. Not fresh, but sustaining, not the healthiest with all additives and preservatives, but..."

"I saw that from your shopping list the other day. You're really into fresh and local. Didn't need to leave the periphery of the store for you." She smiled at Lorne. "So, when you're not running from murderers, what do you do?"

He looked at Catherine, paused, then shrugged and saw her slight nod. "We're both writers, wine and food writers."

"God, have you been following the restaurant review scam thing? Amazing how it's spreading. Gone absolutely viral. The whole planet seems to be adding to it now."

"We've been a bit out of the current events loop, holed-up here." Lorne paused, saw Catherine's, pursed lips and then her nod. "My hypocritic blog post started it. That's why we're here."

"Fuck! Pardon my language, but fuck! What a great post!"

"Pardon granted." Catherine giggled. "We speak it fluently."

"So, you're the Unknown Diner?"

Lorne nodded to her. "Now three people know."

"So, who's K ate? My other favourite reviewer, the one who's pushed this thing to gazillions of likes."

Catherine raised her hand, grinned and wiggled her fingers.

"Fuck! My two favourite foodies, and I'm grocery shopping for you. Oh, my God."

"We haven't had time to do anything but glance at the response. Noticed it had gone viral on Twitter, but we've been buried digging through crap." Lorne shrugged. "Guess we should take a look. We have a hook well sunk now."

"You've someone hooked?"

"We don't know how big yet, but a long way up from a minnow. Connected to the current restaurant scam. I've followed threads back to the restaurant fraud trial at the beginning of the century when the sleazy lawyer got the Mafia off."

"The collapsing restaurant thing? Strange, wasn't that?"

"Stranger that the same person is connected to the current one."

"The same person?"

"Robotham. The lawyer at my trial. I don't know what trickery he pulled to spring the Montreal Family, but I'm sure he earned a lot of favours from it. He's apparently running their current restaurant scam. I'm not sure yet whether it's only locally or regionally or if it's nationally."

"We've wondered where they all went after their drug market began collapsing. It's been pleasantly quiet." She laughed. "Except for the usual real estate scams and the regular stock market corruption, it's been rather peaceful."

Lorne ran his fingers through his hair and stared blankly over the rooftops beyond the balcony railing. "I've found some stuff your people appear to have missed."

"We're aware we miss a lot of things. An overwhelming amount of stuff to handle sometimes. What do you have?"

"Two, and there are likely more, but I've dug through two cases where he's led to acquittals of perverted priests. There's clear evidence through email threads of conspiring fraudulent testimony from Frick. You remember Doctor Frick?"

"Never forget him for what he tried to do to you." She stared at him for a long time. "What an evil man he was."

"We suspect he's also a major player with the restaurant thing, doing the market manipulation."

"This is way too big for you alone, Lorne. Even for the two of you. Far too huge. We need to get you connected. Would you like some support, some help with this?"

"We'd love that." He sighed and nodded to her. "Yeah, we'd really love that. Can I pull you another espresso?"

Chapter Sixty-Two

Denise took out her phone and punched at it as Lorne went in to pull three more espressos. She was still on the phone when he returned with the cups, and he listened to her.

"... we'd need full twenty-four-hour security here. I think it would be better if they were there. Closer contact... I'll ask." She smiled up at Lorne as he set her cup on the table. "We've a secure suite at headquarters. Want to be moved? All the computer geeks are there, the whole investigative team is..."

She saw his nod and turned back to her phone conversation, confirming, and then arranging the details for their transfer. After she had clicked off her phone, she looked up and smiled. "Some things aren't meant to be carried alone."

Catherine put one hand on her own belly and extended her other hand across to Denise's. "Together. We'll go through this together."

"Yeah. Stronger this way." They leaned into a hug, then shuffled it closer. "Yeah, much stronger."

Thirty-five minutes later, they were escorted down the elevator and into a van in the parkade, then driven to E Division headquarters in Surrey and installed in a small suite.

"Spartan, but adequate." Lorne examined the rooms. "Better than some of those airport hotels. God! Remember that horrid place in Santiago when the flight was cancelled?"

"Strange thinking back to then. Five years ago. Five years married to Nathan. I couldn't stop thinking of you in the next room. My friend with whom I could talk. Stupid isn't it? How long it took me to realise I was unhappy with him. Really stupid."

They were beginning to unpack the two bags they had quickly stuffed at the loft, when there was a knock. He looked through the peephole at a uniformed man, then he opened the door to the Staff Sergeant.

"The Deputy Commissioner wishes to meet with you in half an hour. I'll come back in twenty minutes to escort you."

"Thank you, we'll be waiting." Lorne closed the door and looked at Catherine for a moment, then they merged in a hug.

After several silent minutes, Catherine said, "I should finish unpacking, and you should see if there's a response from your message to rubme."

He opened his computer and logged in. "We need access to the net. The wifi code." He thumbed on his iPhone, clicked *Hotspot* and enabled it, then back at his computer, he connected the Bluetooth. "Quite a bit slower this way, but I'm in."

He browsed to the site, clicked on the PM flag and read Catherine the reply:

"Hello, Francis... I'm in Yaletown. Gustav is running marketing for us. You write well, he can give you some work, if you need it. I'd love to do some work on you if you still don't want it. Be well, Bill."

"Interesting. In Yaletown. That has to be why he found *Tastevin* so quickly."

"My thoughts, exactly. So Frick is doing the marketing." He looked up at her from his computer screen. "We'll have to search for a connection between BorNullo and CynCat."

"Yeah, they're both involved in marketing, both into stretching and both on Robotham's bme site, so it should be easy to..." She was interrupted by the knock on the door. "Is that twenty minutes already?"

They were escorted to a small boardroom and introduced to the nine officers who were already waiting there, a Chief Superintendent, a Superintendent, four Inspectors and three Staff Sergeants. Among them were the

Michael Walsh

heads of the Child Exploitation, Homicide Investigation and the Market Enforcement departments, as well as inter-force liaisons with Federal and International Operations and the Vancouver Police Department. Deputy Commissioner Singh came in, acknowledged Catherine and Lorne, and asked everyone to take a seat at the boardroom table.

"Sorry for the short notice on this," Singh said. "But these two have uncovered something huge which crosses the lines between all of your departments, possibly other departments, but we'll start here." He looked at Lorne. "I'm going to let you ramble through this from the beginning, but to ensure they pay attention to you, I'll mention a few topics you'll be hitting."

Singh turned to the group. "Kidnapping, child porn, torture, mutilation, perjury, forgery, bribery, corrupting the courts and now widespread organised fraud and attempted murder." He looked at Lorne. "Have I missed anything?"

Lorne stood and nodded to Singh. "You've mentioned most of it, though I think at least one murder can also be added to the list." Lorne looked at Catherine and then at the group. "I'll not start there, but I'll mention now where I'm heading with the story. The murdered body pieces found in the Gastown alley last November, the boat explosion and fire at Quayside a few days ago and the restaurant fraud thing that's gone viral. Those are some of the places where this has evolved."

He paused and examined each face as he gathered his thoughts. "In 1996 I was chained in a garret and held captive there, sexually abused and mutilated by a priest for seventeen months. Some of you may remember the trial in 2003, and the subsequent ones for the defence lawyer and his expert witness."

Lorne watched as most of them nodded, then he continued the story with only sufficient detail to show the web of corruption and conspiracy which extended back at least a decade and a half and involved the organised crime mobs.

After he had brought the story to their current digging through the body modification and mutilation culture, he paused and scanned the faces again. "Last night, I discovered evidence that shows two child molesting priests were fraudulently acquitted. There are likely more, but my stomach couldn't handle going back any farther at that point." He stood watching the silent faces.

Singh broke the silence. "Ladies, gentlemen. Any questions? Comments?"

A hand popped out, followed by a voice. "Inspector Bourgeois, Child Exploitation. Where are you finding your evidence on what you call fraudulent acquittals?"

"From the computer files which were seized when Robotham was charged. I was beginning to mine the emails."

"And how have you access to these?"

"From Ottawa, Harold pushed it through."

"Harold?"

"Sorry. Commissioner Gillespie." There was silence again.

Singh stood. "Lorne's been working quietly but closely with us for more than a dozen years. Some of you know him by code and will have now related him to that. Ensure his identity remains secret." There was a nodding around the table.

Singh turned to Lorne. "Where should we start?"

Chapter Sixty-Three

Lorne looked at Deputy Commissioner Singh. "It might be best to begin by meeting with key people from each department for twenty or thirty minutes in turn, enough to get everybody started, then we can freelance as needed. Also, we need faster connections; tethering to our phones is a bit slow."

Singh stood. "Hopgood, you get a schedule put together. Let's get going on this. Who can set-up a wifi for them?" Three hands went up. "Good, Stevens, you see to that." He stepped over and shook Lorne's hand, then Catherine's. "We've worked together several times, Lorne. It's good to finally meet you in person. Let Hopgood there know if you need anything."

Lorne nodded to Singh. "We'd appreciate it if you thanked Denise... Staff Sergeant O'Brien for us. It's her initiative that got this thing rolling faster."

Singh looked along the table again. "Hopgood, you know Staff Sergeant O'Brien?"

"Yes, Sir. She's leading one of the Market Enforcement teams... Commercial Fraud, she'll be fully involved with this."

"Have her come see me."

"I'll have it arranged, Sir."

Singh glanced at the wall clock as he turned back to Catherine and Lorne. "Lunch time shortly. I would be honoured if you joined me."

Seeing Lorne's nod, he continued. "Great... I'd love a broad overview of this. Let the departments deal with the details." He motioned for Hopgood to join them.

"Yes, Sir."

"Grab Ferguson. Organise sandwiches for five in my office for twelve thirty." He laughed. "Have them tell the cafeteria they're for restaurant reviewers, maybe we can get something upscale for a change."

"Sir?"

"Joking, Hopgood, only joking."

He turned back to Catherine and Lorne. "Quite the game they're playing; manipulating the reviewers."

Catherine nodded. "The sad part is that many of the reviewers are playing their game. They're turning a blind eye to reality."

"The problem is that reviews are only opinions." Lorne ran his fingers through his hair and shrugged. "The valid ones, though, are unbiased, based on a depth of knowledge and experience, both aesthetic and technical, and importantly, on a proven ability to discern quality. It's a subtle thing. How does one review a reviewer? Is this new marketing approach fair or fraudulent?"

"It appears to be misrepresentation," Singh said. "Similar to bait and switch, to false advertising."

"But the restaurants aren't doing the reviews." Lorne shrugged his shoulders. "What they're doing is wining and dining the reviewers and offering them easy tools to write and illustrate their reviews."

"That's the slick defence lawyer's argument." Singh shook his head. "The courts will likely accept it, even though everyone knows it's fallacious. Everyone but the letter of the law."

"That's the balancing act they're playing; teetering on the edge of legality." Lorne shrugged. "You must admit, it's clever."

Catherine spoke up, "Yes, okay, but what about the sites like Yelp, Tripadvisor, Zomato, DineHere... All those patron review sites? Those are filled with glowing reviews of awful places. I would think that's a big part of Frick's marketing — flooding all those sites with a continuing stream of creative laudatory crap."

Lorne pursed his lips and slowly nodded. "I wonder if Frick is off on an unsupervised tangent with this. It seems to be much less well thought through."

"Our internet teams can dig into that, Lorne. They're good at finding common sources and repeat patterns." Singh glanced again at the clock. "I have a meeting in two minutes. See you in my office at twelve thirty." He signalled to Hopgood, nodded, turned and left.

Hopgood came over and introduced himself. "Have you any questions?"

Catherine pointed at his shoulder insignia. "I'm curious about the badges. I always get lost above sergeant. What's the crown and diamonds?"

He glanced down at his epaulettes, then smiled at her. "That's Chief Superintendent."

"And the crossed swords Singh is wearing?"

"That's actually a sword crossed with its scabbard. It's Deputy Commissioner. There are only seven of them in the RCMP." He turned and scanned the group. "Ferguson!"

"Sir!"

He motioned him over. "We may as well get together now; you'll be joining us for lunch shortly. She's curious about the insignias, so we're having a show and tell." He smiled at Catherine. "His crown and single diamond indicate Superintendent." He scanned the room again, then pointed. "There, the crown, that's Inspector."

They all shook hands and chatted. Ferguson quickly swung the conversation to the Hypocritic Diner theme. Hearing the laughter, others came over to join the group, and they added to the anecdotes. "My son has four dinner reservations this week. He's hoping the scam lasts long enough to get at least one freebie. He's praying it's the mystery dinner place."

Catherine gave Bourgeois her best attempt at a puzzled look as she replied to him. "It seems we've missed all the excitement of this thing. We've been too busy being murdered."

There was silence. A long silence, until she said, "I wanted to suggest there's much more involved with this than dinner." She scanned the faces again. "In the last two days, I've seen a huge amount of sick stuff on the net connected to this." She looked around. "You men might feel this more intensely than we women do, but I'm sure that threats, images and videos of penis amputations and references to displaying the severed parts in trophy cases bring cringes to us all."

After another long silence, she glanced at the clock. "We should refresh for lunch."

Chapter Sixty-Four

The discussion during lunch was less dramatic as they sat and examined the current situation, then worked back through the information Catherine and Lorne had uncovered. The officers related this new information to their awareness of the backlog of unanswered questions and unsolved crimes. They made plausible links between organised crime and the explosion, the restaurant scams, the unsolved murders and the missing body parts. Robotham was prominent in all of these.

After lunch, Lorne and Catherine spent three and a quarter hours in meetings with available senior staff of four departments. While Lorne briefed and supplied data and links for continued searching, Catherine was brought deeper into the complexity. She added observations and insights from her brief experience, but mostly she observed and absorbed.

It was seventeen ten when they returned to their suite and stood in a hug for a long while just inside the room. "Exhausting. More emotionally than anything." He squeezed her tighter. "I feel a huge weight's been lifted from me. Feel strange. Odd, disoriented."

"You should." She kissed his neck and gazed up into his eyes. "You now have a dozen and a half senior police officers trying to figure out how to pick up and continue with the load you've been carrying. You need to let go of it now. Relax. It's not your burden anymore."

He bent to kiss her. "Yeah, I *do* need to. It's tough after carrying it all these years. But it's time to leave them to do the digging through the crap piles. Their job, anyway."

She slid her hands down to his butt and gave it a little shake. "Come, lie down and cuddle. Kick off our shoes and unwind."

They were entwined, and he was still asleep when Catherine heard the knock on the door. She gently unfolded and went to the peephole, then unlocked and opened the door. She held her finger to her lips in a shhh motion as she beckoned Denise in. "He's exhausted," she whispered.

"God, he should be from all that information he presented to us in the briefing and the file walk-through."

"Your department was the mildest one."

"So I've been hearing. Everyone is talking about how placid he is with the whole thing."

"Fifteen years of practice with..."

"What are you girls whispering about?" He leaned up on his elbows.

"We were talking about my graceful swan sweeping across the waters with barely a ripple." Catherine smiled at him. "Did you manage to get a bit of a nap?"

"Until all the noise." He laughed and sat up. "Hi, Denise."

Denise stood staring at him and slowly shaking her head. "So much stuff. *So* much. Why didn't you approach us earlier?"

"I became tired of playing Whack-a-Mole. This time, I wanted to assemble enough for you to tear out the entire garden." He stood from the bed and joined them.

Denise checked her watch. "I'm off at twenty hundred, ten minutes. We could do dinner together."

"Yeah, we'd like that." Catherine saw Lorne's nod, then looked around the small suite. "Seems to be no options except ordering in or dining out. What's good around here?"

Denise shook her head. "You have no idea how silly this is. You're the two most famous foodies on the planet at the moment, and *you're* asking *me* for dining recommendations."

"By far the best way to find out. Local knowledge." Lorne smiled at her and winked. "Unbiased personal recommendations are most often the best."

She shrugged and returned the smile. "There's a marvellous Italian place across on King George, Vita Toscana. We won't need reservations: they're not very busy anymore. I still love the place despite the poor comments online."

They all looked at each other and nodded. "That has to be one of their targeted ones, doesn't it?" Denise nodded more vigorously and lifted her upper lip toward her wrinkling nose. "Amazing. Insidious."

"Yeah, isn't it?" Catherine nodded. "Give us a few minutes to refresh."

"I need to change into street, anyway. Inspector Raadsveld would like to join us if you..."

"Helma, yeah... Feisty. Straight to the point." Lorne smiled and nodded to Catherine. "We enjoyed her energy this afternoon."

"This'll be fun." Catherine hugged Denise and led her to the door. "In fifteen minutes at the reception desk?"

"Make it twenty. I need to swing by the inspector's office, then we have a long walk to the locker room and back."

Forty minutes later, they were shown to a table in the sparsely populated restaurant. "About a third full." Denise glanced at her watch. "Twenty thirty-five. Three months ago there'd be a line-up at this hour. We'd always reserve. Prime location and very popular."

"I began reading through their reviews on Tripadvisor before we left the room." Lorne smiled at the three. "I must be crazy, surrounded by beautiful women and I continue thinking about the scam."

"So what did you find?" Helma asked.

"There are still glowing reviews, but many others talk about slow service, cold food and low quality for the price."

Catherine nodded. "I saw the same on Yelp. Nothing specific. No details, but all mentioning the three major things diners don't want."

"Too obvious when you stop to think about it." Lorne nodded slowly as he opened his menu. "Let's concentrate on enjoying each other, the evening and the dinner. Tomorrow we'll untangle their web."

Chapter Sixty-Five

On Denise's recommendation, they began by sharing a huge piatto di antipasti, and they worked away at it as they talked. The conversation soon swung back to restaurant reviews when Denise asked Lorne, "So, am I right? You don't review on free meals, you dine a minimum of three times, paying each time before you write a review. The money? Who pays for this?"

"Me." He smiled at her. "I love praising fine cuisine. I love to encourage its continuance."

"But compensation for your expenses?"

"Satisfaction." He speared a piece of grilled red pepper with his fork and moved it toward his mouth. "This is a marvellous platter."

"So your writing fees must be large, then."

"I should examine that again. It's two years, more than that, since I last checked. Likely much higher now with its growth in popularity." He popped the piece into his mouth.

Denise shook her head. "You seem to be blasé about income, expenses."

"My accountant keeps track of the details for me, and I simply monitor the big picture, asking random questions to keep him on his toes. He's served me well for fifteen, no sixteen years now."

"Sixteen? Before the trials? You were still a kid."

"Dad's lawyers appointed him when I turned eighteen, and they converted the estate and the inheritances from trust." He speared a small wedge of tomato on a slice of bufala.

Michael Walsh

"This is getting personal now. I should stop here."

Catherine put her hand on Denise's and laughed. "This is also new information to me. You have a smooth interrogation style."

Lorne finished his bite. "Yeah, guess we've not talked about this, have we?" He smiled, slowly looked into each of the women's eyes, then shrugged. "I was the only child of only children." He laughed. "That seems to be one of the few Catholic traditions the family didn't follow. From the sizes of inheritances, it appears they poured all their energy into making fortunes rather than families. Most of it tumbled down to me after the crash."

Helma smiled, then turned to Catherine. "So he doesn't need the writing fees. What about you? You also dine anonymously."

"I get more than enough from my other writing." She speared a long, thick roll of prosciutto e melone and brought it to her plate.

"Other writing?"

"I've written some novels." She sliced the roll in two and moved one piece toward her mouth.

"Catherine Isselstein?" Helma shrugged. "I'm not familiar with anything of yours, but I read mainly romance, my major relief from the heavy stuff with the force. What genre do you write?"

"I do romance. The type that's most often called women's fiction." She popped the piece into her mouth, smiled at Lorne, then shrugged. "You may have heard of Katy Rachelson."

"One of my favourites. Love her style. She always has such hot hunks and steamy scenes. My diddle books." She glanced at Lorne, and blushed. "Sorry, girl talk. So you write like her?"

"Yeah, word for word." Catherine winked at her, then speared the other roll of prosciutto e melone.

Both Helma and Denise were staring open-mouthed at her, shaking their heads. "You're not?"

Catherine smiled and nodded as she slowly licked her lips and seductively mouthed the piece on her fork. *"She licked it as she looked longingly up into his eyes, then slowly slipped the thick piece between her lips and back out as her eyes ran down his broad chest and lower."* She laughed. "Yeah, something like that."

"Oh... My... God. Those drop-dead gorgeous hunks, the scenes. You must be constantly wet writing these." Helma looked again at Lorne and blushed deeper. "Sorry."

He laughed and patted her hand. "Don't worry about it. The first one did the same thing to me a dozen years ago. Her freshly evolving ones still do."

"So where do you get your ideas? Your inspiration for your men. God, what wonderful men you create. Where do they all come from?"

Catherine smiled, stared up into Lorne's eyes and squeezed his arm. "From this magnificent creature. Every one of them. He's been inspiring my imagination since I was four."

"You've known each other that long? God, that's thirty..." Denise was interrupted by the waiters.

"We have fusilli alla carbonara, trofie al pesto, tagliatelle al funghi and gnocchi al quattro formaggi. Who ordered which?"

Lorne looked up. "It doesn't matter, we're going to pass them around so we can each taste all of them."

The two waiters set a plate of pasta in front of each of them. "Another bottle of Pellegrino? Some wine?"

Helma smiled at Lorne. "Unlike these two, neither of us is pregnant. Denise is my designated driver tonight and for the next long while." She winked at Denise then turned back to Lorne. "Share a carafe?"

He saw Catherine's smile and nod. His eyes shifted up to the waiter. "Another Pellegrino. And we could do glasses. What have you open?"

"I'll send the sommelier."

They continued through dinner in an increasingly relaxed manner, accentuated with attentive service and wonderful food. The conversation remained in its shift to writing, and both Denise and Helma admitted to having started writing novels.

They discussed their attempts and their frustrations, comparing experiences and each asking for advice on methods and techniques and over-

Michael Walsh

coming writer's block. After a roundabout discussion, Catherine said, "One of my favourite quotes is from Somerset Maugham: *If you can tell stories, create characters, devise incidents, and have sincerity and passion, it doesn't matter a damn how you write.*"

She smiled at them and threw her hands up in a big shrug. "Just write. Write from your souls, from your hearts from your hot centres, whatever. Don't pause to look back and condemn what you've written. Just write and keep writing. Let your characters tell the story to you, let them drag you along. The first draft looks a mess. It is, and it isn't. It's waiting for those strokes, those touches, the ones which take it over the crest into release."

"Fuck! Like diddling. Nothing happening, nothing, then..." Helma smiled at Lorne. "You understand this, don't you?"

"Oh yeah. It's the same for all of us. Male, female and the full range between. We've the same basic systems and fundamental drives."

Chapter Sixty-Six

On Tuesday morning, the computer analysts in the Commercial Fraud section began combing through the online reviews on the popular sites, starting with Vita Toscana, Nuance and Roberto, searching for patterns and repeats.

By mid-afternoon, they had identified thirty-seven accounts which had posted negative reviews on each of the three restaurants on Yelp, TripAdvisor, EatHere and Zomato. They shared common themes and phrases, and though each was slightly different, it was easy to see their relationship.

"Getting account information from Yelp, TripAdvisor and Zomato will be a long process." Inspector Raadsveld looked up at Lorne and Catherine as she tapped the list. "But we should be able to get something more easily from EatHere, it's Canadian, and we'll have freer access."

"What about CanDine and VanDine?"

Helma looked at Lorne. "I'm not familiar with them. New?"

"I'm not sure... They came up in my Google when I started digging a week or two ago. I saw high praises for a place I was doing research on — Molly's." He looked at Catherine. "That's where I got the idea to go try The Driftwood. Probably them."

"Who?" Raadsveld began slowly nodding, then accelerated it as she rose from her desk and motioned them to follow. "Yeah, good chance it is." She stopped in the lane between cubicles. "New direction, everybody. Comb through..." She paused and turned to Lorne. "The names again?"

"CanDine and VanDine. One word each. Search for the same or similar accounts to those on Yelp, Zomato, the others."

Lorne sat at an unoccupied desk, opened his computer, logged in, entered a url in his browser and clicked for a while. "The IP address for VanDine is a proxy server in Yaletown." He did the same with CanDine and found a different server IP. He clicked on the map link, then turned to Catherine. "Two different servers, but the same coordinates. Appears you're neighbours."

She leaned closer to the screen to see the pin on the map. "Oh, God! That's just around the crescent from us, close to *Tastevin's* berth. He'd know the boat when he talked with George."

Lorne browsed to imBMEX.ru, did some clicking and looked back up at Catherine. "Robotham missed some security basics when he set up his systems, leaving himself wide open here." He chuckled. "He may be a clever lawyer, but as an IT, he totally sucks."

He stood, picked up his computer, grabbed Catherine's hand and led her back to Helma's office, pausing to knock on her open door. She looked up, smiled and beckoned them in. "Find something?"

"Yeah, Robotham." He grinned. "His dining review sites and his body modification site share servers in Yaletown. All three IP addresses point to a townhouse." He tabbed to *GoogleEarth StreetView*. "That one. Residential, not commercial. Too much coincidence. Way too much."

Helma was on the phone to Singh, before Lorne had finished. "Raadsveld here. We need to see you, Sir. Big... Yessir, on our way." She led them along the hall toward the Deputy Commissioner, who was standing at his door as they approached.

Within five minutes, Hopgood, Ferguson, Tung and Bourgeois had joined them. Each gave situation reports on the progress of their investigations, then they began tying pieces together.

When the discussion slowed, Singh stood from behind his desk and paced. "From the private message exchange, Frick's with Robotham, and they're likely at the townhouse on Marinaside. Makes sense they're there with the servers, but we'll find out. Robotham's now eager to meet

Connolly. We've been told the arrest, search and seize warrants will be issued within the hour."

He paused his pacing and looked at each person in turn as he slowly nodded. "I think the next step is to set up a meeting. Can you see any reason we can't have our ghost of Connolly initiate the contact now?"

There was no response except a shaking of heads.

◇◇◇

At nineteen twenty-five, a white-haired man dressed in black walked slowly around the crescent, then turned back to retrace his steps, before he sat on the waterside bench across from Aquarius Mews. He looked at his watch, then pulled out a bag of sunflower seeds and began feeding the gathering pigeons.

Seven minutes later a young man in jogging clothes stopped and sat beside him. "You can relax now. We nabbed Robotham and Frick shortly after they came out through the front door. The team's inside now. Another nice quiet one." He laughed. "The gun lobby will be disappointed again."

The white-haired man looked up, smiled and extended the bag. "Care for some sunflower seeds?"

Chapter Sixty-Seven

Over the following days, the seized computers and servers were mined for information, and the large collection of plastinated amputation trophies was sent for DNA analysis to try to match them to mutilation and murder victims. A team of officers was assigned to study recent emails and to continue the routine correspondence as the members of the Canada-wide web were identified.

Lorne and Catherine had been moved back to the loft on the morning after the arrests, and Denise visited them daily with updates and groceries. On Saturday morning, Catherine had two broad parallel strips of pink paper taped to the belly of her yoga pants when she opened the door to greet her. Denise screamed. "Told you they work. Mine worked at four days too."

They hugged and kissed and played like silly schoolgirls as they slowly giggled their way toward the kitchen. Lorne locked the door and followed, enjoying the bubbling energy of the pregnant pair. *We knew it. Pleased science agrees with us.*

A lot of baby talk later, Denise looked up from her coffee. "They arrested George yesterday afternoon in Calgary, so it's safe again for you outside for short spells."

Catherine looked up and winced. "Cynthia? You've still found nothing to connect her? Tough, isn't it? Re-establishing trust." She ran her finger around the rim of her cup. "Still no connections beyond the initial marketing and the opening promotions?"

"She appears to be completely clean. We've done a full search, a thorough record check. Nothing. She dealt by email directly with the Montreal office, and the communication is all business. There's no mention of either Frick or Robotham in any of it."

"Same we're finding with the body mod site." Lorne combed his fingers through his hair. "They don't seem to know each other there either." He laughed. "I'm pleased to see you're back to Gustav Frick and Bill Robotham. Malek Jandali and Samir Azmeh were a bit strange for me to use."

"Yeah, we've gone back to their fingerprint names. We have to do a lot of sorting and matching the next while. Not one among the hundreds we've identified so far has a criminal record."

"So they've also an identity theft thing going?"

"That, but most of them have emerged onto the records as refugees. We've uncovered a hole in the system — a huge one. It appears they've infiltrated, and they've been creating new identities at will."

"That makes sense. Use the system, be official and unique. It's a great base for them to start over — clean." He drained his coffee. "So what's the next step?"

"We've been setting up a lot. I'm not sufficiently high in the loop to know for sure, but from what we've been asked to contribute, everything points to something big happening soon. A coordinated Canada-wide sweep the next day or two."

"I should wait until after that's done before I contact Cynthia." Catherine shook her head. "Trust. So hard to... So hard. I've never before had to think like this."

Lorne wrapped his arm around her shoulder and hugged her into his side. "Trust. Yeah, so easily broken, so hard to repair. The doubts, the questions. They continue to linger."

She turned her head to him and drew a twisted smile, then she looked back at Denise. "What about the DNA?" She put her hand to her mouth. "God! It's so sickening to think about that. Any more matches besides Nathan?"

"Yeah, six more unsolved murders linked — seven now and they still have so many pieces unidentified. God, so sick."

"Coffee!" He stood and looked into the empty cups. "We need more coffee and something lighter to think about." He gathered the cups and went to the machine.

They were silent as they sipped the hot espressos. After a long quiet spell, Lorne spoke. "I guess we're still officially dead until the roundup is finished, so no internet presence. No follow-on or response to the blogs, no social media, no emails yet."

"That would be best for the gathering net." Denise looked up from her cup. "Catching them by surprise saves a lot of bullets and a lot of blood. Best if you remain quiet a while longer."

"The only one outside the Mounties I've been in contact with is my lawyer, and he's aware of the situation. He's working with my insurance company. The surveyor was given access to the hulk on Thursday, so the settlement is in process."

"That was quite the fire. I saw the glow through the bridge from our balcony, so I walked down to Spy Glass Place. So sad to see it burn and then sink. Big boat. Very big."

"Yeah, when I had her built, I was dreaming of sailing with a big family."

"Fuck!" Catherine reached out, fell onto his shoulder and held on to him, scrabbling tighter.

He cupped the back of her head and laughed. "Not right at the moment, Gorgeous, we have company."

She sat up and stared at him. "When was that? When did you have her...?"

The sound of Lorne's phone going bing bong interrupted her. Catherine looked at him. "You need to get that, don't you?"

"Yeah, I do. My Mountie email sound." He pulled out his phone, thumbed it on and thumbed in, then clicked on the blinking icon and read a short while before he lifted his head and smiled. "It's from the Commissioner." He read it to them.

Lorne... Here's a press release I've just authorised. Thank you again for your assistance... Harold.

For Immediate Release

The RCMP, the OPP and the SQ completed a coordinated joint operation this afternoon, arresting nearly eight hundred people across Canada. This was the culmination of a long investigation involving a broad range of charges from child pornography and commercial fraud, through to murder.

The active portion of the operation involved more than twelve hundred officers of the Royal Canadian Mounted Police, the Ontario Provincial Police and la Sûreté du Québec. They were armed with more than nine hundred arrest warrants as they moved in on three hundred and six addresses in seventy-four communities across the country.

The number of outstanding warrants is diminishing as the follow-up operations continue. Computers and files have been seized, and the ongoing investigations are adding to the number of suspects. More warrants are being issued. Further details to follow.

-30-

Epilogue

After further discussions with Denise and Lorne, Catherine phoned Cynthia and explained her lack of communication the past week as they had hunkered from Robotham. She left out everything concerning their suspicions of her involvement, aware it would add nothing but tension.

In the following weeks, dozens of additional arrests were made across Canada, and authorities in the US and Britain arrested members of nascent networks there. The DNA from the plastinated amputation trophies led to another four matches with unsolved murders. Included in the long list of offences brought against Robotham, were eleven counts of murder.

Traffic on the online restaurant review sites went into rapid decline as their owners scrambled to purge the fraudulent and questionable reviews. Advertising rates on most of the sites were slashed in futile attempts to stem the flow of fleeing clients. Many dining review blogs fell idle, leaving the few well-established and unbiased ones to regain their prominence.

Lorne and Catherine were married in a quiet ceremony in the vineyards at Mosscrop in late July, then they headed to Europe on an extended honeymoon, beginning in Rotterdam to sign contracts for the construction of the new *Tastevin*. Their honeymoon continued through the German, Austrian, Italian, French, Spanish and Portuguese vineyards as they received splendid hospitality from the producers.

An ultrasound after their return to Vancouver in late October showed Catherine was carrying healthy twins, a boy and a girl.